OF LIGHT AND NIGHTMARES

THE ASHES OF MAGIC TRILOGY: VOLUME I

OF LIGHT AND NIGHTMARES

ALEX B. HARPER

Copyright © 2023 by Alex B. Harper
All rights reserved.

Visit my website at www.alexbharper.com
Cover Designer: Sarah Lahay, www.cestbeaudesigns.com
Editor: Jovana Shirley, Unforeseen Editing,
www.unforeseenediting.com
Contributing Editor: Laura Lakhian

No part of this book may be reproduced or transmitted in any form or by any means, electronic or mechanical, including photocopying, recording, or by any information storage and retrieval system without the written permission of the author, except for the use of brief quotations in a book review.

This book is a work of fiction. Names, characters, places, and incidents are either products of the author's imagination or are used fictitiously. Any resemblance to actual persons, living or dead, events, or locales is entirely coincidental.

ISBN: 9781738906406

AUTHOR'S NOTE

I wrote this story to provide a short reprieve from reality, and in the process of bringing this tale to life, I've included topics that might be traumatic for some readers. I have tried to capture all triggers in the warnings, but if something was missed, it was not intentional.

Stories are magical adventures that let us live countless dreams, and although providing warnings might hint at spoilers, I accept that risk to keep the joy of reading a safe and accessible space.

I hope you enjoy Emmeline's journey as much as I loved writing it.

With much love and gratitude,
Alex B. Harper

Book Classification: Adult Contemporary/Urban Fantasy

Trigger Warnings (in alphabetical order): mentions of ableism, antisocial personality disorder, child abandonment, child abuse, death of loved ones, domestic abuse, drug use, execution, genocide, hostage situations, infertility, mental illness, misogyny, murder, physical assault, scars, sexual assault, stalking, suicide and self-harm, violence.

Content Warnings (in no particular order): mature subject matters, sexual content, gore and graphic violence, profanity.

For those of us who look for the smallest spark of magic everywhere we go.

But most of all, for the love of my life, my family, and my bestest of friends.

I love you all to the banana moon and back.

CONTENTS

PART I: PAPER AURAS

Chapter 1	Heirs Apparent	3
Chapter 2	Hallucinations	13
Chapter 3	Of Things to Come	19
Chapter 4	Fairy Tales	27
Chapter 5	Dumplings	37
Chapter 6	Curiosity	43
Chapter 7	Trespassers	52
Chapter 8	One of Two	60

PART II: TITANS

Chapter 9	·New Beginnings	69
Chapter 10	Road to Hell	76
Chapter 11	Hostile Introductions	85
Chapter 12	Vultures	92
Chapter 13	Boundaries	95
Chapter 14	Into the Monster's Belly	109
Chapter 15	And Out the Other Side	117
Chapter 16	The Salt in Memories	128
Chapter 17	Aftermath	137

PART III: STUDIES AND STORIES

Chapter 18	Safeguards	151
Chapter 19	All That Glitters	163
Chapter 20	Executioners	174
Chapter 21	A Shadow in the Dark	181
Chapter 22	Sanctuaries	192
Chapter 23	Of Dreams and More	197
Chapter 24	Late Bloomer	207
Chapter 25	Sanctity of Life	213
Chapter 26	Fury	225
Chapter 27	Counterbalance	233

PART IV: FIRSTS

Chapter 28	Premonition	247
Chapter 29	Early Warnings	257
Chapter 30	Remarkable	262
Chapter 31	A Seeker Who Cannot See	270
Chapter 32	Stalked	275
Chapter 33	Momentum	280
Chapter 34	Just a Name	284
Chapter 35	Deception	298
Chapter 36	Past Lives	306
Chapter 37	The Tower	317

PART V: SECONDS

Chapter 38	When Monsters Follow	331
Chapter 39	Realizations	341
Chapter 40	Lines Crossed	348
Chapter 41	Right Beside You	363
Chapter 42	Ambushed	372
Chapter 43	Reckless	383
Chapter 44	Unfinished Business	389
Chapter 45	The Connection	401
Chapter 46	Beneath the Mid-Autumn Moon	409
Chapter 47	Collateral	417
Chapter 48	Two of Two	428

PART VI: THE CATASTROPHE OF OATHS

Chapter 49	The Beginning of the End	439
Chapter 50	Denmark	448
Chapter 51	Cracked Glass	458
Chapter 52	Powerless	462
Chapter 53	Burden of Responsibility	472
Chapter 54	Look At Me	476
Chapter 55	A Thousand Lifetimes	485
Chapter 56	Angel of Death	489

PART I:

PAPER AURAS

CHAPTER ONE

HEIRS APPARENT

Emmeline sighed as she thumbed through the couture section of her dressing room. She narrowed her eyes at the offending sea of designer silk and lace, and blew a stray hair out of her face.

"Let's start with color," she murmured to herself.

Pointing her finger at the long rack of dresses, she moved across the hangers and mentally crossed off gowns as she passed each one.

You and you.

She plucked out two dresses—a strapless floor-length emerald-green gown and a knee-length cobalt-blue cheongsam.

"Ms. Rose, should I wear green or blue for tonight's gala?" Emmeline called out.

The click of Ms. Rose's slippers came down the hallway and stopped at the doorway of Emmeline's dressing room. Ms. Rose peered over her glasses and tapped her manicured fingernails against her lips. Her short sandy-brown and gray-streaked hair bobbed as she nodded at Emmeline's dress choices.

"You know you'd look beautiful in either dress. You could wear a paper bag and still be a princess," Ms. Rose said.

"That's not true, and you know it." Emmeline eyed her two choices and selected the blue cheongsam.

"You look like you've decided that you're not going to have a good time tonight."

"There's so much gossip at these events, and I'm constantly dodging nonstop questions from all the aunties and uncles. I feel like I'm under interrogation sometimes."

From an early age, Emmeline and her brother had been taught to address their parents' close friends and business partners as auntie and uncle despite not being related. She often had to bite her tongue to stop herself from calling her friends' parents as such.

"That's because you only show up when the family foundation's a title donor. I worry some people might think you're too good to go to lower-profile events, and nobody likes a snob. If you went to more events, people might talk less," Ms. Rose countered.

"Or maybe they'll realize I'm boring and leave me alone." Emmeline smiled delightfully at the thought. "Why don't you come with us? You haven't been at one of these events in years."

"Absolutely not. Can you imagine the gossip columns in the society pages?" Ms. Rose waved her hand in the air to imitate a newspaper headline. "*Emmeline Taylor-Wu mocks high society by bringing her governess to the gala to keep potential suitors at bay.*" She pressed one hand to her chest and laid the other dramatically on her forehead, pretending to feel faint.

"No one would dare mess with you," Emmeline giggled.

"It'd be scandalous!" Ms. Rose straightened and wrinkled her nose. "In any case, Mattie's accompanying you."

Emmeline rolled her eyes. "Mattie's the opposite of helpful. He doesn't keep the aunties off my back as to why I'm not married with two perfect little children running around. The aunties love him so much; he could commit a crime, and they'd clamber over each other to protect him. I'm pretty sure they love him because he's the exact opposite of charming, which makes him even more charming."

"They also love him because they want to set him up with their single daughters. Who wouldn't want a hardworking, well-connected doctor who comes from money?" Ms. Rose walked over to Emmeline's jewelry chest and picked up the stack of eight thin pure-gold bangles that had once belonged to Emmeline's mother. "These would look wonderful with your dress. Your grandma gave these to your mother when you were born. They were your mother's favorite, and she adored the sound they made when she moved her wrist."

"They're my favorite too." Emmeline looked away. "You're right; those would look beautiful with my dress. I'll wear them tonight."

Ms. Rose put the bangles back into their rightful place, and when she turned back around, all traces of memories were gone from her face.

Emmeline cleared her throat and changed the subject. "I might not like these events, but Mattie hates attending."

"Only your brother could turn escaping charity line dancing into an art form. You'd think he worked for a spy agency based on how fast he disappears off a dance floor," Ms. Rose said.

"The loud music gives him a terrible headache."

"That's true, but he also has a million pairs of those little things that go in his ears and cancel noise. I know because I keep ordering them for him."

"Even I keep a pair in my purse for him in case of emergency. Maybe I'll point that out next time I catch him trying to pull a Houdini," Emmeline snickered.

When they had been children, Matthew had avoided loud noises by hiding in nooks and crannies. Their parents would find him hunched over in odd corners, covering his ears and rocking back and forth. They thought he would eventually grow out of it, but when they finally understood his sensory oversensitivity, they made sure he always had a pair of noise-dampening headphones with him. When she had been younger, Emmeline had started carrying her own set to be like her older brother.

"There must be some eligible bachelors at these events. Give them a chance, and a few might surprise you. And if nothing works out"—Ms. Rose shrugged—"you'll have made a friend—or at least another potential donor to the many causes the family foundation supports."

Emmeline gently shooed Ms. Rose out of the doorway. "Time for me to get fabulous. You know how particular Mattie gets about being on time. Nothing irritates him more than being late, and the last thing I want is to give him another reason to be grumpy."

Emmeline changed into her cheongsam before adding a pair of brilliant diamond studs and the gold heirloom bangles Ms. Rose had picked up earlier. She applied a touch of luminous makeup to her wide, almond-shaped eyes that were the color of a midnight sky. If one looked close enough, they'd find bright amber flecks dotting her deep irises like stars. After winding her long, wavy black hair into a low bun, she picked out a small clutch and pale gold heels to complete her look. She grabbed her favorite pair of leather ballet flats for the car ride and walked over to her backlit mirror.

You are confident. You are smart. You are beautiful.

After repeating her pep talk, Emmeline went to her bedside table and picked up a delicate gold band. She ran her finger along the inside, feeling the comforting inscription.

Forever and always.

She slipped her mother's ring onto her index finger.

Ready.

Just like her mother had taught her, she straightened her posture, held her head back, and left her bedroom.

Matthew didn't look up from his tablet when Emmeline walked into the kitchen and dropped her clutch on the island, where he was working.

"We're going to be late, Emia," Matthew frowned.

Emmeline rolled her eyes. "We're not going to be late."

She looked over her brother in his slim-cut tuxedo and resisted picking off a stray piece of lint on his shoulder. They were both tall, like their father, and lean and lithe, like their mother. Throughout Matthew's early teenage years, her mother had worried he would be petite like her, but the summer that he turned sixteen, he'd shot up like a beanstalk. Emmeline and Matthew both had their mother's high cheekbones and midnight eyes, flecked with amber, and their rosy-gold skin was an even blend of their parents' English-Australian and Chinese origins. All in all, they looked alike, except Matthew's golden-brown hair contrasted dramatically against Emmeline's ink-black tresses. Emmeline had always thought Matthew's many freckles made him exceptionally handsome, and she loved how the light smattering across the bridge of her nose made her look like she had just returned from a trip to the beach.

"Mattie, are those glasses new? The navy looks good on you. It brings out your freckles," Emmeline asked innocently.

Matthew pushed up his glasses and ignored her.

Emmeline's grin widened. "Ms. Sun and the other aunties are going to love this look. I'll be sure to point it out to them." She giggled as Matthew looked up at the ceiling.

"Do we really need to go to the gala tonight?" Matthew grumbled.

"We're going because our family's the title donor for the Royal Children's Rehabilitation Hospital. They need our help to build the new wing."

"Can't we just give them more money?"

Emmeline snorted. "Believe me, we've already made a generous donation from the family foundation."

"So, why do we still have to go?"

"Because we're the title donor, and that's what title donors do," Emmeline repeated impatiently. "Stop trying to get out of it because it's not going to work."

Ms. Rose entered the kitchen and flew to Matthew's side, careful not to get too close. "Mattie, you look so handsome!" she gushed. She looked over Emmeline and Matthew, and her eyes shone with pride. "You both clean up so well. I don't understand how neither of you has found a partner yet. Emia, you hide at home, working all the time, so that doesn't surprise me much. But, Mattie, you're handsome, rich, and a successful doctor. Surely, you meet people at the hospital. How is it possible that you still haven't found someone yet?" Ms. Rose sighed. "No worries, my dear. The right person's out there for you. May I hug you?"

Matthew nodded and hunched over so Ms. Rose could hug him.

"Can I hug you too?" Emmeline asked.

Matthew nodded again, and Emmeline wrapped her arms around him and Ms. Rose.

"We should get going. Am I driving, or are you?" Emmeline asked.

"Me." Matthew grinned and held up a shiny, new key fob.

Another new car? Emmeline's mouth fell open.

"I don't want to know." Ms. Rose held up her hands and swept gracefully out of the kitchen. "Drive safe and have fun. Make sure you put on your best faces and thank everyone for their donations. Also, remember your goal is to keep people donating, so be nice!" she called out over her shoulder.

"Yes, Ms. Rose," Emmeline and Matthew chimed in unison.

Emmeline turned back to her brother. "Instead of buying a new car, you could've personally donated that money to the hospital, and I would've excused you from coming to this event."

"One, you know that's a lie. You would've made me come anyway. Two, I work hard for my money. And three, it brings me joy." Matthew looked at Emmeline pointedly. "And what do we do with things that bring us joy?"

Emmeline only sighed.

Emmeline slid into the plush leather passenger seat of her brother's new sports car and dropped her heels on the car floor.

This car must have cost the equivalent of a down payment for a property, and everyone knows real estate in Toronto is outrageous.

"Where are the *oh-shit* handles?" Emmeline looked up to her right.

"Oh, please. Your driving's way more questionable than mine," Matthew snorted. He revved the engine and drove down the steep driveway. Once he turned onto the winding single-lane road, he pressed a button, and the moonroof slid open, letting in the cool evening breeze.

"Mattie, how come the sound of a car engine doesn't bother you, but other sounds do?"

"Because it reminds me of Dad."

Emmeline lapsed back into silence, and she stared out the passenger window.

"What's on your mind, Emia?"

"I was thinking about the little speech I promised to make. I'm also dreading the questions about my work and love life—or lack thereof. You know how the society columns write things and how much the aunties and uncles love to gossip. To them, I'm just a bratty kid who was left a fortune by her unlucky parents."

"They were my unlucky parents too," Matthew murmured.

"You made something of yourself. You keep people healthy, and you save lives. Mom and Dad would be so proud of you if they were alive. All I do is manage the family trust and hide at home."

Matthew glanced at her before focusing back on the road. "That's not true. What you do is ensure Mom and Dad's legacy lives on and all the good philanthropic work they did endures. You make sure the family trust has longevity and can continue to fund causes that support those who are underprivileged, even when you and I are no longer here. You're not just some bratty kid."

"A lonely, bratty kid." Emmeline's eyes didn't leave the road. "Do you ever get lonely?"

"Not really. I don't mind being alone. Do you feel lonely?"

"Sometimes, I do. Mom and Dad have been gone for over ten years, and I still miss them very much. I'm finding it harder to connect with people as the years pass. It feels like there's something wrong with me."

"Maybe you're like me," Matthew said.

"Maybe." Emmeline smiled.

Matthew turned into the entrance of Casa Loma, the historic castle that had been transformed into one of the city's top event venues.

"Ms. Rose is right. You should stop being so reclusive and get out more. Even I get out more than you do. I know you're terrified of having another seizure in public, but you haven't had one in a few years. Don't let fear stop you from doing what you want."

"Thanks, Doctor," Emmeline muttered as Matthew pulled up to the valet.

"Oh good. We're here!" Matthew said with mocking cheerfulness, and they both rolled their eyes.

Emmeline changed into her heels as the passenger door glided upward. She stepped out of the car and waited as Matthew handed his key fob to the valet and then took his place beside her.

What a formidable and handsome duo we make.

With brilliant, well-practiced smiles and poise from years of training, Emmeline and Matthew posed briefly for the cameras before strolling into the famous castle.

CHAPTER TWO

HALLUCINATIONS

Emmeline's eyes widened as soon as she stepped into the grand hall. The castle had been transformed into this year's theme of Chinese mythical creatures. A forest-green dragon with glittering scales hung from the ceiling and curled around half the hall, its mouth twisting into a wide, toothy grin. Facing off the dragon was a gold phoenix with its wings unfurled in all their glory, challenging the dragon for its place in the heavens. Muted light bulbs draped across the ceiling, and at each table was a glass centerpiece representing a different mythical creature.

"Emmeline Taylor-Wu, it's so nice to finally see you at an event!"

Emmeline felt the shrill voice in her spine before it reached her ears, but her smile was genuine as she turned to face Carmen, vice president of the fundraising committee. Carmen grasped Emmeline's hands and leaned in to kiss her on both cheeks.

"Every year I see you, you get more beautiful. You look stunning," Carmen gushed.

Emmeline blushed and tried not to shift uncomfortably. "You look fabulous yourself."

"I know we already spoke over the phone, but I wanted to thank you and your family again for the generous donation to the hospital. It alone accounted for ten percent of our goal."

"My brother spent many years at the hospital as a child, and even after he stopped attending, my late parents remained patrons. I can't think of a better cause to continue supporting," Emmeline replied.

"Well, with that, plus all your usual annual donations, we're campaigning to have the new wing named after your family." Carmen patted Emmeline's hand.

Emmeline cleared her throat. "That's not something my parents would've ever wanted."

Carmen frowned and patted Emmeline's hands again. "Let's talk about it later. I will continue making my rounds and hope to get more donors to open their hearts and wallets a little wider. I'll be back later to introduce some friends who are eager to meet you. Tell your brother to work his magic with the ladies. They adore him." She winked at Emmeline and, with a whirl, disappeared back into the crowd.

Emmeline turned around to look for Matthew, but he was nowhere to be found.

Figures he'd disappear at his first chance, she thought irritably. *I might as well freshen up before the welcoming ceremony.*

Emmeline made her way to the restroom, passing several gala attendees and making light conversation with those she knew. Most partygoers had already moved to the main hall and settled into their seats. A few boisterous stragglers remained behind, laughing with each other as they held on to their drinks.

I'd better be quick. I don't want to be late.

She pushed open the door to the restroom and rushed toward an empty stall. Just as she was about to enter, another attendee stepped out and collided into her. Emmeline cried out as a flash of bright white light blinded her. She stumbled backward, desperately grasping for something to hold on to.

I'm having a seizure!

Her mouth went dry, and no sound came out as she fell.

I can't see.

A pair of arms caught her just before she hit the cool marble floor.

I can't breathe.

Emmeline gasped for air.

Mattie, help!

The light began to fade, and Emmeline's heart stopped as she looked up at the woman who had caught her. Fiery copper irises covered the woman's eyes, and paper-gray skin stretched across her face, dipping into the harsh shadows of the sunken crevices of her bone structure.

What the hell?

Emmeline's eyes widened in terror, and she let out a blood-curdling scream.

The woman startled and fell back, taking Emmeline with her. Right before Emmeline's eyes, the woman's irises shrank back to normal, and her skin smoothed to light chocolate. Her hair transformed into a dark Afro, but the white aura stayed, illuminating her like a halo.

"What's happening?" Emmeline sputtered.

As if she had been scalded, the woman dropped Emmeline to the floor just as a gala attendant ran into the restroom. The attendant rushed to Emmeline's side and knelt beside her.

"Ms. Taylor-Wu, are you all right? Should I call emergency services?" the attendant asked.

Emmeline sat up and pushed her hair off her face. Her eyes darted around, looking for the strange woman.

Where did she go?

"Ms. Taylor-Wu?" The attendant looked at her with concern.

Emmeline shook her head. "I'm okay. No need to call emergency services."

"Can you stand up?"

Emmeline nodded, and the attendant helped her to her feet.

"I'm a little shaken, but I'll be fine."

"Are you sure?" the attendant asked.

"I'm sure."

"At least let me walk you back to your seat."

"That would be great."

Emmeline glanced over herself in the mirror and smoothed out her cheongsam. Her face had lost some color, but otherwise, she looked normal. The attendant picked up Emmeline's clutch off the floor and placed it into her shaking hands. Emmeline took another deep breath and exhaled slowly.

I must be going crazy.

Matthew was seated at the table when the attendant walked over with Emmeline.

"Emia, are you okay?" Matthew asked.

"I collided with a woman in the restroom, and then I was blinded by a flash of light. I thought I was having a seizure, but I didn't black out. When I lost my balance, the woman caught me and stopped me from hitting the floor."

"You saw a flash of light?"

"Yes." Emmeline shifted in her seat. "There was something else."

I can't tell him about the eyes and face. I must've been hallucinating.

"Just tell me what happened," Matthew said impatiently.

"The light stayed with the woman. It was like there was an aura around her."

"Seeing auras isn't uncommon with seizures, and you've always said you see bright flashes of light before losing consciousness. Because you were focused on the woman, it looked like the aura was around her." Matthew scanned the banquet hall. "Do you see the woman now? Is she here?"

Emmeline shook her head. "I don't see her, but she's a guest."

"How do you feel now?"

"Normal," Emmeline admitted.

"Have you been keeping up with your appointments with Dr. Li? You know how important it is."

"You know I have."

"Do you want to go home?"

"Mattie, we can't go home. Stop trying to get out of attending this gala!"

Matthew glared at her. "That's not what I meant."

"Sorry, habit," Emmeline muttered.

"Just let me know if you want to leave. You know I hate these things."

Emmeline rolled her eyes. "Before I forget, Carmen wants you to make some rounds with the aunties and inspire them to open their wallets wider. You know they control the bank accounts."

Matthew cursed under his breath and ignored her.

CHAPTER THREE

OF THINGS TO COME

Emmeline looked down at the place cards at her table and raised an eyebrow. The table was clearly for the VIPs. She and Matthew were seated with the hospital's president and CEO, the fundraising committee's president, Carmen, the mayor of Toronto, and the premier of Ontario.

Emmeline looked up just as Patrick, the fundraising committee's president, and Lauren, the hospital's president and CEO, headed toward their table. In between them were the mayor and premier. She coughed to get Matthew's attention, and they both stood up with brilliant smiles.

"Ah, Dr. Matthew Taylor-Wu and Ms. Emmeline Taylor-Wu, there you two are." Patrick shook Matthew's hand vigorously and slapped him on the shoulder, making Matthew grimace. Patrick turned to Emmeline. "And you are blindingly beautiful, as usual." He kissed her on both cheeks.

"You're too generous, Patrick," Emmeline replied.

"Only when it's deserved." Patrick winked at her. "Well, I know everyone knows who each other is, but has everyone been introduced?"

"Not formally, but of course, I know who our newly appointed mayor and illustrious premier are," Emmeline said.

"Then, I must do some introductions!" Patrick puffed out his chest. "I'm pleased to introduce the Honorable Willow Phan, premier of Ontario, and Philip Vil, mayor of Toronto. And you both know Dr. Lauren High, our hospital's own president and CEO." He turned his toothy grin to the mayor and premier. "I'm delighted to introduce you to our title donors, Dr. Matthew Taylor-Wu and Ms. Emmeline Taylor-Wu."

A round of handshakes ensued. As Emmeline got to Mayor Vil, he turned her hand over and kissed it. His hand lingered on hers, and she blushed.

"It's nice to make your acquaintance, Ms. Taylor-Wu. I've heard nothing but flattering accounts of your philanthropic work," Philip said smoothly.

"It's nice to meet you, Mayor Vil." Emmeline took her hand back.

"Please, call me Philip."

"Then, extend me the same courtesy and call me Emmeline."

Philip pulled out Emmeline's chair, and she sat back down, murmuring her thanks. She appraised him from beneath her dark eyelashes.

He's handsome, charming, and very put-together.

Philip looked several years older than she and Matthew and had an air of confidence, apparent from how he jutted his chin out and held his shoulders back. His light-olive skin was subtly lined, offsetting his deep brown eyes and dark hair. He was dressed in a perfectly cut, classic black tuxedo that highlighted his athletic figure. Emmeline flushed again and pretended to look for something in her clutch. Her phone buzzed.

Mattie:	The mayor kissed your hand. Was he flirting with you?
Emia:	I don't think so. He's handsome. What's his history?
Mattie:	Born in British Columbia, great-grandparents from France, mid-forties, divorced, no kids, former entrepreneur, ambitious.
Emia:	You need to get out more.
Mattie:	Look who's talking.

Emmeline put her phone facedown and kicked her brother under the table.

～

Emmeline stifled a yawn.

The night was proceeding precisely as she had expected. Numerous award presentations followed speeches and extravagant prize draws. The only saving grace was the magic show and the cover band.

"Emmeline, you're up after the next speech." Carmen appeared at her side like a puff of smoke. "Don't be nervous; you're one of the most genuine people I know. Well, once you get past the whole ice-queen exterior." She pretended to sprinkle her fingers like mock snow.

"Only for you, Carmen."

"I know, and for that, I'm annually grateful." Carmen looked around and turned back to Emmeline, dropping her voice next to her ear. "I completely forgot to tell you earlier. Mr. Mayor seemed to change his mind about attending tonight's gala when he heard you and Matthew would be here. His assistant requested that you both be at the same table as him and Ms. Phan. He's very eligible."

Emmeline was about to reply when Carmen straightened.

"You're up," she whispered.

The master of ceremonies introduced Emmeline and Matthew as representing The Taylor-Wu Foundation, and the spotlight floated over to their table as she and Matthew stood to face the crowd, each giving a short wave.

Suddenly, a flash of bright white blinded Emmeline, and her hand automatically gripped Matthew's arm to steady herself. She blinked as the brilliant light dimmed into an aura.

What is that?

It almost seemed as if the aura was beside another.

Are the auras ... at a table?

Emmeline squinted in the darkness.

And she swore she made eye contact.

Emmeline faced the audience, purposely keeping the auras to the side of her vision. She gripped the podium and lifted her voice, knowing it would take the tremor out.

"Good evening. My name is Emmeline Taylor-Wu, and on behalf of The Taylor-Wu Foundation and my brother, Dr. Matthew Taylor-Wu, I want to thank you for having us. The Royal Children's Rehabilitation Hospital was close to our parents' hearts and will forever have a special place in ours. Matthew spent much of his childhood at the hospital, and the research and generous donations of others helped our family understand how to best support his potential."

Emmeline glanced at her brother, and he nodded encouragingly. She looked around and the auras came into her center vision, glowing dimly at the back of the room.

"I ..." she stammered before clearing her throat. "Our family was lucky. We had many resources at our disposal, but there are countless families who aren't as fortunate as ours. For them, help is just a dream."

Get through this. Focus!

"The Royal Children's Rehabilitation Hospital is in its next phase of providing care to more families, and our foundation has granted it a significant contribution. Please join us in helping the hospital reach its donation goal. To all of you who've already contributed, I know you have more in you to give, so please don't be shy." Emmeline tried to smile. "Thank you. Be generous and kind."

The aura stayed in the same place, and Emmeline stared at the hazy light as it faded with each passing second.

The master of ceremonies hopped back on the podium with a wide smile. "Thank you to The Taylor-Wu Foundation for your incredible generosity!" He held out his hand to help Emmeline down the stairs before turning back to the audience. "Please have some dessert, do some dancing, and visit the beautiful garden. We'll be back shortly."

"What happened?" Matthew asked Emmeline after she settled back in her seat.

Emmeline leaned toward Matthew's ear. "I saw another flash of light, but again, no seizure."

"Maybe we should leave, just in case. Let me give Dr. Li a call."

"Don't bother Dr. Li now. It's late. I'll call her in the morning."

"Emia, this could be serious. I want you to do another MRI exam. It's been a few years, and I think it's time." Matthew raised an eyebrow at her. "Don't roll your eyes at me, or I'll tell Ms. Rose about this. Not only will you never hear the end of it, but you'll end up doing the MRI anyway."

Emmeline stopped her eye roll just in time. "Fine."

"That was a wonderful speech, Emmeline." Philip's deep voice came from behind her.

"Thank you." Emmeline smiled, and Matthew leaned back in his chair.

"Can I buy you a drink?"

"I don't drink alcohol," Emmeline replied.

She felt a light kick from Matthew, and she side-eyed her brother as he stared straight ahead at absolutely nothing.

Philip's smile waned. "I haven't seen the garden yet, and everyone's said it's spectacular. Care to accompany me?"

Emmeline felt another light kick on her knee and narrowed her eyes. *Mattie, you're going to ruin my dress with your dirty shoes. This cheongsam is vintage!*

"Yes, of course, Philip."

Philip pulled back her chair so she could stand, and she looked around the room for the aura.

Maybe it's gone?

～

Strings of lights outlined the beautiful garden and illuminated the night. Flowers of every imaginable color swayed to ethereal music coaxed to life by the graceful fingers of a lone pianist.

"If we walked into heaven, this is what it'd look like, wouldn't it?" Philip broke through Emmeline's thoughts. He kept a respectable distance and held his hands clasped behind his back.

"I suppose," Emmeline replied.

Philip walked purposefully, smiling at various guests as they waved and nodded to him. Every few steps, someone would stop to shake his hand and congratulate him on his new appointment.

"You're quite popular, aren't you, Mr. Mayor?"

"A requirement for the job."

"Mayor Vil! There you are. I've been looking for you all night!" a silky voice called out.

Emmeline looked to her left, just as a beautiful, willowy brunette in a black sequined gown sashayed over.

"Excuse me for a moment, Emmeline." Philip stepped to the side as the brunette slipped into his arm and whispered something against his ear.

"I'm quite tired, and I'd prefer to retire for the night. It's been a long day." Emmeline gave Philip a gracious smile. "It was nice to make your acquaintance."

"I understand. Can I send you a quick message later to see how you're doing?"

"Carmen has my contact information. Good night."

CHAPTER FOUR

FAIRY TALES

Emia: Mattie, where are you?

Mattie: I'm in my car.

Emia: Is it line-dancing time?

Mattie: Yes.

Emia: I'm on my way.

Mattie: Are you done with the mayor already?

Emia: Yes.

Emmeline walked through the garden as quickly as her heels would let her with dignity.

I can't wait to take off these death traps.

Emmeline almost groaned, thinking of her soft ballet flats, waiting for her in Matthew's car. She looked down and slipped her phone back in her clutch.

Suddenly, something stepped in front of her, and she gasped and looked up with irritation.

And it glowed.

Emmeline stumbled back, and a hand gripped her arm to steady her. Another manicured hand grabbed her wrist, hauling her to a dark corner of the garden before letting go.

"If you scream, I'll clamp my hand down so fast on your mouth that it'll definitely ruin your makeup," a bell-like voice hissed.

Emmeline snapped her mouth shut and looked at her assailant.

Correction: two assailants.

The woman with the manicured hand had straight, chin-length black hair, swept back, and her icy-gray eyes stood stark against her alabaster skin and pale, heart-shaped lips. She was statuesque and seemed to have poured her graceful body into a three-piece dark blue suit.

She's stunning.

Beside her stood the woman who had steadied her.

That's the woman I crashed into!

The other woman's chocolate skin, warm copper eyes, and full lips were framed by a loose, medium-length Afro. A simple white dress draped across her left shoulder, skimming her curves and making her silky skin gleam.

She looks like a goddess.

Emmeline gaped at the two women, and they stared back at her.

"You!" Emmeline pointed at the Black woman. "I ran into you in the restroom. You were ... you looked different." She squinted at the woman in white. "And why are the two of you glowing?"

I must be going crazy.

The two women glanced at each other before turning back to her. Emmeline looked back and forth between the two women. "And why are you both looking at me like that?"

"You're the one staring at us like we're ghosts," the manicured woman retorted, earning herself a reproachful look from the woman in white.

"Who are you? *What* are you?" Emmeline reached out and touched the Black woman's arm to make sure she was solid.

The Black woman covered Emmeline's hand with hers. "My name is Lesedi, and this is my partner, Anja."

Anja frowned. "What do you mean, we're glowing?"

"I'm going crazy, aren't I?" Emmeline glanced up at the sky before returning to Lesedi and Anja.

They're still glowing.

She let out a breath and fumbled through her clutch for her phone.

Emia: Mattie, can you come to the garden as soon as possible?

Anja narrowed her eyes, and Emmeline returned an equal glare.

"My brother is coming to get me because I don't trust my judgment right now, and more importantly, I don't trust you," Emmeline said. She drew herself to her full height. "Now, I ask again, who are you?"

"We just told you who we are," Anja retorted.

"You haven't told me anything. I couldn't care less what your names are," Emmeline snapped.

Lesedi placed a hand on Anja's arm. "We informally represent the LGBTQIA-plus community. I know your family makes a generous annual donation to Pride. That's very kind of you."

"We try to support voices that need to be amplified," Emmeline replied automatically. She heard quick footsteps coming in their direction.

"Emia, are you okay?" Matthew bent to look at her face. He pulled down on her lower eyelid and scanned her pupils.

Emmeline swatted his hand away and gestured to the two women. "Do you see auras around them?"

Matthew turned to Anja and Lesedi, taken aback by their presence. "No auras. Do you see an aura?"

"Yes! I see two." Emmeline held up two fingers to make a point. "Though they seem to be fading."

Anja's icy eyes scanned the garden. "Can we find somewhere more private to talk? With you, alone."

"If you want to talk, it'll be with the two of us. I don't keep anything from my brother, so you might as well save me time and talk to us together," Emmeline said.

Anja narrowed her eyes before turning to Lesedi. "It's against the rules."

"Since when do you pay attention to rules?" Lesedi sighed. "I don't like it either, and neither will Javier."

"I could just kidnap her," Anja offered.

"I can hear you; you know that, right?" Emmeline stared at Anja.

Lesedi held up a hand. "Let's just find somewhere more private, where we can all talk."

Emmeline raised an eyebrow at Matthew, but he only shrugged.

Anja sniffed. "Relax. If we wanted to hurt you, it wouldn't be while dressed in these fabulous outfits."

"You just suggested kidnapping me," Emmeline reminded her.

"I changed my mind. I don't want to ruin my clothes and makeup."

"Fair," Emmeline muttered.

I wouldn't risk it either if I looked like her.

⁓

Emmeline pushed open a door to one of the smaller rooms used by volunteers to rest.

"No one's here right now. We can use this room."

Anja walked in first with her head held high and surveyed the room.

That woman walks with the grace of royalty.

"Should we lock the door?" Anja asked.

"We aren't staying in a locked room with two strangers," Emmeline interrupted. She stood beside the door with her back against the wall.

This probably wasn't a smart move. And now, I've dragged Mattie into this.

"You might want to sit." Lesedi gestured to a chair.

"We're fine. Be quick," Matthew clipped.

"Just try to keep an open mind." Lesedi paused. "Anja and I are different from normal human beings. We have the unique job of ensuring bad things that don't belong in this world don't end up here." She paused again and contemplated her next words. "For simplicity, you can think of us like demon hunters. We stop bad things from crossing a barrier between this world and another, and when they somehow make it across, we dispose of them."

Emmeline looked at Matthew incredulously, and he gave her his infamous *why am I here?* glare before straightening up, signaling that he was more than done.

"I'm a little old for fairy tales," Emmeline said. "I don't believe in ghosts, goblins, or gargoyles anymore. Good night."

Emmeline opened the door when it was wrenched from her grasp and slammed shut.

"We're not finished," Anja hissed.

"Move out of the way, or the next conversation you'll be having will be with our lawyer," Emmeline snapped.

"Good luck finding me."

"Anja, that's not necessary." Lesedi waved for Anja to come back to her side. "Emmeline, you haven't asked what any of this has to do with you."

"We haven't asked because it has nothing to do with us," Matthew replied.

"You noticed us because we have an aura, but we noticed you because you have magic in you. It's faint, but it's there."

Emmeline's mouth fell open. "You both must think I'm a rich idiot."

Anja's cool eyes pierced into Emmeline's. "You're not a normal human."

"I can assure you, I'm as normal and boring as they come."

Matthew tilted his head at Anja in a challenge. "If you can prove you are who or what you say you are, then please do so."

"Fine." Anja turned to face the two of them.

The room seemed to darken into shadows as Anja's ashy irises widened until all the white was covered. Her pupils stretched to span the height of her eyes, and the silver flecks in her irises deepened in brilliance.

And then, she smiled wickedly, showcasing two rows of perfect, sharp teeth.

"Matthew, you're looking a little bit green," Anja purred.

"Dr. Taylor-Wu," Matthew corrected her. His voice was incredulous as he gaped.

"Is someone overcompensating?"

"Only when someone's an asshole."

Emmeline backed up against the wall, and she couldn't stop staring at Anja's eyes and teeth.

That's what I saw earlier! But it was Lesedi and not Anja. And her skin was gray, but Anja's isn't. Emmeline looked wildly between the two women.

"Anja, can you please be kind?" Lesedi frowned.

"They're the ones who wanted proof, so I gave it to them," Anja said. "I already went easy on them. You should be giving me a pat on the back and commending me on my incredible self-control."

"That's what I saw in the restroom! I thought I was hallucinating." Emmeline pointed a finger at Lesedi. "I remember seeing your eyes like Anja's, but your skin was gray and brittle. This can't be real. Did somebody spike my water?"

Anja smirked. "No one spiked your drink."

"Mattie, please tell me you're seeing this as well?"

Matthew nodded and looked curiously at Anja. "May I?"

Anja dipped her head in permission, and Matthew tilted her chin up to examine her eyes. He reached to the left of his chest but was met by the crisp pocket square of his tuxedo. He looked down and muttered a single unintelligible curse. Looking around the room for better lighting, he grimaced as he guided Anja a few steps back. He repositioned her shoulders and pulled her lower eyelid down to get a better look.

"Watch the makeup," Anja muttered.

"Can you move your eyes?"

Anja did as she had been asked.

"Fascinating." Matthew pulled down her lower lip. "Can you smile?"

Anja grinned, baring all her sharp teeth. Matthew knocked on her teeth with his finger, and she frowned.

"Thank you." Matthew let go of Anja's face and stepped back.

Anja blinked, and her eyes returned to normal. "You're very odd. Most people would be cowering by now, yet all you want to do is examine."

Emmeline stepped beside Matthew. "I don't understand what this has to do with us."

"You," Lesedi corrected her. "This has nothing to do with your brother."

"What does this have to do with me?"

"Do you still see a glow around Anja and me?"

"Barely."

"I think you have the gift of sight. You can see our kind, where normal people cannot."

"Great. What does that mean?"

"It's not just the ability to see us that makes you special. Humans with this gift can foresee those who will become like us." Lesedi gestured to Emmeline. "There aren't many of you in the world. You're quite rare."

"You mean, I can see the future? Like a seer or a fortune teller?" Emmeline was confused. "I've never had an inkling of a vision."

Lesedi waved her hand to brush away Emmeline's questions. "Things will become clearer with time. I don't have enough knowledge of this subject, so I need to discuss it with those who have studied this. I know this is a lot to take in, but I'd like you to meet some of our family soon."

"Family?" Matthew's eyes flickered away from the wall and over to Lesedi.

"Well, not family in the traditional sense," Lesedi said. "No blood relation, except for one odd instance in our history. All we have are each other, so we consider each other family."

I must be dreaming. Do I believe this is happening?

"Don't worry; I'll be in contact with you soon. In the meantime, I'd appreciate it if you didn't share this encounter with anyone. We value our privacy and would hate to get off on the wrong foot," Lesedi said.

"What would happen if we did?" Matthew asked, half-listening to what was happening in the room and half in his own world, cataloging what he had just seen.

Ever the multitasker.

"Then, I'd have to kill you," Anja said sweetly.

Matthew turned to stare at Anja, and Emmeline shivered.

There's something seriously wrong with that woman.

"I'm pleased to have found you, Emmeline, and I hope to get to know you better soon." Lesedi opened the French doors that led to the balcony. "Good night."

"Good night, Doctor. See you soon, Emmeline," Anja drawled, and followed Lesedi to the balcony.

With a blur of gray and a gust of wind, they vanished into the cool summer evening air.

"Wait!" Emmeline rushed to the balcony.

Her hands gripped the stone ledge, and she craned her neck over the railing to look around the night sky. Light music filtered up as the smell of late summer blossoms wafted through the room.

Soon, the gentle breeze whispered as it curled itself around Emmeline, soothing the blood thundering through her veins.

CHAPTER FIVE

DUMPLINGS

"They could've just used the front entrance. It's not like we would've made a scene," Emmeline grumbled as she and Matthew walked through the main hall.

She looked at Matthew and sighed.

He's not listening to me.

"Emmeline, there you are! I've been looking all over for you." Carmen hurried over, a bright smile gracing her face.

Emmeline looked at Carmen for a few seconds before it registered who was talking to her.

Carmen cupped Emmeline's hands. "Are you ill?"

"I'm not feeling well," Emmeline lied. "I've had a headache all day, and it won't go away."

"Get some rest. I'll message you tomorrow with the details of the fundraiser."

"Thank you, Carmen. I'll talk to you soon."

Emia: Ms. Rose, we'll be home soon. Is there anything to eat?

Ms. Rose: I'll fry up some pork and leek dumplings. Just you, or will Mattie be joining?

Emia: Both of us. Thank you.

Emmeline sank into the plush leather seat of Matthew's new sports car and closed her eyes. Matthew was still silent and seemed to be driving on autopilot through the quiet roads that led home. The moonroof was open, and she could hear the crickets calling every time the car slowed and the engine rested.

"I still don't believe what we saw," Matthew stated, startling Emmeline out of her thoughts.

"Do you think it's an elaborate hoax? Because I can't make sense of it either."

"Her eyes and teeth were real. How is that possible?" Matthew stared ahead. "But if it's a hoax, it's probably about money. It's always about money."

Emmeline turned to Matthew. "I've been seeing auras and having seizures since university. Could this be why? I don't get them often, but every time I've seen an aura, it's always been blinding, and I always black out after."

"But this time, you didn't have a seizure."

"True, and it was only blinding for a moment. I have a feeling it's related."

Matthew turned into their driveway, but instead of parking close to the front door, he pressed an invisible button, and the underground parking garage door rose.

"You're staying at home?" Emmeline asked.

"After tonight, I think it's best to stay close to home for a few days. To be safe."

"Are you scared to go back to your condominium?"

"It isn't me they care about," Matthew replied as he backed into his favorite parking spot.

Emmeline sobered at the thought and looked at her feet. "It's nice to have you home, Mattie."

"It's nice to be home."

Emmeline could smell the fragrant mix of leeks, garlic chives, and minced pork frying on the stove as she made her way up the stairs from the basement. Matthew followed behind her, desperately trying to shed his bow tie and jacket.

"It's like being in a straitjacket," he muttered.

"Emia, Mattie, you're just in time," Ms. Rose called out from the kitchen.

"Ms. Rose, can you call Mr. Jae to meet us in the kitchen?" Matthew asked. "I know it's late, but we need his assistance."

"Yes, of course."

Matthew quickened his steps and passed Emmeline to make his way to his bedroom.

Emmeline rolled her eyes. *Weak. Try wearing weapons on your feet for hours.*

Emmeline slipped out of her cheongsam and carefully hung it up. After divesting herself of her heirloom jewelry and placing each item back into their rightful spots, she pulled her hair into a ponytail and washed her face. She looked through her closet and thumbed through the cashmere tank dresses that hung in pristine color-coded order before selecting a charcoal gray.

Her stomach grumbled again.

I know, I know, it's time to eat!

She tucked her feet into a pair of slippers and left her bedroom.

"Mr. Jae!" she greeted the property manager seated at the kitchen island.

Mr. Jae and Ms. Rose had been with the Taylor-Wu family since Emmeline had been a child and Matthew barely a teenager. As they had grown older and not needed as much help, most of the property keepers had left the household until only Mr. Jae and Ms. Rose remained. Emmeline and Matthew considered them family.

"Hello, Ms. Emia. You're home earlier than I expected, and you brought a guest!" Mr. Jae laughed after Emmeline gave him a quick kiss on the cheek.

"Ms. Rose, that smells delicious." Emmeline gazed at the sizzling plate of dumplings.

Emmeline grabbed four plates, chopsticks, and dipping sauces and laid them out on the quartz countertop. After retrieving a jar of fresh kimchi from the refrigerator, she plopped down on a barstool.

"Mr. Jae, Ms. Rose." Matthew walked into the kitchen. He had changed into his favorite white T-shirt and black joggers and sat beside Emmeline. He piled a mountain of dumplings and kimchi onto his plate.

"I should tell you both what happened tonight." Matthew set his chopsticks down. "We left earlier than usual because Emia was accosted by two gala attendees."

Ms. Rose frowned. "What did they want?"

"I'm not sure. They were persistent, so I'm going to stay home for a few nights."

"Mr. Jae, can you do a round of the estate and check that all the doors and windows are locked and have the safety latches on? Ms. Rose, can you make sure the security system is on and the cameras are all working?" Emmeline asked.

Mr. Jae nodded and tapped his smartphone. "I'll go take care of this right now. Don't worry; the security is very good, and nobody comes in or out without me knowing. I'll be back once it's done." He popped a couple dumplings into his mouth. "Don't let the two bottomless pits finish the entire plate." He winked at Ms. Rose and jogged out of the kitchen.

"Are you worried they'll come here?" Ms. Rose tapped on a tablet to make sure each camera was working. "Once Mr. Jae is back, I'll arm the system, and I'll include the ones on the second and third floors." She looked pointedly at Emmeline, who was notorious for sleeping with a window open.

"I don't think they'll come here, but I'd feel safer if we took some additional precautions for a little while," Emmeline said.

"Do you want me to bring in a security detail?" Ms. Rose peered at both Emmeline and Matthew.

Emmeline answered, "No," just as Matthew said, "Yes."

"No," Emmeline repeated. "I don't want a stranger in this house. We have a top-of-the-line security system that's supposed to keep us safe. I also don't think those two women would go so far as to come here."

"Fine. I'm going to bed." Matthew stood up and brought his empty dish to the sink. "Ms. Rose, good night. Please tell Mr. Jae good night for me. See you both in the morning."

CHAPTER SIX

CURIOSITY

Help!

Emmeline squeezed her eyes shut to block the light searing into her brain.

Please stop!

Pain shot through her spine, making her back arch and limbs tremble. Tears pricked the sides of her eyes, and she braced herself for the next assault.

Someone, please help me …

∼

Emmeline woke with a start and sat up.

Where am I?

She pushed her damp hair off her face and looked around.

I'm in my room.

She kicked off her blanket and flopped back onto her bed.

I haven't had a dream for so long, and the first thing I dream about is having a seizure. She sighed and glanced at the clock. *It's early. I might as well get up and do some work.*

Emmeline grabbed her phone to check her messages, and there was one from a number she didn't recognize.

Unknown: Hi, Emmeline. This is Philip. I hope you had a good time at the gala. I meant to talk to you about the other causes your family foundation supports. Let me know when you have time for us to connect. Take care.

Emia: Good morning, Philip. I always try to support causes close to the family's heart. Happy to chat later.

After she hit Send, her phone chimed immediately.

Philip: How about coffee this coming Thursday morning? I have a private balcony at the Harbor Yacht Club.

Emia: You're up early.

Philip: No rest for the wicked.

Emmeline smiled as she looked through her schedule.

Emia: Thursday morning works.

Philip: Great. See you then.

Emia: See you.

Emmeline put her phone down and headed to her bathroom en suite. She turned on the hot water in her marble-encased shower and let the steam wrap her in its embrace. She peeled off her sticky tank dress and stepped into the shower, allowing the scorching water to roll off her skin and carry away with it the remnants of her nightmare.

~

Emmeline crept up behind Matthew as he sat at the patio table on their backyard deck. She snickered as she watched him type on his laptop while inhaling a chocolate croissant. She leaned over his shoulder, just inches away from his face, and cleared her throat.

Matthew didn't flinch.

"You know that doesn't work." He continued his latest correspondence without looking up.

Emmeline harrumphed. "I'll get you one day."

"You also know we're fully grown adults and not children."

"Better late than never."

Emmeline poured herself a steaming cup of black coffee and sat in the chair beside her brother.

"Mattie, you're wearing the same thing you were wearing last night. How many sets of white T-shirts and black joggers do you own?"

Matthew squinted at his screen. "Sixteen."

Emmeline almost spat out her coffee. "Sixteen sets? Why?"

"So that I can go a few weeks without having to do laundry. You should try it. It's efficient."

"I guess it's a good thing we invested in that little start-up in British Columbia."

"Yes, their version of technical cashmere is excellent. I own most of their line."

"And I thought I was the one who was boosting the company up. No wonder they're doing so well," Emmeline muttered.

"Can you ask Carmen if she knows anything about the two women from the gala?" Matthew asked.

"Good idea."

Emia: Carmen, the gala was lovely, and I'm sorry I had to leave early. Last night, I was accosted by two women. I think they were at a table close to the east exit doors. One was white and wearing a three-piece suit, and the other was Black and wearing a one-shouldered white gown. Can you find their names and contacts?

Carmen: Good morning, Emmeline! Let me check the records and see what I can find. I'm sorry this happened. Our guests are always well-behaved. Are you okay?

Emia: I'm fine. I just want to know who I'm dealing with if I run into them again.

Carmen: Found it. Amy Wild and Leslie Serene. It doesn't say they were representing any organization.

Emmeline groaned and turned to Matthew. "Fake names."

Emia: They mentioned Pride. I'll check with my contact there.

Carmen: Okay. Let me know how else I can help.

"I'm not surprised they used fake names. We don't even know if the names they gave us were real," Matthew said as he continued typing on his laptop.

"But why were they at the gala?"

"I've been wondering the same thing. It didn't seem like they were there for you. They looked equally surprised to learn about you."

Emmeline couldn't help the curiosity that bubbled up. "I don't think they're out to hurt me, and I get the feeling they aren't after money." She shivered as she remembered Anja's glittering irises and sharp smile. "I want to find out more about them."

"Why?"

"For my whole adult life, I've lived in the shadow of my seizures. The flash of light I saw when I first met Lesedi and Anja felt similar to what I see right before a seizure. What if they have the answer as to why I get the seizures? Or it's one hell of a coincidence."

Matthew looked at Emmeline for the first time that morning. "Let me know if they contact you again."

"I will."

∼

"Gus!" Emmeline waved to her best friend, August, as she strode into the garden.

August's tight brown curls bounced against her shoulders, and her deep caramel skin glowed under the sunlight. Her green eyes lit up at the pastry and fruit platter on the patio table.

"Hey, Emia, Mattie. Oh, yum, chocolate croissants!" August grabbed one and wolfed it down in three bites.

Emmeline raised her eyebrow. "I thought you were on a low-carb diet?"

"Selectively."

"I don't even know why you're on a diet. You're beautiful. I'd kill for just a portion of your curves." Emmeline looked down at her own modest chest.

"And this is why you're my best friend." August leaned over and kissed Emmeline on the cheek, flashing her a brilliant smile that showcased the beautiful gap between her two front teeth.

Matthew shut his laptop and packed up his backpack. "I need to get to the hospital." He stood and turned to August. "You don't need to diet. Eat balanced meals, exercise regularly, and manage your stress by not letting Emia work you twenty-four/seven. Set healthy boundaries for yourself."

Emmeline glared at Matthew. "I don't work her twenty-four/seven."

"She's the finance controller for our foundation's entire portfolio. That's not a nine-to-five job."

"You're too sweet, Mattie, but I'm fine, and I love my job," August replied.

"If you need help, just ask." Matthew threw his backpack over his shoulder and went back inside the house.

August turned back to Emmeline. "How was the party last night?"

"Something happened. Well, a few things happened," Emmeline said.

August put down her second croissant. "What things?"

"I saw a couple of auras and thought I was going to have a seizure."

August sat up, and Emmeline could see the alarm in her eyes.

"I didn't have a seizure," Emmeline added hastily.

"Jeez, Emia. You waited until now to tell me this?"

"There's more." Emmeline winced as August narrowed her eyes at her. "There were two women who kind of harassed me at the gala."

"What did they do?"

"They cornered me and told me they wanted to talk. Then, they told me they'd be in touch and find me later, and disappeared."

I can't tell her about the eyes and teeth and the disappearing off a balcony. Gus would think I'm going crazy.

"Do you have their names? I can do some digging for you. Were they representing an organization?" August asked.

"No. They registered with fake names."

"Fake names? At a charity gala?"

"This event was a big one, and both the premier and the mayor showed up."

"Whoa, stacked. Did the women mention anything that might be a clue as to who they were?" August furrowed her brow.

"They knew that our foundation makes an annual donation

to Pride. We always donate under our foundation name to show our support, so many people know about this."

"I have a few contacts at Pride. Let me see what I can find."

"Thanks." Emmeline shifted uncomfortably.

"Spit it out, Emia."

Emmeline blushed. "I think I might be going on a date."

August slapped the table with both her hands, and Emmeline jumped. "What? Why didn't you lead with this?"

"It's not an official date. We're having breakfast to talk about our foundation's charity work. That's it."

August leaned her face in. "With who?"

"Philip Vil."

"Philip Vil, *the mayor*?" August shrieked.

Emmeline winced. "Yes, but don't make a big deal about it, or next time, I'm not going to tell you."

"Fine, but I want all the details, and don't you dare leave a thing out. I tell you everything, Emmeline Taylor-Wu. Everything! I want you to remember that," August huffed.

Emmeline cringed at August's fiery glare. "We'd better get to work. It's almost lunchtime."

August fixed Emmeline with another deathly glare and pulled out her laptop. Before they knew how much time had passed, Ms. Rose stepped onto the deck with a trolley to serve lunch.

"Thank you for making us lunch, Ms. Rose. Why don't you join us? It's a beautiful day," Emmeline said.

"And listen to you both drone on and on about numbers and money? No, thank you." Ms. Rose placed their lunch on the table. She turned to Emmeline and squinted at her face. "Sweetheart, did you put on sunscreen this morning?"

"Yes. I wouldn't dare risk another lecture."

August snorted. "Don't listen to her, Ms. Rose. I take all your advice seriously. I wear sunscreen every day."

Ms. Rose patted August's arm. "Good girl. Don't take too long to eat. Your kickboxing instructor will be here at three, and you need enough time to digest your food." With that, she swept out of the garden.

"Way to put a damper on such a delicious meal," August groaned.

Emmeline laughed and put her arm around August, giving her shoulder a squeeze.

CHAPTER SEVEN

TRESPASSERS

Emmeline flopped down on her couch and looked longingly at her bed.

I should shower first.

She groaned and pushed herself off her bed. After their kickboxing class, she and August cooled off in the pool before returning to the audit reports until dinnertime. August left for a late dinner date with her husband, Ryan, while Emmeline continued to work until the sun set to a brilliant orange and her cashmere wrap begged her to go back inside.

Emmeline stretched and rolled out her shoulders and neck. She undid her ponytail and shook out the salt-coated strands before heading to her bathroom.

Emia:	Mattie, when are you coming home?
Mattie:	I'm done with all my appointments. I will be home soon.
Emia:	If you're too tired to drive, stay at your condo.

Mattie: I'm coming home for the night.

Emia: Okay. See you soon.

Emmeline put her phone on the bathroom counter and washed her face as she waited for the steam to fill the room. She began stripping off her clothes when her phone vibrated.

Unknown: Emmeline, this is Lesedi. Let me know when you can talk. I'm outside.

Outside?

Emia: What do you mean, you're outside? Outside where?

Lesedi: Outside your room. No rush. I can wait.

Emmeline threw her tank top back on and tapped open her security application on her phone. Her thumb hovered over the Panic button as she opened her bathroom door and looked around her empty room.
They wouldn't dare!
Everything looked exactly as she had left it a few minutes ago. Her bedroom and sliding balcony doors were both closed and locked. Her phone vibrated again in her hands.

Lesedi: I'm on the balcony.

Emmeline stared, wide-eyed, at the light-gray curtains that covered the balcony doors.

Lesedi: You don't need to worry. If I wanted to hurt you, it would've already been done. If you call security, I'll be long gone by the time they get here.

Emmeline walked over to the balcony and flipped on the outdoor lights before pulling back the heavy curtains. Lesedi was perched on the arm of the double lounge chaise and dressed head to toe in a formfitting matte-black outfit. Her cap-sleeved T-shirt was covered with a stiff-looking vest that looked like armor, revealing toned arms. Two leather straps crossed over her chest, and her leggings were tucked into mid-calf leather boots that looked ready for combat. Despite her intimidating outfit, Lesedi was regal, and her copper eyes radiated warmth.

Emmeline unlocked the glass sliding doors, and she stepped barefoot out onto her balcony.

"Good evening, Emmeline."

Good evening? Anger rolled over Emmeline like a tidal wave.

"This is private property, and you're trespassing. This is my home. Who do you think you are?" Emmeline demanded. "Not only would I like to know how you got my contact information and address, but I also want to know why you couldn't be civilized and book a fucking appointment."

"I apologize. I know this is a bit of an intrusion, but we need to talk privately."

Emmeline narrowed her eyes. "How did you get up here anyway? We're on the third floor."

"If you give me enough time, I'll show you later."

Emmeline's phone buzzed.

Mattie: Home.

Emia: Come to my room right away.

Lesedi raised an eyebrow, and Emmeline stared back at her.

"I'm going to hazard a guess and say that was your brother. We might as well wait for him," Lesedi sighed.

Within seconds, footsteps came running down the hallway, followed by loud knocking on Emmeline's bedroom door.

"Emia, the door is locked," Matthew called out as he jiggled the door handle.

Emmeline ran to unlock the door and let Matthew in. He looked disheveled in his white dress shirt and dark dress pants, like she had interrupted him while he was changing.

"What's the emergency?" Matthew asked.

"I have an unannounced visitor."

"Who?" Matthew looked past Emmeline, and recognition registered across his face. "Why is Lesedi on your balcony?"

"That's what I'm trying to find out. I certainly didn't invite her here. She just showed up."

"Why didn't you call the police? Trigger the alarm? Press the panic button? You know, all the expensive things we pay for and have been trained on in case of emergencies?"

Emmeline stared at Matthew. *Why didn't I?*

"I don't know."

Matthew glared back at her. "Really?"

"I can hear everything you're saying," Lesedi called out. "If you give me time, I'll answer your questions and more."

Emmeline and Matthew gave each other a look and headed out to the balcony.

"You understand that you're trespassing on private property," Matthew stated as he evaluated Lesedi.

"Yes, Emmeline has already informed me."

"Whatever you want to say, you'd better do it quickly. I'm infinitely less patient than my sister."

"Before we get started, I brought two friends with me. I didn't want to surprise you with the unannounced visit of three of us on your balcony."

"How considerate," Emmeline said.

"I try." Lesedi looked up at the roof. "Anja, you and Asadi can join us now."

Anja landed with solid footing on the balcony, and Asadi arrived behind her several seconds later. Emmeline raised one hand to shield her eyes from Asadi's flash of light, and her body automatically braced itself for a seizure. She closed her eyes and took a deep breath to steady herself.

No seizure.

Emmeline opened her eyes and lowered her hand as Asadi's aura dimmed to a faint glow. In front of her stood a tall, older gentleman with a deep olive complexion and dark hair, curled out at the nape of his neck. Unlike Lesedi and Anja, he had broad shoulders and a brawny build that reminded Emmeline of a middleweight boxer with a stern expression to match.

Matthew looked at Emmeline. "Aura?"

"Only for the new person, and it's subsided now. There's no aura around Lesedi or Anja anymore."

"And you didn't have a seizure. Very interesting."

Lesedi cleared her throat. "I trust you both remember Anja?"

"How could we forget?" Emmeline muttered.

She glanced at Anja, who was dressed similarly to Lesedi, highlighting her slender figure. Instead of the high, swept-back hairstyle she'd had at the gala, her chin-length hair framed her face and softened her angular features. Her kohl-rimmed eyes were just as clear and icy as Emmeline remembered.

She's gorgeous.

Emmeline tugged self-consciously at her tank top and tried to smooth down her hair by tucking it behind her ears.

"Dr. Matthew, I told you I'd see you soon. I bet this isn't how you envisioned us meeting again." Anja flashed him a brilliant grin.

"I don't understand why you think I would've spent any time thinking about that."

Lesedi smiled. "Isn't this nice? We're all getting along just fine. Now, let me introduce you to one of my friends. Asadi is our senior historian."

"It's nice to meet you both." Asadi nodded to Emmeline and Matthew. His voice was deep and soothing, and as he stepped into the light, Emmeline could see his dark hair and short beard were tinged with gray.

"I've asked Asadi to join us and help answer some of your questions." Lesedi paused. "He's also concerned that Matthew knows about this, and he's here to ensure that you both take our request for secrecy and discretion seriously."

Matthew pushed his glasses up. "That sounds like a threat."

"It can be," Asadi replied.

"Don't talk to my brother like that," Emmeline snapped. "The three of you have some nerve, seeing as you've instigated every encounter." She stepped in front of Matthew and pointed to the balcony rail. "You can take your attitude and penchant for trespassing and get the fuck off my property. Leave the same way you came."

"And just when I thought we were all beginning to get along." Lesedi sighed, earning herself another glare from Emmeline. "Can we please have a conversation? Give us one hour, and I promise we'll all behave."

Emmeline looked at Matthew, who, as usual, only shrugged. "Fine. You get one hour in the garden. I'm sure you know the way," she retorted.

Emmeline turned and grabbed Matthew's arm, making him wince as she hauled him back into her bedroom. She slammed the door harder than needed and locked it behind her.

The nerve of some people!

∼

"One hour? And in the garden? What will you tell Ms. Rose or Mr. Jae? Ms. Rose will want to serve them drinks."

"I don't know. I just wanted them off my balcony. I was also cold and wanted to put on something warmer." Emmeline pulled the curtains over the balcony doors.

"I'll see you downstairs in a few minutes." Without waiting for her response, Matthew turned and left her room.

Emmeline changed out of her clothes and put on a hooded sweater and thick leggings. After combing out her hair and setting it in a neat bun on top of her head, she picked up her phone and messaged Ms. Rose.

Emia:	Ms. Rose, I have some guests in the garden. They'll only be here for a short while, so no need to bring out anything. I'll turn on the security system once they're gone. Please don't wait up.

Ms. Rose: Okay, dear. Have a good night. If you need anything, message me. I'm in my room, catching up on some TV shows.

Emia: Good night, Ms. Rose.

Emmeline grabbed an extra shawl for herself and headed downstairs.

~

Emmeline walked into the kitchen and almost ran straight into Matthew. Sure enough, he had changed back into his standard uniform with the addition of a black hoodie. In his hand was a small pouch that she knew all too well.

"Why did you bring your medical equipment with you?" Emmeline asked.

"I want another demonstration."

"I'm going to make coffee for myself. Do you want one?"

"No. I want to get this over with and go to bed. I have a long day of appointments tomorrow."

"You can go out first if you want to make small talk."

"I'd rather stab myself in the eye with a syringe," Matthew said irritably. "Are you going to offer our guests anything?"

"Nope."

Matthew raised his eyebrow but didn't comment. The coffee machine buzzed, and Emmeline took her cup off the drip tray.

"Come on, Mattie. Let's get this done."

CHAPTER EIGHT

ONE OF TWO

Lesedi, Anja, and Asadi were seated at the patio table when Emmeline and Matthew walked out. The steam from Emmeline's coffee curled lazily in the cool summer air as she set her cup down and settled into her seat. From the corner of her eye, she caught Anja gazing at her cup.

I'm such a pushover.

"Would anybody like a coffee or water?" Emmeline asked through clenched teeth. She avoided looking at her brother.

Anja perked up in her seat. "I'd love a coffee—one-quarter milk. Please," she added hastily.

Emmeline went back inside and fixed a cup of coffee with freshly steamed milk. Anja beamed when Emmeline reappeared and handed her the piping hot mug.

So, she is capable of a genuine smile.

Lesedi cleared her throat and nodded at Asadi.

"Dr. Taylor-Wu, I'm often told that I'm too blunt. I apologize for my earlier comment." Asadi dipped his head.

"I don't have a problem with anyone being blunt, but I do have a problem with threats. Don't ever threaten my sister or me," Matthew replied.

Asadi was about to respond when Lesedi held up her hand to stop him.

"There won't be threats of any kind from us," Lesedi said. "Asadi's just very protective of our family. We operate under complete secrecy, and you're one of a handful of humans who knows who we are. I know what I'm about to say might be perceived as a threat, but I want to be honest. We take betrayal of our secret very seriously, and we'll do anything to ensure it remains a secret."

"We barely know anything about you, and even if we were to tell anyone, nobody would believe us," Emmeline interjected.

"When you say I'm one of a handful of humans who knows about you, why did you only direct that comment at me? Why's my sister exempt from this warning?" Matthew asked.

"That's a good question, and I think that's where we'll start today." Lesedi turned to Emmeline. "When we met yesterday, I told you that you have the gift of sight. We believe you can see humans who will become one of us."

"You also said it was related to the auras I see."

"Our kind has always been aided by two seekers. The job of a seeker is to locate humans who've been marked. Seekers have magic within them that allows them to sense a potential, and once a potential has been identified, it becomes our job to find the potential and help them transition from their human form to our form."

Asadi leaned forward and clasped his hands on the table. "The formal name of a seeker is elystier. They ensure the survival of our race and, ultimately, the human race."

Emmeline looked over at Matthew, but his face remained unreadable. "And what exactly are you?" she asked.

Asadi looked at Lesedi, who nodded. "We are the nainthe. We're the guardians of the gateway between this world and the raizour world. You can think of it like a gate that separates us from hell, except it isn't hell—or at least, not the hell humans believe in. Without a seeker, it's challenging for us to find potentials, and without potentials to take our places, we will eventually die off. Without us guarding against the raizour, they'll come through the gateway and take over this world."

"Are seekers also nainthe?" Emmeline asked.

Asadi shook his head. "Seekers are human."

"Are you the same as Anja?"

"We're all the same."

"Show me again," Emmeline demanded.

Asadi gave Lesedi a questioning look.

"It's fine. Just as Anja did," Lesedi replied.

Matthew pushed his chair back and gestured for Asadi to stand. Asadi hesitated but let Matthew guide him to stand with his back toward the patio doors. Emmeline grabbed Matthew's medical pouch and went to his side.

"Wait." Matthew rummaged through his bag and pulled out his ophthalmoscope. He flicked on the little light. "Continue."

Asadi faced Matthew, and his brown irises expanded until all the white was covered. His pupils stretched and widened, touching the top and bottom of his eyelids.

"Can you switch between your human and nainthe forms?" Matthew asked.

"I can, but you're making me feel uncomfortable."

"I know."

Matthew shone his ophthalmoscope into Asadi's eyes while his irises shrank back to normal before expanding again. Matthew put the ophthalmoscope back and unwrapped a disposable tongue depressor.

"Can you open your mouth?" Matthew asked.

Asadi opened his mouth, and Emmeline watched in horror as his perfectly straight teeth sharpened to gleaming points. Matthew tapped Asadi's teeth with the tongue depressor.

"Real?" Emmeline whispered to Matthew.

He nodded and tossed the tongue depressor into the garbage bin. Emmeline backed up when she felt a presence beside her. She jumped and came face-to-face with two rows of sharp white teeth. Emmeline shrieked, and Anja's hand clamped over her mouth, muffling the sudden noise. Anja laughed, and Emmeline pushed her away.

"Anja!" Lesedi barked. "Stop scaring her!"

Anja sobered and turned back to Emmeline. "Sorry. You're so jumpy, and it's too tempting." She waved her hand at Matthew. "And your brother doesn't seem bothered at all, so that's no fun."

Matthew turned to Anja. "I'm plenty of fun."

"I'm sure you are."

"See if I ever offer you another cup of coffee again," Emmeline muttered. "Assuming I believe what you're all saying, why do you think I'm one of these seekers?"

Anja turned serious. "When I saw you at the gala, I felt nothing. It wasn't until you looked straight at me that I felt it. But it was also different. When I first met Lana and Chin, I knew who they were right away. I don't feel that with you. The pull is much weaker."

"Same for all of us," Asadi confirmed as he sat back down. "I haven't encountered this before, and I checked the historical accounts and couldn't find anything that described a similar experience. My guess is that you haven't fully come into your gift, or maybe your gift is muted or dialed down."

"What happened to Lana and Chin?" Emmeline asked.

Anja turned to look at the garden. "Lana and Chin both died about twenty years ago. Lana from old age and Chin from a stroke. We've been searching for other seekers since and haven't had any luck until last night."

"Does this mean there haven't been any new nainthe for the past twenty years?"

"We've found a handful of potentials, which is a fraction of what two elystiers could find. Our ability to find potentials is limited to physically seeing them," Lesedi said. "But an elystier feels the call. They don't need to see the potential to know they're there."

"I don't remember feeling any call."

"We're hoping we can help with that," Lesedi said.

"I still think you have the wrong person. I don't have any special gifts, and there certainly isn't anything exceptional about me."

"I'm never wrong," Anja said.

"It's true. She's rarely wrong," Lesedi confirmed, and Anja gave Emmeline a smug smile.

Emmeline ignored them both. "So, if you believe I'm a seeker, there's still another seeker out there somewhere?"

Asadi nodded. "In all the historical accounts I've studied, there have always been two. Sometimes, there's a slight gap of a few months or, at most, a few years. To have gone this long without seekers is unprecedented."

"What are the raizour?" Matthew spoke up.

"For now, you can think of them as demons. They want to leave their world and enter ours. They're intelligent and more like us than we'd care to admit." Asadi stopped and shared a glance with Lesedi. "I think this part of the explanation should be saved for later. This was a lot for one night."

"I agree." Lesedi placed her hand on Emmeline's arm. "I'd like you to visit us and meet the rest of our family. I'm sure you have many questions, but it's late, and we all need rest. I can't stress just how important you are to our survival and how far we'll go to protect you. You're the hope that we've been searching for."

"I have one more question before you go." Emmeline looked at Lesedi, Anja, and then Asadi. "How did you get on and off my balcony?"

Anja threw her head back and laughed a genuine bell-like laugh. "I'll show you later, but I don't think you'll like it very much."

That woman is insufferable.

"Fine." Emmeline stood up. "It's past the one-hour mark anyway."

"Good night, Emmeline, Dr. Taylor-Wu. We'll be in touch soon. If you have any questions, you have my contact now." Lesedi sounded tired. "And please remember not to mention us to anyone."

Matthew stood, and he and Emmeline both walked toward the patio doors.

Before opening the door, Emmeline looked over her shoulder. "Who gave you my contact information?"

"No one did. I pilfered it." Anja's smile widened. "Though I imagine you wouldn't mind if the mayor had it. Shall I pass it to him?"

Emmeline reddened. "He already has it."

Anja's laugh rang through the night air again, and Matthew looked at her strangely.

Emmeline turned and headed inside.

Completely insufferable.

PART II:

TITANS

CHAPTER NINE

NEW BEGINNINGS

Emmeline's alarm went off in a succession of chimes, and she threw her arm over her eyes.

Come on. You can do it. You will roll out of bed in ten seconds.

Emmeline counted down as loudly as she could in her head and threw back her fluffy duvet. Swinging her legs over the side of her bed, she grabbed her phone off her nightstand to check her messages.

Still no messages from Lesedi. It's been a few days now, and I wonder why I haven't heard from her. I hope she's okay. She shook the thoughts out of her head. *You and Mattie probably just entertained a bunch of crazies.*

She straightened.

I have breakfast with Philip today. I'd better get ready if I want to do some work done beforehand.

Emmeline went to the bathroom and hopped into her shower, opting for a quick rinse instead of her usual extended soak. After drying herself off with a towel, she threw her head upside down and blow-dried her hair. When she flipped her long black hair over, it fell in silky, voluminous waves down her back.

She plucked out a cream sweater tank, which highlighted her toned shoulders, and black leggings that masqueraded as dress pants. She threw on a pale blue linen blazer and hoisted her trusty leather tote bag over her shoulder before heading downstairs to her office.

∼

Emmeline closed her laptop and gathered her things into her bag. As she passed Matthew's office, she almost tripped over her feet. There Matthew was, sitting at his desk, hunched over a file folder with a pen in his hand.

Emmeline knocked on the door and poked her head in. "Mattie, do you know what time it is? Shouldn't you be at the hospital?"

Matthew looked up, his glasses perched precariously on his nose. "I start all my appointments at one o'clock on Thursdays."

"Why?"

"Because I can."

Emmeline narrowed her eyes at him.

"Because I want the time to go over files in more detail and make sure I didn't miss anything," Matthew added. "Where are you going?"

"I'm having breakfast with Philip."

"That's good." Matthew turned his attention back to his report. "Have you heard from Lesedi?"

"No, and I'm kind of surprised," Emmeline admitted. "She said she'd be in touch soon, but I don't know what that means. Should I message her?"

Matthew didn't look up from his work. "If they haven't contacted you, either something's wrong in their world or they got something wrong about you. I trust they'll be in touch if they need to be."

"I need to go, or I'm going to be late."

"Have fun. Be yourself."

"Thanks, Mattie."

Emmeline beamed as she walked downstairs to the garage entrance. She reached for her key fob when she spotted Matthew's new one.

Why the hell not? He's not using it right now. I'll be back before he needs to go to the hospital.

She snapped up Matthew's key fob and headed out to the garage. As she approached the sleek black sports car, it automatically unlocked itself with a barely audible click. The driver's door rose, beckoning Emmeline to enter its dark interior. She dropped her heels on the floor and placed her bag on the passenger seat, draping her blazer on top of it. Sliding into the driver's seat, she pressed the ignition button and sighed in pleasure as the engine purred to life. She shifted into first gear, and the car growled in response.

A thrill ran through her body, and she grinned.

I could get used to this.

Emmeline parked close to the entrance of the Harbor Yacht Club and did a quick mirror check before heading inside.

I haven't been here in so many years. I think the last time I was here, Mom was still alive.

Emmeline stopped at the concierge and looked around.

It looks the same.

The club had done some minor renovations, but most of what she remembered remained intact. Tonal striped wallpaper, French doors, and deep leather dining seats decorated the space, and although dated, it brought back happy memories.

The concierge hung up the phone and greeted Emmeline. "Good morning, ma'am. How can I assist you today?"

"Good morning. I'm here to meet Mayor Vil."

"And who should I say is here?"

"Emmeline Taylor-Wu."

Recognition dawned on the concierge's features. "Welcome back, Ms. Taylor-Wu. It's wonderful to have you join us on this beautiful day. I will let him know you're here." The concierge made a short phone call, dipping his head in understanding before hanging up. "Ms. Taylor-Wu, let me show you to Mayor Vil's table."

The concierge led Emmeline to a private covered balcony and knocked on the French doors.

Philip stood up as soon as he saw her. "Emmeline, I'm so glad you could make it this morning. I've been looking forward to our meeting all week." He took her hand and pressed a kiss on top. "You look beautiful."

Emmeline blushed. "The Harbor has always been one of my favorite clubs."

He fits in so well here.

Philip was dressed in slim khakis and a tailored navy blazer, reminding her of a model straight out of a country club magazine.

"Please." Philip pulled out a chair for her, and Emmeline obliged. He sat down after her, and they made small talk until a waiter came by with an assortment of charcuterie, fruit, and pastries on a marble platter. "I hope you don't mind, but I preordered various items off the menu."

"It's fine. I remember all the items on the menu being delicious." Emmeline eyed the flaky almond croissant.

"You're probably wondering why I asked you to meet me. I'll confess, I have a couple of motives." Philip winked at her.

"You mentioned having questions about The Taylor-Wu Foundation. Ask away."

"I noticed your foundation focuses on neuro care. It's impressive how much your family donates." Philip leaned forward in his chair. "Would your family consider expanding its support to charities outside of health care?"

"Health care holds a special place in our family's heart and was a passion for my mother and father. We support areas outside of health care, just on a smaller scale. We accept new applications for funding if they meet the guidelines set out by our audit committee and if there's room in the annual budget to do so. We've made exceptions in times of crisis, but those are rare."

"Definitely not just a pretty face." Philip's teeth gleamed in the sunlight.

"Not when it comes to the foundation or anything else that matters," Emmeline replied.

"That's good. What a waste it would be if you were."

Emmeline stiffened, but her face remained impassive.

"Philip, what foundation are you seeking additional support for?"

"Before I became mayor, I supported the Canadian Children's Literacy Club. Now that I'm mayor, I thought I would use my clout to inspire some of the most influential people in the city to support it."

"It isn't currently one of our recipients. Why don't you send a request to The Taylor-Wu Foundation, and we can see what can be done to help?"

"That's all I can ask for," Philip said.

Emmeline heard her phone vibrate, and she had a feeling she knew who it was, even before fishing it out of her tote bag. "Excuse me for a minute."

Mattie: Did you take my car?

Emia: Yes.

Mattie: I need to go to work. When do you plan on returning it?

Emmeline looked at the time. *Noon already? No wonder he's annoyed.*

Emia: Sorry, I completely lost track of time.

Mattie: I'll take your SUV. It'd better be charged. And clean.

Emia: If it's any consolation, your car is fabulous. I might keep it.

Mattie: Buy your own. Please bring mine back in one piece. This breakfast had better be worth it.

Emia: See you tonight.

Mattie: Don't scratch my car.

Emmeline put her phone back in her bag. "Apologies, Philip. Seems time flies when you're having fun. I need to head out to another meeting."

"I should get back to the office as well."

"Thank you for having me. I'll be in touch regarding the Literacy Club."

"Emmeline, I have something else I'd like to ask you." Philip flashed her a charming grin. "I'd like you to join me for dinner. I promise we won't talk about work. Social only. I want to get to know you better."

Emmeline faltered. It had been at least a year since she'd been out on a proper date.

Smile, woman! Don't just stare at him.

"Yes, that'd be lovely, Philip."

"Are you free on Saturday night?"

Emmeline nodded, not trusting her voice.

"Great. I'll send you a few restaurant choices, and you can choose what catches your eye."

Emmeline stood up, and Philip leaned over to kiss her on the cheek.

Her skin stayed warm all the way home.

CHAPTER TEN

ROAD TO HELL

Emmeline backed Matthew's car into his favorite parking spot in the garage and shifted into second gear before shutting off the engine.

Old habits die hard.

She heard her phone ring in her bag, and she rolled her eyes as she reached for it.

Probably Mattie, wondering if his car's back in one piece.

She looked at the unknown number and frowned, declining the call. The number called back, and she rejected it again. The third time, her phone vibrated with a message.

Unknown: It's Anja. Call me.

Rude. Emmeline's mood soured. *Leave it to Anja.*

Emia: Later. I'm busy. Where's Lesedi?

Anja: It'd help if you picked up the phone or called me, like I asked.

Emmeline glared at her phone.

Nope, not doing this. I'm going to be late for my meeting.

She tucked her phone back into her tote bag and headed to her office. As she was about to dial into her meeting, she heard her phone vibrate again.

Anja: If you don't call me, I'll come to your house.

Emia: I'll call you after my meeting. Do NOT show up at my house.

Anja: Why can't you call me now?

Emia: If you want me to call you, stop being you.

Anja: Fine. Call me as soon as possible.

~

Emmeline unlocked her phone screen and sighed in resignation as she dialed Anja's number.

Anja picked up immediately. "What took you so long?"

"I was busy. I'm not sitting here at your beck and call. I have real work to do."

The line went silent.

"Hello?" Emmeline looked down at her phone screen.

"Still here."

Emmeline crinkled her nose. "Are you going to tell me why you wanted me to call you so urgently?"

"Lessie was hurt a few days ago."

"Is she all right?" Emmeline asked with alarm. "What happened? Who would want to hurt her?"

"I don't know if she's going to be okay."

The line went silent again, and Emmeline waited for Anja to continue.

"When we left your house, we were ambushed by several raizour. Normally, we could handle a few without problems, but we didn't have our weapons that night. We'd left them in the car."

"You carry weapons with you?"

"Yes."

"How come you left them in your car?"

"Lessie insisted we leave them behind. She didn't want to scare you."

Emmeline remembered how all three nainthe had leather straps crossed over their chests. "Does Lesedi need medical assistance? If so, you need to take her to the hospital."

"We can't go to a hospital. Technically, none of us exists. If we went to a hospital, they'd figure out quickly that we weren't fully human."

"What do you do when you get hurt or sick?"

"Some of us are trained with basic medical knowledge, and we can usually care for our own. We rarely get sick, and we heal fast."

Suddenly, Emmeline realized why Anja was calling. "Are you calling to ask for Mattie's help?"

"Would he? I haven't been very kind to him, and he doesn't like me much." Anja's voice sounded small.

"Mattie isn't like that. If you had taken the time to get to know him, you would've figured that out," Emmeline snapped.

"Can you ask him if he'd be willing to see Lessie?"

"I'll ask him. How was she hurt?"

"She was stabbed in her lower abdomen. One of our medics closed the wound, but it's not healing. We tried antibiotics, but they didn't help. Her fever's very high, and she's suffering from hallucinations."

"Where should we meet you?"

"I can't tell you where we are."

"This isn't going to work out very well, now is it? Mattie does virtual consultations, but this doesn't meet the criteria for one," Emmeline said sarcastically.

"I can pick you up. I would bring Lessie to you, but I don't think she should be moved. My people also don't know that a human knows about us."

"Are you putting Mattie in danger? If you put him in danger, I'll kill you myself."

"They won't hurt him. He'll be protected because he's with you. We need you more than you need us," Anja said. "If Matthew's willing to help Lessie, I promise I'll protect him. You have my word."

Emmeline sighed. "Let me see if I can find him."

Emia: Mattie, can you call me if you're not with a patient? It's important.

Her phone rang a few minutes later.

"Hey, Mattie," Emmeline rushed on. "The reason I haven't heard from Lesedi is because she was hurt after leaving our house. Anja asked if you'd be willing to see her. Their medics haven't been able to stop her infection and fever."

"Emia, I'm a radiologist, and you know I don't have specialized training in trauma. I've done my emergency rotations in medical school and early residency, but I haven't practiced those skills in years. Lesedi needs to be treated at a hospital."

"They won't go. It would put them at risk."

"I can't give her the care she might need. They're putting her at more risk by delaying bringing her to a hospital."

"It was Anja who called me. Her people don't know about you yet."

"Right."

"Her asking for your help goes against their rules."

"I can go see Lesedi, but there's very little I can do."

"When can you come home?"

"Let me check my schedule." Matthew paused to scan his calendar. "It doesn't look like there's anything critical, so I'll ask my assistant to clear my late afternoon appointments. I'll be home in about two hours."

"Mattie, this might be dangerous for us. Maybe more dangerous for you than me."

"I guess it's a good thing I'm me."

"Anja promised she'd protect you if you were willing to see Lesedi."

"I'll see you soon."

Emmeline sighed and hung up.

Emia: Anja, Mattie will be home in about two hours. Just message me when you're outside my house.

Anja: I'll be there. Thank you.

Emmeline furrowed her brow.

Am I doing the right thing? Do I trust these people? I hope I'm not dragging Mattie into something dangerous.

Emmeline rubbed her temples. This took away from the anticipation of a dinner date with Philip.

I have a feeling this won't end well.

Emmeline heard Matthew come up the stairs from the garage and ran over to meet him. He was lugging a large duffel bag in one hand, and in the other was an extra-large backpack.

"I don't remember your emergency kit being so robust," Emmeline said.

Matthew shrugged. "I might have made some adjustments over the years to account for more situations."

"Like an apocalypse?"

Matthew ignored her last comment and shook off his blazer.

"Go change if you want. Anja isn't here yet." Emmeline glanced at her watch.

"She is. She's sitting in a black SUV on the driveway."

Emmeline looked at her phone, but there weren't any missed messages or calls.

Emia:	Anja, are you outside? Why didn't you message me?
Anja:	Not two hours yet.

Emmeline rolled her eyes.

Emia: We'll be out soon.

Emmeline grabbed her backpack and folded a sweater hoodie for later. Running to the kitchen, she packed a couple of water bottles and energy bars for her and Matthew before making a coffee for herself.

A little voice nagged as she remembered Anja's smile at the sight of a hot coffee. She grumbled and made another coffee, adding an ungodly amount of milk just as Matthew entered the kitchen.

"Seriously, Mattie, you need a different outfit. They're going to think you only have one set of clothes."

"Let's go. I'll have to put in extra time at the hospital tomorrow to make up for today, so I'd like to be home before midnight."

Emmeline handed Matthew a bottle of water. "Me too."

Emmeline opened the passenger door of the nondescript black SUV and looked in. Anja was in the same black outfit she'd worn the last time Emmeline saw her, and a pair of dark aviators hid the shadows beneath her eyes.

Emmeline sat down and handed Anja a tumbler. "The way you like it."

Anja held the tumbler and looked at it. "Thank you." She flipped open the lid and took a long sip.

Matthew opened the trunk and loaded his duffel bag and backpack. He climbed into the backseat and buckled his seat belt. "Anja, I'm sorry to hear about Lesedi. I hope I can help her, but there's only so much I can do without the right equipment and knowledge. I strongly recommend you bring Lesedi to a hospital. They'll be able to get her the best possible care."

"There's so much you don't know about us." Anja's voice was stoic, as if she was trying not to cry. "If humans found out about us, they'd hunt every one of us down. No matter how much I want to save Lessie, I can't bring her to a hospital. I can't risk everyone else's life to save her one life."

Matthew stared at her through the rearview mirror. "Your people don't know you're bringing me, do they? How dangerous is this for my sister and me?"

"I don't know, but you both have my word that I'll protect you. My brother will as well."

"Your brother?" Matthew's midnight irises flickered. "Are you and your brother the one historical instance of a blood relation Lesedi mentioned?"

"You have a good memory, Dr. Matthew," Anja murmured before glancing at Emmeline. "Your sister's presence alone should be enough to protect you."

"This isn't instilling much confidence." Emmeline squirmed in her seat.

"You haven't met my brother yet."

"After today, you owe us a full explanation of what you are."

"I agree." Anja opened the center console, pulled out two black scarves, and held them up.

Emmeline stared at the scarves and then at Anja. "Nope."

"Can you at least put it on when we get close and say you had it on the whole time?"

"Yes," Matthew answered on behalf of him and Emmeline.

Emmeline turned her head and glared at her brother. "No."

Matthew met her glare. "I want to get this done. I don't care where they live. I don't plan to go back."

"Fine," Emmeline muttered.

They all sat in silence as Anja made her way through the winding roads and headed farther into the city, right into rush-hour gridlock.

"You shouldn't have taken this route," Emmeline said.

"I don't usually use a car." Anja narrowed her eyes at the road. "I also don't travel during this horrid rush-hour traffic."

After getting off the main road and taking a few back streets, Anja motioned at the two scarves. "It's time."

Emmeline looked around in surprise. "We're still in the city."

Emmeline and Matthew put the scarves around their eyes, and she felt Anja make a few more turns before descending. The echo of wind and whirl of fans rumbled against the car.

We must be in a tunnel of some sort.

Anja stopped the car and turned off the engine. "Keep the scarves on. I'll lead you into our home and make an introduction first. My friend's here, waiting to help us."

Emmeline heard Anja leave the driver's seat and open Matthew's door before her footsteps made their way over to the passenger side. She opened the door for Emmeline and helped her out of the car.

"Dr. Matthew, I can carry the duffel bag. Can you take the backpack?" Anja asked.

"I can carry both."

Emmeline heard the rustle of Matthew putting on his backpack and shifting his weight to take on the duffel bag. She shivered in anticipation.

Here we go.

CHAPTER ELEVEN

HOSTILE INTRODUCTIONS

"Quinn, meet Emmeline and Matthew," Anja said.

"Nice to meet you both." Quinn's voice was low and smooth. "Emmeline, you can take my arm. I'm sorry we're meeting under such grim circumstances."

"Dr. Matthew, you can take my arm," Anja said, but Emmeline didn't hear a response from her brother.

"He doesn't like to be touched," Emmeline said. "Just use your voice to guide him."

"I'm fine, Emia," Matthew replied.

"It seems like there's a lot for us to learn about you, Dr. Matthew," Anja murmured. "Quinn, did you ask Javier, Michael, and Maira to go to the courtyard?"

"They're waiting for us, as are the others. We should get going."

Quinn let Emmeline set the pace. Emmeline heard footsteps behind her and could tell Anja and Matthew were keeping up with her and Quinn.

"I feel like we've been walking for a while," Emmeline said under her breath. Her footsteps made quiet clicks against the stone floor. "I should've dressed warmer. Are we underground right now?"

"We're in an underground tunnel system and about to approach ground level. It'll be warmer once we get to the courtyard," Quinn replied.

They walked a bit longer, and Emmeline felt the air warm, as promised. Quinn stopped, and Emmeline removed her arm and stretched out her fingers.

"Can I take off this blindfold?" Emmeline asked.

"Yes, please do," a low voice replied.

Emmeline removed the scarf and opened her eyes. She cried out and stumbled back into Anja as the force of multiple auras flashed and burned until they melded into a single blazing light. She squeezed her eyes shut and fell to her hands and knees as she gasped for air. Panic rose in her, and she tried to push down the urge to retch.

"Mattie!" Emmeline clawed at the floor, her fingers slipping over the stone.

Matthew gripped her shoulders. "Focus on my voice and your breathing."

Emmeline forced herself to take deep breaths, and after a couple of minutes, her heart rate slowed, and the panic subsided. She opened her eyes, and the blinding light dimmed to a glow that stretched across the courtyard.

"Better?" Mattie asked.

Emmeline nodded, and her eyes dropped down to her hands. She stared at her bloodied fingers in horror and then at the floor, which was marked with red claw strokes.

"It's just a surface wound. I have bandages in my backpack," Matthew said.

He helped Emmeline off the ground and rummaged through his backpack for some antibiotic ointment and a roll of gauze. Emmeline looked around, and realized that a significant number of people, all with a subtle aura, were staring back at her.

"That was embarrassing. What a great first impression," Emmeline muttered as she sized up her surroundings.

They were standing in the middle of a large courtyard, bathed in the orange glow of a setting sun. Shadows flickered as the evening breeze swirled through, bringing the early hints of autumn. Half the courtyard was covered with lush green grass while the other half was paved with smooth concrete. A large, raised platform with a louvered roof sat at the center, and on either side were patio seats under high gazebos. The buildings that enclosed the courtyard were three to six stories high, and surrounding the square were perfectly spaced sliding doors, encased by light-gray concrete walls.

Emmeline straightened, letting her bloodied hands fall to her sides. She lifted her chin, composed her features with an air of indifference, and faced the crowd.

Don't show your nerves.

She locked eyes with a towering man seated at the center of all the others. Everyone else stood rigid, fanning out around the man in the chair, and he studied her, as she did him.

She was about to introduce herself when he spoke first. "You must be Emmeline Taylor-Wu."

"Yes, I am," Emmeline replied. "And you are?"

"My name is Javier." The man dipped his tanned face.

Javier's skin was lined, and his voice was deep and gruff. His short, dark hair was streaked with gray, matching the groomed beard along his strong jaw.

"It's nice to meet you, Javier." Emmeline gestured to Matthew. "This is my brother, Dr. Matthew Taylor-Wu. He's here to see Lesedi."

"And who requested your brother to come here?"

Emmeline looked at Javier and then at Anja. "Why do you ask a question you already know the answer to? Don't use me to make a point."

Javier regarded Emmeline before turning to Anja. "Anja, can you explain why you thought it was a good idea to bring a human here and endanger us all?"

"Lessie's not getting better, and we can't send her to a hospital to get the care she needs. There isn't anyone here who has the medical knowledge to help her. I trust Emmeline and Dr. Taylor-Wu not to put us in danger."

"You trust them?" Javier asked. "You barely know them!"

"Are you willing to let Lessie die? Is that how little you care about her?" Anja clenched her fists.

Javier leaned forward and narrowed his eyes. "Watch your choice of words, Anja Loren. It would be wise of you to remember who you're talking to."

From the corner of Emmeline's eye, a tall, lean figure stepped forward at the opposite side of the courtyard, and she turned to look at his profile. He had short, wavy black hair swept back, alabaster skin, angular features, and a slight shadow of stubble. The air between Emmeline's fingertips sparked and crackled as his icy-gray eyes flickered over and locked with her midnight ones. A flutter ran down her spine as realization hit her.

That must be Anja's brother.

Emmeline looked back at Anja and winced as she placed her hand on Anja's arm.

"Javier, I understand you're not happy that we're here," Emmeline said.

"I'm unhappy your brother's here. On the other hand, you have every right to be here."

"My brother and I come as a pair. You can either accept both of us or neither. I'll leave it to your choice," Emmeline replied. She glanced at Matthew, who didn't look the least bit bothered by the tension in the room.

Thanks a lot for the support, Mattie. Could you at least pretend to look interested?

The man to Javier's right stepped forward, and his dark eyes flashed. "I'll give you the benefit of the doubt since you're new here and you don't know who you're talking to. Javier is our leader, and we follow his direction. You humans have no respect for authority. We operate differently here, and you're in our territory now."

Emmeline forced her hands to relax as she evaluated the tall, wiry man in front of her. He had black hair, shaved down close to his scalp, and heavy eyebrows that furrowed into a fierce scowl.

A hushed breeze moved over Emmeline, and Anja's brother dropped in front of her. He turned his head briefly to look at Emmeline and Matthew, his icy irises glinting under the last rays of the setting sun.

Anja's presence was already intimidating, but her brother was terrifying. Up close, he was taller than both Anja and Matthew. His broad shoulders were pulled back, and Emmeline could see the outline of his tense muscles beneath his black T-shirt. Where Anja wore her emotions on her pale features, her brother's face was cold and blank. Despite having the same light-gray eyes, his resembled shards of ice while Anja's constantly moved alongside her mood. Anja's brother's hands were bare, but he had two long, narrow blades crossed along his back.

Emmeline looked back at where he had stood a few minutes ago and then back to where he was now.

How did he get here? Did he fly? No, they can't fly. Can they? Is that how they got onto my balcony?

"Don't be so fucking rude, Michael," Anja hissed.

"That's enough," Javier growled.

Matthew cleared his throat. "I'd like to speak, if I may."

Anja and her brother moved out of his way, and Javier eyed Matthew.

"You may speak," Javier said.

"The issue is me being here, but I'm already here, so arguing about it is irrelevant. All I care about is seeing if I can help Lesedi. I've already provided my recommendation that she belongs in a hospital, but seeing as you're unwilling to do that, I'll try my best to help. Lesedi told me you protect our world, and I assume that means you save lives. I save lives, too, so maybe we aren't so different. After I do what I can, I'd be happy to be on my way. Your secret's safe with me because I couldn't care less how you choose to live your lives." Matthew looked straight at Javier. "I'd like to do what I came here to do and put this behind me. I don't want to be here any more than you want me here."

Emmeline tried not to shift her feet as Javier weighed Matthew's words.

"Michael, accompany Dr. Taylor-Wu to see Lesedi." Javier turned back to Matthew. "Dr. Taylor-Wu, I trust you'll only do what's necessary for Lesedi's care, nothing more and nothing less."

"If you trusted me, you wouldn't be sending Michael to watch over me, but I understand why you would." Matthew picked up his emergency kits and hauled both over his shoulders. "I'm ready, Michael. Lead the way."

"Wait." Anja held up a hand to stop Matthew and turned to her brother. "Erik, I want you to go with Dr. Taylor-Wu."

He has a name. Erik.

Michael narrowed his eyes. "You don't trust me to return your precious doctor in one piece?"

"Do I look like I trust you?" Anja snapped.

Emmeline blanched, and she almost reached for Matthew's arm. "Mattie, you don't have to go."

"You know I'll go."

"Be careful."

"Anja, keep my sister safe," Matthew said before turning to follow Michael.

Emmeline looked up at Erik, and her brilliant midnight eyes again met his clear, frosty ones.

"I'll keep Dr. Taylor-Wu safe."

His smooth timbre and warm, musical lilt made her voice die in her throat. Before she could respond, he turned and followed Michael and Matthew out of the courtyard.

CHAPTER TWELVE

VULTURES

"I would've accompanied them, but your brother's safer with Erik. You don't need to worry," Anja said. "Javier will want to talk to you while we wait for them."

Emmeline could see Javier making his way over to her, and she straightened her posture.

Anja lowered her voice. "Remember, we need you more than you need us. I'll stay with you."

"Emmeline, I'd like to talk to you in my office," Javier said.

"I'm going to wash my hands and get cleaned up first. Anja will accompany me and show me the way afterward."

"Very well," Javier clipped, and he turned and left the courtyard.

Anja picked up Emmeline's backpack and motioned for Emmeline to follow her. "Let me show you where the restroom is."

Emmeline sucked in a breath from the sting as she washed her hands with soap and warm water.

"Anja, can you help me wrap gauze around my fingertips?"

"Sure."

Anja unzipped Emmeline's backpack and retrieved the antibiotic ointment and gauze Matthew had placed inside. She washed her own hands and applied a thin layer of ointment on Emmeline's fingers.

Emmeline watched Anja concentrate as she cut the gauze and wrapped Emmeline's right hand.

"I'm sorry about Lesedi. I know you want to be there with her, but instead, you're here with me," Emmeline said. "I hope Mattie can help her."

Anja secured the gauze with tape. "Me too."

"How long have you and Lesedi been partners?" Emmeline asked.

"I'm not sure how to tally up the time, but linearly, about a year." Anja wrapped Emmeline's left hand with gauze. "We have an open relationship."

"Why?" Emmeline asked before mentally slapping herself. "Sorry, that was rude. You don't have to answer that."

"It works for us, and I'm okay with it. I like Lessie for who she is, and this is what she wants. She's kind, fair, and strong. She's everything I'm not. I wouldn't dream of keeping her to myself." Anja shrugged. "When you become a nainthe, everything changes."

"What do you mean?"

"Later. It would take too much time to explain."

Emmeline changed the subject. "Who is Michael, and why is he so hostile?"

"Our leadership council is voted in, and Michael hasn't made it a secret that he thinks he should've been elected to Javier's position. Compared to Javier, Michael is much more authoritarian, and I bet if he could change the leadership to a dictatorship, he would."

"Is Javier a good guy or a bad guy?"

"He can be both. I've known him for a long time, and sometimes, I can't tell which side he's playing. He can be unforgiving, but I doubt he'll hurt you or your brother." Anja tucked the first aid supplies back into Emmeline's backpack. "Just be cautious with what you say to him, though you don't seem to have trouble holding your own."

"Many years of training. The vultures come out in droves when your parents are rich and die young."

"Is that why you're such a hermit?"

Emmeline opened and closed her mouth before looking away.

"I can't understand what it's like, but I think I can imagine." Anja picked up Emmeline's backpack and tossed it over her shoulder. "Let's go before Javier sends his lapdogs to look for us."

CHAPTER THIRTEEN

BOUNDARIES

Anja knocked on a large glass door, which slid open automatically.

Javier looked up from his desk and stood up. "Anja, you can wait outside. I want to speak to Emmeline alone."

"I want Anja to stay," Emmeline interjected.

"Are you worried about your safety?" Javier raised an eyebrow.

"Can you blame me? Neither you nor anyone else has been kind to my brother or me, especially considering my brother's only here to help. You treated him with contempt the moment he set foot in this place."

"You don't understand how dangerous it is when a human knows about our existence."

"That's not my problem. That's yours. We were asked to come here."

"Not by me."

"Then, I'll happily leave as soon as my brother's done."

"That doesn't change the fact that your brother knows about us."

"He knew about you before today, so being here now makes no difference."

"You're trying my patience," Javier growled.

"Likewise." Emmeline glared back.

"Javier," a calm, foreign voice spoke out.

Emmeline spun around, and an elegant South Asian woman stepped out of the shadows. Long lashes framed her wide espresso eyes, and her straight, dark hair was knotted in a neat bun close to her neck. Her terra-cotta skin was smooth and rich, and she was dressed similarly to Anja, but instead of a black T-shirt, she wore a black tunic with subtle tonal embroidery that reached her knees.

"Emmeline, this is Maira," Anja introduced. "She's third-in-command on our leadership council."

"Nice to meet you, Maira."

"It's nice to meet you as well. We've been looking for you for a long time," Maira replied.

"That's what I keep hearing."

Javier gestured to the large conference table at the center of his office. "Shall we talk?"

Emmeline sat down and looked at Javier. "I assume you're first-in-command. Who's second-in-command?"

"Michael," Anja replied.

It took every ounce of Emmeline's training and self-control not to let the surprise show on her face. "Interesting."

Javier ignored her. "Anja, how much have you told Emmeline?"

"Not that much," Anja admitted. "We told her about the elystier and how we haven't had one in over two decades. We also told her what an elystier does and how they and the nainthe are connected."

"I apologize if this comes off as rude, and I've said this to Anja and Lesedi already," Emmeline interrupted, "but I'm not sure I'm who you're looking for. I see auras when I look at you, but I don't think I'm an elystier. Maybe I just have the gift of being able to see you."

"What do you see right now?" Javier asked.

"A very faint glow. It starts off blinding but dissipates until it disappears completely. I don't see an aura around Anja anymore."

"Are all our auras the same?"

Emmeline looked at Javier and Maira. "Pretty much."

"I don't recall elystiers seeing auras. Lana and Chin could feel a nainthe nearby, almost like a sixth sense, but it was never a physical aura." Javier leaned back in his chair. "But I'm certain you're the seeker we've been looking for. I can sense your magic even though it feels weak."

Maira spoke up. "Do you ever feel like you're supposed to be somewhere or you're supposed to find someone?"

Emmeline shook her head. "Well, not aside from the normal existential crisis that thirty-something-year-olds generally have," she replied dryly.

"Do you have dreams?" Javier asked.

"Rarely. I do get seizures sometimes."

Maira straightened. "Tell me more about your seizures."

"I don't know why I get them, and it doesn't happen often. It started during my undergraduate studies and ramped up when I was completing my master's. Afterwards, it slowed down. It usually starts with a dim aura that grows to a blinding light, and then I have a seizure and black out. I don't remember much of it when I wake up." Emmeline looked at Anja. "I have anxiety over my seizures, and that's why I reacted the way I did at the gala." She looked at Javier and held up her hands. "And that's why I reacted the way I did today."

"When you have seizures, do you ever see or sense anything? Like a place or person? Or a feeling or smell?" Maira asked.

"Nothing. It's like time has disappeared."

"That's very odd." Javier looked perturbed.

"How do elystiers find potentials?" Emmeline asked.

Maira frowned. "From what I understand, they receive a vision that gives them a sense of location. There's usually a hint of who the person is—from a physical characteristic to a personality trait. It's a mixed bag."

"Did the last two elystiers, Lana and Chin, get the same visions?"

"They didn't."

There was a sharp knock on the door before it slid open, and Matthew stepped back into the room with Erik and Michael at his heels.

Anja rushed over and grabbed Matthew's arm. "Is Lessie going to be all right?"

Matthew flinched and pulled his arm away.

"Sorry, I forgot."

"Most people do. Just warn me next time."

"Dr. Taylor-Wu, we're all eager for an update. Please." Javier gestured to the conference table.

"Lesedi has a bad infection where her wound is. I talked to the medic, and he's been using penicillin to treat her. Normally, it should work, but for some reason, it isn't. I believe the infection has become systemic, meaning the bacterial infection from her wound has now entered her bloodstream. It can lead to death."

The blood drained from Anja's face, and she crossed her arms over her chest.

"Are you able to treat her?" Emmeline asked.

"I've started her on a broad-spectrum intravenous antibiotic."

"How quickly will we know if it's working?" Anja asked.

"If effective, we should see her condition stabilize soon."

Suddenly, Anja looked around angrily. "Who's watching over Lessie right now? Did you guys leave her there by herself?"

"Anja"—Erik's melodic voice floated from the doorway—"we would never do that to Lessie. Ben's looking after her."

"I need to go see her." Anja walked to the door, stopping beside Erik. "Stay with Dr. Matthew and Emmeline."

Erik tipped his head in acknowledgment, and Anja disappeared through the doorway.

"Mattie, what happens if the antibiotics don't work?" Emmeline asked.

"I can't test for other types of infections here." Matthew turned to Javier. "Would you allow me to take some samples to the hospital for testing?"

"No."

"Then, your options are limited, and the probability of Lesedi dying is higher. Lesedi belongs in a hospital, and that's my professional opinion."

"You know we can't do that," Javier replied.

Emmeline scrutinized Javier's face. His mouth was set in a firm line, and his eyes were hard, but there was sadness behind his unwavering stare.

Matthew removed his glasses and rubbed his eyes. "Then, let's hope the new antibiotics work quickly."

Maira studied Emmeline and Matthew before she decided to speak. "You must be tired and hungry. I'll send for some food. Any preferences?"

Emmeline's stomach growled at the mention of food. "What time is it?" She grabbed her backpack and rummaged through it, looking for her phone.

Maira coughed, and Emmeline looked up. Her phone was sitting in Maira's outstretched hand.

Emmeline snatched her phone out of Maira's hand and glared at her. "Why did you have my phone?"

Maira reached into her pocket, pulled Matthew's phone out, and handed it to him. Matthew took it and flipped it back and forth before examining its contents.

"Impressive," Matthew muttered as he swiped through various screens and applications. "When and how did you find time to do this?"

"When you were both distracted."

"And when was that?"

Maira shrugged and changed the subject. "I needed to be sure neither of you would do something you shouldn't do with your devices."

"Like what exactly?" Emmeline snapped.

"Photos, videos. If it helps, I didn't go through any of your personal items."

"First, that doesn't help. This was an invasion of privacy. Second, you people tend to apologize a lot. This whole *beg for forgiveness later* strategy doesn't work with me. Do something like this again, and it'll be the last you ever see of us." Emmeline's face reddened, and she didn't bother trying to control her anger.

"Aren't you going to ask if I did anything to your phones? Not that I did anything," Maira added hastily. "I couldn't do anything anyway. The security on your phones is excellent."

Emmeline unlocked her phone and gaped at the numerous missed messages. She turned her glare to Javier.

Maira wouldn't have done this without your direction.

Emmeline cocked her head. "I don't care if you did anything. How much longer do you think I'll have this phone now that I know you've touched it?"

Maira looked contrite, but Javier's face remained impassive.

The arrogance of that man! At least Maira looks thoroughly ashamed, Emmeline screamed in her head.

"It seems we need to work on trusting each other," Javier stated.

"No shit, Sherlock."

"Maybe it's time we take a break." Maira held her hands up. "Emmeline and Dr. Taylor-Wu, I'm sorry, and I want to be clear; the decision was mine and mine alone. You have my word that it won't happen again. Can I have some food brought over?"

"I'm having trust issues at the moment," Emmeline said sarcastically. "I have energy bars and water. You may all leave and come back in an hour."

"Are you dismissing me out of my own office?" Javier gawked at Emmeline, and Michael's head looked like it was about to explode.

"I'd like some peace while I answer the missed messages on my misappropriated phone. Either you can leave this room or we can. Regardless, we'll leave this place when Anja's back."

"Javier, let's give them some space. This is all very hard to digest," Maira said.

Javier turned to Erik. "Were you able to capture any raizour last night?"

"Three."

"Emmeline, before you go today, we'd like to show you something. We were going to save this for later, but now's as good a time as any. We'll come back in an hour, as you've requested," Javier said. He walked out the door, followed closely by Maira and Michael.

After they left the room, Erik looked over his shoulder, and Emmeline tried not to shrink against his cold gaze. "I'll be outside the door. If you need anything, come find me."

"Thank you, Erik."

But he was gone before the words left Emmeline's lips.

∽

"Are you okay, Mattie?"

"I'm fine."

Emmeline pulled out her sweater hoodie and shrugged it on, zipping it up over her thin T-shirt. She threw her head upside down and shook out her long hair before digging through her backpack for the water bottles and flattened energy bars. She handed one of each to Matthew. He helped Emmeline open her energy bar and water bottle before ripping open his and finishing it in two bites. He chugged half his water bottle before setting it down on the conference table.

Matthew took off his glasses and massaged the bridge of his nose. "I'm worried Lesedi won't respond to the antibiotics. There isn't much else I can do for her here."

"I know."

"The equipment here could use some upgrades and additions." Matthew leaned back in his chair. "Ben, the person overseeing

Lesedi's care, has some medical training and is doing his best, but he doesn't have the background or support to provide the care she requires. In a hospital, teams of trained professionals have repeatedly seen these cases, and still, the mortality rate of those who go into septic shock is high."

"It's a good thing you had antibiotics in your bag."

Matthew changed the subject. "You didn't need to be so rude to Maira."

"If I hadn't been, they'd have thought it was okay to walk all over us. I won't be a doormat."

"I'm sure they haven't mistaken you for a doormat."

"That's the point."

"Anyway, you did good today." Matthew looked at Emmeline tiredly. "Mom taught you well. Good job."

"Fake it till you make it. That's my motto."

Matthew didn't respond and only gave her an amused half-smile.

"I need to check my messages and see if anything's burning down. You should get some rest."

Matthew nodded and crossed his arms over the table. He took off his glasses and leaned his head down on the crook of his arm. "Wake me up when it's time to go."

Emmeline found her stylus and flipped through the different messaging apps on her phone. She smiled when she saw a message from Philip.

Philip: Hi, Emmeline. I had a wonderful time this morning, and I'm looking forward to having dinner with you on Saturday. I have three recommendations—Shishito Sushi Hut, The Grand Schoolhouse, or Junos Thai Bar. Let me know what you prefer, and I'll make a reservation. Does seven o'clock work?

All good choices. The man knows his restaurants.

Philip: I haven't heard back from you. Is everything okay?

Emia: Apologies, Philip. I've been tied up with an emergency all day. Let's go with Junos Thai Bar, and seven is perfect.

Philip: I thought you'd disappeared on me. I'll make a reservation at Junos and pick you up at seven.

Emia: I can have a driver drop me off.

Philip: I'll pick you up. It's the gentlemanly thing to do.

Emmeline frowned but shook herself out of her headspace.
Maybe I've been out of the dating scene for too long. It's nice of him to offer to pick me up.

Emia: That's kind of you. Good night.

Philip: Have a good night.

Emmeline flipped through a few more missed messages.

Gus: How'd it go?

Gus: Stop ignoring me.

Gus: DO NOT IGNORE ME.

Gus: Don't make me call you.

Gus: EMMELINE TAYLOR-WU. ANSWER YOUR MESSAGES.

I miss you, Gus! I wish I could tell you about everything happening, but I don't want to put you in danger.

Emia: Sorry, Gus. I was tied up in an emergency. Breakfast with Philip was good. He asked me to go to dinner this Saturday.

Gus: Is everything okay?

Emia: I'm fine. Just a family thing I needed to take care of.

Gus: Back to your date. Was he a perfect Prince Charming at breakfast? I need details!

Emia: I'll tell you more later. Still working through some family things with Mattie right now.

Gus: He must be smitten by the beautiful but elusive

Emia. I'll come over Saturday afternoon and help you get ready.

Emmeline's heart warmed despite her irritation from earlier.

Emia: Ms. Rose, Mattie and I will be home late tonight, so don't wait up for us. Could you do me a favor and ask Eva to order two new mobile phones for Mattie and me?

Ms. Rose: She usually keeps a stash at her office. You're lucky she's one of your best friends.

She was about to move to her calendar when there was a knock on the door. The sliding door glided open, and Erik walked across the entrance with Anja behind him. Her normally icy eyes were dim, and her sideswept hair hung across her eyes.

"Anja, how's Lesedi?" Emmeline asked.

"She's stable."

Erik glanced at his watch. "Javier will be back soon. I need to change. You should too, Anja."

"I'll be fine. I should stay with Emmeline and Dr. Matthew."

"You should give our guests an idea of what they're about to witness."

And with that, Erik was gone.

He's like a ghost.

"Mattie, it's time to wake up. Anja's back."

Matthew lifted his head and rubbed his eyes before placing his glasses back on his nose. He ran his fingers through his hair several times.

"You look great, Mattie. Messy chic," Emmeline said.

"I want to check on Lesedi." Matthew pushed his chair back and stood up.

Anja shook her head. "Later. Ben's looking after her now, and he will message me if anything changes. We should be here when Javier returns."

"What does Javier want us to see? Your brother said he caught three raizour?" Emmeline asked.

"I never told you Erik was my brother."

"You look alike. Dark hair, tall, lean, pale skin, and those eyes. You both have extraordinary eyes. I don't think I've met anyone with eyes like yours." Emmeline paused. "Javier mentioned your surname was Loren. That sounds Scandinavian."

"Danish, but we were born on Canadian soil. Our parents were first-generation immigrants," Anja murmured.

"Same for us, except my parents were not Danish," Emmeline said, grimacing at the obviousness of her statement. "My mother was from Hong Kong, and my father was from Australia." She started to pack her stuff into her backpack. "You and Erik are very different from each other."

"How so?"

"You have a big heart you hopelessly try to hide. If you were a child, I'd probably label you as mischievous. But your brother's the opposite, where his mind and heart are completely elsewhere. He gave me the impression of being very detached."

"My brother goes through more than anyone should ever have to. If you get to know him better, maybe, one day, he'll tell you himself."

Emmeline held Anja's gaze and then pointedly looked at Matthew. Anja looked down at her hands.

Good. She understands.

"What surprise is in store for us?" Emmeline asked.

"You're about to come face-to-face with three raizour," Anja replied.

Matthew's head snapped up. "This I want to see."

Both Emmeline and Anja stared at Matthew.

"I don't," Emmeline sputtered.

"Dr. Matthew, are you not even the slightest bit afraid?"

"Why would I be?"

Anja looked up at the ceiling in exasperation just as there was a sharp knock. Javier, Maira, and Michael stepped back into the office, all dressed in black and covered with flexible armor. The armor wrapped around their torso from the upper neck to the waist and around their elbows and knees. They each had a single blade strapped across their back and were carrying a helmet under their arm.

Maira handed Anja a set of armor. "I didn't have time to get yours, but you can use this spare one for tonight."

Anja gave the outfit a distasteful glance, and Maira rolled her eyes.

"It's clean. If you cared so much, you should've made the time to get changed."

Emmeline raised her hand. "I would like protective equipment as well." She looked down at her leggings and felt very bare.

Anja strapped on her armor. "I'm your protective equipment."

"Emmeline and Dr. Taylor-Wu, it's time for you to see what we're up against. Follow me." Javier turned on his heel and stepped back out into the night.

CHAPTER FOURTEEN

INTO THE MONSTER'S BELLY

Javier led the group across the courtyard and past the concrete platform. Emmeline shivered and zipped her hoodie up to her neck as the cool night air bit at her bare ankles. The sun had disappeared beneath the horizon, and the courtyard was now lit with lanterns hanging along the walls. Emmeline looked up at the clear midnight sky and took a deep breath.

I still can't believe we're in the middle of the city.

A few nainthe were milling around the courtyard, enjoying the peaceful night. Some were using the square as a shortcut to their next destination while others sat in quiet conversation. Every so often, a bright light would flare up and dim, and Emmeline would look away until her eyes adjusted.

As their group cut across the lawn, other nainthe would stop what they were doing and whisper between each other. Emmeline quickened her pace and tugged at her light-gray hoodie.

I should've dressed in black. I stick out like a sore thumb. At least Mattie blends in.

"Do they know where we're going?" Emmeline whispered to Anja, nodding to the nainthe they were passing by.

Anja looked around. "They probably know something's up since we have a small entourage and are dressed for combat." She half-smirked. "And we also have a human and a seeker with us."

"I feel like a specimen." Emmeline fought the urge to cross her arms and hug herself.

"Get used to it. We've been looking for you for over twenty years. To some younger ones, an elystier is just a legend."

"I still think you guys got it wrong. I just don't know how to prove it to you," Emmeline said before switching the subject. "Where are we going?"

"To the underground caverns."

"What do you use it for?"

"It's a multipurpose event space." Anja shrugged. "We use it for the three *p*'s—prisoners, parties, and practice, though not necessarily in that order. The raizour prisoners are kept in the underground caverns because the entrance can be barred with a solid metal gate. There's no way to escape."

"Are there normally prisoners?"

"No, we don't usually keep prisoners." Anja looked at Emmeline briefly, but she didn't elaborate further.

Javier stopped before a massive arched gateway and turned to face the group. Two intricate stone carvings of massive winged creatures guarded each side of the entrance, and they reminded Emmeline of the gargoyles she had seen in history books and on her trips to Notre-Dame, except their features were far more grotesque. Rather than perched on a rooftop, the creatures were grounded in a fighting stance, each holding a long, thin blade in its hand. The wings were not the gorgeous, feathered creations of children's books, but were sharp and monstrous. The hollows of the creatures' cheeks were sunken in, and their foreheads protruded with their fierce scowls. Pulled back into wide sneers, their mouths showed two rows of ferocious teeth.

Those teeth.

Emmeline looked at Matthew, who studied the archway and statues like a scholar. She knew he had mapped the details into his brain in a way only he could understand. He finally looked at Anja, and Emmeline understood Matthew's unspoken question.

Is this what you are?

Anja broke her gaze from Matthew, and she spoke so quietly that Emmeline almost didn't hear her. "I hope you'll remember that we're not the monsters."

Javier eyed both Emmeline and Matthew from underneath the archway.

"Before we enter, I'd like to warn you that what you're about to meet is disturbing, but you'll be perfectly safe and protected. Dr. Taylor-Wu, as much as I'm fully against you being here, it seems you'll be with us at your sister's insistence." He frowned at Emmeline before turning back to Matthew. "I can count on one hand the number of humans who know about us; out of those, you'll be one of two who will have met a raizour while under my care. If you wish to remain above ground, now's the time to make that choice."

Emmeline felt her stomach drop into a pit. "Mattie, Javier's right. Maybe you shouldn't come down with us. I've already dragged you into this mess, and I don't want to put you in any more danger."

"I want to see." Matthew pushed his glasses up.

"Very well." Javier pressed his palm against the stone wall, and the heavy gate groaned as it slid open.

Michael trailed behind Javier as he entered the darkness, and Maira looked over her shoulder at Emmeline.

"Can you follow our auras in the tunnel?" she asked.

"I'm not sure." Emmeline watched as the darkness of the entrance swallowed Javier. "I can still see your auras, but it doesn't act like a light. It doesn't illuminate anything."

"Strange." Maira looked perplexed. "Let your eyes adjust to the darkness. We don't have lights in the tunnel, so hold on to Anja if needed. Our eyes adapt quickly to the dark, but the human eye will not adjust well."

Anja moved in between Matthew and Emmeline. "Emmeline, hold on to my arm. Dr. Matthew, stay close to me and follow my voice."

Anja began to hum a soft tune that reminded Emmeline of an old lullaby. Her sweet voice was haunting, filling the air with quiet sorrow. Matthew tilted his head and closed his eyes as he adjusted his senses to his surroundings.

Emmeline took Anja's arm and gave it a squeeze. *Thank you for your offer to Mattie.*

Emmeline looked up and caught Michael's stare just as he turned his head back to look at her. His dark eyes were fully expanded and cold, but she didn't flinch, and she stared at him until he turned back around. She let out a breath, and her grip tightened against Anja.

"What's wrong?" Anja stopped humming and turned her full, glossy irises to Emmeline.

"I just realized why you can see so well in the dark."

Emmeline could almost hear Anja laughing through her humming as they descended into the darkness.

And into the monster's belly we go.

The group moved through the deathly quiet tunnels that led to the underground caverns. Emmeline could hear light footsteps, but there weren't any echoes or dripping of water or any other sound one would expect to hear in tunnels that led underground. There was a distinct sour, metallic smell in the air.

"How far down are we going?" Emmeline asked.

Anja didn't stop humming. "About six stories."

"Mattie, are you okay?"

"I'm fine."

They settled back into the steady rhythm of steps while listening to Anja hum softly.

"Does cellular service work down here?" Emmeline asked.

"Up until about halfway."

Emmeline almost cursed herself. "My phone has a light. Why are we walking in the dark?" She reached for her backpack.

"I have a flashlight, but I prefer this. It's nice," Matthew said.

You've had a flashlight this whole time and never said anything? That's just great, Mattie.

"We're here," Maira's voice rang out from in front.

Emmeline was jolted out of her thoughts as the group stopped in front of another door. The door creaked as it slid into the wall, and warm light from the caverns flooded into the tunnel. Emmeline sighed with relief as she extricated her arm from Anja's and rubbed her hands together for warmth.

Just then, a bloodcurdling howl echoed through the caverns, followed by successively louder screams. Emmeline shrieked in terror and latched back on to Anja's arm.

"Oh, right. I should've warned you about that," Anja muttered. "Apparently, raizour highly object to being held as prisoners."

Guttural rasps and barks thundered against the crash of metal chains raking across the stone floor. Matthew lurched forward, and his hands flew to cover his ears. He winced as he fumbled through his backpack with one hand.

"Let me help you." Emmeline grabbed Matthew's backpack and searched the pockets as deafening shrieks continued to echo from the caverns and into the tunnels.

Finally, she found his noise-canceling earbuds and pressed them into his trembling hand. He pushed the earbuds into his ears and tapped the side, and after a few seconds, his body relaxed.

Anja watched their exchange, and her icy irises glittered as they settled back on Matthew. Matthew looked away, but Anja waved her hand in front of his face. When he looked over, she raised her eyebrows in question and gave him a thumbs-up. Matthew nodded and raised a thumbs-up in return. Emmeline felt her heart lift, and she smiled gratefully at Anja.

Anja pursed her lips. "Both of you, stay with me at all times."

"You weren't exaggerating when you said this was an event space." Emmeline's mouth dropped open as she entered the expansive room.

The caverns stretched out into a perfect circle several stories high, culminating in a peaked ceiling. Recessed into the walls were smaller versions of the stone statues that stood guard outside the entrance, and while each figure was in a different fighting stance, they all had the same fierce, toothy scowl. The floor was covered with smooth stones, tiled in an intricate mosaic pattern of various shades of white that transitioned into cool gray walls. A few of the hollow spaces appeared to be a tunnel, and dual-ended light sconces spiraled up the walls, intermixed with protruding platforms and giving the illusion of an endless staircase.

"Dr. Matthew!" Anja cried out.

Emmeline whirled around and saw that Matthew had broken away from the group and was studying the statues. His fingers traced the patterns surrounding each figure while his eyes roamed the circular room in wonder. Emmeline was about to run after him when Anja pulled her back.

"Don't leave the group," Anja hissed.

Javier frowned at them and gestured for Anja to bring Matthew back. She sprinted forward and planted herself in front of Matthew with her hands on her hips, but he ignored her scowl and pointed to different statues on the wall.

"Are these modeled after historical figures?"

"Yes!" Anja exhaled loudly and threw up her hands. She grabbed Matthew by the arm and hauled him back to the group. "Stay with the group."

Matthew rubbed his arm before turning to Emmeline and pointing at the walls. "The statues are impressive."

Emmeline rolled her eyes and didn't bother answering him.

A tall figure, dressed in fitted black armor, walked out of the tunnel to the group's left and stopped to talk to Javier. Two blades were strapped to his back, and a lower mask stretched over the front of his helmet, obscuring everything, except his eyes. Emmeline startled when his icy irises flickered over to her.

Emmeline poked Anja. "Is that Erik?"

"Yes."

"What's going to happen now?" Emmeline asked.

"They'll bring out the raizour to show you."

"And what happens after show-and-tell?"

"They die."

Emmeline fell silent, and her stomach twisted.

"They were going to die anyway, so don't feel guilty. Your presence has only delayed their death sentence," Anja added.

"Will your brother kill them?"

"Yes."

"Why Erik? Why not you or anyone else?"

Anja's frosty irises flickered over, and her voice chilled Emmeline to her bones.

"Because he's our Executioner."

CHAPTER FIFTEEN

AND OUT THE OTHER SIDE

Matthew braced himself and tapped his earbud to disable the noise-canceling function as Javier strode over to meet him and Emmeline.

"Emmeline, Dr. Taylor-Wu, we're bringing out the raizour now, so please prepare yourselves accordingly. I recommend you not use devices that could distort your ability to hear what's happening around you," Javier said.

Matthew took out his earbuds and shoved them into his pocket. He winced and fought against the urge to cover his ears as the shrieks from within the tunnels came closer.

Erik stepped into the center of the room. Two large, leathery wings unfolded behind him, and his skin transformed to a paper-gray with ridges forming around his forehead and at the top of his now-sunken cheekbones. Wisps of his hair escaped from under his helmet and were now a lighter shade of ash. Erik leaped up and used his wings to carry him to a platform. He crouched in a ready position, blending in with the other stone statues circling the space.

Emmeline's mouth gaped. "That's what Lesedi looked like at the gala! Mattie, am I hallucinating?"

Matthew stared up at Erik. "I don't think so, or we both are."

"Anja, did you drug us?" Emmeline sputtered.

"Of course not! That's offensive," Anja huffed. "Stop talking and pay attention."

Another nainthe came out of the tunnel, dragging a thick metal chain that appeared to be attached to something still hidden. The howls became louder until sharp, taloned feet appeared.

Emmeline gripped Anja's arm. "I don't want to be here anymore."

"I'm perfectly capable of protecting you and Dr. Matthew. My brother is also watching from above. You guys will be fine." Anja paused. "Plus, there are only three."

The nainthe yanked the chain, and a great creature stumbled into the room. Suddenly, the creature sprang forward with its claws and teeth bared but was jerked back by another nainthe, holding a chain from behind. The raizour slammed against the floor and howled in pain as the two nainthe hooked the chains to floor anchors along the wall.

Emmeline pointed to the nainthe with a ponytail underneath her helmet. "Was the second nainthe that just came out Quinn?"

"Yes."

Emmeline stayed behind Anja and peered over her shoulder as the creature snarled and snapped its teeth at them, jerking at the chains and whipping them against the stone floor. The creature's skin was translucent and marked with the faint outline of its muscles and veins in its bare body. It had wide pitch-black eyes that were glossy and unblinking, taking up almost a third of its face. Faint vertical openings lined the sides of its jaw, like the gills on a fish. Its teeth were long and sharp, resembling rows of fangs, just like the nainthe. The ridges along the creature's neck and above its chest pulsed as it panted and dragged its sharp claws against the floor, marking jagged lines into the stone. The two nainthe reappeared from the tunnel and dragged another raizour into the room, securing it to another set of floor anchors. Both raizour took turns trying to lurch forward but were held back in place by the chains.

Emmeline covered her mouth in horror when one of the raizour turned around. Its wings were pressed flat to its back with large metal hooks.

"One more." Anja looked up at her brother.

Unlike his earlier graceful movements, Erik's body was tense as he balanced on the edge of the narrow platform. He was terrifying with his papery skin and leathery wings, but his icy irises had become cloudy.

"Anja, is your brother okay?" Emmeline's voice trailed off as the two nainthe brought in the last raizour.

"He just wants to get this over with. He doesn't enjoy his job."

"No, I mean, he doesn't look well."

"He's fine."

The last raizour was leaner than the other two, and its black eyes followed Quinn and the other nainthe. It didn't try to escape and only snarled as the two nainthe secured its chains to the floor anchors.

After the nainthe moved away, the third raizour stood and growled at Javier. Javier stayed in human form and stared back, holding the raizour's gaze. The other two raizour howled and bared their teeth, but the third raizour barked, and they both fell silent. The third raizour turned back to Javier and then looked at Maira and Michael. It sneered as it shifted its weight across the floor, and its black eyes assessed Matthew, who stiffened under its scrutiny.

The raizour slunk toward the group, its eyes alternating between Emmeline and Matthew until the chains pulled tight and scraped against its anchors.

I see two filthy humans here, the raizour hissed.

"Maira, get Asadi," Javier commanded, his eyes never leaving the creature.

Maira sprinted out of the room, and there was the distinct flapping of wings before the heavy door closed behind her. The creature turned to Javier and cocked its head.

You are the fearless leader of the nainthe. Your day of reckoning is coming. We will destroy you and all your followers, the raizour sneered.

A sharp tug in Emmeline's head pierced behind her eyes, and she clenched her fingers to stop her hands from shaking. All the nainthe clasped their hands behind their backs and steeled their features, betraying no emotion.

"Why aren't you responding to it?" Emmeline whispered to Anja.

"We don't speak their language. The historians have some documented knowledge, which is why Javier has summoned Asadi. There isn't usually much conversing when nainthe and raizour meet."

"You can't understand them?" Emmeline's eyes widened, and her palms started to sweat.

"No."

"I can."

Anja whirled around to face Emmeline. "What do you mean?"

The raizour snapped its head at Anja and hissed.

"I can hear it in my head," Emmeline said.

"Anja!" Javier barked.

Disobedience among the ranks. That does not bode well for you, fearless leader. The raizour smirked before turning its attention back to Emmeline. It paced from side to side, and its black eyes never left her face. *You are rather interesting.*

Emmeline stared into the creature's eyes as the pain in her head subsided. It pulled her forward, and her feet carried her past Anja and Matthew.

Matthew grabbed her arm. "Emia, what are you doing?"

"It wants to talk to me."

"It wants to kill you, not talk to you."

Emmeline didn't look at Matthew. "It knows what I am."

"Let her go, Dr. Taylor-Wu," Javier commanded.

"Don't tell me what to do. I'm not one of your soldiers," Matthew retorted.

"Mattie, it's okay. Let me go," Emmeline said. Her sight started to close in, blackening her vision and clouding her senses. Her mouth tasted like cardboard, and all she could smell was ash.

"I got her." Anja stayed one step to the side of Emmeline. She glanced up at Erik before pulling her blade from her harness and balancing it at her side.

Ah, the last one. Come closer, seeker, and let me see you. Curious little human, are you not? the raizour taunted.

Emmeline stopped several feet before the raizour and the fog in her mind cleared.

Just a little bit closer, it crooned.

Emmeline stared back at the creature. "Why do you find me interesting?"

Fascinating. You can understand me. The raizour cocked its head.

"Yes, and you can understand me as well."

The metal door that guarded the caverns slid open, and quick footsteps on the stone floor stopped behind Emmeline.

Tell me, seeker, why are you here? Have the almighty nainthe asked you to witness our deaths at the hands of the Executioner?

"I'm here to see what you are."

What is more interesting is what you are and why you are here. Tell me, human.

"They think I'm a seeker."

It seems you elystiers are hard to come by. The precious seeker. The all-seeing one.

"Am I?" Emmeline asked.

The raizour paced side to side and smirked, as if it was mocking her. *There are usually two of your kind. Where is the other one?*

"They don't know where the other seeker is."

Of course they do not. The nainthe are blind, and when they fall, we will rejoice in their defeat, the raizour sneered.

"How do you know the nainthe will fall?" Emmeline felt Javier's presence come up beside her.

We will ensure it. The nainthe's time is almost up, and the rise of the raizour is coming. The creature's smirk widened. *Tell the nainthe leader the monsters are on their tail, and they do not even know it.*

Emmeline repeated the raizour's words for Javier, her eyes never leaving the creature.

"Ask it what the raizour are planning," Javier said.

It is a surprise, it mocked after Emmeline repeated Javier's question.

Maira leaped up and landed on the back of the raizour. She plunged a short blade into its shoulder and twisted it before pulling it out. The creature howled in pain and thrashed at Maira, who somersaulted off and fell back behind Javier. Deep blue liquid seeped out of the wound and down the front of the raizour's torso.

"Ask it again and tell it we can either give it a quick and merciful death or a long, painful one," Javier commanded.

We are not afraid of death. Death is inevitable, and it will come for you soon enough. Your own house is crumbling from within, and you cannot see it.

Emmeline's heart pounded in her ears. "What do you mean?"

It is unfortunate the nainthe found you, but it is fortunate for us. The raizour's grin widened further as it panted. The creature shifted its gaze to Anja and flexed its claws. *The Executioner's family. Quite the rare coincidence, is it not, to have someone you know who has the same noble calling, let alone a sibling?*

"What did it say?" Anja's icy eyes flashed.

"It knows that you and Erik are related."

Anja's eyes flickered up to Erik before falling back to the creature.

The Executioner will pay dearly for his atrocities against our kind. Tell me, seeker, shall we kill him first, or make him watch his sibling die instead?

Blood rushed to Emmeline's head, and she reached out to hold on to Anja to steady herself. She looked past the creature and to the two behind it.

Something's not right. They're too calm. It's like they're waiting, she thought.

Emmeline panicked and looked behind her. "It's a trap. Mattie, get back!" she cried out.

The creature broke free from one of the chains and swiped its claw at Anja. Anja lurched backward and slid into a hunched position, narrowly avoiding the razor-sharp tips. The creature sprang forward, but the remaining chains held it back. Erik's boots slammed into the stone, and he brandished a blade in each hand. His icy irises surged with rage, and he raised his blades to strike.

"Don't you dare kill it, Erik. This bitch is mine," Anja hissed and transformed into nainthe form.

Enough! Time for this to end. The raizour threw its head back and howled.

The two raizour behind snapped free from their chains, sending the metal scraping across the concrete. They jumped on their nainthe guards and pulled back their heads. Sinking their sharp teeth just under the nainthe's chins, they ripped out the nainthe's throats and flung the torn flesh across the stone floor. The raizour threw the lifeless bodies to the ground and wiped their mouths with the backs of their claws.

"Quinn!" Anja screamed.

Erik leaped into the air, and Anja pushed Emmeline back toward Matthew. Emmeline cried out in pain as she hit the ground.

She watched in horror as Erik decapitated the two screaming raizour. Anja cradled Quinn's broken body, and Asadi picked up the other nainthe's body. She forced herself to blink when she found herself staring into the black eyes of the raizour still chained in front of her.

Seeker. The raizour slipped out of its chains and slunk toward her.

Matthew stepped in front of Emmeline and raised his hand to block the raizour, but the raizour swiped at him with the back of its claw, launching him through the air.

Filthy human. Who do you think you are? it snapped.

"What do you want with me?" Emmeline stammered.

The creature grinned. *There is nothing I want from you. You are of more value to us when you are dead.* It wrapped its large claws around Emmeline's throat and squeezed, cutting off her air supply. *You humans are so fragile. How easy it would be to crush your feeble existence.*

Emmeline clawed at her neck, and her mouth fell open as her vision darkened. The raizour released her throat, and she choked as she sucked air into her lungs. It grabbed her hair and forced her head back, exposing her neck. Emmeline screamed and kicked against the raizour as it bared its razor-sharp teeth and opened its mouth to bite down.

Suddenly, a deafening blow knocked the creature off her. Erik drove his boot into the creature's head and snapped it back, breaking its neck.

I might have failed, but the others will not. Blue liquid leaked from the raizour's mouth and eyes as it lay, panting, on the floor. *Your time will come, Executioner, and you will mourn the day we take everything you care about.*

"What did it say?" Erik turned to Emmeline, his irises hard as ice.

"It threatened Anja's life."

Emmeline exhaled as she lay her head on the cold stone floor. She barely saw Erik move, but the air burned around him as his blade swung down and decapitated the raizour in one swift motion.

Emmeline lay still on the floor despite the frenzied commotion around her. In the distance, she could hear wings echoing in the tunnels and boots slamming on the ground. She closed her eyes to block out the flashes of light as angry shouts punctured the air around her.

Mattie, where are you?

She lifted her head to look for her brother. Matthew was kneeling on the floor, and his hands gripped the stone as he tried to steady himself. He took a deep breath and hoisted himself up, his hands pressing down on his chest to check for fractures.

"Michael! I want the emergency teams on the lookout immediately!" Javier barked. "Maira, I want everyone on high alert."

Loud commands followed, and footsteps pounded against the stone floor.

Javier turned to Emmeline as she tried to push herself off the floor.

"Erik, get the seeker and the human above ground now. Take them to Ben and Lucia immediately." Javier looked around grimly. "I want my team, the seeker, and her brother in my office in one hour. Erik, that includes you and Anja." He turned on his heel and stalked out of the caverns.

Matthew limped over to Emmeline's side. "Are you okay?"

Emmeline nodded. "I think so. I can feel everything, but my chest and throat hurt," she whispered.

Erik took off his face mask and helmet and knelt beside them. He changed back into his human form, but his irises still encompassed his eyes.

"Emmeline, as a precaution, I will carry you up to the surface." Erik's melodic timbre halted with each word he spoke. "Dr. Taylor-Wu, are you able to walk? If not, I'll have one of the other nainthe come and assist you. It's a long walk back up."

"I'm fine," Matthew replied.

Erik nodded. "Let's get you both out of here."

CHAPTER SIXTEEN

THE SALT IN MEMORIES

Erik's strong arms slipped under Emmeline's head and knees, lifting her against him. She closed her eyes and welcomed the respite on her heavy limbs, letting her body soften in his arms despite the wailing voices battling in the background. The faint scent of citrus and cedar reminded her of a soap she used to use as a child.

Emmeline opened her eyes to look up at Erik as he climbed steadily through the dark tunnel that led up to the surface. His hair was messy, and his mouth was pulled taut, as were the muscles underneath his armor.

"Are the two guards dead?" Emmeline whispered, trying not to aggravate her sore throat.

"Yes."

"What will you do with the raizour bodies?"

"Burn them."

"Where are you going to do that?"

"There's a crematorium underground. Anything or anyone who dies is brought there," Erik replied.

Emmeline leaned back into Erik's arms.

"Try not to fall asleep until your brother or Ben has examined you." Erik glanced at her, and she shivered at his icy stare. "We're almost at the surface."

Emmeline closed her eyes and let Erik's footsteps and the rise and fall of his erratic breathing rock her like a gentle lullaby.

∼

The cool air touched Emmeline's skin, and she opened her eyes to look around the courtyard.

"We're close to the infirmary," Erik said.

His footsteps were silent on the soft grass, and the dimmed lights glowed peacefully, oblivious to the violence just six stories below ground. He turned down a long, sterile hallway and used his back to push open the heavy double doors at the end. Bright fluorescent lights and a metallic odor invaded Emmeline's senses, and she lifted her arm to cover her eyes as Erik placed her upright on a hospital bed.

"Do you want to lie down?" he asked.

Emmeline shook her head. "I'll sit and wait for Mattie."

Erik gave her a curt nod and made his way over to Anja. Emmeline blinked to let her eyes adjust, and her hand flew to her mouth as she looked around. Quinn and the other nainthe guard were each lying on a hospital table. There were gaping holes where their throats used to be, and torn, bloodied flesh hung down the sides. Their arms were placed across the black armor that protected their chests, and sticky blood seeped to a halt on the cold metal table they lay on. Their eyes were closed and their mouths were drawn into a straight line.

Anja sat beside Quinn, and she stared at a white wall. Asadi knelt on a small carpet, praying with his forehead against the floor. He was facing a wall, which Emmeline thought must be east to Mecca.

Emmeline looked around for Matthew and found him sitting in a chair while a man with a mop of curly brown hair shone a light into his eyes.

There's a faint aura around that man. I must've seen him earlier.

"Dr. Taylor-Wu, how are you feeling? What you just witnessed was incredibly traumatizing," the man asked, his hazel eyes darting between Matthew's left and right eyes.

That must be Ben.

"I'm fine," Matthew replied.

"Do you remember what just happened?"

Matthew looked at Ben strangely. "Why wouldn't I remember what happened?"

Ben snapped his mouth shut as he stared at Matthew. "Er, no reason." He ran his fingers through his hair and pushed up his wire-framed glasses.

Matthew stood up and walked over to Emmeline.

"Mattie." Emmeline's eyes widened as all her fear and terror rushed forward. She reached out blindly for her brother. "Mattie!"

Matthew grabbed a garbage can and held it to Emmeline's face, and she emptied her stomach into it. Ben handed her a clean paper towel.

"I want you to lie down on your side." Matthew gently helped her lean back and bent down to rummage through his backpack for one of his medical kits.

He checked her pulse and breathing, and she stared at the little light until he was satisfied with what he saw. He touched her head in different spots and moved her hair away to look closer.

"Did you hit your head?"

Emmeline shook her head. "I think I might have to throw up again."

"Any ringing in your ears?"

"None."

"You have a notoriously weak stomach. Can you tilt your chin back?" Matthew squinted at the bruises forming around her neck. "You need to rest your voice. You're lucky that thing didn't break your neck."

"Agreed."

Matthew stood back. "Ben, can you stay with my sister? I'm going to check on Lesedi."

"I'll keep an eye on her."

Emmeline looked over at Anja, and her heart hurt at the anguish in Anja's eyes.

I hope Lesedi makes a full recovery. I can't imagine what will happen to Anja if Lesedi doesn't make it.

Anja had shed her armor, leaving it piled up in a corner. Erik was beside her, and they talked in hushed voices, neither looking up nor at each other. Emmeline couldn't see Erik's face, but his body was tense, and his hands gripped the hospital bed so tightly that the veins were raised against his skin. Emmeline pushed herself upright and steadied herself.

"Maybe you should stay lying down for a bit," Ben suggested.

"I want to check on Anja." Emmeline took a deep breath and shifted herself off the hospital bed, pausing to ensure she didn't need to vomit again.

She crossed her arms over her chest and shuffled over to Anja and Erik, clearing her throat to announce her presence. Anja turned to the wall and wiped her face with her hands.

Emmeline looked at Erik and swallowed her surprise. "How come your eyes are still like that?"

Erik turned his face away from her and stayed silent.

"I'm sorry. I didn't mean to pry," Emmeline said.

Erik crouched beside Anja. "I need to go back to my room."

Anja only nodded in response, and Erik stood up and left the room without another word. Emmeline rolled up a chair beside Anja and sat down.

"May I give you a hug?" Emmeline asked.

Anja nodded, and fresh tears rolled down her cheeks. Emmeline wrapped her arms around Anja and pulled her close. She held Anja tight as her tears became desperate sobs.

I'm sorry this happened to your friend.

Emmeline heard footsteps and looked up just as Matthew came around the corner. He grabbed a box of tissues and placed it on the hospital bed, pushing it close to Anja.

"I'm sorry about Quinn. I know she was your friend," Matthew said. "Do you want me to cover her with a sheet?"

"No, this is a normal part of our lives." Anja looked up at Matthew, and her eyes were puffy and red. "Why do you seem unaffected by what just happened?"

"This is just who I am." Matthew's eyes flickered to Emmeline. "Just because it happens often doesn't mean it's normal. What's normal is grief. It's okay to grieve."

"Then, it seems we're destined to spend our entire lives grieving." Anja stood up and rubbed her eyes. "How's Lessie?"

"She's showing progress. The antibiotics seem to be working."

"I'd like to go see her."

Matthew moved out of Anja's path. "We didn't mention anything about the raizour attack. It's up to you if you want to tell Lesedi, though I'd recommend keeping her focused on recovery."

"I won't tell her yet. She'd be livid if she knew about the danger we put you and Emmeline in."

Anja began walking toward the hallway Matthew had just come back from, but before turning the corner, she tilted her head over her shoulder, not quite making eye contact with him.

"Dr. Matthew, thank you for taking care of Lessie." Anja clenched her jaw. "I was supposed to protect you and your sister, but I failed. If my brother hadn't been there, you'd both be dead. For that, I'm sorry. Please forgive me."

And just like her brother, she left the room like a ghost.

"She feels tremendous guilt, but it wasn't her fault. She didn't kill the two guards, and she didn't try to kill you," Matthew said to Emmeline.

"I know," Emmeline murmured.

"Ben, who was the other guard?" Matthew asked.

"That was Mihal. He was one of our newer members and one of the youngest here. He was called upon when he was about twenty, and that was five years ago. He was one of the few potentials we found without the help of a seeker."

"What's your natural life span?"

"More than twice that of a human. If we survive long enough to die of natural causes, we can live to about two hundred, give or take a few decades. It's different for every nainthe."

"I can understand why Javier is so protective of the nainthe."

"Best-case scenario would be humans trying to experiment and genetically duplicate us. The worst case is them trying to exterminate us."

Emmeline looked around. "Where did Asadi go?"

"He probably went to the reflection room. Asadi was one of Mihal's mentors, and this is hard on him." Ben looked at the clock. "It's past four in the morning. You should get home and try to rest."

Ms. Rose will be worried sick if she doesn't see us this morning. We'd better get home soon.

Matthew pulled out his phone from the inner pocket of his hoodie and frowned. His phone screen was shattered, and it stayed black, unable to turn on.

"Emia, can I borrow your phone? I need to message my assistant to cancel today's appointments."

Emmeline went to her backpack to get her phone and handed it to Matthew. Ben looked past Emmeline and Matthew at a woman with long, wavy brown hair and strong, arched eyebrows standing at the doorway.

"Hey, Lucia," Ben called out.

"Hey, Ben. I'm here to relieve you of your shift." Lucia's dark eyes hardened as they fell on the two nainthe bodies.

Ben motioned to Emmeline and Matthew. "Lucia, this is Emmeline and Dr. Taylor-Wu. Emmeline and Dr. Taylor-Wu, this is Lucia, another resident medic."

"What's a human doing here?" Lucia pressed her thin lips together. "It's against the rules."

"Dr. Taylor-Wu was asked to come here and help Lesedi. Javier wasn't happy either, but he cleared it."

"Javier shouldn't get to choose when to bend the rules." Lucia pointed at Matthew and glared at him. "You shouldn't even know about us, let alone be in our home."

"Don't talk to my brother like that," Emmeline snapped.

Matthew shot her a look. *Back down.*

"As I told Javier, I don't want to be here any more than you want me here. I've already given my word that I won't say anything about the nainthe," Matthew said.

"Your word isn't worth anything to me," Lucia replied coldly.

"Then, it's a good thing I care very little about what you think," Matthew retorted.

You tell her, Mattie, Emmeline thought.

Ben looked back and forth between Lucia and Matthew. "Er, Lucia, Javier said we can bring Quinn's and Mihal's bodies to the crematorium tomorrow night after everyone's had a chance to pay their respects. In the morning, we can bring them to the reflection room." He looked down the hallway. "Lesedi's recovering in room D. The full report and instructions from Dr. Taylor-Wu are here." He held out a tablet to Lucia.

Lucia snatched the tablet from Ben's hand and stalked out of the room without another word.

The nainthe are the most inhospitable people I've ever met.

"Mattie, we need to get to Javier's office," Emmeline said. "I want to know what the hell just happened." She saw Anja's shadow behind Ben and almost jumped out of her skin.

"Yes, it's time. We owe you an explanation, but I don't think we'll have one that'll make you happy. Ben, I can take them to Javier's office since my presence has also been requested," Anja said.

"Dr. Taylor-Wu, will you visit again? There's so much we can learn from you," Ben asked.

"I'm not sure." Matthew looked around and picked up a pen from a nearby table. He jotted down his contact information on a paper towel and handed it to Ben. "If you have any questions, send me a note. I will try to help as best I can."

Anja looked wistfully at Quinn's body, and Emmeline gave her a hug.

"You're a hugger, aren't you?" Anja sniffled.

"Only when I think someone needs one. My father was a big believer in hugs. He believed hugs could cure everything," Emmeline murmured.

"Not everything," Matthew replied.

"My father believed the sea could cure everything," Anja said absently. She seemed lost in a hazy memory.

"Your father sounds like he knows what he's talking about."

"Sounded. My father passed away many years ago." Anja snapped out of her daydream. "Let's get this over with, so you guys can go home."

CHAPTER SEVENTEEN

AFTERMATH

Emmeline stepped back into Javier's office, and she stiffened at the tension in the room. Everyone had shed their armor and was gathered around the conference table. The lines on Javier's face cut far deeper than earlier, and although his eyes were still hard and sharp, he looked like he had aged many years.

"Sit," Javier commanded.

Emmeline and Matthew looked at each other before they took a spot at the table. Anja remained standing and moved to the side.

"Where's your brother, Anja?" Javier glowered.

"Recovering."

Recovering? Emmeline looked at Anja and Javier with surprise.

"Erik needs to be here. I don't care if he is recovering or not. We have two dead nainthe!"

"And if he hadn't been there, you'd have more, including a dead seeker and a dead doctor," Anja shot back.

"It was his responsibility!" Javier thundered, and he slammed his fist on the table.

Emmeline let out a high-pitched squeak, and Matthew winced.

"What was my responsibility?" Erik emerged silently from the shadows. He had also shed his armor, and his icy irises had returned to normal.

"You know exactly what your responsibility was," Michael growled. "It was your responsibility to ensure the raizour were properly secured."

"I did do that. Quinn, Mihal, and I checked all the locks together," Erik retorted.

"Are you blaming my brother for what happened?" Anja went to stand beside Erik, folding her arms across her chest.

"How else do you explain it?" Michael stood and gripped the table. "There were only three individuals who came in contact with the raizour. Two of those individuals are dead."

"Why would you think I'd want to hurt Quinn and Mihal? Quinn was my friend too. I might not have known Mihal very well, but he was just a kid."

"Erik, you were by far the most experienced out of the three, and I stand by what I said: it was your responsibility," Javier stated. "Why couldn't you anticipate what the raizour would do?"

"You know my ability isn't always within my control. Unlike Michael, I didn't make a mistake, and I don't often do."

"I don't make mistakes, you arrogant asshole! I ought to teach you a lesson in humility." Michael's face contorted, and he leaned over the table.

"You think you're going to be the one to teach me a lesson?" Erik replied coldly.

"*Enough!*" Javier bellowed. "Enough of this!" He looked at each of them angrily.

Emmeline caught Matthew's eye, who watched the exchange with interest. She raised her eyebrow at him, and he gave her a nod. Emmeline rapped her fist on the table, and everyone turned to look at her and Matthew. Javier stared at her and blinked, as if he'd just remembered they were in the room.

Emmeline's voice burned in her throat. "I know everyone's upset right now, and we can spend all night talking about whose fault it was, but I would much rather talk about what happened."

"With all due respect," Michael drawled out his sarcasm, "you're speaking about matters you know nothing about."

Emmeline pulled her long hair away and traced her neck with her fingers, lightly treading along the thick bruised lines of where the raizour had wrapped its claws. "You might think so, Michael, but my neck would beg to differ."

Anja looked away at the sight of Emmeline's bruises, and Maira held her hand up to silence Michael from speaking further. Maira walked over to Emmeline and gently tilted her head back for a better look.

"We certainly are terrible hosts, aren't we?" Maira sighed. "We never even asked if you're okay."

"I'll be fine." Emmeline shrugged her head out of Maira's grasp. "If it hadn't been for Erik, I wouldn't be sitting here at this table." She tried not to flinch as his icy eyes turned to her. "Erik, thank you for saving my life."

"I shouldn't have had to save your life. None of this should've happened," Erik replied.

"But you did save my life, and that's what matters." Emmeline turned back to Javier, and her voice hardened. "This was your idea. You put my life and my brother's life in danger. What you did was unnecessary; if I had known how dangerous it would be, I would never have agreed to it. You owe us an apology."

Javier's face softened. "You're right. You have my apologies. There was never any intention to put your lives in danger. I wanted to show you what we're up against, hoping it would convince you why you're so important to us."

Emmeline looked around the room. "How come those creatures knew who I was? And why am I the only one who could understand what they were saying?"

"Raizour can sense seekers and nainthe the same way we can sense you and them. They knew just by sight alone that there was magic in you," Maira replied.

Javier sat down. "I've never encountered an elystier—or anyone, for that matter—who could communicate with a raizour, which is why I summoned Asadi. As one of our historians, he's studied what little of the raizour language we have documented. Dr. Taylor-Wu, could you understand what the creature was saying?"

"Not a word."

"Emmeline, you were speaking to it in English, but it seemed to understand everything you were saying. How is that possible?"

"I could feel its language in my mind. When I first saw the creature, I had a pain in my head, and then the pain was gone. Kind of like your auras."

"What else did the raizour say to you?" Javier asked.

"It knew you were the leader of the nainthe and Erik was the Executioner. It also knew that Anja and Erik were family." Emmeline looked at Anja. "The raizour asked if they should kill you first and make your brother watch."

"The raizour seem to know much more about us than we know about them," Erik stated.

"Erik, on your next few hunts, I want you to bring a raizour back alive. I want to interrogate it," Javier said.

"You trust him to do it?" Michael glared at Erik. "Look at what happened tonight."

"Then, you do it, Michael. Or has sitting up here in the ivory tower made you soft?" Erik snapped.

"I don't want to hear another word from either of you," Javier barked.

Emmeline sucked another breath down her burning throat. "Is it safe for us to go home? I'm exhausted and in pain. I want to get some sleep."

Javier looked out the window. "The sun's beginning to rise, so it's safe for you to go home. Raizour are sensitive to light and heat, and only appear at night. Michael and Maira will arrange regular patrols around your residence during the evenings. The magic in you is weak, and I hope your gift continues to go unnoticed for the time being."

Anja stood up. "I'll take you both home."

"That's not necessary," Emmeline said. "Since it's safe for us to go home, I'd prefer you all get some rest. I'll call a driver to pick us up if someone can show us out."

"Absolutely not," Michael said. "Javier, they can't know where we are. It's too dangerous, especially since one is just a human."

"We're both sitting here, so don't talk about us as if we were beneath you," Emmeline snapped. "This human you so condescendingly refer to risked his own life to come here and save one of yours. Also, I've lived in this city my entire life. I might not know exactly where we are, but I have a pretty good idea."

"Actually, I know exactly where we are." Matthew fidgeted with his bricked phone and pushed his glasses back up. "I've already told you I won't tell anyone."

"How do you know this? Didn't Anja keep our location secret?" Michael threw a scowl in her direction.

"She made us wear a blindfold on the car ride over. I just have a good sense of direction and an almost-perfect memory, courtesy of my mother." Matthew shrugged.

Emmeline stood up. "That's enough. I wasn't asking for permission to leave, so unless you plan on keeping us prisoner here, show us out."

"Why should I trust you?" Michael narrowed his eyes.

Emmeline leaned forward, and her eyes darkened until her irises resembled the coldest winter nights. It was a look she had practiced repeatedly with her mother until she could summon it on will.

"If I wasn't clear enough before, let me make it crystal clear for you again. I do not give a fuck what you think." Emmeline turned her chilly gaze to Javier. "Show us out. Now."

"This is a mistake, Javier," Michael warned.

Javier stood and ignored Michael. "Emmeline and Dr. Taylor-Wu, we're entrusting you with our secret and our lives. Rest well, Emmeline. I wish you a quick recovery."

The sky hinted at the promise of morning with the first rays of light peeking over the edge of the buildings. Emmeline took a deep breath and welcomed the refreshing chill of morning dew. Anja led the way, and Erik followed at the back as they walked in single file through the courtyard. Anja's hunched shoulders tugged at Emmeline's heart.

I don't understand how she's even functioning right now.

They passed under several arched doorways and into a darkened great hall. Long dining tables sat in the center, and seating booths bordered the walls. Curved floor-to-ceiling windows rose from the smooth concrete floor and filled the wall that faced the courtyard, giving occupants an all-encompassing view.

"This is our dining hall, but we mostly use it like a family room." Anja spoke for the first time since they had left Javier's office. "The communal kitchen is on the left."

A wide spiral staircase stood at the end of the space, leading to the upper platform.

"There are several ways out of this complex, but I chose this one since it's the nicest. The other paths involve darker hallways and steeper stairs. There's an elevator and accessibility ramp on the other side of the complex, but they don't get used often," Anja continued.

They fell back into silence as they climbed the spiral staircase. Anja led them through a long corridor and used her handprint to unlock several doors. They finally stopped in front of a fire exit.

"We're here." Anja pushed open the door and stepped out onto the street.

Bright streetlights lined the sidewalk and narrow roads, and Emmeline immediately recognized where they were. She looked at Matthew with wide eyes.

"You knew where we were this whole time?" Emmeline asked.

Matthew looked confused. "Why are you surprised?"

"You're right. I shouldn't be."

Emmeline tapped Anja's shoulder. "You live behind these shops and low-rise complexes?"

"We own this entire block, and it conveniently hides us. The renters think they back onto a factory and storage facility, which is true for a small part."

"Do you know how much this land is worth?"

Anja snorted. "A lot."

Emmeline gave Anja a look and took out her phone to message her private car service.

This land is worth more than just "a lot."

"The car service will be here in eight minutes." Emmeline tucked her phone back into her pocket.

"Will you come back?" Anja asked.

"I don't know. I keep thinking this is a bad dream and I'll wake up at any moment."

"I don't blame you. This was probably the worst introduction in the history of the nainthe." Anja looked away. "We need you, Emmeline."

"That's the thing; I'm not sure you need me or if I'm of any use to you. I don't get any visions or dreams or anything that would make me think I'm an elystier."

"You can see us, and you can understand the raizour. There's something about you that ties you to us," Erik said.

Emmeline's phone buzzed, indicating that her car service was a minute away.

"Maybe there's something that ties me to your crazy world, but why me, and why now? Your people didn't want us here, and they made it clear we are outsiders despite us only trying to help. I don't want to be somewhere we're not wanted. If I wanted to do that, there are many places I could choose from," Emmeline murmured.

"You might not feel wanted, but you're needed." Anja's eyes were sunken, and shadows hung underneath. "We'll need to spend time with you to see what you're capable of and how we can help you hone your skills."

"Give her time, Anja," Erik said.

An electric vehicle pulled up along the curb, and Emmeline checked the license plate for a match.

"I'm grateful you took care of us. Even though you don't believe it, you did keep your promise," Emmeline said. "I'm sorry about Quinn and Mihal."

Anja's eyes looked watery, but Emmeline couldn't tell if it was from utter physical or emotional exhaustion or both.

"Dr. Matthew, thank you again for coming to help Lessie," Anja said.

"I know you know how to use my proper name, but you purposely choose not to. You can call me Matthew or Mattie." He gave her a rare small smile.

Emmeline raised an eyebrow at her brother. He only let family and very close friends use his childhood nickname.

Anja glanced at Emmeline before turning back to Matthew. She hesitated and seemed unsure of how to ask. "Would it be okay if I gave you a hug?"

Matthew nodded, and Anja hugged him, mouthing a low thank-you into his ear. He patted her awkwardly on the back, barely touching her.

After they got into the backseat of the car, Emmeline lowered the window.

"Anja, Erik, be careful," she said.

Erik slipped out of the shadows and into the light. "Why do you say that?"

Emmeline glanced at the driver before she leaned out the window and lowered her voice. "I didn't tell the others this because I didn't know who I could trust. When the raizour spoke to me, it said the nainthe were broken from the inside. At first, I thought it was trying to get inside my head, but then I realized that it had no intention of letting me live." She tried to choose her words carefully but couldn't think of a way to say it delicately. "I think you might be dealing with traitors within the nainthe."

Emmeline shrank back into her seat as Erik's eyes flashed in anger. His irises swelled and snapped to her, but as quickly as his eyes had changed, they changed back.

"Was there anything else the raizour said that you haven't told us?" Erik asked.

"The raizour referred to you as *the Executioner*, but it was more than just knowing who you were with the nainthe."

"What do you mean?"

"I'm not sure how to explain it, but it didn't seem as if it was referring to you by your ability or reputation. It almost seemed as if it was referring to you by name."

Anja glanced at Erik. "They also knew you and I were family, but they shouldn't know anything about us. How could they have known this information? Every time we come across one, we kill it. It's not like we know their names or anything about them."

"If there are traitors, I'll find and kill them myself." Erik turned and disappeared through the fire exit door.

Emmeline gave a small wave to Anja and leaned back in her seat, signaling to the driver that it was time to go.

I hope I did the right thing by telling them.

She glanced at Matthew, who had already closed his eyes and was leaning against the passenger window.

For all our sakes.

PART III:

STUDIES AND STORIES

CHAPTER EIGHTEEN

SAFEGUARDS

Emmeline plodded to the kitchen in the early afternoon. Her hair was askew and piled high on her head, and she was still in the T-shirt dress she had slept in. Before going downstairs, she had circled a thin scarf around her neck, shrugged on a cardigan to cover her bruises, and replaced the gauze on her fingers with discreet bandages.

"Morning, Ms. Rose." Emmeline yawned.

Ms. Rose glanced up. "It's not morning anymore, sweetheart. Seems like someone had a late night—or a very early morning."

"Coffee, please." Emmeline sat down at the kitchen island and laid her head on the cool stone countertop.

"It's on its way." Ms. Rose patted her shoulder.

"Please, coffee," Emmeline repeated pitifully. Her voice was still raspy from the previous night, and she wanted something hot to soothe it.

The coffee machine beeped, and Emmeline breathed in the rich aroma. A magical cup slid across the counter and came to rest beside her tired face.

"Where did you and Mattie go last night?" Ms. Rose asked.

"We were hanging out with Gus and Ryan and lost track of time."

What's a little white lie?

"You and Mattie are full-grown adults now. You don't need to lie to me about your whereabouts. If you want to have fun and let loose, that's perfectly fine. At least you did it safely and didn't drive." Ms. Rose walked past Emmeline and patted her on the shoulder again. "It's good to have some fun. All I care about is that you're both safe and happy. Nothing else matters."

"How did you know I didn't drive?"

"I know everything." Ms. Rose turned to the tablet on the wall and tapped a few times. "Garage door wasn't opened, and all cars remained inside." She tapped the tablet again. "And you and Mattie didn't come home until six this morning. It must've been some night."

"Do you know where Mattie is? Is he still sleeping?"

Ms. Rose narrowed her eyes. "Why does your voice sound like that?"

Emmeline clammed up, and her hands went to her scarf.

"I'm going to make you a hot lemon water instead." Ms. Rose reached over to take Emmeline's coffee away.

Emmeline looked up in horror and wrapped her hand protectively around her piping hot cup. "No, don't take my coffee away. I promise I'll drink both. Leave the coffee!"

Ms. Rose rolled her eyes and let go of the coffee cup. "Your brother was up earlier and had lunch with me and Mr. Jae. I think he's in his office, working, as usual." She grabbed a new mug for the lemon water. "I saw the state of destruction of Mattie's phone. I don't even want to know what happened last night."

Emmeline thanked Ms. Rose and picked up both mugs, one in each hand.

Time to find my brother.

Emmeline knocked on Matthew's office door with her foot before sliding the door open with her elbow. He didn't look up from his papers as she set down her two mugs on his desk and sat across from him.

"Is one of those for me?" Matthew asked.

"Nope. Both are mine."

Matthew continued to work. "How's your neck?"

"Sore and bruised. Looks and feels worse than yesterday, but bearable."

"That's expected."

"I need to burn some energy. Want to do some kickboxing with me?" Emmeline asked.

"Not especially."

"Come on. Let's go," Emmeline said. "We should do some strength training as well."

Matthew looked up at her. "Are you worried?"

"I'd like to improve my chances of being able to defend myself."

"You understand that as humans, we are wholly and unequivocally outmatched? You could be a professional mixed martial artist and still not stand a chance. Both species have a completely different physique than us."

"You weren't scared at all?"

"No. I was irrelevant to them, though I was fearful for you." Matthew seemed to contemplate something and stood up. "Maybe it's a good idea to brush up on your self-defense. I'll meet you downstairs in ten minutes."

~

Matthew was already warming up and waiting for Emmeline when she arrived in the basement. She joined him on the mat and began her warm-up.

"Will you go back to the nainthe's home?" Matthew asked.

"I haven't decided." Emmeline held her head to her knees to stretch out her leg muscles. Her younger years in gymnastics and later years in various types of yoga kept her agile and flexible.

"We both know you will."

Emmeline glared at her brother. "Are you trying to get me riled up so that I kick your ass later?"

"As if you could." Matthew wrapped his hands. "If you weren't thinking of seeing them again, we wouldn't be doing this right now."

"Why do you have to be so damn logical all the time? Can't you be, you know, irrational and emotional, like the rest of us?" Emmeline instantly regretted the words that had left her mouth.

"I wish I were." Matthew finished wrapping his hands. "You know I do."

"I'm sorry about what I said." Emmeline lay down on the floor and stared at the ceiling. "I feel like I am going crazy."

Matthew motioned for her to stand up. "You're not crazy. I believe what we saw was real, though I don't understand the dynamics of how the nainthe work. There seems to be unrest among them."

"That's an understatement." Emmeline wrapped her hands, careful to avoid her bandaged fingers, and got her gloves, head protection, and mouthguard. "No matter what I choose, I don't want you involved in this mess. At first, it was interesting, but now, it's dangerous."

Matthew held up two mitts and motioned to Emmeline to begin. "Too late. This is far too fascinating for me to ignore."

"Do you mean from an academic standpoint?" Emmeline kept her hands at eye-level and attacked her brother multiple times. Her fingers ached from the last punch, and she ground her teeth.

"Yes." Matthew swiped at Emmeline and launched a kick at her head, which she evaded. "This is a once-in-a-lifetime opportunity to learn about two species we never knew existed."

"Oh, really?" Emmeline blew a stray hair out of her eyes. "How come you let Anja call you Mattie?"

Matthew faltered, and Emmeline took the opportunity to side-kick him in the chest. He stumbled back and grunted as the air left his body.

"I can count five people who are allowed to call you Mattie," Emmeline continued. "Ms. Rose, Mr. Jae, me, Gus, and Sam, my ex-boyfriend. This makes Anja number six. The rest of us have mostly known you your entire life while you only just met Anja."

Matthew took off his mitts and grabbed his gloves and head protection. He placed his glasses on a shelf and put in his mouthguard. "It's just a name, nothing more."

"I'm your sister, so don't bullshit me."

Emmeline blocked several attacks before one kick landed against her arm and another at her shoulder, knocking her to the floor.

"Not even Eva's allowed to call you Mattie, and she's one of my best friends. You pointedly ignore her every time she uses that name, which is rude, by the way." Emmeline readied herself. "She's bringing our new devices tomorrow."

Matthew motioned Emmeline to continue.

Shit, he's extra focused now.

Matthew fluidly blocked each of Emmeline's attempts and tapped her on the head with his fist. "Knockout."

Emmeline groaned. "I love practicing with you, and I also hate practicing with you."

Matthew took off his gear and went to drink some water. "Kickboxing isn't going to help you or me in this new situation. We should focus on defense that relies less on strength."

"I have a date on Saturday," Emmeline said, changing the subject.

"With the mayor?"

Emmeline nodded as she shed her gear into a basket and gave it a few sprays of fabric refresher.

"How come you don't seem excited about it?" Matthew asked.

"I feel like he's out of my league. He's charismatic, charming, and he could have his pick of women. I'm just me." Emmeline saw Matthew about to correct her, and she held up her hand. "I can't help how I feel."

"Don't think about it too much. Just enjoy the date."

"What are you doing tonight?"

"Working."

"You should go out and do something fun too. Take that shiny, expensive, new toy out for a spin."

"Last night was enough 'fun' for a lifetime," Matthew replied.

Emmeline laughed. "See you later."

Gus: Sweetie, I'll be at your place in 30 minutes. We'll pick out an outfit that will knock Philip off his feet. He's so handsome, it makes me want to hurl. Don't tell Ryan I said that.

Oh no, I forgot that Gus was coming over!
Emmeline slapped her forehead, and her scarf felt warm around her neck.
She can't see me like this.

Emia: Sorry, Gus, I can't meet today. Do you and Ryan want to come over on Sunday for a barbecue?

Gus: Why can't you meet today?

Emia: I'm feeling tired. I might cancel my date with Philip.

Gus: Don't you dare. Go take a shower and go on that date. You always chicken out and sabotage yourself.

Emia: I don't want to make a big deal out of this.

Gus: Where's he taking you?

Emia: Junos Thai Bar. What should I wear?

Gus: Your black vegan-leather leggings, that cute puff-sleeved light-pink blouse, and pointy black mules. Don't forget jewelry.

Emia: You're the best. I'll see you on Sunday.

Gus: If you need a rescue, message me. Ryan and I will come and "bump into" you guys.

Emmeline recorded a video of herself blowing a kiss and sent it to August. She tied her hair into a bun and stared at the bruises around her neck. They had started to turn into a deep purple with tinges of yellow and green around the edges.

How am I going to cover this up?

∽

Emmeline showered and changed into the outfit August had recommended but swapped out the top for a high-neck blouse in the same color to cover her bruises. She tucked the billowy top into her pants to create a sleek silhouette and opted to go barefaced with only a light smoky eye and lip gloss. She left her long, wavy hair down and gave it a few spritzes of styling spray to give it a beachy, tousled look.

What do I do about jewelry?

Emmeline settled on her classic diamond stud earrings, a delicate knotted gold bracelet, and her favorite watch. Her hand hovered over her mother's ring before she picked it up and ran her finger along the inscription on the inside. She slipped the ring onto her index finger, relishing in its familiar, comforting weight.

Ms. Rose: Emia, darling, Eva's here in the kitchen with your new phone. Mattie picked his up earlier.

Emia: Thanks, Ms. Rose. I'll be right down.

Emmeline selected a small vintage clutch and a dark gray wrap and ran down the stairs.

Eva was standing at the kitchen island, her red lips moving silently as her fingers slid across the smooth glass of her tablet. Her long, straight black hair that typically fell just above her waist was tied up in a high ponytail, and her transparent-framed glasses were perched low on her dainty nose.

"Eva!" Emmeline engulfed her friend in a hug. "I've missed you."

Eva returned her hug and kissed her on each cheek. "Sorry, hon. I've been super swamped at work lately. We're working on upgrading our security platform." She handed Emmeline her new phone. "Latest model, updated with the highest security protocols. I've always told you to be more careful with your phone. What happened to your old one? Matthew's was destroyed."

"Matthew fell on his phone." Emmeline cringed at her lie. "Someone showed me they were able to access my phone and change some of my settings."

"Don't worry; it won't happen again. But if it does, I'd like to hire that person," Eva replied.

"Pretty sure you wouldn't want to hire that person," Emmeline muttered as she reset her security passcodes. She handed her phone back to Eva. "Please show me all the new things I need to know, oh wise one."

Eva snorted and took Emmeline through a condensed version of the new security features.

Emmeline looked at the time. "Oh shoot, it's almost seven! Philip will be here soon."

"I've never heard you mention a Philip before. Are you going on a date?"

"It's just a first date. We met at the annual Royal Children's Rehabilitation Hospital gala." Emmeline paused. "It's Philip Vil."

Eva's jaw dropped. "Like, as in the mayor?"

"That's the one."

Eva whistled. "No pressure."

"I know, right?"

"But the Emia I know eats these situations for breakfast."

Emmeline rolled her eyes. "This isn't a business meeting. It's a date."

"Hmm, that's true. I guess he should be the one doing all the eating." Eva winked and laughed as Emmeline covered her face in mortification.

"I walked into that one, didn't I?"

"One hundred percent." Eva laughed again. She gathered her items from the kitchen island and packed them into her backpack. "It's just a first date. I'm assuming you have a fail-safe in place with Gus?"

"Of course"

"Good. I need to get back to work and then back to Sally."

"You're such a workaholic, just like Mattie. I don't know how Sally puts up with you."

"She puts up with me because I'm great in bed." Eva tilted her head thoughtfully. "And she has the patience of a saint."

"Unlike you," Emmeline snickered. "Tell her I said hi. You need to work less, so we can spend time together again. I never see you anymore."

"After this project, I should get some of my life back."

"Send Ms. Rose the bill for the phones and services, and she'll settle it for Mattie and me."

Eva rolled her eyes. "I'm not going to charge you for this. You're one of my best friends, and you certainly give me enough business on the corporate side."

"Stop rolling your eyes at me. Business is good?" Emmeline asked.

"Very good."

Emmeline felt a burst of pride for her best friend. She had watched Eva scrape, claw, and bully her way through while getting knocked down along the way, only to get back up on her feet and dust herself off.

"I'm so proud of you. Take on as many interns as you can from the tech programs. They need someone awesome to look up to."

"We have and will always do so." Eva shrugged on her backpack. "Go get ready for your date. I'll show myself out. Message me after!"

Emmeline blew Eva a kiss and watched her leave. She tried to steady her nerves as the clock ticked closer to seven.

∼

Mr. Jae threw open the front door as soon as the doorbell chimed. Philip stood on the doorstep, impeccably dressed and holding a colorful bouquet of Gerbera daisies.

"Ah, Mayor Vil. Please come in. Emmeline will be down at any moment," Mr. Jae called out just as she came around the corner.

"Ms. Emia, you look resplendent!" Mr. Jae said.

"Mr. Jae, you're embarrassing me." Emmeline laughed. "Philip, it's nice to see you again." She leaned in so that Philip could kiss her on the cheek.

"You look beautiful. These are for you." Philip handed her the small bouquet.

"You look very handsome as well. Blue suits you."

Emmeline heard Matthew's footsteps coming down the hall before she saw him. Philip stretched out his hand to shake Matthew's, but Matthew kept his hands in his pockets.

"Philip." Matthew nodded his head in acknowledgment. "Emia, I'm heading out now."

Philip retracted his hand. "Where are you off to, Dr. Taylor-Wu?"

"The hospital."

"We're about to head out to Junos Thai Bar."

"I've been there. I thought it was too noisy and had to use my earbuds. I ended up leaving early."

"I've been to the restaurant many times and never had a problem with the noise level," Philip said.

"Most people don't," Matthew replied before turning back to Emmeline. "I'm going to take your SUV to the hospital."

"What's wrong with your car?" Emmeline asked.

"It's raining."

Emmeline rolled her eyes. "Keys are in the box." She paused and smirked. "Don't scratch my car."

Matthew shook his head as she flipped her hair over her shoulder and walked out the door with Philip.

CHAPTER NINETEEN

ALL THAT GLITTERS

Philip held open the door of his luxury sports car for Emmeline as the pitter-patter of rain echoed off the driveway. The air was cool, humid, and lively, reminding Emmeline of her childhood summers at the family cottage. When it was raining, her father would wake her and Matthew up early in the morning, and the whole family would trudge out to the lake to go fly fishing.

Philip slid into the driver's seat and started the car. "What's up with your brother?" he asked, keeping his eyes on the road.

"What do you mean?"

"I don't think he likes me very much, and I barely know him."

"Why do you think he doesn't like you?"

"He didn't shake my hand. It's disrespectful not to shake hands when one's extended to you."

"Mattie wasn't being disrespectful. He probably thinks he doesn't need to do it again since he's already shaken your hand. He prefers not to touch anyone if he doesn't have to."

"It's not because of my policies or political viewpoints?" Philip asked.

"I doubt it. We're both aligned with most of your platform."

Philip raised an eyebrow. "Most?"

Emmeline cleared her throat. "Let's not start the night with politics."

"Good call." He changed the topic. "I heard your brother call you Emia. Is that a nickname you go by? It's nice."

"It's just a silly childhood nickname. Very few people call me that now."

"Can I use it?" The sides of Philip's eyes crinkled.

"You're going to have to earn the right to call me that," Emmeline teased.

"That shouldn't be hard. I'm pretty good at getting what I want." Philip winked at her.

Emmeline blinked and made a mental note to make it as hard as possible. Philip kept the rest of the car ride light with talk about the latest news in the city, touching a little on everything—from social events to traffic initiatives to crime rates.

"We're here." Philip parked at a nearby public lot and took an umbrella out of the trunk. He offered Emmeline his arm again as they walked underneath the umbrella to the restaurant.

He's such a gentleman, and so charming.

Emmeline's heart skipped a beat, and she felt a blush creep up her neck again. As they turned the corner, she heard several voices call out shrilly.

"Look, it's the mayor!"

"Who's he with?"

"Mayor Vil, look over here!"

Emmeline's feet stumbled as the clamor of shoes and boots on the ground rushed toward them. Philip slipped his hand around her waist and steadied her as he waved and smiled for the cameras. Lights flashed in Emmeline's face, and she resisted holding up her hands to block it. She kept her features neutral and gritted her teeth behind a small, tight smile.

"Philip, I'm going to head inside the restaurant first so you can do your press thing," Emmeline murmured.

"Nonsense. It'll make me look bad if you leave now." Philip leaned in close to her ear. "Just hold on to me, smile, and wave."

He kissed her lightly on the cheek, and the cameras flashed as the shouts intensified.

Emmeline faltered and started to pull away from Philip, but he tightened his grip around her waist.

"Emmeline!"

Emmeline turned toward the sound of her name.

Anja!

With a smile plastered across her face, Anja pulled Emmeline from Philip's grasp. She angled her back to the crowd and kissed Emmeline on both cheeks.

"Mr. Mayor, I'm going to steal Emmeline away for a moment. It's raining, so we'll be inside."

Philip narrowed his eyes at Anja, but in a flash, the look was gone. Anja linked her arm with Emmeline's, and they took shelter in the warmly lit foyer of the restaurant.

Emmeline stared at Anja in shock. Her hair was swept up regally, as it had been at the gala, and her makeup was flawless. She looked like a supermodel from the '90s with her motorcycle-style leather jacket and tight black jeans, and her icy eyes were reflective against her pale skin. If Emmeline didn't know to look, she would've missed the outlines of exhaustion beneath Anja's perfect exterior.

"Anja, what are you doing here?"

"Is that how you thank someone who just rescued you?"

"I didn't need rescuing."

Anja raised an eyebrow at her.

"Fine. Maybe a small rescue. Thank you. But still, what are you doing here?" Emmeline asked.

"Matthew told me you were here," Anja replied.

"You spoke to him?"

"Yes, but that's not important right now. I'm here because you're under the protection of the nainthe." Anja looked up and narrowed her eyes as two men walked past them, neither making eye contact with her.

"You know, if you're going for subtle, it's not working."

"Do I look like a subtle person to you? You should know me better than that by now."

"I've known you for about a week," Emmeline pointed out.

Anja watched Philip wave to the crowd and wrinkled her perfect nose. "This is the one you chose? Seems pompous."

"My love life is none of your business."

"He's using you as a prop. Whatever. You can do better." Anja rolled her eyes. "He's returning from his photo shoot and adoring fans. I'll make myself scarce, but I'll be around, so don't worry."

Anja disappeared just as quickly as she'd appeared.

Emmeline looked at the ceiling and sighed.

Someone, save me.

"Apologies, Emmeline. That's life in public office." Philip shrugged, but his smile was wide, and there was an extra pep in his step.

"I understand." Emmeline smiled and tried to push down her annoyance.

"Let's go to our table." Philip put his arm around her waist and signaled to the hostess.

The hostess led them upstairs to a small table by the open balcony. Emmeline looked out onto the bustling street below, and to her relief, the photographers and crowds had dispersed and were nowhere to be found. People milled around beneath the balcony—some out for a short break and chattering with friends while others waited for their table. The rain had stopped, and the city air had turned clean and crisp.

"Would you like a drink, Emmeline?"

She snapped her attention back to Philip and shook herself out of the clouds. "Just sparkling water, thank you."

"I preordered the full-tasting menu so that you could try everything."

"That sounds wonderful."

"The woman who pulled you away, was she a close friend?" Philip asked.

Emmeline racked her brain. "She's an acquaintance I met at a charity gala."

"That must be where I recognize her from. She was at the gala. I remember seeing her with you."

Emmeline started to panic. "You remember her?"

"You don't forget a woman like that."

Did he compliment another woman while on a date with me? Emmeline blinked, but she kept her features blank.

Philip continued, "I don't know who she is, and I take great pride in knowing everyone important to know. She also doesn't look very approachable."

Emmeline picked up her sparkling water to give her hands something to do. "She doesn't need to be approachable. Do you find her intimidating?"

Because you should. She could tear you apart with her bare hands.

"I don't find anyone intimidating." Philip's eyes glinted under the dim lights of the restaurant.

Careful, Philip. She might be listening. I wouldn't put it past her to toy with you for her own amusement.

A playful gleam came back into Philip's eyes. "Enough about her. Tell me what's been happening in the world of philanthropy."

Emmeline welcomed the change of topic and gave him a quick overview of upcoming events and essential programs across the city.

"Will you be attending all those events?" Philip asked.

"I only attend the ones where the foundation is a platinum or title donor. If I attended every event we sponsored, it'd be a full-time job. And honestly, these events aren't all that interesting. Necessary and important, but not interesting."

"Would you like me to attend the ones you're going to?"

Emmeline couldn't stop the look of surprise that crossed her face. "I usually go alone or sometimes with Mattie if he's available. I think it's a little early for us to be attending public events together."

Philip looked disappointed, but he was quickly all smiles again. "You're right; I'm getting ahead of myself. Maybe it's because you're so beautiful and I'm already smitten."

Emmeline blushed again and looked away.

Philip glanced around the loft. "The music isn't too loud here. Isn't it odd your brother needed earplugs? That's overkill, isn't it?"

"Many people probably find it odd, but most don't understand what it's like to be autistic."

"But he's a doctor."

"Yes, he is, and he's a very good and successful one."

"Why does he need earplugs?"

"Mattie has a hearing sensitivity, and loud noises irritate him. He told me that, sometimes, it can feel like a physical assault on his senses."

"Don't his patients mind that their doctor is autistic?"

"Would you mind?" Emmeline asked.

Philip faltered at her direct question. "I don't know."

"Why would they mind? I think being autistic makes him a better doctor," Emmeline said. "He's hyperaware of his challenges, and he works twice as hard to care for his patients, sometimes at the expense of his own health."

He has absolutely no knowledge of this topic.

"Philip, do you understand what it's like to be autistic? I assumed you did since you were at the Royal Children's Rehabilitation Hospital gala, but maybe that was presumptuous of me."

"Of course I know what autism is," Philip scoffed. "I just didn't know that Dr. Taylor-Wu was autistic."

"Why does it matter what the label is?"

Philip paused and stared at her. "You're right; it doesn't."

Emmeline folded her napkin and set it down in front of her. "Philip, thank you for inviting me to dinner, but I think we should end the date now." She pushed back her chair and stood up.

Philip grabbed her arm. "I'm sorry if what I said was offensive. Why don't you stay and help me understand then? Please?"

Emmeline was about to open her mouth when the waiter came by with their first course. She sighed and sat back down. The waiter gave a rundown of the item and explained the ingredients, highlighting which flavors to pay attention to.

Philip lifted his glass to Emmeline and smiled. "To new friends and new relationships."

The rest of the night was filled with light chatter on the food, city gossip, and entertainment happenings.

"Philip, this restaurant was a wonderful choice." It took all Emmeline's self-control not to settle back in her chair and pat her stomach.

"Glad you enjoyed it. This is one of my go-to restaurants."

"Mayor Vil! It's so nice to see you here again," a sweet voice rang out.

Emmeline looked up to see a beautiful ebony-skinned woman strut over. Philip stood and kissed her on both cheeks.

"Nellie, meet Emmeline Taylor-Wu. Emmeline, this is Nellie Vaye. She's co-owner of this restaurant," Philip introduced the two women.

Emmeline stood to shake Nellie's hand. "Pleasure to meet you."

Nellie clasped her hands and looked at Philip. "She's adorable!"

Emmeline stood there awkwardly as Philip and Nellie chatted in low voices.

Finally, Nellie took Philip's arm. "Emmeline, I'm going to steal the mayor away for a moment, but I promise to return him promptly." She looked at Philip. "There are a few people you absolutely must meet!"

Philip looked at Emmeline apologetically and left with Nellie. Emmeline sighed and pulled out her phone to keep herself busy.

Emia: Where are you hiding?

Anja: On the roof.

Emia: I didn't get the chance to ask you earlier—How's Lesedi doing?

Anja: The antibiotics are working, and the fever is completely gone. I don't know what would have happened if Matthew hadn't been there. How's your date with Mr. Popular going?

Emia: I'm glad Lesedi is doing better. I hope her recovery is quick.

Anja: Ignoring my question on the date?

Emia: Love life is not up for discussion.

Anja: Fine, be boring.

Emia: How's everyone else doing?

Anja: Business as usual. We cremated Quinn and Mihal tonight.

Emmeline mentally slapped herself.
Here I am, on a date, and Anja's coming from a funeral for her friends.

Emia: I'm sorry. I've been very insensitive. How are you holding up?

Anja: I'm fine.

Emia: Come back to my house after this. I'll make you a coffee.

Anja: That would be nice.

I should tell Mattie that I invited Anja over.
She looked around for Philip and saw him in the bar area. He was surrounded by people, all hanging off his every word.
He's Mr. Popular, and those women are drop-dead gorgeous. Even the men are drop-dead gorgeous.

Emia: Mattie, Anja's coming over tonight for coffee.

Mattie: I'll be home soon. Still at the hospital.

Emia: You're going to join us?

Mattie: Yes.

Emmeline raised an eyebrow at her brother's last message and put her phone back in her clutch. She looked up just as Philip came strolling back to their table.
"Sorry, Emmeline. Duty calls sometimes." Philip sat back down with a big smile. "Would you like to go for a drink somewhere else?"
Emmeline looked at her watch. "It's late, and I should get home. I have a long day tomorrow that starts early."
Philip nodded and signaled for the check. "Will you be attending the Inspire Gala? I was reminded that it's coming up in a couple of weeks and that I'll be in attendance."

"I wasn't planning on going. Our foundation makes an annual donation, but I usually decline to attend in person."

"Would you like to come as my guest?" Philip held up his hands in defense. "Not as a date—unless, of course, you want to—but as my special guest."

Emmeline hesitated.

What's the harm? Maybe I should get out of my comfort zone.

"I'd be happy to be your guest."

"Great." Philip's teeth gleamed. "Let's get you home."

⁓

Philip parked his car on Emmeline's driveway and walked around to open her door. As they made their way to the front door, she could hear the faint rumble of an idle motorcycle in the background.

Of course Anja rides a motorcycle.

"Thank you for a nice evening, Philip."

"You're welcome. I hope we can do this again soon." Philip leaned in and kissed her cheek. "I'll call you later, beautiful."

Emmeline reddened as she walked into her home and closed the door behind her.

CHAPTER TWENTY

EXECUTIONERS

Emmeline heard Anja's motorcycle pull up to the front of the house. She threw on a T-shirt and leggings, then grabbed one of her favorite wraps before hurrying to the kitchen to make two cups of coffee and a decaf for Matthew. Balancing all three on a tray, she pushed open the sliding doors and stepped out onto the patio. Anja was standing at the edge, looking out over the garden.

Anja glanced over her shoulder at Emmeline. "I never noticed what a beautiful garden you have."

Emmeline set the tray on the table. "You're welcome to use the garden when you need a place to escape. The only people who use it are me, Ms. Rose, and sometimes, Mr. Jae. Mattie doesn't usually live here anymore, so he barely uses it."

Anja walked over and sat down. "How come he doesn't live here?"

"He wanted to be closer to the hospital, and I think he wanted a break from this place. It's our family home, and there are a lot of memories here."

"Happy or sad?"

"Happy. At least, I believe the memories are happy. Hard to tell with Mattie sometimes."

Anja looked around. "Is that why you stay?"

"I love this house. It's my childhood home, and I can't bear to let it go. I know it's too big for me, and more than half the house isn't in use, but I feel the closest to my parents here." Emmeline shrugged. "Plus, where else would I go? Anywhere I go, I'd take Ms. Rose and Mr. Jae with me, so we might as well all stay put."

Emmeline handed Anja her coffee and saw her glance at the third cup.

"That's for Mattie. Decaf," Emmeline said.

"He's joining us?"

"I think so."

On cue, the patio doors slid open, and Matthew stepped through, still dressed in his office clothes. He had discarded his blazer and rolled up the sleeves of his white dress shirt.

"Emia, Anja," Matthew greeted and pushed up his glasses.

"Dr. Matthew." Anja's icy eyes brightened at his presence.

A smile fleeted across Matthew's mouth at the incorrect use of his name.

"Come sit with us, Mattie." Emmeline handed him his cup. "Decaf."

Matthew thanked Emmeline and sat down beside her. "Anja, how is Lesedi doing?"

"She's doing better, thanks to you."

"Did the nainthe cremate Quinn and Mihal yet?"

Anja nodded. "It happened earlier tonight."

"How are you doing?"

"I'll be fine." Anja looked away.

"If you don't mind, could I ask you some questions?" Matthew asked.

Anja dipped her head but stayed silent.

"What exactly do the nainthe do? You said before that you guard the gateway between the worlds."

"The gateway isn't like a door. Think of it like a giant piece of fabric, held together by magic, but the magic is fragile and can tear, creating holes between our world and the raizour's. The raizour come through these holes."

Emmeline perked up. "Magic? Can you show us?"

Anja looked at them skeptically. "I could show you magic, except you wouldn't be able to see it. Emmeline should be able to feel it, just like I can."

Anja held up her hand, and the air hummed and crackled. Emmeline watched in awe as tiny tendrils of light radiated from Anja's hand.

"I can see it. It's very faint, but I can see it." Emmeline looked at Anja with wide eyes.

"Really?"

Emmeline nodded.

"Interesting." Anja wrinkled her nose and looked curiously at Emmeline. "What does it look like to you?"

"Sort of like a faint electric current with a heartbeat."

"You really can see it?"

Emmeline nodded again.

"Is the gateway everywhere?" Matthew asked. "Are there nainthe all around the world?"

Anja shook her head. "The gateway shifts, on average, every fifty years or so, but no one knows when a move is coming and where it'll be next. The current gateway hasn't moved for the past eighty years. There are nainthe all around the world, but most of us are here. We situate nainthe where we believe the gateway might shift to, and we also have nainthe that travel around the world."

"Why?" Emmeline asked.

Anja's eyes glittered. "To look for you and your other half. We've been looking for over twenty years, and so far, we've only found you. And you were right under our noses this whole time." She shook her head in disbelief. "We don't know when or if we'll find the other elystier."

Suddenly, Emmeline smacked her hands onto the patio table. Matthew winced, and Anja jumped, almost spilling her coffee.

Anja narrowed her eyes. "Listen, only I'm allowed to do that to you. You're not allowed to do it to me." She turned to Matthew. "Why did that do nothing to you?"

Emmeline waved her hand. "Loud noises don't scare him. Nothing scares him. It just hurts. Believe me, I've been trying my whole life."

"Why did you hit the table? Are you mad that we haven't found the other elystier? It's not for lack of trying."

"No, I just remembered something from the previous night." Emmeline searched her brain for the details. "When the raizour was talking to me, it knew I was a seeker, but it also called me the last one."

Anja's eyes hardened, and she pulled her phone out of her jacket and tapped furiously. "I think you might be right about traitors within the nainthe. I just messaged Erik, but he's out on a hunt. I asked him to come here if he can."

"What do you mean, the last one?" Matthew's midnight eyes flickered with concern.

"And, um, if in fact I'm actually a seeker, I certainly don't want to be the last one," Emmeline added.

"I have no idea what the raizour meant by that, and I don't know who to ask because I don't know who I can trust. I'll have to do some investigating when I get back home," Anja replied.

"Erik's on a hunt?" Emmeline shivered as she remembered the cold indifference in the way he dispatched the three raizour.

"The magic that holds together the fabric between the worlds constantly needs to be strengthened. When weak spots come up, the raizour get through. We're always reinforcing the fabric and patrolling for raizour that escape." Anja stood up and walked to the edge of the patio. "We all take turns doing patrols, and we do it in teams. As you've seen, the raizour are strong, and if they get out into the human population, they will wreak havoc."

"I believe that," Emmeline said.

"My brother's the strongest and most skilled of all the nainthe, and he does all his patrols on his own, and he goes almost every night. That's why we've given him the nickname 'Executioner.' In our history, there hasn't been another nainthe with the same abilities as my brother, so he's definitely an anomaly, and nobody knows why. Just try not to call him Executioner to his face. He hates that name, and it usually puts him in a bad mood."

Anja looked over her shoulder, and her icy eyes darkened.

"But truthfully, we're all executioners. My brother's just better at it than the rest of us."

"Was Erik able to capture any raizour alive?" Emmeline asked.

"No, every time we get close to capturing one, they do something that makes us kill them."

"Then, the three that night must have allowed themselves to get captured." Emmeline looked at Anja in horror. "They knew exactly what they were doing."

"That's what we think too."

"But why do they want to come to our world? What do they need or want on Earth?" Matthew asked.

"As far as we know, raizour get energy from our atmosphere. No nainthe has entered the raizour world in over a millennium, so we're not sure what's there. We don't know if we could survive in their world."

Matthew walked to the edge of the garden and stood beside Anja. "Have you checked how the raizour are built? I mean, if they get energy from our atmosphere, it must mean whatever they get here is missing or in scarce supply in their world. It would be important to know what that is."

"We've never cared."

"Why not?"

"Because it's never mattered."

"Why doesn't it matter? If you understood what they needed, maybe you could help them solve their problem."

"It doesn't matter because we aren't interested in solving their problem. Our job is to make sure they stay in their world." Anja's eyes flashed.

Emmeline's senses shifted to high alert, but Matthew only furrowed his brow as he tried to make sense of the information.

"That's dangerous reasoning. I can name many examples in our world where that belief has led to tragedy," Matthew said.

"Maybe it's dangerous, and maybe we don't care," Anja replied. Her irises expanded until they resembled shards of glass.

"But you should care."

"You know nothing of our life," Anja retorted.

Emmeline stood up and slipped in between Anja and Matthew. "We're just trying to understand your world. You're right; there's a lot we don't know, and yes, that means we'll ask lots of questions and have opinions that don't always match yours. We have every right to."

Anja's eyes returned to normal, and she stared into the dark garden. "If you only knew how many nainthe had sacrificed their lives and souls to keep you safe." She strode over to the patio table and grabbed her helmet. "I've overstayed my welcome." She put her helmet under her arm and walked out of the garden without looking back.

Matthew took off his glasses and rubbed his eyes. "I think I made her upset."

"You did," Emmeline murmured.

"I didn't mean to."

"I know you didn't."

"Should I apologize?"

"Give her some time to cool off. I think she owes you an apology too."

Matthew nodded and put his glasses back on. He looked in the direction where Anja had left. "How was your date with Philip?"

"It was fine. He asked me to be his guest at the Inspire Gala in a couple of weeks."

"Do you like him?"

"I don't know yet. He's charming, but maybe a little too charming sometimes. He's always surrounded by beautiful people. How do I compete with that?"

"It's not a competition."

"Thanks, Dr. Matthew," Emmeline mimicked Anja and rolled her eyes.

"I'm going to bed." Matthew turned on his heel and stalked back into the house.

Seems like I got under someone's skin.

CHAPTER TWENTY-ONE

A SHADOW IN THE DARK

Emmeline felt a weighted presence and looked up at her bedroom ceiling. She took off her headphones and strained her ears to listen for the slightest dips in sound.

Am I imagining things?

Emmeline glanced at her balcony door, though it remained silent and unmoving. She picked up her phone and tapped through her home security, checking several security cameras and motion detectors, but there wasn't a log of movement anywhere. She did a double-check to make sure all the systems were armed.

I'm being paranoid. It's late, and I should go to bed. It's been a long week. Maybe I'm just tired.

She hadn't heard from Anja since the night on her patio and thought it would be best to give her some space. She also hadn't heard from Philip, except for periodic messages, inquiring how she was doing.

The house creaked, and Emmeline jumped.

It's just the house settling.
Emmeline pressed her lips together.
Maybe I should message Anja. Just in case.

Emia: Hey, Anja. You wouldn't happen to be around the area? It's probably nothing, but I thought I could feel something around the house, and maybe it was you or another nainthe. Anyway, I'm just being paranoid. I hope you're okay and Lesedi's doing better.

She waited a few minutes to see if Anja would respond, but all she got back was silence.
I'm going to take a quick look around. Should I wake up Mr. Jae?
Emmeline bit her lip before deciding not to.
I wish Mattie were home. Of all nights, he had to go back to his condo to sleep.
Emmeline climbed out of bed and grabbed her cashmere wrap. She tapped into the panic application on her phone.
At least no one's awake to witness my paranoia.
She opened the door to her bedroom and looked down the dark hallway before stepping out and padding to the staircase. Moonlight filtered through the skylight spanned over the majestic split-level staircase, coaxing out large shadows across the upper foyer. Emmeline tucked her hair behind her ear and walked down the stairs to the central landing. She stopped to listen, but there was only stillness in the air. She let out a breath.
I'm clearly out of my mind.
She walked down the central staircase and went to the kitchen for a glass of water. As she moved through the darkened hallway,

silvery light streamed in each arched window, reminding her of old ghost stories. The moonlight bathed her face and bare legs in eerie incandescent light, making her skin seem luminescent. She walked up to one of the windows and touched the cool glass that overlooked the west side of the garden. All was still outside, as if frozen in time.

Such forgiving light.

Emmeline's phone vibrated in her hand, and she jumped, letting out a small yelp. She swore under her breath.

Anja: Where are you in the house?

Emia: On my way to the kitchen.

A shadow flickered across the window, and Emmeline almost dropped her phone. She whipped her head around and scanned outside, but everything was as still as it had been seconds ago. She could still feel a presence around her and pulled her wrap closer.

Anja: We're on our way. Erik will get there before I do. Stay away from the windows and keep the lights off.

Backing away from the window, Emmeline hurried to the kitchen and stood with her back against the corner, her eyes darting around, looking for the slightest movement.

If I wasn't paranoid enough before, Anja certainly kicked it into high gear. Should I message Mattie? I don't want to worry him. It's probably nothing.

Emmeline took a mug from the cupboard and clutched it to her chest. She looked out the window above the sink, and the shadows in the garden remained still. Remembering Anja's warning, she shifted a few steps over to the hot water dispenser, her eyes never leaving the window. After filling her mug with warm water, she took a shaky gulp.

I swear there's something out there. I can feel it.

Something flew by the corner of her eye, and she jumped back from the window. Her back slammed into something hard, and she screamed just as a large hand clamped down over her mouth and another over her arms and waist.

Help!

Her mug fell from her hands and crashed onto the stone floor, shattering into pieces and flinging water across the kitchen. She kicked and screamed against her captor until she felt herself being lifted off the floor.

"Be quiet!" a melodic voice hissed. "It's me, Erik."

She nodded into Erik's hand, and he removed his hand from her mouth while stepping over the broken glass and puddle spreading across the floor. After setting her down, he turned and looked out the window and then at the ceiling before settling on the patio doors.

Erik was in full protective armor with two blades strapped to his back. He turned his chilly gaze to Emmeline and placed his finger against his lips. His irises expanded, and he pulled one blade from his harness. Soundlessly, he walked to the patio doors before his eyes snapped back to the hallway, his body stilling as he listened. Suddenly, he relaxed and sheathed his blade back into its place.

Erik removed his mask and helmet. "A raizour was here, but it's gone now. It might come back though."

Emmeline nodded and wiped the tear tracks from her face.

"Are you okay?" Erik asked, his icy eyes drifting over her reddened cheeks.

Even in the dark, Emmeline could see the cool glint in his eyes. She pulled her wrap tighter over her tank top and shorts.

"I'm good. What happens if it comes back?"

"I'll kill it." Erik looked at his watch and walked over to the patio doors. "Anja's outside."

"Wait." Emmeline went to the tablet mounted on the wall and turned off the security in the kitchen zone. She furrowed her brow and looked at Erik. "How did you get in my house?"

"Skylight."

Emmeline balked at him. "There are cameras and sensors everywhere."

"Not on the roof."

"You could've just called me, and I would've opened the front door."

Emmeline was about to ask him more questions, but she saw a light flicker on and heard sleepy footsteps coming down the hallway. She covered her eyes and groaned.

"I think we woke up Ms. Rose."

Erik looked around for a place to hide before sliding open the patio doors. "I'll be outside."

"Don't bother. Ms. Rose will know something's up, and if she checks the cameras, she'll know you were in the house. Just stay, and I'll figure out an explanation. Can you hide your weapons?"

Erik unhooked his blades and tucked them behind the kitchen island. He pulled out his phone and tapped a message to Anja. Emmeline shook her hair loose to help cover the fading bruises on her neck just as Ms. Rose entered the kitchen, yawning. She flicked on the kitchen light and let out a short gasp of surprise as she saw Emmeline in the kitchen.

"Emia, darling, what are you doing up? And why are you here in the dark? I heard a crash and thought maybe I hadn't put something away properly."

"Oh, I just came downstairs for a glass of water, and it slipped out of my hand." Emmeline hesitated and gestured to Erik. "My friend decided to visit, so we were just chatting."

Ms. Rose turned and jumped out of her skin. She clutched her chest and looked at Emmeline and then at Erik and back and forth several times before remembering her manners.

Erik cleared his throat and extended his hand, which Ms. Rose shook daintily.

"A pleasure to meet you, Ms. Rose. My name is Erik. Emmeline has spoken warmly of you."

"It's nice to meet you, Erik." Ms. Rose brushed back her hair and looked over Erik and his attire, taking in the matte-black body armor.

"Why are you two talking in the dark?" Ms. Rose asked with confusion. Realization dawned on her face just as the words left her mouth. "Please, no details. I don't want to know."

"It's not that! We were only talking. Erik's eyes are sensitive to light, so he prefers the dark," Emmeline stammered through her lie and sneaked a peek at the amusement on Erik's face.

Ms. Rose raised her eyebrows and looked at Emmeline and her outfit pointedly. Emmeline adjusted her wrap, which suddenly felt extremely thin and short.

"I'm going back to bed," Ms. Rose announced. "Erik, I trust you'll assist Emia with cleaning up the glass on the floor?"

"No need. I can take care of it." Emmeline reddened until she resembled an overripe tomato.

"I will help clean up the glass." Erik dipped his head.

Ms. Rose left the kitchen, and Emmeline went to dim the lights.

"I don't have a light sensitivity," Erik said dryly.

"Now that I've told the little white lie, I need to act the part. Ms. Rose already thinks we're doing unmentionable things in the kitchen in the middle of the night, and now, I'm going to have to answer many questions in the morning. What a mess this is. I won't be able to keep up with all the little lies I've been telling," Emmeline muttered.

Erik went to the patio doors and opened them for Anja. She stepped through the doorway, dressed in her full-body armor, and her helmet under her arm.

"What did I miss? Were there raizour here?" She asked.

"It left. It must've known I was here," Erik replied.

"What did you detect?"

"One. Fury, hatred, bloodthirst."

After securing his helmet over his head, Erik picked up his blades and strapped them back into his harness.

"Anja, I'm going to try to hunt down the raizour. I don't want to lose its trail. Will you stay?"

"Yes. Be careful."

"Emmeline, Anja will give you my contact for emergencies." Erik looked at the broken glass on the floor.

"Don't worry about the glass. I'm not completely useless." Emmeline gave Erik a rueful smile. "Thank you again. I hope this whole *saving my life* thing isn't an emerging pattern."

"Same."

Erik stepped onto the patio and pulled his face mask over the front of his helmet. He crouched down, and his sharp wings unfolded high behind him. He leaped up, and like a gust of wind passing through, he was gone without a trace.

Emmeline locked the patio doors. "Um, I have cameras in the garden. Should I erase the footage?"

"Yes, to be on the safe side."

Emmeline unhooked the tablet and tapped into the security application. She backtracked the footage to where Anja had landed on her garden.

"How come I can barely see your wings? I wouldn't have noticed them if I hadn't known where to look."

Emmeline fast-forwarded to Erik leaving. His tall, intimidating presence was as clear as the midnight sky, but his transformation was like Anja's and barely noticeable in the recording.

It's like he jumped and disappeared.

"When we're in the moonlight, our nainthe form takes on a camouflage cover. We don't know why, but we think it protects us from being seen by humans. Unless you know to look for it, you won't see it."

"Are you … invisible?"

"No, not invisible. Just unnoticeable. But if you know about us, you'd be able to see us. It's kind of like how a soldier wears camouflage when in battle. Those who are unaware won't notice the soldier, but someone with experience would be able to spot them."

"What happens when it's cloudy?"

Anja's mouth twitched. "Still camouflaged."

"What happens if you're indoors, but it's nighttime?"

"No camouflage." Anja held her hand up. "And before you ask, if we're indoors at night but standing beside a window that's not covered, we're partially camouflaged and partially not."

Emmeline got a broom and a dust pan from a cupboard and began clearing up the broken glass on the floor. Anja bent down to help dry the floor with a towel.

"What happens in the sunlight?" Emmeline asked.

"In the sunlight, we don't have any protection. Anyone and everyone can see us in our nainthe form if we use it. We don't usually go out too much during the day unless there's a threat that we're aware of. Accidents happen, and it's too risky. There's also the risk of encountering someone who might recognize us."

"Do the raizour have the same benefit?"

"Nope."

"Is that why they only come out at night?"

Anja shook her head. "Humans are inconsequential to them, and they're not afraid of them. Raizour are very sensitive to sunlight. Their eyesight diminishes, and because of the translucency of their skin, they heat up much faster than humans. Sunlight won't kill them unless they overheat, but it puts them at a significant disadvantage."

"Are you still mad at Mattie?" Emmeline switched topics.

"No, I'm not mad at him anymore. I think I overreacted."

Emmeline stayed silent to see if Anja wanted to say anything more.

"Erik puts his life on the line almost every single night, and each time he leaves on a hunt, I never know if he's going to make it back. I dread the day I must go out to look for him and retrieve his body or the day he needs to find mine. Some of the nainthe think we're lucky to have each other, but I wouldn't wish this on anyone. I wish I had been called into this life and that he had been spared, though I know he also wishes I had never been called. Lessie told me that he was inconsolable when the seekers found me."

"I can understand why you feel that way," Emmeline said. "Mattie was only trying to understand the situation, and he needs to understand motivation and logic for things to make sense to him. He doesn't have a single mean bone in his body, and he doesn't say anything with the intent to hurt. He's genuinely kind, selfless, and brave."

"Not being able to be scared doesn't count as being brave," Anja pointed out.

"He doesn't fear for himself, but for the people he cares about—me, Ms. Rose, Mr. Jae, a handful of friends, and his patients. Mattie doesn't need to work, and probably three future generations of Taylor-Wus wouldn't have to if we manage our investments properly. He chooses to put himself at the mercy of other people's scrutiny and judgment to provide care for others."

"I know he's kind and selfless."

"He might have upset you, but you also hurt him."

"I know," Anja murmured.

Emmeline looked around. "What do I do now? I sure as hell will not be able to sleep after what just happened."

"You should try to rest. I'll stay for the remainder of the night."

"I have a lot of guest rooms, and you can take your pick. Though I prefer you pick the one closest to my room," Emmeline said.

"I was going to camp out on the roof."

"What kind of host would I be if I made the person trying to keep me alive sleep on the roof? And what if a neighbor saw you? It'd be a circus."

"Emmeline, your neighbors, as you so generously call them, are so far away that it would be almost impossible for them to see me with the naked eye."

"You can take the guest room next to mine. There's a balcony in that room, so you can come and go as you please without having to go through the house. There's a large en suite, and if you'd like, I'll ask Mr. Jae to put in a minibar. Think of it like a hotel room."

Anja looked at Emmeline as if she had sprouted a set of wings. "I'm not moving in."

"I never said you were, but you'll be here more often. What if the raizour come back? I'm giving you your own space, so you don't have to worry about Ms. Rose and Mr. Jae."

"A bed does sound more comfortable than the roof," Anja admitted.

"What did you used to do with the other elystiers? How did you keep them safe?"

"They moved in with the nainthe and learned all about us. Once they were confident in their abilities, they were free to move on with their lives, though they could stay with us if they wanted to."

"Oh, that's nice, but that's not going to happen with me. I'm staying in my own home."

Anja sighed. "Show me to the guest room."

CHAPTER TWENTY-TWO

SANCTUARIES

Emmeline threw her forearm over her eyes. Her room was still dark from the blackout drapes that covered her windows and balcony doors, but she knew that it was probably late morning.

I should get up.

She rubbed her bleary eyes and massaged her cheeks with her fingertips to wake herself up. After she was partially awake, she checked her messages.

Philip: Hi, Emmeline. How's my favorite philanthropist doing? I know it's late notice, but would you like to have lunch today? I have a reservation on the patio at La Patron at one o'clock.

Emmeline bit her lip and checked her calendar.
I don't want to end up in the pages of society news again.
She narrowed her eyes at herself.
Get a grip. If you date someone like the mayor, you need to be able to handle these minor inconveniences.

Emia:	I'd love to. I have some errands to run beforehand, but I'll meet you there.
Philip:	Great, and before I forget, the Inspire Gala is next Saturday. I hope you'll still accompany me as my guest. We can talk about it at lunch. See you soon.

Emmeline scrolled through some of her other messages.

Anja:	I left this morning at sunrise and went back home. I didn't have a way to lock the balcony door from the outside, so you'll have to remember to lock it from the inside. I sent you Erik's contact and gave him yours. Also, Javier's eager for you to return to the Sanctuary to start some of your training. Can you come tonight after dinner?

So, that's what they call that entire block.

Emia:	Thanks for staying last night. If you hadn't been here, I probably wouldn't have slept a wink. I'm having dinner with Ms. Rose and Mattie, and I will come by afterward.
Anja:	On the north side of the block, there's underground public parking. Go to the second level, and there's a set of garage doors, marked Out of Service. Use code 0820, and it'll let you into our private garage.

Emmeline clicked off her phone screen and stared at the ceiling.

Let's go face Ms. Rose.

Emmeline walked into the kitchen, dressed for her lunch date with Philip. She had chosen a high-necked black top, tucked into a pair of distressed jeans that fit her like a second skin. She'd piled her hair into a clean, elegant bun on top of her head and finished off her face with concealer and blush to hide her sleepiness.

Ms. Rose and Mr. Jae were out on the patio, enjoying the last sunny days of late summer. After downing a tall glass of warm water, Emmeline made herself a coffee and joined them outside.

Mr. Jae turned around as Emmeline walked through the patio doors. "Ah, Ms. Emia awakes! Did you have a late night?"

Ms. Rose snorted into her cup of tea, and Emmeline blushed.

"I had a friend visit last night," Emmeline replied.

"Mayor Vil? I sense something promising there." Mr. Jae's eyes twinkled.

Ms. Rose snorted again, and Emmeline glared at her petulantly.

"No, a different friend. We just spent some time talking—that's it." Emmeline tried to emphasize the last part.

"I've never seen this friend of yours before, nor have I ever heard you mention him. He certainly had an interesting choice of clothing," Ms. Rose commented.

"I just met him recently, and he was dressed like that because he rides a motorcycle," Emmeline said.

"Hmm, he's quite handsome, if I may say so. Those eyes of his, it's like looking into a thunderstorm."

"He's just a friend, and even that might be generous. I'd call him more of an acquaintance."

"Acquaintances don't have midnight conversations in a kitchen, half-naked," Ms. Rose said, and Emmeline almost spat out her coffee.

"I wasn't half-naked!"

"Emia, whatever you choose to do is your choice. I've always maintained you should get out more and that it's not good for you to be holed up in this giant house with just me and Mr. Jae for company. As long as you're being safe, of course."

Emmeline covered her eyes and groaned. "Nothing happened, and nothing is happening. As far as I know, you both will be stuck with me for the rest of your lives. I'd really prefer not to talk about my nonexistent love life."

Mr. Jae laughed and slapped his leg. "Trust me, we don't want the details either, but we do want what's best for you. If anyone treats you poorly, let me know, and I'll find a nice spot in the garden for them."

"Oh, Mr. Jae, you always spoil me." Emmeline smiled sweetly, and he patted her hand before turning back to his newspaper.

"Why ruin a beautifully landscaped garden when there's a perfectly good ravine right behind it?" Ms. Rose sniffed.

Ms. Rose and Mr. Jae looked at each other and proceeded to cackle.

"You two are hilarious," Emmeline giggled. "Ms. Rose, I have a lunch date with Philip, but Mattie and I'll be home for dinner. Afterward, I'm going out with some friends."

"No wonder you're all dressed up. I'll order sushi for tonight."

"I'm heading out now." Emmeline got up and gave Ms. Rose and Mr. Jae a kiss on the cheek.

She stopped at the patio doors and turned around. "Um, Mr. Jae, I need a few favors. Can you check out the skylights? I thought I felt a draft coming from one. Also, in the guest room beside mine, can you install a lock on the balcony that locks from inside and outside? Oh, and add a minibar if possible. I might have a friend coming to stay for a bit."

"Of course, Ms. Emia. Consider it done."

Emmeline grabbed her purse and sunglasses and headed to the underground garage.

Too bad Mattie's new toy isn't here.

CHAPTER TWENTY-THREE

OF DREAMS AND MORE

Matthew stacked all the dishes and chopsticks into a neat pile on the dining table while the little soy sauce dishes teetered on top.

"Mattie, bring over the dishes, and I'll load the dishwasher," Emmeline called over her shoulder.

Emmeline handed a towel and her favorite citrus cleaner to Mr. Jae, who wiped down the dinner table while whistling his favorite Korean soap opera tune.

Matthew pushed up his glasses and carried the stack of dishes to Emmeline. "You said your lunch date with Philip went well?"

"It was nice."

"But?"

Emmeline shrugged as she eyed the dishwasher. "I don't know if I can get used to seeing someone who's so public." She slotted several plates into their rightful spots. "It feels like he's never quite there with me, like every outing has a purpose. And there are always other people demanding his attention, and I have to pretend

I'm fine with it even though I'm not. I'd much rather spend a quiet meal together without thinking about the press or others."

"You shouldn't have to pretend."

"I know. And if it's like this now, what's it going to be like if we end up getting more serious?"

"Do you like him enough that you see it getting more serious?"

Emmeline closed the dishwasher and started it. "I'm not sure he's the one for me. Anyway, we're going to go to the Inspire Gala together. I'm going as his guest and not as an official date."

"Does it matter what you call it? The entire city—well, the portion that cares about these matters—already knows you two are seeing each other."

"I just don't like being in the spotlight." Emmeline found a travel tumbler and prepped the coffee machine.

"Are you going out?" Matthew asked.

"The nainthe want me to start some training tonight, so I'm going to the Sanctuary—that's what they call their home."

"Did you talk to Anja?"

"Oh, I didn't get a chance to tell you what happened last night." Emmeline did a recap of the previous evening and how Erik had felt the presence of a raizour close to their home.

Matthew listened intently. "Normally, I'd say we should hire security, but I don't think it would help in this situation. I'm going to move back home until we can find a better way to keep you safe."

"You being home doesn't keep me any safer than you being at the condo. Not that I don't love having you home," Emmeline said. "Anja said I'm under the protection of the nainthe and they'll be watching over me. I've given her the guest room close to mine."

"Is she still upset with me?"

Emmeline shook her head. "She told me she feels bad about our last meeting."

"I should come with you tonight. I want to apologize to her." Matthew put his hands in his pockets.

"I didn't ask you to come because I don't want you mixed up in this anymore. At first, we were both skeptical of this whole thing, but this has turned into something much more serious, and I don't want to put you in danger."

"That's not for you to decide."

"Isn't it? I'm the one they're after."

Matthew just stared at her and didn't budge.

"You're seriously the most stubborn person I've ever met," Emmeline muttered.

"I'm not stubborn."

"I guess we'd better get going. I'd ask who's driving, but I already know." Emmeline held out her hand.

"Buy your own. I'm driving."

Emmeline leaned back into the luxury seat as the exotic car growled through the historic tree-lined hills, the streetlights blurring through the thick, tinted windows.

She looked at her brother and admired his stoic profile. His golden-brown hair was short and messy, and the city lights reflected off his glasses. His elbow rested on the edge of the driver's door, and his knuckles hovered above his mouth while his other hand steered.

He even drives like Dad.

Emmeline turned to look out the window.

"We're close to the Sanctuary. Where should I park?" Matthew asked.

Emmeline pulled out her phone and repeated Anja's instructions. Matthew turned into the public parking garage, stopped at the Out of Service door, and punched in the code Anja had provided. The garage door rolled up, revealing a dark tunnel.

"Would it kill them to put in some lights?" Matthew muttered as he flashed on his high beams.

After their car passed the entrance, the garage door rolled down behind them. As they descended through the curved tunnel, dim lights appeared in the distance, and finally, they entered a mostly empty parking lot. There were several black motorcycles parked in a row and multiple variations of black SUVs. Matthew backed his car into a spot close to the entrance of the building and killed the engine.

Two flares of bright white flashed and subsided to a sheer aura, revealing two nainthe waiting for them. They were both tall and muscular, seemingly mirror images of each other. Dressed in fitted black, they each had a single long blade strapped to their back. One had a tanned complexion; short, dark hair; and equally dark, deeply set eyes. The other had sideswept black hair, tucked behind his ears, and a light-golden complexion. His sharp almond-shaped eyes widened at the sight of Matthew's car.

Emmeline stepped out of the car while Matthew went to the trunk and pulled out a backpack and a slim crewneck sweatshirt. They walked in lockstep over to the two waiting nainthe.

"Hello. I'm Emmeline, and this is my brother, Dr. Matthew Taylor-Wu. We're here to see Anja."

The nainthe with the tanned skin spoke first. "My name is Saadah, and this is Ellis. Anja sent us to escort you to the meditation building. We've been waiting for you for a long time." Saadah's voice fumbled as the words left his mouth. "What I meant was that we've been waiting to find you for a long time, not that we've been waiting here, at this moment, for a very long time."

Ellis covered his eyes with his hand and groaned.

"So I've been told," Emmeline murmured. "Saadah's a beautiful name. What's your background?"

Saadah dipped his head. "I was born and raised in Egypt. Our family's tradition is for each firstborn to be named Saadah, regardless of gender. I come from an extensive family, and there are many Saadahs."

"That's a wonderful family tradition." Emmeline turned to Ellis. "Ellis is English, isn't it?"

"It is." Ellis smiled.

"You look Chinese, but I detect a slight accent. Are you from Great Britain?"

Ellis grinned and greeted her in Cantonese. "My parents immigrated to London from Hong Kong after they got married. My brother and I have British first names and Chinese middle names."

Emmeline laughed. "We have Chinese middle names too! Your Cantonese is excellent. Unlike my brother and me, I don't detect an accent at all."

"Speak for yourself, Emia," Matthew replied in perfect Cantonese.

Ellis responded in Mandarin. "I have a knack for languages. I'm also fluent in French and Spanish. Saadah's recently started teaching me Arabic."

"That's impressive," Emmeline replied in Mandarin.

Ellis shrugged, and his grin widened. "It's a bit of a useless gift in my current profession, but it does impress the ladies." He turned to greet Matthew. "Dr. Taylor-Wu."

Matthew raised his hand to stop him. "Please, Matthew is fine."

"We heard—well, everyone has heard—how you came to Lesedi's aid. Thank you for saving her," Saadah said, and he and Ellis both placed their right hands over their hearts. "We're indebted to you."

"I didn't do anything more or less than any other doctor would've done." Matthew pushed his glasses up.

"Can I ask you a question?" Ellis piped up.

"Of course."

Ellis eyed Matthew's car. "How does it drive? Is it truly what dreams are made of?"

Matthew erupted into a big smile. "Of dreams and more. If there's an opportunity later, I'll take you for a drive."

Ellis and Saadah looked at Matthew like he was a demigod, and Emmeline rolled her eyes.

My brother smiles, like, five times a year, but throw in talk about an exotic car, and all bets are off.

"Your car has a fan club now," Emmeline said.

Matthew turned to her. "I recall you driving it and liking it very much."

"Come on. Let's get going," Emmeline laughed.

Saadah and Ellis led them up multiple flights of stairs. By the time they reached the top, Emmeline felt close to being out of breath. She glanced at Matthew, who looked no different from when he had started.

"I keep telling you to stay active, Emia."

"I am active."

"Not as much or as regular as you should be."

"Leave me alone." Emmeline looked up at their two guides. "Saadah, Ellis, is there another entrance from the garage, or are there more underground garages? The last time I was here, Anja took us through a series of tunnels, though, we were blindfolded."

Saadah looked over his shoulder as he led them through the courtyard. "There's only one parking garage since we don't normally have too much use for vehicles. The tunnel you came through last time is on the other side of the garage. The stairs were just faster."

"We only use the cars or motorcycles when we need to do something during the day. At night, we have our special editions." Ellis pointed to his back.

"What do you do during the day?"

"Depends on our assignments and what rotation we're on." Saadah shrugged. "Most of us work in rotating shifts of four to eight weeks, depending on the job. Ellis and I are both part of the hunt teams, and we do four weeks on and four weeks off. Right now, we're in our off rotation, so we use this time to train and assist with the upkeep of the Sanctuary. We do repairs, renovations, and for those of us who are technically inclined, we do technology upgrades. This place is enormous, and it takes a lot of work to maintain."

Ellis raised an eyebrow at Saadah. "Those of us who are technically inclined? Are you calling me technically challenged?"

"Well, if it walks like a duck and quacks like a duck…"

Ellis punched Saadah in the shoulder, and Saadah snorted.

"Listen, if it wasn't for me designing better menus, we'd all be subjected to the same crappy meals over and over again," Ellis said.

"You two sound like siblings." Emmeline looked at Ellis and then at Saadah. "If you're on the hunt team, don't you need to sleep during the day?"

"We do sleep, but the amount we need is less than when we were human. If we are hurt or need to recover, we'll sleep more so our bodies can repair themselves," Saadah replied.

Matthew stopped walking. "What do you mean by your bodies repairing themselves?"

Saadah and Ellis both stopped and turned around, but it was Saadah who answered, "We heal fast. If the physical wound isn't severe or mortal, we'll recover quickly. Much faster than the human body can."

Matthew furrowed his brow. "Why did I need to treat Lesedi? Shouldn't she have been able to self-heal? I looked at her wound, and it wasn't mortal when it happened."

Ellis shook his head. "Normally, we don't get infections, and our bodies work fast enough to heal our wounds. We also don't get sick. Things like the common cold, the flu, strep throat, you name it—we usually don't get it. Sometimes, our wounds don't heal as fast as they should, and someone might get sick on rare occasions. I don't understand why, and I don't know anyone here who could tell you why." He grinned at Matthew. "Maybe that's why you're here."

"I'm sure that's not why I am here," Matthew replied.

Ellis raised his eyebrows and looked back and forth between Matthew and Emmeline. "Want to know who sounds like siblings? You both have the same intonation."

Emmeline clasped her heart and looked at Ellis in mock horror. "And here I thought, we were about to become fast friends." She laughed at Ellis's chagrin.

"But we are siblings, and you knew that already." Matthew looked at Ellis with confusion.

"He's making fun of us, Mattie," Emmeline said.

"Before we say anything more that we shouldn't and risk offending you both, we should keep walking. We're close to the meditation space, where Anja and Ember are waiting for you." Saadah tapped Ellis's shoulder, and they both turned around.

Emmeline and Matthew followed them through the courtyard and tried not to disturb the other nainthe who were milling about. Emmeline was aware of the stares and whispers that followed her as she passed by, and every so often, she would see a flash of bright white when a nainthe she hadn't met before came into her vision.

"Mattie," Emmeline whispered, "the flashes of light are getting shorter and less intense, or maybe I'm getting used to it. The auras are also fully disappearing."

"You haven't had a single seizure either. We could run some experiments here."

"Thanks, but no thanks."

"Ellis!" a high-pitched voice called out.

Emmeline turned and saw a curvy woman with long, riotous chocolate curls and wide, sparkling brown eyes run over to them.

No burst of light and only a very faint aura. I must've seen her before.

"Sophia! What are you doing here?" Ellis's eyes brightened.

"I saw you walking through the courtyard with our two famous guests and thought you could do an introduction." Sophia's cheeks flushed to a rosy pink.

"Of course." Ellis did a quick round of introductions.

"It's an honor to meet you, Emmeline," Sophia said.

"Please don't say that. The honor is mine," Emmeline replied.

"Ellis, Lucia and I are going to have a drink before doing some training. Do you want to join us?" Sophia asked.

Ellis nodded mutely, and Sophia gave him a sweet smile. She said her good-byes and returned the way she had come.

"What am I, chopped liver?" Saadah slapped a dumbfounded Ellis on the shoulder. "I think being seen with Emmeline has made you more popular, Mr. Wong."

"Be quiet, Saadah," Ellis huffed. "Let's go, or Anja's going to kill us."

Saadah and Ellis continued on their way and stopped in front of a set of steps that led up to wide sliding glass doors.

"We're here. Anja and Ember are inside, prepping for your training session. Thank you for allowing us to escort you," Saadah said. He and Ellis pressed their right palms to their hearts and dipped their heads.

"Thank you. I hope I get to see you both again soon. Don't forget my brother owes you a car ride," Emmeline said.

Ellis grinned. "I definitely won't forget!"

Saadah laughed at Ellis, and they both turned around and melted into the courtyard shadows.

"Shall we, Mattie?"

Matthew nodded, and they both walked up the steps and through the sliding glass doors.

CHAPTER TWENTY-FOUR

LATE BLOOMER

The glass doors closed behind Emmeline and Matthew and it immediately silenced the ambient sounds from the courtyard. Beyond the glass doors was a second set of wooden doors that floated open once the first set of doors closed.

Emmeline slipped off her flats, and Matthew did the same with his sneakers, and they tucked them into the wooden cubbies off to the side. They stepped past the wooden doors into an open space with soft lights, highlighting symmetrical wood floor planks. The wall on the right was filled from floor to ceiling with a living garden while the other was painted with hazy blues and greens, reminiscent of sunlight beaming down on calm, open water. Emmeline looked up at the massive skylight that showcased the night sky and its brilliant stars.

This must be breathtaking in the morning.

"This is my kind of space. Maybe we should build something like this at home. We have the room." Matthew stared up at the skylight.

"It would be nice to have a meditation room at home. If you oversee the renovation, go for it."

"So, do what you would and hire a project manager."

Emmeline narrowed her eyes. "You're ruining my zen."

Light voices came around the corner of a hidden hallway at the end of the room, and as the voices got closer, she braced herself for the bright flash of light.

Anja and Ember entered the room and walked toward the center of the space to meet Emmeline and Matthew. Anja was dressed in a fitted black outfit with no armor or blade, and her features and icy irises were softer and more relaxed. Even the dark shadows under her eyes seemed lighter. Ember was shorter than Anja, and her curly honey-brown hair was tied into a tidy ballerina bun on top of her head. Her face was round with plump cheeks and lips, and her dark brown eyes were bright. She was dressed head to toe in soft gray, matching the serenity of the space.

"Anja." Emmeline smiled in greeting before turning to Ember and holding out her hand. "You must be Ember."

Ember shook her hand vigorously. "It's nice to meet you finally." She held out her hand to Matthew. "Dr. Taylor-Wu, it's very nice to meet you as well. You're also quite famous around here."

There was a pause before Matthew took Ember's hand, a delay so slight that even the most intuitive people would've missed it.

You're getting very good at pretending, Mattie.

Emmeline's heart hurt for her brother. From the corner of her eye, she saw Anja flinch.

"Anja, it's nice to see you again," Matthew said.

Anja nodded and looked away.

I hope these two apologize to each other soon instead of just talking about doing it sometime in the future.

Emmeline cleared her throat. "Ember, I know you're here to help train me to be a seeker. Should we get started?"

"I'm not going to be doing much training in the traditional sense. I can't teach you how to be a seeker since all I have to go on is what's been recorded and my experience with Lana and Chin. In all the documented accounts, seekers have come into their full abilities on their own, and the nainthe help them refine and understand their abilities and what it means. Seekers would be drawn to potentials and see them in visions and dreams, which would help us find them. When I met Lana and Chin, the connection was as clear as the sun in the sky." Ember glanced at Anja. "From what Anja has told me, you haven't exhibited any of the traditional afflictions, but I can feel it when I look at you. It's like my connection with Lana and Chin, except it's very soft. I hope that makes some sense."

"It doesn't make sense to me, but I know something connects me to your world. Has Anja told you about the auras I see?"

Ember nodded. "The only thing I can think of is, there's some sort of glitch. I don't know if this means anything, but you're also older than when most seekers come into their abilities. Usually, it happens in the late teens or early twenties."

"I started getting seizures in my early twenties."

"The timing seems right." Ember gave Emmeline a perplexed look. "It's so odd you haven't come into your abilities yet."

"This feels like puberty all over again," Emmeline muttered. Anja snickered.

Emmeline shrugged. "It's true. I was a late bloomer."

"Me too!" Ember laughed. "Anyhow, my job is to help you unlock your abilities. I want to begin with meditation to see if I can help you focus your mind. We'll start with improving your awareness of the nainthe around you without you having to see us physically. If that works, we'll switch to seeking out the nainthe presence in the unknown, so you'll be able to feel them without knowing they're there. Lastly, and most challenging, will be to reach out farther with your mind to find potentials."

Emmeline let out a breath. "Well, no time like the present. Let's get started."

"I'm going to get several floor pillows for us to use." Ember headed to the far corner, where there were stacks of large square pillows.

"Let me help you." Matthew jogged over to Ember.

"You're staying, Dr. Taylor-Wu?"

"Yes, I'd like to observe. And please, call me Matthew."

"This might get dull from an observer's standpoint. Don't say I didn't warn you." Ember handed him two pillows. She grabbed two more pillows and headed back to Emmeline and Anja. "Emmeline, does one of the walls speak more to you?"

Emmeline pointed to the watercolors stretching across the left wall. "This wall's breathtaking. It reminds me of the sea."

"Good. We'll practice facing it." Ember laid a pillow for herself and placed a pillow down for Emmeline. "Matthew, you can sit behind us."

Matthew laid down two pillows farther back, and they all took a seat and crossed their legs.

Ember softened her voice. "Close your eyes, Emmeline. We'll spend time focusing on our breathing and nothing else. Center yourself on taking deep breaths and feel it fill your body with life. With that same thread, follow your breath as it leaves your body."

Emmeline followed Ember's instructions, slowly taking deep breaths and letting it out. After some time, her mind slowly began to wander to the previous night until she found herself standing at the hallway windows of her home, overlooking the moonlit garden.

Still as death itself.

From the corner of her eyes, the garden began to turn gray and brittle. She watched in horror as everything crumbled and turned to ash, suspending itself in the air, as if stopped in time. Emmeline's heart fell into her stomach, and she clenched her fists over her knees.

Ember hummed lowly before speaking. "It's okay if your mind wanders to other places. It happens, and it's natural. Part of this process is helping you recognize when your mind has shifted and how to refocus yourself back on breathing."

Keeping her eyes closed, Emmeline pushed her thoughts down and concentrated on inhaling and exhaling. Her breathing and heart rate calmed, and she felt her body relax again.

"Emmeline, I know you can see auras around the nainthe. Try to focus your mind on a vision of that aura."

Emmeline took a deep breath and tried to visualize an aura. The one that came into her sight was like hazy smoke, unlike what she saw after the flash of white when she met a new nainthe.

"Focus on the aura." Ember's voice soothed. "Keep your attention on it but listen to the direction of my voice. Now, slowly split your focus between the aura and me."

Emmeline envisioned Ember on her right and placed the image of the aura to her left, letting it float in the darkness. She felt a spark to her right, just tiny flickers clustered together. She gasped, and her eyes flew open.

"What happened? Did you see something? Feel something?" Anja's voice demanded from behind.

Ember turned and gave Anja a stern look.

"Sorry," Anja grumbled under her breath.

She is capable of apologizing. Just not to Mattie.

"Emmeline, did something happen?" Ember asked.

"I can't tell if I saw something or if my imagination took over, but I think it was pieces of your aura." Emmeline frowned. "I call it an aura, but it looks different from what I see after meeting a nainthe for the first time."

"Did you feel anything?"

Emmeline shook her head. "Nothing."

"It's a promising start. I'd like you to take some time out of each day and try this exercise. Would you be open to that?"

"I am, but don't I need to be around one of you?"

Ember hesitated. "Would you be willing to spend more time at the Sanctuary? It would be ideal if you moved here."

"I normally work from my home office, so shifting some of my time around to be here can be done, but I'm not moving in. Unless you want to take in my whole family."

"I don't agree to moving in," Matthew spoke up.

"There you go. No moving in," Emmeline said.

"This means we'll need more resources to keep you safe," Anja sighed dramatically. She stretched out her legs and touched her toes with her fingers, her limbs bending fluidly at her will. "All right, Ms. Socialite, tell us what your schedule permits, and I'll work on negotiating with you from there."

Emmeline nodded and stood on her tippy-toes, stretching out her stiff muscles. "If we're done here, I'd like to see Lesedi."

CHAPTER TWENTY-FIVE

SANCTITY OF LIFE

After bidding Ember good-bye, Emmeline and Matthew cut through the courtyard with Anja leading the way. The square was quiet with only a few nainthe out and about. Crickets chirped in the cool night, and the faint scent of charred firewood lingered in the breeze.

As they rounded the corner of the concrete platform, Emmeline saw several nainthe training and sparring with each other. A few nainthe made eye contact with her and waved. She shyly raised her hand in acknowledgment and quickened her pace to keep up with Anja and Matthew.

Anja kept several steps ahead, her head held high and her pace graceful. Emmeline nudged her brother and gestured to Anja with her chin. He glared at her and shook his head.

"Not now," Matthew muttered.

Anja looked over her shoulder before turning back, her icy-ash eyes glinting.

Emmeline rolled her eyes at Matthew and pointed to her ear.

Above average hearing, remember?

Anja led them up a long set of narrow stairs to the second floor, showcasing individual rooms outlining the courtyard. Above the second floor were two more stories, both with identical layouts. Each room had a solid wood door; some were bare while others were decorated and personalized, and to the right of each entry was a large window, giving its inhabitants a broad view of the courtyard.

"Are all of these private rooms?" Emmeline asked.

Anja nodded and pointed across the courtyard. "My room's on the third story on the south side of the courtyard, and so's my brother's. Ground floor rooms are mainly common-use spaces and private offices. Last time you were here, we were at the infirmary and Javier's office." She pointed at the ground level to the east and southeast corners. "I don't know if you remember the great room, but it's directly across from the courtyard platform. The courtyard platform is on the west side, and the great room is on the east side."

"Could I get a map?" Matthew asked, pushing up his glasses.

Emmeline gaped at her brother, and she thought the world was about to collapse on top of her.

A map is the last thing you need, Mattie. Are you making a joke to Anja, of all people?

Anja laughed, and her bell-like voice rang through the air. "You, Dr. Matthew, Mr. Perfect Memory, are the last person who needs a map."

Emmeline watched as Matthew's mouth twitched into a half-smile, and her mouth fell open.

I'm in the twilight zone.

Anja stopped in front of a door. "This is Lessie's room. I've already let her know that you wanted to visit. Just wait here, and I'll come to get you."

She knocked and entered Lesedi's darkened room, closing the door behind her. A light flickered on and illuminated the covered window.

Emmeline whirled around. "Were you just flirting?"

"Of course not." Matthew clasped his hands behind his back.

"She has a partner—a female partner—whom she cares about very much and whose life you just saved. She's also not human."

"She's just a friend. I was rude to her the other night, and I'm trying to make up for it."

"So, apologizing without apologizing?" Emmeline stared at the dark wooden door, waiting for it to open at any moment.

The air between them dipped into silence, and Emmeline assumed Matthew had chosen not to continue the conversation.

"I will apologize," Matthew finally said.

Emmeline heard a click, and the door opened into a brightly lit room.

Anja stepped to the side. "You can come in now. Lessie's ready to see you."

Matthew stepped over the threshold, and Emmeline's heart sank just a little bit for him.

This might get messy.

~

Lesedi's room was decorated with warm yellow and burnt-red accents, and the scent of apples and cinnamon filled the air, making Emmeline's stomach growl with hunger. She stood in the foyer with Matthew and noticed Anja's short black boots were placed on a mud mat. She reached into her tote bag and rummaged around until she found her ankle socks and put them on her feet, tucking her flats beside Anja's boots. Matthew followed suit, his sneakers looking comically large beside her and Anja's shoes.

"You keep socks in your purse?" Anja looked at Emmeline incredulously.

"I don't like walking barefoot around someone's home."

"What else do you keep in there?"

"Everything. It's the purse that keeps on giving."

Anja laughed at Emmeline's comment. "Lessie's in the kitchen. She's heating an apple pie for all of us."

Avoiding eye contact with Matthew, Anja turned and headed around the corner. Emmeline peeked at Matthew's face as he followed closely behind Anja, but his features were unreadable. As they walked into the kitchen, Lesedi was at the oven, her hair beautifully free, holding a browned apple pie between two oven mitts.

"Dr. Taylor-Wu! I'm so happy to see you." Lesedi broke into a smile at the sight of Matthew. She put down the apple pie and walked over to Matthew with her arms stretched out, ready to pull him into a hug.

"Lessie, he doesn't like to be touched." Anja's arm shot out to pull Lesedi back.

Lesedi's smile faltered, and she stopped in her tracks.

"It's okay, Anja." Matthew pushed up his glasses.

"I'm sorry. I just assumed it was fine, and I shouldn't have." Lesedi clasped her hands in front of her. "Thank you for coming to my aid when I needed it. I know we can be a challenging bunch, and being here mustn't have been easy."

"That's an understatement," Emmeline snorted.

"You're welcome, Lesedi, and like I tell almost everyone, please call me Matthew."

Lesedi raised an eyebrow. "Almost everyone?"

"Only the ones I don't mind." Matthew's eyes flitted to Anja before coming back to Lesedi.

Careful, Mattie.

Emmeline looked at Lesedi's face and saw her pause. She smiled brightly. "How are you feeling, Lesedi?"

"I'm still drained, and the wound is sore, but overall, I'm doing much better."

"Would you like me to take a look?" Matthew asked.

"Please, Dr. Taylor-Wu."

"Matthew."

"Matthew," Lesedi echoed. She lifted the side of her shirt and peeled off the wound dressing.

Matthew went to the kitchen sink, washed his hands, and dried them off with a paper towel. He knelt on one knee and gently touched Lesedi's skin, peering at it from different angles. Satisfied, he stood up and returned to the sink to wash his hands.

"Your wound is healing faster than normal."

"You just touched me, and you were fine," Lesedi said.

Matthew went to his duffel bag to get a new dressing pack for Lesedi, but he didn't look at her. "I can tolerate it enough."

"What do you mean?"

Emmeline looked sharply at Lesedi and was about to tell her to back off, but a quick look from Matthew stopped her: *Don't fight my battles.*

She got her brother's message loud and clear.

Matthew pushed up his glasses. "Light touches sometimes make my skin feel like it's burning. I knew I was going to touch you, so I was fine. I've conditioned myself to tolerate it when I expect it, but if I don't have to, I'd prefer not to."

"What happens with touches that are not light?"

"As long as I expect it, it's fine." Matthew pulled taut the zipper to his duffel bag. "Do you have any more questions for me?"

Lesedi seemed taken aback by his bluntness. "No, I don't."

Matthew nodded and handed her a new sterile dressing pack. "You should wash, dry, and put a patch back on."

Lesedi excused herself to go to the bathroom, and the tension in the room lifted.

Anja coughed and held up a knife and some plates. "So, who wants pie?"

Emmeline pulled out a chair, sat at the small wooden dining table, and put her head down on her arms.

"Pie?" Anja repeated.

Without looking up, Emmeline raised her hand. "Is there vanilla ice cream? I only want pie if there's vanilla ice cream."

"Lessie has vanilla ice cream."

Emmeline heard the freezer door open and close and the gentle clink of the cutlery drawer as Anja rummaged for an ice cream scoop. The chair beside her scraped across the floor, and she knew Matthew had sat down. Sighing, she straightened up and pulled her long hair out of her face.

"Are you okay?" Emmeline asked Matthew as quietly as she could.

"Why wouldn't I be?"

Anja handed Emmeline and Matthew each a slice of apple pie with a generous scoop of vanilla ice cream on top. She went back, grabbed two more plates, and set one for herself and one for Lesedi. Lesedi walked back into the kitchen, and Anja pulled out a chair for her.

Emmeline looked around the small kitchen. "Sitting here almost makes me forget we're at the Sanctuary. It feels so normal."

"We try. Our rooms are our escape." Lesedi changed the subject. "Anja told me a raizour attacked you. How's your neck healing?"

"The bruising's almost all gone. Unfortunately, I don't heal as fast as the nainthe." Emmeline pulled down the high neck of her sleeveless top and showed Lesedi. She caught Anja averting her eyes.

Matthew held a forkful of pie and ice cream but did not attempt to eat it. "It's not your fault, Anja. Stop blaming yourself."

Anja's cloudy eyes flickered to Matthew, but she didn't say anything.

"This never should've happened. We would never intentionally put you in danger." There was a hint of anger in Lesedi's voice, and she placed a protective hand over Anja's.

Emmeline watched Matthew's face, but his features remained blank.

"Anja, have you made any progress finding out what happened?" Emmeline asked.

"My brother, Asadi, and one of Asadi's apprentices, Finn, are looking into it." Anja took a deep breath. "We all agree the raizour knew what they were doing and might have allowed themselves to be caught. If you remember, our armor covers the lower part of our neck. The raizour knew their teeth wouldn't be able to get through the armor, so they purposely aimed for under the chin."

"How come the nainthe only fight the raizour with blades? There must be a more efficient way to destroy the raizour. Are your blades made of a special material?" Emmeline asked.

Anja nodded. "Our blades are made of scryress and have been passed down from each generation of nainthe."

"What is scryress?"

"It's an ancient material that feels like metal and is black with a slight blue tinge. It's the only substance we know of that can kill a raizour."

Matthew frowned. "Do you know what it's composed of?"

"We don't. What's in our arsenal is all we have, and so our blades are precious to us," Anja replied.

"But it must be made of some compound of elements. If you can break it down, you can re-create it."

Lesedi shook her head. "It is not made of any elements we know."

"But all things are made from the elements," Matthew stated.

"Dr. Matthew, I have wings. Nothing in our world makes sense in yours." Anja gave him a wry look.

Matthew's mouth clamped shut, and he sat back.

"I don't understand. Why would you wear armor that doesn't protect you?" Emmeline looked at Lesedi with confusion.

"The armor is regular human-made armor but customized to our specifications. It gives us an extra layer of protection and helps us to last longer in battle, but it can't stop a weapon made of scryress, nor can it stop a raizour's sharp wings, though it does protect us from a raizour's teeth and claws. Our nainthe form can also deflect some human weapons for a period, such as bullets, metal, and surprisingly, radiation. Be very careful of a raizour's wings," Lesedi warned. "Their wings are coated with a substance that's venomous to both nainthe and humans."

"So, that's why the raizour's wings were bound that night," Emmeline murmured in understanding, but then she frowned. "The raizour knew what they were doing when they went after the nainthe guards."

"Their names are Quinn and Mihal," Anja murmured.

Emmeline bent her head. "I'm sorry, Anja. Quinn and Mihal."

"Don't be too hard on Emmeline. Our world is completely foreign to her." Lesedi squeezed Anja's hand.

"I'm not trying to be hard on her. I just don't want anyone to forget." Anja took her hand back and crossed her arms.

The four sat in silence, picking at the apple pie and ice cream. Finally, Matthew wiped his mouth and put his napkin on the dining table.

"Anja, a few days ago, I said some things to you that were insensitive. I've been meaning to apologize, and I was trying to find the right time to do it. I'm sorry. I believe in the sanctity of life, and that includes the nainthe. I wasn't implying the nainthe do not believe or deserve the same respect. Please forgive me," Matthew said, and the golden flecks in his midnight irises deepened.

Anja met Matthew's gaze for the first time since he stepped into the Sanctuary. "I also owe you an apology. I might have overreacted when you've been nothing but kind. I know you didn't mean it. I was angry, and I took it out on you." She looked away. "I'm still angry, but not at you."

"My Anja, apologizing?" Lesedi pretended to look shocked.

Matthew stood up abruptly, signaling that he was ready to leave. "Lesedi, thank you for having us over. I'm happy with your progress, and if you need additional consultations, feel free to call me anytime. Though I expect you to make a full and quick recovery."

Emmeline tried to finish her plate as fast as she could.

Mattie, you'd better not turn around and leave me here by myself.

She wiped her mouth and stood up as well.

"Are you leaving?" Anja sat up straighter, her eyes sharp.

"Yes, my services are no longer required here." Matthew turned back to Emmeline. "I'd like to visit the infirmary before we leave and speak to Ben, or are you too tired and would rather go home?"

"We can go to the infirmary first. Just don't spend three hours talking about medical equipment," Emmeline muttered.

Anja stood up. "I can take you both there. Not everyone knows you yet; it'll be safer if I accompany you. Lessie, I can take care of the dishes when I get back. You get some rest."

Matthew and Emmeline picked up their belongings and thanked Lesedi for hosting them. As Lesedi's door closed behind them, the crisp night air wafted through Emmeline's hair, and she let out a sigh of relief.

As they walked down the staircase back to the ground floor, Emmeline slowed her pace so that she fell several steps behind Matthew and Anja. She watched as Matthew deliberately shortened his pace so he could walk beside Anja.

It's getting chilly. Emmeline pulled out her sweater and shrugged it over her head and shoulders.

Matthew glanced back at Emmeline before tilting his head to Anja. "Are you cold?"

"No, I'm not," Anja replied.

Matthew nodded, and they continued to walk in silence.

"Will you come back to visit?" Anja asked.

"I don't think there's a need for me to be here. My presence isn't exactly welcome." Matthew put his hands in his pockets and looked at Anja's profile. "If you have any questions or need anything from me, you can call me. You know where I live."

"I only know where Emmeline lives."

"I'm moving back home temporarily. It's not as convenient to get to the hospital, but I feel better at home, given what happened the other night."

"We'll protect her. I promised you I would protect you both with my life, and I meant it."

"I know you will."

Matthew and Anja fell back into silence.

I feel like I'm intruding on a private moment.

Emmeline turned and looked at the courtyard and saw a familiar face.

Ellis! I have an out.

She stood on her toes and stretched out her arm, waving at Ellis.

"Anja, would you mind if I stayed in the courtyard while Mattie visits the infirmary?" Emmeline asked.

"Of course not," Anja replied.

Matthew turned around just as Ellis jogged over.

"Emmeline, Matthew, it's nice to see you again. We just finished training, and we're taking a breather before our next round." Ellis gave Anja a side-fist bump.

"Ellis, could you show me around? I'd love to watch a training demonstration." Emmeline motioned to Matthew. "My brother is on his way to the infirmary to talk about medical equipment, and I'd much rather meet some nainthe and get to know the Sanctuary instead." She paused, realizing how overbearing she sounded. "As long as it doesn't interfere with your training."

"It'd be an honor. You watching will make us bring our A game," Ellis said.

"Always looking for a chance to show off for the ladies," Anja teased.

"Constantly." Ellis laughed. "Emmeline, I'll introduce you to the rest of the crew. See you later, Matthew. And don't worry, Anja; I'll take good care of her."

"Thanks, Ellis," Emmeline said with relief.

Ellis pointed at Matthew and grinned. "I'm not going to forget about that car ride you promised me."

Anja raised an eyebrow at Matthew, her mouth twitching. "Car ride? Is that as awkward as it sounds?"

Matthew pushed up his glasses. "It's not awkward. Ellis has a commendable appreciation for the finer things in life. He likes my car."

Emmeline covered her eyes with her hand.

Mattie, that's not helping.

"Message me when you're done at the infirmary."

Emmeline turned around and followed Ellis into the courtyard.

CHAPTER TWENTY-SIX

FURY

"How were drinks with Sophia and Lucia?" Emmeline hurried to catch up with him.

"It was fine." Ellis blushed.

"Hmm, I'm sure it was," Emmeline teased him. "How come Lucia's so rude to Mattie? She wasn't outright hostile to me, but when she met Mattie, she seemed upset he was here."

"I'm not sure how much I should say, but as you get to know us, you'll realize that nobody wants to be here. None of us had the choice to become a nainthe, and we each deal with our loss and grief differently. Lucia blames humans. If it wasn't for humans, there wouldn't be nainthe."

"She was also once human."

"Everything was taken away from her—family, fiancé, and her dream of becoming a doctor to help her community."

"Blaming humans is a stretch though, isn't it?"

"Maybe, but until you've experienced the loss every nainthe in this place has gone through, it's hard to understand."

"That's fair."

Emmeline padded beside Ellis and looked up at the sky.

"Ellis, this courtyard is enormous, and I know the nainthe own this entire block, but how do humans not know about this place? There are high-rises, aircraft, and drones. How does this all stay hidden? We're in the middle of the most populous city in the country."

Ellis stopped walking and turned to Emmeline. "Did Anja already talk to you about our magic?"

Emmeline nodded.

"The magic we use to protect the fabric that separates our world and the raizour's world is also used to create a ward. It's like a giant shield stretching over the middle of this block. Not only does it protect the sanctuary from the raizour, it has a reflective quality, rendering the space dull and unnoticeable. It would be like looking at nothing."

"What if someone took a picture?"

"You've been watching too many supernatural movies and television shows," Ellis said.

"Can you show me? The magic, I mean."

Ellis held up his hand, stretching out his fingers above Emmeline. She watched in awe as the air sparked and delicate threads of light shimmered over their heads.

"You can see it?" Ellis asked.

Emmeline nodded in wide-eyed wonder.

"I didn't think elystiers could see magic, but then again, what do I know?"

"Can you show me again?"

Ellis held out his hands and closed his eyes; this time, the air crackled and hummed. The light brightened and stretched out wider, illuminating the air above them.

Emmeline felt the urge to touch the light, and she reached out and hovered her hand beneath it. Closing her eyes, she moved her hand back and forth, feeling the warmth of the light as it caressed the palm of her hand and followed her movements.

Is this what magic feels like?

Suddenly, Emmeline was jolted out of her peace, and her eyes snapped open. The warmth was replaced with the brisk night air, and she heard loud footsteps and sharp commands.

"Shit!" Ellis looked up at the sky and changed into his nainthe form.

He pulled Emmeline to him and shielded her with one of his wings. Before she could cover her head, she heard a high-pitched whistling and then a loud crash.

"I need to get you away from the courtyard." Ellis changed back into his human form.

"What's happening?" Emmeline saw the crumpled body of a raizour lying in the middle of the courtyard. She looked back up at the sky. "Are there more?"

"Probably, but likely dead. I'm sorry. I wasn't paying attention and panicked. I thought you might accidentally get hit with a falling body. If anything happens to you, Anja will skin me alive." Ellis looked ashamed.

"Why are there falling bodies?"

Ellis pointed to the sky. "That'll be answered shortly."

Within seconds, a nainthe slammed onto the ground. He held two raizour bodies by the necks with long, bloody gashes across their torsos. The nainthe dropped the two bodies onto the grassy lawn and fell to his knees, clutching his chest.

"He's hurt!" Emmeline tried to rush over.

"Wait! It's too dangerous right now." Ellis grabbed her arm and pulled her back.

"How come no one's helping him?" Emmeline pointed at the nainthe crouched on the ground.

"That's not how it works. We need to give him space," Ellis said in a hushed voice, keeping his grip on Emmeline.

A harsh breeze whipped through Emmeline's hair, carrying a raspy, disembodied message.

"There are three more in the Donlands. I've taken care of them all. Bring the bodies back."

Emmeline's heart stopped. She'd recognize that voice anywhere.

Erik.

Emmeline took out her phone and tried to call Anja, but only got the message of an inactive voice mail service. She tapped out a message, hoping Anja would check it soon.

Emia:	Erik just returned to the Sanctuary, and I think he's hurt. He's in the courtyard. You should come. They won't let me get close to him.

"I'm going to help bring back the other raizour bodies. Will you be fine here by yourself? Or I can bring you to the great room or the infirmary." Ellis looked up just as another nainthe ran past him and tossed him a helmet.

Emmeline looked over Ellis's shoulder, and Erik was still kneeling on the ground. "I'll wait here for Anja and Matthew."

"I'm sorry we didn't get to spend more time together." Ellis turned and walked away as he tightened the straps on his armor.

Emmeline spotted Saadah in the distance and he lifted his hand in acknowledgment.

After Ellis was a distance away, Emmeline ran toward Erik's hunched form. Erik craned his neck and tilted his mask-covered face toward the midnight sky, letting out a hoarse groan. He stretched out his wings and launched himself into the air.

"Erik, wait!" Emmeline cried out.

Emmeline reached out her hand in his direction, but he flew over her and toward the opposite end of the courtyard before disappearing into the dark third-story corridor.

That must be where his room is.

Emmeline ran to the stairs and climbed the steps two at a time until she reached the top. She looked around the shadowed hallway, debating which way to go.

It's a fifty-fifty chance, but I think he went this way.

She walked up to each door and listened closely. She passed by several doors until she came across one that had a large plaque, covered with labels from different indie and popular coffee brands.

This must be Anja's room, which means Erik's room must be close by.

She went back one door and listened, but it was silent. She knocked and waited, but there was no answer. She walked over to the next door and was about to knock when she noticed the door was ajar. The room was dark, and she leaned her ear in closer, straining to hear any sounds.

"Erik?" Emmeline called out and knocked on the door.

There was no response, so she knocked harder.

"Erik, are you there?"

Again, there was only silence.

Should I go in? What if this isn't his room?

She pushed the door open and stepped into the dark room. Closing the door behind her, she peered around the corner. This room was set up differently from Lesedi's and seemed narrower but much longer. A minimalist galley kitchen at the front extended into a small sitting room, and the only light was from the moon high above the windows.

Emmeline jumped as a sudden guttural cry echoed through the room, followed by harsh scraping against the floor.

"Erik?"

Emmeline rushed around the corner and ran past the open concept bedroom to the bathroom. She pushed open the door and skidded to a stop.

Erik was hunched over on the floor with his wings sprawled over him, their sharp edges and leathery covering reflecting the faint moonlight. He was still in his armor but had thrown his helmet and mask to the side. His eyes were closed tight against his papery skin, and his chest heaved with each breath he took.

Emmeline knelt on the floor beside him. "Erik, should I call for Ben or Lucia? Or maybe Mattie?"

She reached for his hand, and Erik's eyes flew open. He rounded on her and grabbed her wrist.

"Why are you here? You shouldn't be here!" Erik roared.

Emmeline tried to pull her hand away, but he held on to her with a viselike grip.

"Erik, it's me, Emmeline. You're hurting me!"

Emmeline tried to twist her wrist out of his grasp, and tears formed in her eyes as he pulled her close to his face. His icy irises were blind, and his razor-sharp teeth glinted.

"Let me go!" Emmeline pulled at her wrist.

She slammed the heel of her foot into Erik's chest, but his body barely moved. She did it again, but his iron grip on her wrist held fast. Using all her strength, she twisted her body over his arm and used her other heel to kick at his neck. Erik hissed at the impact and bared his teeth at her.

"It's me, Emmeline! You're scaring me."

Erik blinked and a hint of recognition seemed to temper his anger. "Emmeline."

He loosened his grip on her wrist and flung it away, as if it'd burned his hand. His chest heaved again, and he dry retched over the floor.

"Get out," Erik choked out through gritted teeth.

Emmeline backed up and scrambled to her feet. She fled Erik's room and ran down the dark hallway, slamming straight into Anja. Anja groaned and doubled over in pain.

"What are you doing? What happened?" Anja peered closer at Emmeline's face and grabbed her shoulders.

"Something's wrong with your brother. You need to check on him. I thought he was going to hurt me."

Anja looked over Emmeline's shoulder and frowned. "You shouldn't have gone to look for him after he came back from a hunt."

"Excuse me?" Emmeline wiped her face with her hands. "You have some nerve. I went to check on him because I was concerned for him, and you're blaming me for him almost hurting me?"

Anja looked stunned as Emmeline pushed her hands off her shoulders. "That's not what I meant," she sputtered.

"Go find your brother and leave me alone."

Emmeline raced down the stairs and into the deserted courtyard. She looked around for a more secluded spot to hide while she waited for Matthew. There were several outdoor couches under a large, covered pergola at the far end, close to the platform. She stalked over and sat cross-legged in the corner of a sectional couch.

Mattie, where are you?

She reached into her tote to grab her phone, but her hand only met empty space.

Where's my bag?

She placed both her hands over her eyes.

I must've dropped it in Erik's room.

Pulling her knees to her chest, she was grateful for her sweater that kept out the night chill. Resting her head on the cushions, she looked resignedly at the night sky and its smattering of bright stars.

As the minutes stretched out, Emmeline's heart calmed, and her eyelids drooped. She rubbed her bruised wrist and closed her eyes, shifting her body to lie on its side. The cool air and silence lulled her exhausted body to sleep, pulling at her like an unraveling spiderweb into a dark, dreamless sleep.

CHAPTER TWENTY-SEVEN

COUNTERBALANCE

Sunlight began to drift over the buildings and illuminate the courtyard, its golden rays warming the air and bringing with it the fresh scent of morning dew.

Emmeline yawned and stretched. She rubbed her eyes before opening them and blinking.

Where am I?

She lifted her head and groaned. She flopped back down on the cushions and threw her arm over her eyes to block out the light.

I can't believe I fell asleep in the courtyard. Where's Mattie? He wouldn't have left me here on my own. I'd better look for him.

Emmeline sat up and stretched out her arms and back. She looked down in surprise as a light blanket fell off her chest and onto her lap.

Where did this blanket come from?

She looked around, and her eyes settled on a familiar head of shoulder-length black hair at the far end of the sectional.

"Decided to wake up, princess?" Anja murmured. She didn't look up from the book she was reading. Her feet were propped up on the ottoman, and instead of her usual all-black ensemble, she was dressed in a fitted bright pink racerback tank and black leggings.

Emmeline ignored her. "Where's Mattie?"

Anja pointed forward, and Emmeline followed her finger to Matthew's sleeping form stretch out on another sectional couch.

Sorry for making you sleep on a couch, Mattie.

"How's Erik?" Emmeline asked curtly.

"He's fine. Next time, don't go searching for him after a hunt."

"He wasn't fine last night. What happened to him?"

Anja put her book down. "I think he should tell you himself."

"Well, he's not here, and even if he were here, I wouldn't want to see him." Emmeline rubbed her wrist, where a faint bruise had started forming.

"He probably doesn't want to see you either."

"I need my tote bag. I think I left it in Erik's room."

Anja sighed and reached beside her to pick up Emmeline's bag off the floor. She walked over to Emmeline and dropped the bag on the couch before plopping down beside her.

"Thanks," Emmeline muttered as she rummaged through her bag for her phone to message Ms. Rose. She pulled out her travel pouch, rubbed her face quickly with a face wipe, and massaged in some fresh moisturizer and sunscreen.

Anja pointed to a small hallway. "There's a shared restroom."

Emmeline folded the blanket and handed it back to Anja. "Was Mattie okay last night?"

Anja rolled her eyes. "He had a great time with Ben. All they did was talk about medical technology and equipment, and I think Ben now has a small crush on your brother. I left the infirmary to look for you, and after your little meltdown, I went to check on my brother."

Emmeline narrowed her eyes. "I didn't have a meltdown."

"Afterwards, I went to look for you to ensure you were okay and found you passed out here. Then, I went back to check on your brother, and he was still talking to Ben about the same things! I had to practically drag him out of the infirmary."

"That sounds like Mattie." Emmeline stood up. "I'll be back."

"I'm going to tell my brother to come here. You two need to talk, especially after last night."

"I don't want to see him right now."

"I already told you, he feels the same way."

Emmeline glared at Anja and held up her wrist. "You don't understand, do you? I was terrified of Erik yesterday. I thought he was going to hurt me. He didn't even recognize me."

"Look, the sooner you both have a conversation about it, the better, so let's get it over with. Trust me, my brother will hate this way more than you." Anja paused, and sadness flickered across her gray eyes. "He's still the same person who saved your life twice, and he's still the same person who risks his life every night to keep everyone else safe. Try not to forget that when you talk to him."

Emmeline felt a pang of guilt. "I'm going to freshen up. I'm leaving if he's not here by the time I get back."

She turned and stalked off to the restroom.

～

Emmeline brushed her teeth and ran a wet hairbrush through her long hair before shaking it out. The dampness brought out the loose waves and erased all signs of the previous night's sleep. She patted some cream blush onto her cheeks, shrugged off her sweater, and tossed her drying hair over one shoulder before leaving the restroom.

Matthew had woken up and was sitting on the sectional, rubbing his eyes. Anja picked up his glasses from the side table and handed them to him, being extra careful not to touch him.

Emmeline watched as Matthew mouthed, *Thanks*, and his eyes followed Anja as she sat back down to read her book.

"I guess Erik isn't coming," Emmeline stated.

Anja pressed her lips together, and her sharp eyes scanned the courtyard.

"Mattie, we should get home. I already messaged Ms. Rose and told her we fell asleep at Gus's house."

Matthew stood up and picked up his backpack from the floor. Emmeline dropped her travel pouch into her tote bag and threw it over her shoulder. When she looked up, her heart stopped. Erik was walking across the courtyard in long, graceful strides. He was dressed casually in a fitted black crewneck shirt, slim gray joggers, and what Emmeline immediately recognized as a pair of highly coveted red-and-white high-top sneakers.

Mattie's going to have a field day. First a social gathering on medical equipment and now a fellow sneakerhead.

Erik's dark hair was messy, but he was cleanly shaven, and despite the dark shadows underneath them, his gray eyes were clear and held no trace of the turbulence from the previous night. In his hand was a tray that held four cups of coffee, tucked into sleeves from a local coffee shop.

Emmeline steeled herself and sat back down on the couch as Erik approached. She eyed the coffee hungrily.

I could almost forgive him if one of those is for me.

"May I?" Erik gestured to the ottoman.

Emmeline only nodded, not trusting her voice.

"I brought you a coffee. Anja suggested an IV drip, but I thought I'd start with a store-bought cup."

Matthew snorted, and Emmeline felt her mouth twitch in amusement despite her irritation.

I'm going to kill you, Anja.

"Black, as per Anja." Erik freed one of the cups and handed it to Emmeline. His fingers brushed against hers, and she shivered at the contact.

"You're welcome." Anja smirked at Emmeline after she murmured her thanks. She held out her hand expectantly at Erik.

"Anja, your milk with a splash of coffee." Erik handed her a cup, earning himself a glare. He gave the third cup to Matthew. "I didn't know how you took yours, so I went with black. There's cream and sugar in the bag."

"Black is perfect. Thanks." Matthew accepted the cup while eyeing Erik's shoes. "Nice kicks. I have the same pair. Did you get the black and red too?"

Erik turned his entire body to Matthew. "I did. They were hard to get."

"Yes, they're popular."

Erik glanced at Matthew's neon-yellow runners. "Nice retros."

"They're my go-to, but I don't get to wear them often. If you want anything, let Emia or me know. We have a few contacts and can get new releases."

"Speak for yourself, Mattie." Emmeline took the lid off her cup and tucked her feet under her, settling into the couch.

"This sneaker talk is so interesting, but do you know what would be even more interesting?" Anja stood up and didn't wait for anyone to answer. "Breakfast. Dr. Matthew, would you like to accompany me to the great room? We can pick up breakfast for all of us." She smiled brilliantly.

He has no chance against that smile.

"Of course. We'll be right back." Matthew avoided looking at Emmeline.

Emmeline glared at the backs of Anja and Matthew as they walked away.

I'm going to kill you too, Mattie.

Emmeline let awkward silence fill the air as she tried to gather her thoughts. Finally, she looked at Erik and caught him staring at her wrist.

"I did that." He seemed to be speaking to himself rather than her.

He held his hand to Emmeline, and she placed her wrist in his palm. His hand was warm against hers, and she felt the sudden urge to take her hand back. Her wrist looked small against his long fingers as he traced the forming bruise, his thumb leaving a trail of warmth across her skin.

"Staring at my wrist won't make it better."

"I know." Erik let go of her hand. "I'm sorry about your wrist and for frightening you."

"I don't think you meant to hurt me, but you did scare me last night."

"Everybody knows not to come near me after a hunt."

"Nobody told me."

Ellis did hint at it.

"Well, not exactly, and nobody told me why," Emmeline corrected herself and narrowed her eyes at Erik. "You'd better not be insinuating it was my fault I got hurt. If you do, it'll be the last time you and I ever talk."

Erik finally looked at her, and her breath caught at the sight of the silver that burned bright against his icy irises.

"I didn't say it was your fault, but I could've seriously hurt you if I hadn't come to my senses and realized it was you."

They fell back into silence and stared at the courtyard. The nainthe were starting to wake up, and some were cutting across the space or using it to stretch and have their breakfast.

"What happened last night?" Emmeline asked.

"Can I sit beside you? This ottoman isn't the most comfortable."

"You can sit anywhere you want."

Erik sat next to Emmeline but kept a careful distance between them. He leaned back against the couch and stretched out his long legs.

"I know you've heard from others about me and my reputation. It's no secret everyone calls me the Executioner. I hate that name. Don't ever call me that to my face." Erik's eyes turned brittle.

"Noted." Emmeline leaned back into the corner of the sofa, watching his serious profile.

"I'm very good at what I do. I have this sixth sense for raizour, and I can feel them before anyone else. I can usually anticipate what they're about to do. I'm also faster and stronger than the rest of the nainthe."

"And no one else has these abilities?" Emmeline asked.

"All nainthe can feel raizour, but my senses seem to be amplified. I feel it sooner, and my range is wider. No one else can anticipate their actions though. They can learn how to react efficiently through training, but that's about it."

"Why are you the only one who has these superpowers?"

"I guess I got lucky," Erik said bitterly.

"I don't understand." Emmeline paused, and she tried to choose her words more carefully. "In your line of work, the heightened ability would only help you, and from what I remember from that night in the underground caverns, it would be a good ability to have. Why do you seem to despise it?" She touched her neck.

"How's your neck healing?" Erik's cool eyes flickered over to her.

Emmeline pulled down the neck of her top. "Much better."

Erik looked away and stared at the nainthe setting up mats on the raised platform.

"Why do my injuries bother you and Anja so much?"

"Because it never should've happened. If that raizour had succeeded, the first elystier we'd found in over twenty years would've disappeared from our grasp under our watch. Your bruising is a reminder of how close we came to failing."

Emmeline raised her eyebrow. "And here I thought, it was because you all cared so much about me."

Erik laughed, and the sides of his eyes crinkled.

Even his laugh has a musical lilt to it.

Emmeline's heart warmed, and she smiled despite herself.

He should laugh more.

"So, your ability to sense and anticipate raizour makes you better at your job than everyone else. Does anyone else have other superpowers?" Emmeline asked.

Erik shook his head. "No other superpowers. Well, besides our nainthe form, but we all have that. Requirement of the job." He turned his head to focus on the platform again, where several nainthe had started their morning warm-ups.

He looks like he'd rather be getting a cavity filled than sit here.

"Erik." Emmeline looked at him curiously.

His head snapped back to her, and he blinked. "Sorry."

She gave him a moment to clear his head. "I still don't understand what happened last night. What do your abilities have to do with it?"

"My abilities have a counterbalance. When I take a raizour's life, I feel every single emotion as its life drains away." Erik looked at the platform again. "Hatred and fury for us. Pain and anguish when they realize they'll never see their loved ones again. Heartbreak and acceptance of their fate. But never peace."

"What do you mean, you feel it?"

Erik pressed his hand over his chest. "I feel it physically. I feel it in my heart, head, and entire being. On bad days, like the one you saw yesterday, it keeps me in nainthe form. The historians think it's the universe's way of ensuring I never forget what it means to take a life, no matter how easy it is for me. I remember every life I've taken."

"You're kind of like an empath," Emmeline breathed.

"Call it whatever you want; it makes me vulnerable."

"Empathy is not a weakness. Having your abilities without empathy would not only be a weakness, but also downright dangerous."

"It's a weakness in my line of work." Erik's eyes flashed.

"Maybe that's what separates you from being a psychopath," Emmeline countered. She shrank back into the cushions, and her grip tightened around her coffee cup. She uncrossed her legs and drew up her knees on the couch, creating a barrier between them.

The anger in Erik's eyes disappeared, and he shifted his body away from her. "Are you going to kick me again?"

"I don't kick people for no reason," Emmeline snapped.

"You didn't answer my question."

"No, I'm not going to kick you. It's not like kicking you would hurt you anyway."

"It would most definitely hurt when I'm in human form."

Emmeline only glowered at him.

Calm down. Just change the topic.

Emmeline looked up at the bright blue sky and mentally rubbed her temples. "How long do the effects last? Last night, you looked terrible, but now, you seem fine."

"It's different every time. The night the raizour took Quinn's and Mihal's lives, I could control it, but for some reason, I couldn't anticipate what the raizour would do. I can't explain it." Erik exhaled. "Last night, I could anticipate every move the raizour made, but I felt like I was dying afterward. It took a couple of hours before I could change back."

"Everyone leaves you to suffer on your own? That hardly seems fair."

"It's safer for everyone to let my affliction run its course. It's been like this for decades, and everyone knows to stay away."

"Still, it doesn't seem right."

You've been doing this for decades?

"Erik, how old are you and Anja? You don't look much older than Mattie and me."

Erik's eyes glittered in amusement. "I'm a little more than twice your age, and Anja's three years younger than me."

"You're both old," Emmeline said, and she immediately covered her mouth with her hand. "I mean ..." she stammered and then shrugged. "There's no coming back from that. I'm sorry. That was rude. I'm usually much better at controlling my reactions."

Erik laughed again, and Emmeline blushed from embarrassment. She looked up, and Anja and Matthew were walking through the courtyard. Anja was talking animatedly, and Matthew was leaning toward her, his glasses sliding down his nose while he listened to her every word. Emmeline looked at Erik, and he was also watching Anja and Matthew as they approached.

He sees it too.

"That took you both a long time to get breakfast." Emmeline smiled sweetly at her brother.

Matthew handed Emmeline an egg sandwich and gave her a look as he passed another to Erik.

He would've chucked that sandwich at me if Anja wasn't beside him.

The sweet smile never left her face.

"We decided to eat first before coming back. No sense in all of us eating a cold breakfast," Anja replied.

"You're so kind." Erik rolled his eyes and stood up. "Emmeline, Matthew, I need to go help with training. It was nice seeing you again." With that, he turned and disappeared among the rest of the nainthe.

"I would like to be trained as well," Emmeline said.

Anja looked confused. "What are you talking about? Ember is training you, remember?"

"No, I mean, I want combat training." Emmeline pointed to the platform. "Like them. I don't want to feel helpless every time a raizour shows up, and I don't want to always rely on you, Erik, or another nainthe to save the day. It would make me feel much better to be able to protect myself."

"It's not that we can't train you, because we can. It's literally what most of us do all day, every day. But you're not us, and you're no match for a raizour, no matter how much training you do."

"I don't care. I want training."

"Fine, but it just means you'll have to spend more time here. It really would be easier if you moved into the Sanctuary."

"Good, and no."

"Great," Anja muttered.

Matthew cleared his throat. "I'd like to be trained too."

"Really, Dr. Matthew?" Anja sighed.

"Yes."

Anja rolled her eyes. "Fine."

PART IV:

FIRSTS

CHAPTER TWENTY-EIGHT

PREMONITION

Emmeline popped her head into Matthew's office and knocked on the open door.

"Mattie, you should come to the Inspire Gala with me tonight."

Matthew didn't bother looking up. "I know you're nervous about going with the mayor to a public event, but it would be even worse if you brought me along. I'm not a chaperone. I also don't have a ticket, and therefore, I don't have a seat. As far as I know, the event has been sold out for weeks."

"You don't think they'd make space if Dr. Taylor-Wu decided he wanted to join the festivities and make a nice, sizable donation? They'd bring in a bigger table if they had to."

"No." Matthew still didn't look up from his work.

"Anja will be there." Emmeline watched as her brother's hand stilled for a moment and then continued writing.

"Is Anja coming with you?" Matthew asked.

"No, she's going with Lesedi. Each time they go to an event, Anja and Lesedi must make a case to Javier and get clearance beforehand."

"Interesting how the nainthe have to keep a low profile, but Javier lets Anja and Lesedi go to events."

"Probably because it's Anja, and he doesn't want to hear it any more than he has to." Emmeline paused. "And likely because he knows Anja will do what she wants, and Lesedi helps keep her out of trouble."

Matthew looked up at Emmeline as she sat across from him.

"It wouldn't be a good idea for me to join. I've been neglecting my work at the hospital, and I have a lot to catch up on."

"Is that the real reason you want to stay away?" Emmeline asked.

Matthew looked back down at his work and ignored her question.

Emmeline leaned across the table. "Mattie."

Matthew looked up, but his face stayed blank.

"Mattie, you're my brother, and I know you. I know you like Anja. I can see it on your face every time you look at her."

"There's just something about her that draws me to her. I don't know why."

"Well, she's honest, to the point of being too blunt; she cares about others way more than she shows or even knows; she's dysfunctionally charismatic; and she can be terrifying when she wants to be. Oh, and not to mention, she's also drop-dead gorgeous. Besides being terrifying, she's pretty much you, but in a different format."

"I don't know why I bother with you," Matthew grumbled.

"It's because I'm your amazing sister."

Matthew sighed and put his pen down. "I can't stop how I feel, but I'll try. I won't go to the gala and will keep my distance.

You're right that no good can come of this. Besides, Anja's in a relationship with Lesedi, whom I also don't mind."

"Open relationship," Emmeline reminded him. "Don't get me wrong. I'm not encouraging you to pursue her because, for one, she likes women, and two, she's not human, which seems to be a pretty important detail."

"I don't even understand what being in an open relationship means," Matthew muttered.

"I don't know either, but it seems to work for them." Emmeline shrugged. "Let me know if you change your mind. Philip said he'll pick me up at five, so I need to get fabulous now."

"I won't change my mind."

Emmeline left Matthew's office and hesitated. She turned back to ask Matthew if he was sure he didn't want to join her, but she stopped and watched him instead. He had picked up his pen again, and it was poised above his file.

Emmeline turned around and made her way back to her room. *He's right. He shouldn't go. I don't want his heart to get broken.*

˜

Emmeline heard the doorbell ring and Mr. Jae's footsteps as he went to open the door. She put on her mother's ring and gave herself a once-over in the mirror before heading downstairs.

Philip was dressed in a tuxedo, and he smiled at Emmeline as she floated down the staircase.

"You look stunning," Philip said.

Emmeline flushed and gave a demure curtsy. The strapless floor-length emerald-green silk gown she had chosen had a sweetheart neckline, fitted bodice, and a flowing skirt. She had tied up her hair into a knot at the nape of her neck, purposely showing off her slender neck and delicate collarbone, and finished off the look with diamond drop earrings and light makeup.

"Shall we?" Philip offered Emmeline his arm.

"You kids have fun and don't stay out too late!" Mr. Jae called out as he closed the door behind them.

Philip parked his car at the grand hall entrance and handed the valet his key before walking over to open the door for Emmeline. She could already see the photographers at the front gate, snapping away at partygoers.

At least these photographers were hired through the organizers. And this time, I'm ready.

Philip extended his hand, and she hesitated before taking it. She stepped out of the car, and her gown fell around her legs, the whisper-light silk flowing in the wind. She settled her arm in Philip's, and they walked toward the photographers.

"Mayor Vil, Ms. Taylor-Wu, may we please have a photograph?" a photographer asked.

"Certainly." Philip placed his arm around Emmeline's silk-clad waist and pulled her close. He leaned into her ear. "Please smile better this time."

Emmeline stiffened but turned to the photographers and gave them a brilliant smile. Philip kissed her on the cheek as the lights flashed, and he waved to the photographers, thanking them for their support. Emmeline looked around and could see partygoers waiting behind them.

"Philip, I think that's enough press pictures. There are people behind us, waiting to get through," Emmeline murmured into his ear, but her smile never left her face.

"Nonsense. They can wait."

He turned back to the photographers and continued to answer questions. Finally, he waved to signal the end of the session, and he and Emmeline walked through the long hallway into the dining hall.

Emmeline took in the opulence of the decorations. Millions of little white lights hung in waves from the ceiling, reflecting off large crystal centerpieces with candles in the middle.

Philip led Emmeline to a table at the center of the hall and pulled out a chair for her. A waiter materialized beside her with a flute of champagne.

"Ms. Taylor-Wu, would you like something to drink?" he asked.

"Just a glass of sparkling water, please. Thank you very much."

Philip raised his finger. "Scotch on the rocks."

"I'll be right back with your requests." The waiter disappeared gracefully.

"You seem quiet, Emmeline."

"I don't enjoy doing press pictures," Emmeline said. She softened her tone. "It's not my style, and I've never been one for it. Also, I don't appreciate being told to *smile better*."

Philip shrugged. "It's a requirement of my job, and it's something you'll have to get used to doing. We all do things we don't particularly enjoy." He touched her cheek and leaned in to kiss her. "I only said you should smile because you light up a room when you do. The last time we took a press picture, you were so uptight. It looked like you didn't want to be there."

That's because I didn't want to be there. At least, not in the picture.

Philip looked around. "I need to make some rounds. Do you want to accompany me? I can do introductions."

"Why don't you go ahead? I need to reply to a few urgent emails that came through tonight. I could use a few minutes to catch up on work." Emmeline hoped her lie was convincing.

The last thing I want to do is schmooze. I really should've stuck to my original plan and come separately—or not at all.

She pulled out her smartphone after Philip left and went through her emails, answering and filing away anything she could. After a few minutes, Emmeline felt a prickly sensation at the back of her neck. She looked around and caught the eye of a man standing at the back of the hall. She went back to her phone and when she turned around again, the man was gone.

Why did it feel like that man was watching me?

Suddenly, a cool presence appeared beside Emmeline, and she yelped.

"Anja, don't do that!" Emmeline gasped.

Anja grinned. "Too easy. Works every time!"

"Lesedi, I don't know how you put up with her. She's like an overgrown child, wrapped in a ridiculously hot body," Emmeline grumbled.

"That feels like an insult and also a compliment. Which one is it?" Anja asked.

"I'm not sure myself." Emmeline turned to Lesedi and smiled appreciatively at her slim-cut white tuxedo. "You are a vision in white, and you look like you're feeling much better."

"I'm fully recovered, thank you. Sometimes, we take our special abilities for granted, and it takes an incident to make us realize what's truly important." Lesedi glanced at Anja, who looked away.

And this is now awkward. I need to stop putting myself in these situations. Why didn't I stay home? I could be reading a good book with a face mask and warm, fuzzy socks on.

"Emmeline, we should talk. Let's go out to the balcony," Anja said. "Lessie, do you mind if I steal her away for a moment?"

"Of course not. I'll get us some drinks."

⁓

Heads turned as Emmeline and Anja walked out onto the balcony. Anja's hair was swept back, and her kohl-rimmed eyes drew all the attention to her icy irises. She wore a midnight-blue halter gown that was short in the front but trailed off into a train in the back. It was a simple dress, but she made it majestic.

I bet there isn't a single person in this room who would be brave enough to approach Anja. She'd devour them on the spot.

"I see you've come with the mayor," Anja said.

Emmeline looked over the balcony and out into the brightly lit city. "Philip wanted to come together. He thought it would bring good publicity for the event."

Anja raised a perfect eyebrow. "Remember what I said about being a prop?"

"I don't think that's what he wants. If all he wanted was a prop, there are so many better options to choose from. Picking a reclusive and opinionated heiress would be on the bottom of the prop list."

"Or maybe at the top of the list."

Emmeline looked at Anja. "You don't like him very much."

"There's something about him that doesn't sit right with me. He doesn't seem truthful. I can see it in his eyes. I usually have a knack for these things." Anja shrugged and looked around. "This is what you'll be doing a lot more of if you continue seeing him."

Emmeline exhaled. "I'm not meant for this type of life. There's a reason why I only attend a handful of events every year. I love doing philanthropic work, but only behind the scenes. I think I'm too much of a homebody."

"You have a much greater purpose now," Anja said.

"I'm pretty sure I'm still useless to the nainthe."

"It'll come. There's no other choice."

Emmeline changed the topic. "What did you want to talk to me about?"

"Do you remember how we had a conversation about there potentially being a traitor among us?" Anja asked.

Emmeline nodded, her heart sinking into the pit of her stomach.

"My brother has been doing some investigating. He found that the locks had been tampered with internally. You wouldn't be able to tell just from looking at the surface."

"How did he know to look inside?"

"He was adamant he had secured the locks himself, and Quinn and Mihal had taken turns double-checking his work. That night, after the attack, Erik took one of the locks because he wanted to know what had gone wrong. The lock appeared to be in working order, and if you only looked at it superficially, you would assume that it failed because it wasn't secured. When my brother took apart the lock, he noticed the locking mechanism had been disabled and manually shifted to one side, so the raizour only needed to twist it to get out."

"But whoever did this would've known they'd be discovered."

Anja's eyes sharpened as she leaned against the balcony, staring over the streets below. "Agreed. Erik went back to check the other locks, which were in perfect working order. Whoever did this must have gone back and fixed the other locks. My brother still blames himself for Quinn's and Mihal's deaths, and he's been pushing himself harder every night to try to make up for it."

"But it wasn't his fault. He didn't kill them. The raizour did."

"Many of us have told him that." Anja scowled. "Believe me, when I find out who did this, I'll make them suffer."

I believe you. I would never want to be on your bad side.

Emmeline racked her brain. "I saw Javier use his handprint to get into the underground caverns. There must be a log of who went in and out of the place. Did anyone check the history?"

"Erik checked, and no one besides him, Quinn, and Mihal had gone in and out of the prison area between the previous night and the night you came to the Sanctuary. Erik couldn't pinpoint any activity afterward since they left the door open due to the complete shit show that happened. There were so many nainthe going in and out that it would be impossible to narrow it down to a list of suspects."

"I wish I could be of more help with this," Emmeline sighed.

"The fact that you're still talking to us is more than any of us could've hoped for."

"I should head back inside. Philip's probably wondering where I am." Emmeline turned around, and she stopped in her tracks.

That man again!

Emmeline could see the reflection of the same man who had been watching her earlier in one of the large windows.

"Anja, don't look right away, but I think there's someone following me. I've seen the same person twice now, watching me from a distance. He's by the large window in a dark suit and is bald with olive skin," Emmeline whispered.

Anja plastered a fun smile on her face and turned toward the windows, her sharp eyes scanning the area. "If he was there, he's gone now." She took out her phone. "I'll ask Lessie to look around."

"Am I imagining things? I can't tell anymore."

"I felt the same way when I first became a nainthe."

Emmeline started walking back to the balcony doors when Anja pulled on her arm.

"Did Matthew come with you? I haven't seen him yet," Anja asked.

"No, I asked him to come with me, but he said he had too much work to catch up on."

"Oh." Anja fidgeted with the ring on her finger.

"Have you spoken to him since we were last at the Sanctuary?"

"No." The ring twirled around between Anja's fingers, and then it stopped. "Let's go back inside. I'll keep an eye out for that man you mentioned. Are you making any speeches tonight?"

Emmeline shook her head.

"Good, because your last speech was terrible."

"That's one hundred percent your and Lesedi's fault," Emmeline shot back.

Anja laughed, and Emmeline stuck out her tongue at Anja's regal back as she walked inside the dining hall.

CHAPTER TWENTY-NINE

EARLY WARNINGS

The valet pulled up with Philip's car and handed him the keys. Philip opened the passenger door for Emmeline and closed it with a soft click once she and her gown were safely inside. He drove off to the side and put the car in park.

"Emmeline, I forgot to give something to Juliette Pak, the fundraiser organizer. Do you mind waiting a few minutes? I'll be right back."

"I'll be fine here. Take your time."

Philip left the ignition on and buttoned back up his tuxedo jacket as he jogged back into the grand hall.

Why would you leave the ignition on?

Emmeline reached over and turned off the car engine. She pulled out her phone and messaged Anja.

Emia	I just left the gala. Were you able to find anything on the man who was watching me?
Anja:	Yes. Will be by your house later.

Anja: Saadah is supposed to come tonight to watch over you. I gave him the key to the balcony door.

Emmeline placed her phone on her lap just as Philip climbed back into the car.

He looked at his dashboard and furrowed his brow. "I swear I left the car on."

"Oh, I turned it off. Bad for the environment."

"That was presumptuous of you to do."

Emmeline looked at him with surprise. "Is it really that big of a deal?"

"If it's not a big deal, then why did you do it?"

Emmeline stared at him. "Don't worry—I won't touch your car again."

Philip blinked, and the anger vanished from his eyes. "You're right; it's not a big deal. It's fine." He pushed the ignition button to restart the car.

Someone's neurotic about their car. Emmeline resisted rolling her eyes as she settled back into her seat.

"Did you have a good time tonight?" Philip asked.

"It was no different than any other event I go to."

"But you were with me tonight."

"Did you have a good time?" Emmeline deflected the question back to Philip.

"I had a great time. I was able to make a few connections that I had hoped for, so I'd say the night was an overall success."

"That's good," Emmeline murmured. She stared out the windshield as Anja drove past her in a black SUV.

"You look stunning tonight." Philip leaned over and reached

under her chin to pull her face up to meet his. He pressed his lips to hers and deepened the kiss.

Emmeline pulled away, and her breath caught in her throat. Philip's face was flushed, and she could see the want in his eyes.

"Would you like to come to my place tonight?" Philip asked in a low voice.

Emmeline looked away, clearing her throat. "I don't think I'm ready for that yet."

Philip nodded and let out a deep breath. "Let me take you home."

He shifted stiffly in his seat and pulled the car out of the parking lot. They drove in silence until they reached the tree-lined roads that led back to Emmeline's home.

"I saw you with your friend from that time we went to the Thai restaurant. Her name is Anja, right? Does she happen to be at every event you attend?"

Emmeline froze.

I never told you her name.

Did I?

She looked at Philip and tried to keep her voice neutral. "I have no idea. We aren't close. Why do you ask?"

"Is she single? One of my colleagues was wondering." He glanced at Emmeline before looking back at the road.

"She has a partner."

I'd better ask Anja about her name later. I could've sworn she went by a fake name.

Philip turned onto Emmeline's driveway and parked in front of the main entrance. He got out of the driver's seat and walked around the car to open the door for Emmeline. As soon as she stepped out of the car, he wrapped his arm around her waist and pulled her against him.

"I want you, Emmeline." Philip leaned in and kissed her. He pressed her against the car and groaned into her mouth, his desire acutely evident against her abdomen.

This is too soon.

Emmeline pulled away from him.

"Can I come in?" Philip asked hoarsely.

Emmeline took a deep breath. "It's probably a good idea for us to say good night out here."

"Why?" Philip kept his arm wrapped tightly around her waist.

"I ... I'm just not ready," Emmeline stammered. Her hand went to Philip's chest to create some space between them.

Without warning, the front door swung open, and the bright lights from the foyer flooded the entrance. Mr. Jae stepped onto the landing.

"You kids are back! What a coincidence. I was just about to go out and grab a midnight snack for Ms. Rose and myself. Do you kids want me to pick something up for you as well?"

Philip backed away from Emmeline and straightened his jacket. Emmeline smoothed down the green silk of her gown and stepped to the side.

"I was just about to come inside, Mr. Jae." Emmeline picked up her gown and moved past Philip. "I'll see you later, Philip."

"Good night, Emmeline."

Emmeline only nodded and hurried up the steps. As she stepped over the threshold, Mr. Jae came back inside the house with her and closed the door behind him. He fastened the dead bolt, and the smile disappeared from his face.

"Thanks, Mr. Jae. Which restaurant are you getting food from?"

"I wasn't going to get food. Ms. Rose saw Philip's car pull up the driveway and asked me to open the door for you. I saw your face, and you didn't look like you wanted to be where you were, so I made up an excuse to insert my presence."

"I wasn't ready for what he wanted. Not yet."

Mr. Jae looked hard at her. "You never need to justify why you don't want to do something."

"I know."

"Good."

"Can you let Ms. Rose know I'm going to have some guests in the garden tonight?"

"So late? Some competition for the mayor?" Mr. Jae raised an eyebrow.

"No, just a couple of friends stopping by for a quick chat. That's it. No need for any refreshments or anything."

"You let me or Ms. Rose know if you need anything."

CHAPTER THIRTY

REMARKABLE

Emmeline stepped out onto the patio with two coffees, a pitcher of water and two glasses. Anja and Lesedi were already seated and talking in low voices, both still in their evening wear from the gala.

"Oh, coffee! Thank you. You're the best." Anja batted her long eyelashes at Emmeline.

"Lesedi, I know you don't drink coffee, so I brought you water."

"Thank you, Emmeline." Lesedi poured herself a generous glass.

Anja looked at the extra glass. "Who's that for?"

"Saadah. Do you want to ask him to join us? He doesn't have to hide out in the room." Emmeline noticed a fleeting look of disappointment on Anja's face.

Should I tell Mattie that Anja and Lesedi are here? He can choose whether he wants to join. Emmeline pulled out her phone.

Emia: Mattie, I'm outside on the patio with Anja and Lesedi. You're welcome to join us, but I understand if you prefer not to.

She waited but didn't hear back from her brother. Looking up, she saw Anja and Lesedi watching her.

"What? Do I have something on my face?" Emmeline asked.

"It looked to me that the mayor wanted to get hot and heavy with you, but you weren't in the mood," Anja said.

Lesedi gave Anja a disapproving look. "We weren't spying on you. We just happened to arrive soon after you got home."

"My sex life, or lack thereof, is off-limits for any discussion."

"You had the perfect opportunity, but you didn't want it," Anja pointed out.

Emmeline buried her face in her hands. "It didn't feel like the right time yet. Sometimes, I wish I could separate my heart and body. I'd certainly get a lot more action that way."

"How long has it been?"

"Didn't I just say off-limits?"

"You offered more information. I'm just following your lead."

Emmeline sighed. "Let's just say *too long* and leave it at that."

"Let me know if you want me to remind the mayor where his hands need to stay. I'd be happy to send a strongly worded message... or more." Anja's irises glittered like glass.

Emmeline was about to reply when she felt a faint gust of air to her left. Saadah walked up the patio steps and nodded his head in greeting to the three of them.

"Saadah, when you're here, you're not relegated to the guest room. I've already let Ms. Rose and Mr. Jae know I have guests. It would be strange if they only heard said guests, but never actually saw them," Emmeline said.

"The guest bedroom has everything I need." Saadah helped himself to a glass of water. "Your home is incredible. I get why you don't want to move to the Sanctuary."

"It's too big for just the three of us. Well, now, four again, but still. The maintenance cost of this property is exorbitant, but it's my home, and I love it," Emmeline admitted as she looked around the expansive garden. "Anja, you said you found something on the man who was following me?"

"Yes." Using a napkin, Anja reached into a small bag and pulled out three wallets and put them on the table. "Your description was vague, so we found three people who matched it and lifted their wallets."

Emmeline's mouth dropped. "You stole wallets at a charity gala?"

"Misappropriated," Anja corrected her. "Don't worry; I'll make sure each one gets back to the rightful owner if it was a mistake."

Saadah threw his head back and laughed. He leaned over to Anja and gave her a fist bump.

"What if someone saw you? Or what if you were caught on camera?" Emmeline threw up her hands.

"You need to give us more credit. Trust me, no one saw us, and there aren't cameras in the dining hall. The identifications of three men are there for you to examine. Just don't touch the wallets directly since we wouldn't want anyone to find your fingerprints or DNA on them," Anja replied.

"I'll have Eva do some digging."

Lesedi straightened. "Who's Eva?"

"She's one of my best friends, and she manages all my technology security. She's discreet, and she knows how not to leave a trace. Don't worry; I won't tell her about this thing." Emmeline waved her hand in the air at the three nainthe.

Suddenly, her phone buzzed against the patio table.

Mattie: I'm home.

Emmeline heard the door slide open behind her and turned around just as Matthew stepped out onto the patio. He was still in his office uniform of a white dress shirt, gray blazer, and black dress pants.

"Mattie, did you just come home from the hospital?" Emmeline looked at the time on her phone. "It's past midnight."

"I had a lot of work to catch up on." Matthew pushed up his glasses and ran his hand through his hair. He turned to the nainthe, nodding his head to greet them. "It's nice to see you all again."

Emmeline frowned. "It's not healthy for you to work such long hours. Is this what you do when you live on your own?"

"I'm fine." Matthew's eyes lingered on Anja. "What brings you all here tonight? Did something happen?"

Emmeline updated Matthew on the strange man she'd encountered and the three wallets Anja had procured.

"Do you want me to reach out to Eva?" Matthew asked.

"No, you have enough on your plate. I'll message her in the morning."

Lesedi cleared her throat. "I don't think you should ask your friend to do this. It might raise more questions, and we don't want to risk any exposure."

"I trust Eva. Her entire world is about being discreet."

"I still don't think it's a good idea."

"I wasn't asking for permission, Lesedi. This has nothing to do with the nainthe," Emmeline replied.

Lesedi pressed her lips into a firm line but remained silent.

Saadah pretended to look at his watch. "Well, this was a nice break. I had a long day of training, and our team had to me equipment out of the library basement. I'm going to head back to the guest room and get some sleep. Emmeline, you know how to reach me?"

Emmeline nodded. "Anja sent your contact over to me already. I appreciate you watching over us."

"Saadah, if you're tired, I can take over for tonight," Anja offered.

Saadah's face lit up. "Really? I mean, it's not that I don't want to be here, but I'm just drained."

Lesedi looked at Anja sharply. "We're still dressed in our evening wear. You don't have clothes or armor, and your blade's back at the Sanctuary."

Saadah shifted his feet. "I can handle it tonight, Anja."

"Nonsense. We can't have someone tired on guard duty. It's fine. Just take my next shift. Can you leave me your blade?"

"Deal! All right, I'm going to head out."

Saadah unhooked his blade, took out the balcony door key from his pocket, and handed both to Anja. He jogged off the property, and a few seconds later, Emmeline heard the faint rumble of a motorcycle drive off into the night.

"He really couldn't wait to leave, could he?" Emmeline remarked, a smile pulling at the corners of her mouth.

"That's Saadah for you." Anja shrugged and turned to Lesedi. "Do you want to stay?"

Lesedi stood up, and her copper eyes cooled. "I think I'll head home."

"Take the car. I'll grab a taxi in the morning."

"Anja, I can take you home tomorrow. You're already spending your night here. It's the least I can do," Matthew said.

"Good night, Emmeline, Matthew." Lesedi turned and strode out of the garden.

She didn't say good night to Anja. She must know something's up.

"In hindsight, Saadah and Lesedi could've taken the car together and left you the motorcycle," Emmeline said.

"That's disgusting. I'm not wearing someone else's helmet," Anja sniffed.

"But you're willing to use someone else's weapon?"

"Completely different things."

"Right." Emmeline rolled her eyes. "Let's go inside. I'll get you some spare clothes."

They all stood, and Emmeline walked ahead to open the patio doors. She turned just as Matthew moved a chair out of Anja's way, and she heard his voice even though it was low.

"Anja, you look…" Matthew searched for the right word. "Remarkable."

Anja flashed him a devastating smile. "I know."

Emmeline turned around and headed into the house.

Mattie, you're in big trouble.

∽

Emmeline picked out a brand-new, long-sleeved cashmere shirt and a clean pair of leggings for Anja.

I hope Mattie knows what he's doing. I don't want his heart to get broken. But if I didn't know any better, I'd think Anja might feel something for him too.

Emmeline went to her bathroom and grabbed a small pack of makeup remover wipes, one of her luxury face creams, and a new travel toothbrush.

What good could come out of this? Mattie, you could have your pick of women, but the one who finally catches your interest is only gay, but also isn't human, Emmeline grumbled to herself. *Anja, if you hurt my brother, I'm never speaking to you again.*

She ran back downstairs and followed the faint voices to the kitchen. Glancing at the moonlit windows in the hallway, she quickened her pace and let out a breath when she reached the kitchen. Anja sat at the center island with the train of her gown draped over the low back of the stool. Her forearms were stretched out, and her pale skin glowed against the quartz countertop. Matthew had discarded his blazer and rolled up his shirtsleeves. He sat beside Anja, his elbow resting close to hers, highlighting how his rosy-gold undertones contrasted against her pale Scandinavian skin.

Emmeline stood at the doorway and watched them. She couldn't hear what they were saying, but she could see Anja smiling and talking and Matthew mostly listening. Anja leaned toward Matthew, but she kept a small space between them.

Emmeline pretended to cough.

That was terrible.

Matthew stood up and looked awkwardly at Emmeline. She raised her eyebrows at him.

Are you sure you know what you're doing, Mattie?

He gave her the slightest shrug and looked away.

"Anja, I brought you clothes to change into and some toiletries," Emmeline said.

"Oh good, thank you. I'd love to get out of this dress despite how fabulous it is." Anja took the items from Emmeline's hands and set them down on the counter.

"I'm going to turn in for the night. Mattie, can you remember to arm the security system before going upstairs?"

"Yes, I'll do that after I find something to eat. I haven't had dinner yet." Matthew looked at Anja. "Are you hungry?"

"Famished," Anja admitted. "What do you offer, Dr. Matthew?"

Emmeline waited for Matthew's answer.

This ought to be entertaining.

Matthew looked helplessly at Emmeline, and she rolled her eyes. She went to the freezer and rummaged through a shelf, pulling out two frozen tonkatsu ramen from a local artisan shop.

"Is this acceptable?" Emmeline asked.

Anja eyed the noodles. "Yes, that's perfect!"

Emmeline handed the two packages to Matthew. "Heat on medium and stir until it boils. That's it. Can you handle that, Doctor?"

Matthew glared at her and snatched the frozen noodles from her hands.

You just wait, Emia, he silently threatened.

Emmeline gave him her sweetest sisterly smile, and he followed up with another look.

Please leave.

Emmeline sighed. "Good night, Mattie, Anja. See you in the morning."

CHAPTER THIRTY-ONE

A SEEKER WHO CANNOT SEE

Bile rose in Emmeline's throat, and she bent her head to the side, retching violently. Tears ran down her cheeks as she looked up. Anja's eyes stared back at her, her mouth parted in a silent scream and almost touching the floor. Blood from her torn throat pooled around her perfect face and trickled across the floor.

Anja, I'm sorry!

Emmeline sobbed and turned her head away. She wiped the tears from her face but pulled her sticky hand away in horror. Thick blood clung to her skin, and the sharp, metallic smell assaulted her nose, making her gag again. She looked to her side at a set of pale fingers reaching out toward her, unmoving on the stone floor. Her eyes drifted up the long limb to Erik's lifeless face, his ash eyes devoid of light and his mouth parted in surprise. Blood drained from his torn throat and stained the floor a deep scarlet.

No, Erik! It's all my fault. I'm sorry.

Emmeline heaved again, and the bile burned her throat. She wiped the side of her mouth with the back of her hand and forced herself to her feet. She pulled her matted hair off her face and looked around. There were dead nainthe everywhere, each with their throats torn out, their eyes cold and unseeing, their bodies drenched with blood. A shrill howl echoed through the caverns, and Emmeline ran toward the sound, her bare feet slipping over the stone.

She skidded to a stop.

Don't you fucking dare!

Matthew was on his knees, and a raizour's claw gripped his hair.

"Let my brother go, or I'll kill you myself! Let my brother go, you piece of shit," Emmeline screamed.

The raizour grinned, its sharp teeth gleaming with the blood of dead nainthe.

"Mattie, fight back!"

Matthew looked at her, and she bit back a sob. For the first time in her life, she saw fear in her brother's eyes. He opened his mouth, but no sound came out, though she knew what he was saying.

Emia, run!

Emmeline felt a vicious tug in her head, and her body lurched forward.

What good is a seeker who cannot see? The raizour laughed. *Everyone and everything you love will die, and it will be because you are weak and useless.*

The raizour lifted a sharp claw against Matthew's throat. *Even your Executioner has fallen. You could have stopped all of this and saved your brother. You could have saved them all. All this blood and death is on your hands.*

With a swift flick of its claw, the raizour slit open Matthew's throat. It let go of his head, and his body slumped to the ground.

Emmeline fell to her knees and let out a bloodcurdling scream. Her body warmed, and a spark stopped her heart.

And then she felt herself die.

Emmeline sat up and panted, her heart pounding through her chest. She touched her face and body, and sighed with relief.

Just a dream.

She reached over to her nightstand and switched on the light.

More like a nightmare.

She swung her legs over the side of her bed and stood up. She grimaced as she peeled off her sticky nightdress and welcomed the cool air against her skin.

I need a drink of water.

She slipped into a new dress.

I feel so much safer when Anja's here.

Emmeline paused after she shut her bedroom door. She closed her eyes and focused.

Ember said I should be able to feel the nainthe and raizour when they're near. I can feel Anja's presence, but nothing else.

She jogged down the stairs, past her and Matthew's offices and the great room.

She stopped in her tracks.

What in the world?

The great room was the one room in the house besides the kitchen and office, she used the most. It had a large-screen television and an enormous sofa, accompanied by matching ottomans that could be pushed up against it to make a bed. The high ceilings and embedded sound system made it feel like a private theater. It was her favorite room to relax in, and on occasion, Ms. Rose or Mr. Jae would find her in the morning, fast asleep underneath a cozy blanket with the television still on.

Emmeline doubled back to the great room. Her jaw dropped, and her eyes widened at the sight in front of her. Sitting in her favorite spot was Matthew, sound asleep with his head leaned back against the sofa. He was still in his dress shirt and dress pants, and his glasses were on the side table beside a glass of water and the television remote. Matthew asleep in the great room didn't surprise her, but the lithe body curled up beside him did. Anja's head rested on Matthew's shoulder, and her eyes were closed in peaceful sleep. The moonlight softened her features, and her skin was dewy and devoid of any traces of makeup from the gala.

She looks so young.

A blanket was draped over Anja's torso, and her bare feet poked out from underneath.

At least they still have their clothes on!

Emmeline shuddered at the mental picture and pretended to scrub her brain with bleach.

Maybe they accidentally fell asleep while watching a show?

She tiptoed to the side table and picked up the remote to turn off the television. She grabbed another blanket from the storage bench.

I know you're an adult, Mattie, but I still don't want to see you get hurt.

She shook out the blanket over him and folded his glasses properly. She turned and walked out of the room as quietly as she had entered it. Neither Matthew nor Anja stirred from their sleep.

I'd better warn Ms. Rose and Mr. Jae that Mattie has a guest over and to be quiet in the morning.

Emmeline gave the two of them one last look before unhooking the pocket doors and pulling them shut behind her.

CHAPTER THIRTY-TWO

STALKED

Emia: Eva, I need your help. Off the record.

Eva: Switch over to the BlindBlink app and message me there.

Emmeline left her messaging application and went into BlindBlink. The application had what Eva affectionately termed as "self-destruct mode." All messages disappeared after being read, and no other applications or functions could work while a user was in it.

Eva: What do you need?

Emia: I need to track down the history of three men. Employment, associates, everything. Can you help me? I need it as soon as possible.

Eva: Are you in trouble?

Emia: I'm not sure. I went to the Inspire Gala, and a man was following me. I had an associate try to find out who it was, and I got three names. It could be one of the three or maybe none of the three.

Eva: Give me the names. If he has a digital footprint, I'll find him. I know you don't like it, but you should consider better physical security. I'll let you know as soon as I have something.

Emia: Thanks, Eva. Appreciate your help. If something does stick out, I'll pass the file over to our security.

Emmeline sent Eva the details of the three names and clicked off her phone screen.

Let's see what's happening downstairs.

～

Emmeline expected the door to the great room to still be closed when she came downstairs, but the doors were wide open, and the space was tidy.

Are Mattie and Anja in the kitchen?

She walked into the kitchen, and Ms. Rose was seated at the island, her reading glasses perched on her nose as she flipped through the morning paper.

"Good morning, Ms. Rose." Emmeline kissed her on the cheek. "Have you seen Mattie?"

And his guest.

"I haven't. I came downstairs at eight o'clock, and Mattie and his *friend* had already left. I think he went to take her home. His car isn't in the garage." Ms. Rose took a sip of her tea.

Interesting. You can't avoid us forever.

"Emia, darling, tell me more about this friend of Mattie's."

Emmeline tried to think quickly. "He met her at the Royal Children's Rehabilitation Hospital gala."

Ms. Rose peered at Emmeline. "Mattie doesn't bring friends home, especially not for a sleepover. This one must be special."

Emmeline shrugged. "You know Mattie; he's very private."

"Maybe this one's *the one* for him?"

"Maybe."

∽

Emia: Mattie, I'm going to head to the Sanctuary for my training session with Ember. Are you still at work? You didn't come home for dinner.

Mattie: I'm backed up at the hospital. Still have lots to catch up on. You go ahead. Message me when you get inside the Sanctuary.

Emia: What happened last night?

Emmeline waited but didn't receive a message back from her brother. She tucked her phone back into her tote and headed downstairs to the garage.

If I didn't know better, I'd say he's avoiding Anja again.

She climbed into her SUV and pushed the ignition button.

Or maybe he's avoiding Lesedi. Probably a smart move to stay away.

Emmeline selected her favorite playlist and turned up the volume before heading out. She bobbed her head to the beat of the music as she routinely checked her rearview mirror.

Why does it feel like that black sedan's following me?

She made a few random turns, and without fail, the black sedan followed her at a distance.

Emmeline tapped a button on her steering wheel. "Call Anja."

"What's wrong?" Anja answered after the first ring.

"How do you know something's wrong?"

"Because you never call me. Are you and Mattie okay?"

Oh, it's Mattie now, is it?

"Mattie's fine. He's at work. I'm driving to the Sanctuary, and I think a car is following me. I've made a few turns, and it's still behind me. I don't want to lead them to the Sanctuary. Should I head back home?"

"What kind of car is it, and where are you now?"

"It's a black sedan." Emmeline rattled off the make, license plate, and her location.

"Drive past the intersection six blocks north of the Sanctuary and make a right at the next opportunity. That'll take you to the Square. Make a few loops, as if you were looking for street parking. Two motorcycles will be out to intercept and create enough distance so you can lose whoever's following you. Once you've lost them, you can make your way to the Sanctuary."

"Got it."

Emmeline hung up and focused on driving according to Anja's instructions. As she looped around the Square and slowed down periodically to pretend to look for parking, she could see the black sedan continue to follow her from several cars behind.

Just as she was about to make another loop, she heard a loud rumble. Sure enough, two black sport motorcycles came in between the car behind her and revved their engines. One of the motorcyclists lifted their blacked-out visor, and a pair of sharp ash eyes looked directly at her side mirror, making eye contact with her.

Erik!

Emmeline breathed a sigh of relief as he flipped down his visor and revved his engine again. The traffic light turned green, and it took all of her self-control not to speed off. She drove forward and turned instead of continuing the loop. Looking in her rearview mirror, she could see the two motorcycles stopped in the street, as if stalled.

Time to make myself scarce.

CHAPTER THIRTY-THREE

MOMENTUM

"Have you been practicing?" Ember asked Emmeline.

"Yes, but I haven't had much luck. I think it's because there haven't been any nainthe or raizour around when I get to practice. I usually try before breakfast, during the lunch hour, or after dinner."

"Just continue practicing your focus and letting your mind reach. When you come to the Sanctuary, you can have your pick of nainthe to search for," Ember said. "Let's get to work, so you don't have to spend all night here."

She tossed a floor pillow to Emmeline, and they both sat down cross-legged. Emmeline closed her eyes and took a deep breath to get herself to relax.

"Why is it that, sometimes, I can feel the presence of a nainthe or raizour, but other times, I can't?"

"I don't know," Ember admitted. "It could depend on your state of mind, or it could be something unrelated."

Emmeline steadied her breathing as a small light came into her view. A dark, hazy aura curled around the light tendrils that sparked at the center of the cocoon.

"Ember, I think I can see you."

The aura and lights drifted around her before slowly fading into darkness. Emmeline opened her eyes and looked around.

"I'm over here," Ember called out.

Emmeline turned around, and Ember was on the other side of the room. She skipped back over to Emmeline and grabbed her shoulders.

"Did you see the aura move?" Ember asked.

Emmeline nodded. "It went around me and then disappeared."

"You saw me! Let's keep working on this, and soon, we can move on to stretching your mind to see nainthe you're unaware of."

Emmeline grinned at Ember's enthusiasm, and her heart flipped with exhilaration.

"I'll bring you to Javier. He wanted to see you after tonight's training session. He'll be ecstatic at your improvement!"

"Pretty sure the word *ecstatic* isn't in Javier's vocabulary," Emmeline said dryly.

"You're probably right," Ember laughed.

Finally, some progress. Maybe I'm not so useless after all.

⁓

Emmeline knocked firmly on Javier's office door. Maybe a little too firmly.

Act confident. Don't ever let anyone walk all over you.

The office door slid open, and she stepped through it with her head held high and her mouth set in a firm line.

Javier immediately stood up from behind his desk and walked over to meet her. He was dressed in the nainthe's standard slim-fitted black outfit, and his armor hung on several hooks to the side of his desk.

"Good evening, Emmeline. It's been a while since we've spoken. How's training going?"

"Slow, but there's some progress. I was able to see Ember today."

"That's too slow, and you should practice more. You need to give serious consideration to moving here."

Emmeline stiffened. "Out of the question. I've already addressed this several times and dislike repeating myself."

Javier glared at Emmeline, but she met him unblinkingly.

I've met many people like you, Javier, who think they can tell me what to do or how to behave. Don't you dare think for a minute that I'll be a pushover.

Javier relented. "Then, you need to commit to spending more time here."

"I already spend a lot of time here. You understand I run my family's foundation and sit on several boards, right?"

"Those will be meaningless if you don't develop your ability as a seeker. Your role here far outweighs any other obligations you think you have."

Emmeline narrowed her eyes. "I can see you're great at negotiations. I'd better take my leave before we reach another disagreement."

"We might have disagreements, but we shouldn't stop talking. I can't have distrust among the ranks."

"I'm not here to create distrust, drama, or whatever else you want to call it. I'm trying to become the thing you all keep saying I am."

Javier sighed. "Maybe you're right. Let's continue this conversation another time. I hope, in time, you'll learn to trust me and my judgment even though you don't like how I deliver the message."

"I'll come to see you again the next time I'm here."

Emmeline turned and left Javier's office. It nagged her that maybe—just maybe—he might be right.

CHAPTER THIRTY-FOUR

JUST A NAME

Emmeline was walking back to the underground garage when her phone vibrated.

Maybe it's Anja. I haven't seen her the whole night. Is she avoiding me?

Eva: We need to talk.

Emia: Give me a minute.

Emmeline walked back to the courtyard and found a secluded table. She looked up to search for Anja's and Erik's rooms, but both rooms were dark.

Maybe they're both out on a hunt.

She opened the BlindBlink application on her phone.

Emia: I'm ready. What did you find?

Eva: When I looked into the three names, none seemed out of the ordinary. Regular jobs, families, and

	run-of-the-mill social media profiles, but then I ran the license plate you gave me from the car that was following you, and it linked back to a company one of the men is employed at. The company is a private asset management firm for high-net-worth clients.
Emia:	Why would a private asset management firm be interested in me?
Eva:	It seemed odd to me, too, but one of their privileged client services is investigations.

Why would someone hire a private investigator to follow me?

Emia:	Did you find a file on me?
Eva:	I haven't been able to get past their firewall. I know you've upped your security, but I strongly advise you add physical security. Also, you need to warn Ms. Rose and Mr. Jae. I've asked your security company to come by your house tomorrow, and Sally and I will accompany them on a site check. Don't leave any of your vehicles parked in the driveway, and for the love of any higher power that might exist, don't leave your gates unlocked!
Emia:	I'm worried.

Eva: I know. I'll find out who's behind this, and we'll sic your lawyers on them.

Emia: Thanks, Eva. I'll see you in the morning.

Emmeline logged out of the application and sent a quick note to Ms. Rose and Mr. Jae to remind them to arm the security system. She tapped out a short message to Matthew.

Emia: Mattie, keep aware of your surroundings. I'm being followed, and I don't know if that includes you. Make sure no one follows you home. Saadah's on watch tonight. I'll see if Anja or Ellis can escort me after training.

Mattie: I'm still at the hospital, but I'll leave in the next hour. I'll wait up for you.

Emia: When I get home, you and I are going to have a talk about how much you're working and how important work-life balance is.

She didn't wait for Matthew to respond and clicked off her phone. As she stood to leave, she heard a faint beating of wings and looked up at the midnight sky. A figure barreled toward the courtyard and was holding what looked like a smaller body of a raizour.

Erik's back from a hunt.

Remembering his earlier warning, Emmeline stayed where she was and crossed her arms over her chest. Erik landed with a soft thump close to the platform and dropped a raizour body on the grass. A nainthe in full armor ran over and picked up the body, nodding to Erik before sprinting toward the underground caverns.

He doesn't look as bad as the last time I saw him.
Emmeline twisted her ring as she watched him.
Are you okay, Erik? Why are you breathing so hard?
Before she could finish her thoughts, Erik leaped into the air and flew over her, toward his room. He landed on the balcony edge and hopped off, tilting his shoulders so his wings wouldn't scrape along the overhead. He staggered to his door and clutched the doorframe before pushing it open and disappearing into the darkness.

Emmeline stood, rooted to her spot, and stared at the dark doorway.

He should be fine soon. He seemed to have a much more severe reaction last time.

She touched her wrist as her conscience weighed on her.
I know he told me to stay away.
She picked up her tote bag off the chair and looked uncertainly at the entrance to the parking garage and then back at Erik's room. She steeled herself and walked toward the stairs.
I'll check on him and make sure he's okay.

Emmeline pushed open the door to Erik's room and poked her head in.
He must be in the bedroom or bathroom.

She closed the door and dropped her tote bag on the floor. Tiptoeing past the kitchen and sitting area, she made her way to Erik's bedroom.

He's not in his bedroom.

She approached the bathroom and stood at the doorway, peering through the wide crack.

"I told you that you shouldn't be here." Erik's usually melodic voice was raspy as it came around the corner.

Emmeline pushed open the door and stepped into the bathroom, keeping her back to the wall. Erik was sitting on the floor in nainthe form with his eyes closed, his chest rising and falling sharply.

"It's just me, Emmeline."

"I know."

"You recognize me?"

"Yes."

Emmeline bit her lip. "Last time, you didn't recognize me. How did you know it was me?"

"I remember the sound of your footsteps." Erik opened his eyes, and his icy irises glowed. "Why are you here? You should leave."

Emmeline knelt on the cool tiles and scooted closer to him. "I saw you come back from a hunt and thought I should check on you. The last time I saw you, you didn't look well. You told me it wasn't safe, so I tried to be more careful this time."

"I'll be fine. I just need some time." Erik turned his face away and grimaced in pain.

"You're not fine. Look at you. You can't even change back into your human form. The nainthe shouldn't leave you to suffer on your own."

Emmeline reached over to grip Erik's hand, and his long fingers closed loosely over hers. Her heart dipped as their skin touched, and they sat in silence for several moments with only the sound of Erik's harsh breathing and her own pounding heart for company.

I wish I could take some of your pain away.
She closed her eyes, and her hand warmed. Suddenly, Erik groaned, and his chest constricted.

"I don't want to do this anymore." Erik closed his eyes, and he seemed to be talking to himself.

Emmeline's heart stopped.

He wouldn't hurt himself, would he?

Emmeline slipped her hand out of Erik's and scooted closer to him. She ducked under his outstretched wings and put her arms around his shoulders. He smelled of citrus and cedar, and it reminded her of that fateful night he had saved her life.

"No one should have to go through what you go through alone," Emmeline said.

After a few moments, Erik leaned his cheek against Emmeline's head, and they fell silent. Emmeline closed her eyes, and she felt a wetness against her cheek.

Those tears aren't mine. Oh, Erik, how long have you been carrying this burden?

"Maybe I can distract you a little bit. I can share something about myself, and maybe later, you can share something about yourself with me," Emmeline said.

Darkness settled in her mind and wrapped itself around her and Erik. There was a light pulse against her, but all she could feel was profound sadness.

"When I was a baby, my *poh poh* and *gung gung*, who were my maternal grandparents, came over from Hong Kong to visit my mother and meet me for the first time. They couldn't speak much English and had a lot of trouble pronouncing my name, so my parents shortened my name to Emmie for them. And in classic Chinese fashion, where they loved to end all sentences and expressions with the word *ah*, they ended up calling me Emmie-ah. It stuck, and eventually, I became Emia. No one calls me that anymore, only my family and best friends—and that's only because they've known me for so long."

"Emia—that's what your brother calls you," Erik murmured beside her ear. Her name rolled off his tongue, and most of the roughness was gone from his melodic voice.

Emmeline nodded. "Was I able to distract you with some useless information?" She disentangled herself from him and opened her eyes. "Erik, you've changed back!"

Erik opened his eyes, and his irises were still expanded, but otherwise, he was back in human form. The silver flecks in his eyes burned bright, and he watched her strangely. Emmeline suddenly felt self-conscious about her appearance, and she tucked her hair behind her ear while attempting to smooth out her long waves.

"This is progress, isn't it? How do you feel?"

"Tired and hungry." Erik must've noticed her frown. "But better," he added quickly.

"Doesn't anyone ever come to see if you're okay?"

Erik shook his head. "I could've hurt you. You're lucky this episode wasn't as bad as the others. I've hurt others before, and I hurt you last time." He glanced at her wrist before looking away.

"That was nothing compared to what could've happened. You can't put yourself at risk like that."

"Then, maybe you should lock your door."

"I might have to start doing so."

"You know that's not the answer." Emmeline frowned at him again.

Mattie!

Emmeline panicked and looked at her watch.

It's so late.

Emmeline sprinted to the foyer to grab her phone and ran back to the bathroom.

"I was supposed to be home a while ago. Will you be all right here?" Emmeline asked.

Erik nodded.

"I'll see you later." Emmeline turned to leave.

"Does this mean I can call you Emia now?"

Emmeline turned back and gave him a shy smile. "It's just a name. You can call me that if you want to."

"Please don't say anything to Anja about what I said earlier."

He remembers.

Emmeline knelt beside Erik. "You know I can't promise you that. When my mother passed away, a brilliant woman told me the more you resist your pain, the greater your suffering will be. Anja would lay down her life for you without a single thought. She deserves to know that you're suffering."

Erik looked away. "I'm not going to hurt myself. If I wanted to, I would've done it a long time ago." When he looked back at her, his eyes were clear. "I'll escort you home. It's late, and with what happened earlier today, you should take more precautions."

"Let's get going. My car's in the parking garage."

Emmeline unlocked her phone and tapped out a message to Matthew.

Emia: I got caught up at the Sanctuary. Erik will escort me home. I'll talk to you in the morning.

Mattie: Okay. I'm already home.

Emia: Eva and Sally will be by in the morning to check our security system.

Mattie: Fine.

She rolled her eyes at her brother's short answers.

At least he answered my messages.

She stood up, and Erik followed suit, grimacing as he picked up his helmet and two blades. Squeezing past Emmeline, he went to his bed and reached underneath to pull out two shorter blades. He slid them into his harness and placed the longer ones under his bed.

"Why did you switch out your weapons?"

"It's very uncomfortable to sit in a car with those other ones." Erik tucked his helmet under his arm. "We can go now."

"Wait, how will you get home if we take my car?"

Emmeline looked at Erik's confused expression.

"Right," she muttered. "You have wings."

Emmeline tucked her tote bag into the backseat as Erik got into the front passenger seat. She looked down at his legs, which were bent against the glove compartment.

"You can move the seat back, Erik. Nobody ever sits in the passenger seat, so it's just a glorified purse holder."

He adjusted the seat back and stretched out his legs.

"Seat belt, please," Emmeline said.

Erik gave her a blank stare.

"You do know what a seat belt is, don't you?"

"We don't really use seat belts."

"In my car, you do. A seat belt can save your life if you're in an accident. If we get stopped by the police, you'll get a ticket and pay a hefty fine."

"Emmeline …" Erik paused and corrected himself. "Emia, I have two weapons strapped to my back, and I'm dressed in bulletproof armor. I don't have a driver's license or any identification on me. The last thing I'm worried about is a ticket for not wearing a seat belt. If we get stopped, I'll make myself scarce, and the police will never know I was here."

"This car's not moving until you put your seat belt on." Emmeline placed her hands on her lap.

Erik seemed to contemplate his options before sighing and reaching behind him. He pulled the seat belt forward and snapped it into its place.

"Thank you." Emmeline pulled out of her parking spot and squinted as she drove up the dark ramp. "You guys need to put some lights in here."

"We've never needed to account for a human using our parking garage. Our eyes can see fine in the dark."

Emmeline made a left turn onto the quiet street. Besides a few cars parked on the side, the city was silent and resting.

"Then, why have any lights at all?" Emmeline asked sarcastically.

Erik's icy eyes scanned the streets. "I should've taken a motorcycle and followed you instead."

Emmeline narrowed her eyes in indignation, but her lips betrayed her, and she broke into a big smile. She laughed, and Erik's mouth twitched in response, the silver flecks in his eyes deepening.

"Erik, can I ask you some questions?"

"You can ask as many questions as you'd like."

"You said you've hurt others before when you came back from a hunt. Who did you hurt?"

Erik stiffened and pressed his lips together.

"You don't have to answer if you don't want to." Emmeline glanced at him.

"Many years ago, my partner came to find me after a hunt, but I didn't recognize her. I pushed her so hard that she went through a window."

Emmeline gasped, and her heart dropped into a pit. She pulled the car to the side of the road and turned to stare at Erik with wide eyes.

Erik didn't look at her. "It didn't register to me that there was a window there. Nothing registered to me. I didn't even realize she had gone through a window until I came to my senses hours later."

"What happened to her?"

"She had some common sense and had been in nainthe form when she came to find me." Erik turned to look at Emmeline, his eyes as sharp as slivers of ice. "Even though she was in full nainthe form, I could still push her out a window. She had some scratches and was a bit shaken, but physically, she was fine. What do you think would've happened to her if she were human?"

Emmeline snapped her mouth shut, and Erik turned his head to look out the passenger window.

"You should keep driving."

Emmeline shifted her car into drive and merged back into the right lane.

"I'm glad your partner is okay."

"Past tense. She's no longer my partner and hasn't been for a long time."

"Do you have a new partner? Anja told me you work on your own."

"Partner, as in lover. And, yes, some nainthe do have partners for work. Saadah and Ellis usually work as a team, just like Anja and Lessie. I don't have a partner in either. I'm much more efficient on my own and without distractions."

"Oh, that kind of partner." Emmeline shifted in her seat and stared out the windshield at the winding roads. "I was only thinking of work partners, like police officers."

Emmeline pressed her touch-screen console, and the front gate to her home opened.

"Who was your ex-lover? Have I met her yet?" She drove up the long driveway and stopped at the garage door, waiting for it to open.

"Have you met Aria?"

Emmeline shook her head.

"You will soon. She's one of my closest friends."

"How come it didn't work out between you two?" Emmeline tilted her head and tried to gauge whether she'd overstepped any boundaries.

I probably did.

"You mean, aside from the fact that she went through a window and I was the one who had caused it?"

"She must've forgiven you if you're good friends now."

"Our relationship just didn't work out. We might be nainthe, but our emotions are still human. We want love, family, and friends. We have dreams and desires. We still want the same things we would've wanted if this path hadn't been chosen for us."

Erik's eyes seemed to dim, as if he was lost in his memories, but he blinked, and it was gone. Emmeline drove down the ramp of her underground garage and checked her rearview mirror to ensure the door fully closed behind her.

"Erik, do you see those lights?" Emmeline pointed at the bright lights that lined the ramp floor and ceiling. "It's an amazing invention."

Erik rolled his eyes. "I'll see if we can get some lights installed."

"That wasn't so difficult, was it?"

"It's not my department."

Emmeline laughed, grateful for the light reprieve in the mood. She drove to her favorite parking spot and backed in. After she plugged her car into the electrical outlet, she turned around and saw Erik staring open-mouthed at Matthew's car.

Erik turned to her slowly and pointed. "Is that your brother's car? The one Ellis has been raving about this whole time?"

Emmeline nodded and tried to resist rolling her eyes again.

"I'll be sure to petition to become a doctor in my next life."

"My brother's in a very privileged position. I don't think most doctors can do the same. At least, not for a long time."

"Your brother and I are about to become excellent friends."

"I think that's what Ellis is planning as well. I guess he has some competition now." Emmeline looked at her watch. "Saadah's upstairs if you want to say hello. You can leave from his balcony, or I can give you another guest room, and you can leave in the morning through a more conventional method, like the front door. It's already four o'clock in the morning."

"I'll return to the Sanctuary after seeing Saadah."

"I'll show you to his room." Emmeline eyed Erik's outfit. "You might want to be more discreet with your weapons, just in case we bump into Mr. Jae or Ms. Rose. She wasn't impressed with your full-body armor last time. I wouldn't want to add weapons."

Erik unhooked his blades and held them under his arm. "Better?"

"Not really, but I guess it'll have to do."

CHAPTER THIRTY-FIVE

DECEPTION

Emmeline's phone buzzed.

And buzzed.

And buzzed again.

This'd better be important, or I'm going to throw this phone into the garbage.

She opened one eye.

My arm's asleep.

Finally, she freed her arm from under her body and picked up her phone.

Ms. Rose: Emia, sweetheart, Eva and Sally are here. I just let them into the garage.

Ms. Rose: Time to wake up, sleepyhead. It's already nine o'clock.

Ms. Rose: Mattie's in the kitchen with Eva, and you know they don't always get along. If you don't want a battle on your hands, you'd better get down here soon.

Ms. Rose:	Don't make me call you. I know you can hear these messages.
Ms. Rose:	If you don't reply in a few minutes, I will come upstairs.
Emia:	Morning, Ms. Rose. I'll be right down. Can you make me a double Americano? And please don't let Mattie and Eva kill each other. Love you.

Emmeline tapped out a thank-you message to Saadah and received an acknowledgment from him. After washing her face and changing into a pair of leggings and a tank top, she trudged downstairs to the kitchen.

I'm too old to be staying out so late. I should be in bed by eleven at the latest.

Emmeline walked into the kitchen while securing her hair into a bun. She stopped dead in her tracks as she looked around the room.

Not again.

Ms. Rose handed her a piping hot coffee. "I'll be in the family room. Good luck, sweetie." She patted Emmeline on the shoulder before turning to the petite Chinese woman with the platinum-blonde pixie haircut and black-rimmed glasses.

"Sally, would you like to join me for tea?" Ms. Rose asked.

"Yes, please." Sally gave Ms. Rose a relieved look and grabbed her cup. "Morning, Emmeline! I'll catch up with you later." She didn't wait for Emmeline's response and hurried out of the room with Ms. Rose.

Eva stood with her arms crossed in front of her and glared at Matthew, who returned in kind with his own scowl. Matthew towered over Eva, but what she lacked in height, she made up with sheer hardened grit.

Emmeline looked back and forth between her other best friend and brother before swallowing a sigh.

"Eva, I like your new haircut. It suits your face," Emmeline said, hoping to lighten the mood. She brushed back the silky black strands that had once almost gone down to Eva's waist but were now cut into a sleek long bob. "And before you bite my head off, I'm trying to distract you so that you're less angry. Did it work?"

Eva swatted Emmeline's hand away and narrowed her dark brown eyes at Matthew. "Please tell your brother his condescending attitude is annoying."

"Eva, the chip on your shoulder is unbecoming," Matthew retorted.

"Says the overprivileged doctor who has had everything handed to him his entire life," Eva snapped back.

"Whoa, both of you, back down. We're not in high school anymore." Emmeline held up a hand in mock surrender. "Please, it's early, I've only had about five hours of sleep, and I'm still holding a full cup of coffee." She took an exaggerated long sip from her cup, and then looked at Eva. "Now, what did you find?"

"I checked your security system, and everything looks to be in order. You need to remember to use it every single day. Overall, not much to change."

"That makes me feel better." Emmeline let out a sigh of relief. "So, why are you at each other's throats?"

"I think you should hire physical security," Eva said.

"No," Matthew replied.

"I wasn't talking to you. I don't see anyone stalking you right now. You can have an opinion when that happens."

Emmeline gave Matthew a warning look. *Back down. Let me handle this.*

Matthew nodded and crossed his arms.

"Eva, I know you're concerned for me, and I love you for it, but you know how I feel about strangers and bodyguards," Emmeline said.

Eva opened her mouth to protest, but Emmeline placed a hand on Eva's arm.

"I'll consider it. Can you give me some time to think about it?"

"Fine," Eva huffed.

Emmeline smiled as she watched her friend mentally count to ten.

"I also have some good news and some bad news," Eva said after she let out a breath.

She tapped through her tablet and handed it to Emmeline. Matthew looked over Emmeline's shoulder at what Eva had put in front of her.

"What's the good news?" Emmeline asked.

"The good news is that this morning, I was able to get into the private asset management firm's database."

"You're making me nervous about the bad news."

"What you're looking at is your file."

Emmeline went through the document, and when she looked up at her brother, his face remained unmoved.

"The file doesn't say who's having me followed."

"I'm working on it," Eva said.

"I still don't understand why anyone would want me followed. The file says my whereabouts are to be documented, and detailed backgrounds for all associations are to be provided. I've said this so many times that it's bordering pathetic, but I'm a boring person. I work, sleep, and eat. That's about it. Why would anyone want to follow me?"

Matthew took the tablet from Emmeline's hands and scanned through the file.

"Whoever wants you followed is looking for behavior patterns."

"I think so too," Eva agreed. "I don't know the motivation, but at this point, I would guess it has to do with money. Money can make people do terrible things. You need to be extra careful." She looked at Matthew pointedly. "Get security to accompany you everywhere. I'm serious, Emia. This could be anything from blackmail to a hostage situation. And this might not just be you. It could extend to anyone in this household or your circle of friends. I'd bet whoever is behind this has the means to do it."

The blood drained from Emmeline's face as she struggled to process the information.

"I only noticed this at the gala the other night. Do you know how long this has been going on?"

"There's no date listed, but the file was created several weeks ago. It's also an open contract, meaning there's no end date."

"What's happening here?" Emmeline looked at Matthew. "Why has my life been completely turned upside down lately? I feel like I'm trapped in a bad dream."

"I think we'll need some help to sort this out. I agree we need extra security," Matthew said.

"Finally." Eva threw her hands up in exasperation. "I don't know how long it'll take me to find out who's behind this, but in the meantime, I was able to get a copy of the firm's client list."

Eva took the tablet from Matthew's hands and swiped through the screens. "I compared it to your known associates, and I had Gus give me all the contacts from the family foundation. There were several that popped up as having accounts with this firm."

Eva handed the tablet back to Emmeline. There were over thirty names on the list, but only one screamed out to her.

Philip Vil.

"It's him. Philip." Emmeline's stomach churned, and she felt like throwing up.

Eva eyed the list. "Are you sure it's him? I'm not surprised he's on this list since he's considered high-profile. There are several questionable names here."

Emmeline looked at Matthew. "When I accompanied him to the Inspire Gala, he asked me about Anja by name, but I'd never told him it. If he had looked up her name, he would've only found the pseudonym she uses for events."

"Why didn't you say something sooner?" Matthew frowned.

"I thought it was odd, and then I forgot about it, but this new information triggered my memory."

"Who's Anja? She's not on your list of known associates. Do you want me to do a background check?" Eva looked confused as she scrolled through her document.

"No!" both Emmeline and Matthew said in unison.

"Fine. What do you want me to do then? I assume you want me to do some digging on Mr. Mayor?"

Emmeline nodded. "Check if he has a history of stalking and whether he's in financial trouble. See if you can find anything from his past wife and if there was domestic abuse. If there was, I doubt he's been formally charged since it would've come to light before he became mayor. Can you ask Gus to check into the foundations he supports?"

"I'll get on it. I've sent copies of what I have to you. You should give it to your lawyers and get on that security detail." Eva packed up her backpack. "I know you'll want to confront him, but make sure you consult your security before you do anything. You have no idea what this guy is capable of, and we also don't have proof that it's him."

"I can't believe I almost slept with him. I'm glad I didn't." Emmeline put her face in her hands.

Eva pulled Emmeline into a hug. "Me too. I'm grateful you followed your gut."

Matthew blanched. "I'm still here, and I'd much prefer not to be part of a conversation that involves my sister's sex life."

"Oh, shut up, Mattie," Emmeline snapped. "We haven't even talked about the previous night, where I found you and your friend in the great room."

Matthew reddened and shut his mouth.

"And that's my cue to leave. I'll let you know as soon as I find anything." Eva hugged Emmeline again.

"Thanks, Eva."

Emia: Javier, if you're available, I'll come to see you tonight after training with Ember. There are a few things I'd like to discuss with you: my progress, Erik, and my need for a bodyguard.

Javier: I'll see you tonight. Michael and Maira will join us.

Emmeline felt annoyance at the mention of Michael and Maira.
I'd better make sure Anja's free tonight.

CHAPTER THIRTY-SIX

PAST LIVES

Anja was waiting for Emmeline outside in the courtyard when she finished her training session with Ember. Anja was armorless, but she was in her black ensemble with a single blade strapped to her back.

Emmeline shook her hair out of her bun and shrugged on a fitted black sweater over her tank top.

"I see you've taken to our uniform." Anja took in Emmeline's all-black outfit.

"You know what they say when you can't beat them."

"Are you ready for another conversation with The Three Stooges?"

Emmeline giggled but sobered quickly. "Never, but it must be done."

They ambled through the courtyard, taking their time as they made their way to Javier's office.

"Anja, I need to tell you something important."

"What is it?" Anja looked at Emmeline with concern.

"I don't know if your brother is okay. I can feel that he's in a lot of pain. I don't know him well, and I don't know if he would do this, but I'm worried he might hurt himself."

Anja turned to stare at Emmeline. "When did you see him?"

"Last night, after he came back from a hunt." Emmeline looked away. "He didn't want me to tell you about it."

"I'll talk to him tonight."

"You once told me that Erik goes through more than any nain-the should. I think I understand what you meant."

"If I could take some of the burden off his shoulders, I would, as would others, but no one else can do what he can," Anja murmured.

They fell back into silence as they rounded the corner, and Javier's office came into view.

"What's going on between you and Mattie?" Emmeline asked.

"I don't know." Anja blew out some air before turning to Emmeline. "I mean, I'm not sure."

"Mattie's an adult, and he can do whatever he wants, but he's also my brother and my only blood family member left. He might seem logical, calm, and strong, but his heart's fragile. Please don't hurt him just because you're curious."

"I'm not just curious about him! What do you take me for?" Anja said indignantly.

"What did you expect me to think?" Emmeline threw up her hands. "You're in an open relationship with Lesedi. You're gay. You're not even human! Put yourself in my shoes, and what would you think? And more importantly, what would you do?"

Anja looked away, and her eyes reflected the moonlight. "I would tell Mattie to run as far away as possible and never look back."

They both stood awkwardly, and Emmeline crossed her arms over her chest as she waited for Anja to continue.

"I'm not seeing Lessie anymore," Anja finally said.

Emmeline's eyes widened. "Why? Mattie knew you were in an open relationship with Lesedi. Did he ask you to do something?"

"Mattie has never asked anything of me, though sometimes, I wish he would." Anja cleared her throat. "I'm not gay. I'm bisexual, though I've never been in a relationship with a man before."

"Are you even supposed to have relationships with humans?"

Anja shook her head. "It would be too risky in having something revealed. And the nainthe are all sterile, so it's impossible for us to have families."

"Mattie has the right to choose the path his life should take and whether he accepts the consequences. Just be honest with him and don't lead him on."

"I would never do that to him." Anja's jaw locked, and her nose started to turn pink.

Emmeline reached for Anja and pulled her into a hug.

"You're a good person, Anja Loren. You've stood up for me and stood beside me since this craziness started, and you're so protective of Mattie. I'm just asking you to handle his heart with care. That's all."

Anja nodded into Emmeline's shoulder. "You sure packed a lot of heavy topics into our short walk across the courtyard. Come on, hugger. Let's find Tweedledum, Tweedledee, and Maira."

"Good thing you clarified who was who. I would've thought any of them could carry the titles," Emmeline muttered.

Emmeline entered Javier's office with Anja a few steps behind her.

Remember to keep an open mind. Try not to let your pride and stubbornness get in the way.

Javier, Michael, and Maira were already seated at the table, and they all exchanged clipped greetings with Emmeline. Emmeline sat opposite Javier while Anja stood and leaned against the wall.

"Anja, why are you here?" Michael asked.

"I want her to be here. It seems she's the only one with my best interests at heart," Emmeline replied.

Maira frowned. "That's not true. You haven't given us a chance to prove ourselves to you."

"You also seem to have a problem with authority," Michael snapped.

"That's because I don't believe in it." Emmeline tilted her head in challenge. "I don't answer to anybody inside or outside this room. What are you going to do about it?"

"Michael, mind your tongue! If all you're going to do is antagonize her, leave this room," Javier said.

Michael held up his hands in mock surrender.

Javier turned back to Emmeline. "How's training progressing?"

"I'm sure Ember has been providing you with regular reports. I can see nainthe if I know where they are, up to a certain distance. I've been practicing a lot, but I haven't been able to move past that stage. I want to be able to help you, and I understand how important it is, but at the pace I'm going, I'm not sure if I'll be able to. I think you guys received a defective seeker."

"You're not defective. I don't believe in such a thing in anyone," Maira said. "A seeker is a rarity, and they play an extraordinary role in our ecosystem. There's a reason why your abilities are the way they are, and we need to figure out what that is." She tapped the table. "Javier, maybe we should have the historians scour the archives on other methods?"

"Yes, have Asadi and his team start on it immediately."

"Consider it done." Maira tapped out a few commands on her tablet.

Emmeline cleared her throat. "I also wanted to talk to you about Erik." She tried to hide her nervousness and was aware of Anja's icy eyes boring into her side.

"I've seen the effect the hunts have on him, and I'd like other nainthe to step up so that there's a more even distribution of work." Emmeline looked around the table but avoided looking at Anja.

I can't read what Javier is thinking. Michael's head looks like it's about to explode. Maira looks thoughtful, which is a good thing. Maybe I judged her too early.

"Are you speaking on behalf of Erik, or are you advocating for him?" Javier asked.

"Advocating. How is it that he does the most dangerous job here and does it almost every night and on his own? I haven't been here very long, but when I walk around at night, I see nainthe doing training and other things when they could be on a hunt. Unless you're telling me what they're doing is more important than a hunt, then they should be helping Erik out."

Maira furrowed her brow. "Does Erik know you're speaking to us about this?"

"Yes, Emmeline, does he know?" Anja echoed coolly.

"No, he doesn't, and from the reactions around this table, I'm guessing he's not going to be happy about it. But if I always waited for permission to advocate on someone's behalf, I wouldn't be very good at my day job, now would I?" Emmeline replied.

Michael stood up and placed his hands on the table. "Erik has a gift the rest of us don't. Him doing patrols and hunts saves the lives of other nainthe. You have no idea how this place works and why we have things designed the way they are. When he took a self-proclaimed sabbatical and his friends took over for him, some of them didn't make it back alive. His selfishness cost his friends their lives."

Anja slid so quickly across the long oval table that it didn't register to Emmeline that she had moved from her spot. She stopped in front of Michael, and rested her blade at his throat.

"The guilt you put on my brother's shoulders is the only thing keeping him here," Anja hissed. "Choose your next words very carefully, you little bitch."

Michael sputtered and looked at Javier.

"Anja, I'm reaching over to you, so please don't be startled." Maira brought Anja's hand down.

Emmeline ran over and pulled Anja off the table.

Javier gave Anja a disapproving glare. "Your loyalty to your brother is commendable, but I've always told you that you must be more mindful of your impulsiveness and temper."

Anja narrowed her eyes at Javier but didn't say anything.

"Michael, why don't you break for the night? It's been a long day," Javier said.

Michael nodded stiffly and stalked out of the room.

Good riddance.

Emmeline straightened. "Javier, Maira, the responsibility for what happened doesn't belong on Erik's shoulders. It belongs on yours. You told me the nainthe have operated since the dawn of time, but in all your history, Erik has been the first to have such powerful abilities. What will you do the day Erik's no longer here? As the leaders of the nainthe, it's your job to ensure you've diversified your risk."

Javier held her gaze and seemed to be digesting her words.

Don't offend him. Remember what you're trying to do, Emmeline mentally reminded herself. *Maybe try a different tactic.*

"Javier, if you want to keep the Executioner alive, healthy, and working, then consider what I'm saying. In the human world, we call this burnout."

The silence in the room was deafening, but Emmeline appreciated the moment to gather her thoughts.

I hope Erik won't be upset with me. I'd better tell him before he hears it from someone else, or maybe I should have Anja tell him and beg for forgiveness on my behalf.

"We will consider what you've said." Javier dipped his head.

"Thank you."

"There's something else that you wanted to talk to us about?"

This is so embarrassing. Emmeline cringed.

"I'd like to request a personal bodyguard. I know there are regular patrols at night, but I'd like one around the clock." She looked at the confused faces around the table. "I have no problems hiring a bodyguard, but hiring a human would mean they would accompany me here, and I'm afraid it would be inconvenient."

"Does this have to do with the people following you?" Anja asked, and the iciness in her eyes hardened.

Emmeline nodded. "I'll have separate security for Mattie and the rest of my family. I'm happy to pay whatever I would pay for a personal bodyguard. Running this place must cost a lot, and I don't expect anyone to babysit me for free."

"You seemed to have skipped some important information. If there's a threat against you, it's a threat against all of us. Even though you don't feel it yet, you're one of us, and we most certainly will not charge you to keep you safe," Javier said. "You still don't understand your importance to our survival, do you?"

"Thank you, Javier."

Javier raised an eyebrow. "Two thank-yous in one night? We must be making some progress. Tell me more about this issue you're having."

As quickly as she could, Emmeline filled Javier, Maira, and Anja in on all the details regarding the private asset management firm that was keeping tabs on her.

"Anja, can you see that Emmeline gets around-the-clock protection?" Javier asked.

"I will."

"Emmeline, we are under oath that we will never take a human life. We also can't reveal ourselves to humans, but everything else is fair game. If there's a preference on who you would like to help you, let Anja know. I want you to be comfortable with those who will be around you." Javier nodded to Anja. "You can let the nainthe know it's under my order."

Anja glowered at Emmeline. "I can take care of the mayor if you'd like. I've never liked him."

"I don't want him dead! And Javier just said you're under oath not to take a human life."

"I didn't say I was going to kill him, but he'll wish he were dead."

And there's the daily reminder not to get on Anja's bad side.

"I'm still waiting on proof that it's him." Emmeline studied her hands. "I hope it's not him."

"I know."

~

Emmeline and Anja left Javier's office and stood under the covered walkway. Light raindrops fell from the sky, reflecting the lights from the courtyard.

"Can you tell Erik about what I said? I don't want him to hear it from anyone else." Emmeline braced herself for Anja's wrath.

"You should tell him yourself."

"He's even more unstable than you are." Emmeline paused. "Actually, I'm not sure which of you is more unstable. It's a toss-up."

"Definitely me," Anja smirked.

"Pretty please?" Emmeline batted her eyelashes.

"Nope, but when you do tell him, it might help you to do that." Anja pointed at the sweet smile on Emmeline's face.

Emmeline scowled at her.

"That's not the right face." Anja clicked her tongue.

"What happened to Erik's friends? The ones that Michael mentioned."

"Many years ago, Erik left this place. Back then, Erik would sometimes work with a partner. One night, Kenji, his partner, went on a routine patrol with another nainthe and was killed by a raizour. Erik was devastated, so he just picked up and left. Some weren't happy that he'd abandoned the nainthe, so a few of his friends tried to fill the void by taking on the nightly hunts he used to do in addition to the regularly scheduled hunts. They lasted a while, but the nightly hunts eventually took a toll on them. It was exhausting them physically and mentally, which is why our hunt teams work rotating shifts. One night, four of his friends went out as a team, and two didn't make it back. Julian and Aria survived, but Mala and Sum didn't."

Aria. Erik's ex-lover.

"Is that why Erik came back?"

Anja nodded. "Since then, he's never left the Sanctuary or taken a break. The guilt is what keeps him going. He doesn't keep many friends anymore, and most just steer clear of him. He prefers it that way."

I understand why he wouldn't want to do this anymore.

"I met Julian a few nights ago in the dining hall, but I haven't met Aria yet. I never would've guessed Julian and Erik were good friends or even friends at all."

"They used to be, but ever since Sum died, their friendship has never recovered. Sum was the love of Julian's life."

What a brutal and violent life to live. Emmeline felt a lump in her throat.

"I didn't know you could leave the nainthe," Emmeline said.

"You can, if you abide by the rules and don't break your oaths. But what would be the point of leaving the order? It would be a meaningless and lonely existence—no purpose, family, or friends. At least here, I know my work and sacrifice mean something. I didn't have a choice to become a nainthe, but I can make it count and take down as many raizour as possible." Anja looked at her phone. "I'm on duty tonight. Message Ellis when you're about to leave. He'll escort you home and stay the night."

"I will. Be careful out there. Mattie wanted me to drop something off for Ben, so I'm going to go by the infirmary before I head home."

Emmeline said good-bye to Anja and watched her head to her room.

And after seeing Ben, I'm going to see if Erik's back from a hunt.

CHAPTER THIRTY-SEVEN

THE TOWER

His room is still dark. I don't think he's back yet.

Emmeline looked up at the cloudy sky and half-expected Erik to drop through at any moment. She climbed the stairs slowly, unsure of what to do next.

Maybe I should go home.

Emmeline mentally shook herself and made herself stand straighter.

You helped him last time. Maybe you can help him again.

She walked up to his door and gently rapped on it, but there was no answer. She tested the door handle and heard a light click.

I guess you didn't lock the door, did you, Erik?

She pushed the door open and looked around the dark room.

"Hello? Erik?" Emmeline called out.

She strained her ears to listen for any sounds, but the room was eerily silent.

He's not here.

She stepped back out into the hallway and closed the door.

I'll wait out here for a bit.

Looking for a chair but not seeing one, Emmeline sat on the floor and crossed her legs. She took out her phone and went through her emails. After a while, she turned off her phone and closed her eyes as the silence of the night air lulled her into a light sleep. Suddenly, she was startled awake by someone shaking her shoulder.

"Emmeline, wake up. What are you doing out here?"

Emmeline rubbed her eyes and stifled a yawn. As her eyes focused, she found Ellis crouched in front of her.

"Oh, Ellis, I'm sorry! I was supposed to message you when I was ready to leave. I guess I fell asleep."

"Why did you fall asleep here? Are you waiting for Anja to come back? You can sit in the courtyard to wait for her if you want. It's much more comfortable over there, and she should be back soon."

"What time is it?"

"Just past midnight." Ellis stood up and held his hand out to pull Emmeline off the floor.

"I was waiting for Erik. I need to talk to him about something," Emmeline said.

Ellis gave her a look of absolute horror. "That's a terrible idea." He looked around. "And waiting here might be pointless. He doesn't always come back to his room after a hunt. Sometimes, he goes to the tower."

"The tower?"

Ellis pointed to the tallest building on the opposite side of the courtyard. "It's an inefficient building, so it sits mostly vacant. A few years ago, the attic area was cleared out and remodeled. I think Javier gave the order for the renovation to give Erik a safe space. You can also access the rooftops of the adjacent buildings from there."

"Why does he go there?"

"Maybe he thinks it's safer than anywhere else, there's less of a chance of him hurting someone, and at least he's still in the Sanctuary. That's just my guess though. I've never asked him."

"Can you show me how to get there?"

"Not on your life," Ellis said, and his boyish features became stern.

"What if I promise you can drive Mattie's car?"

Ellis tried to hold back a smile. "Sorry, my fear of Anja outweighs my love of cars. No deal. I'd like to keep my head on my shoulders."

"Fine. I'll find my way there myself. It'll be your fault if I get hurt, lost, or both." Emmeline let out a heavy sigh. She picked up her bag and started walking down the hallway.

"Wait!" Ellis jogged up beside her. "You are used to getting your way, aren't you?"

"Usually. Especially when I believe my requests are reasonable."

"You'd better stand up for me when Anja tries to kill me."

"Of course." Emmeline gave Ellis one of her brilliant smiles.

"It's a bit of a trek to get to the tower."

"You could fly me there."

Ellis gaped at her. "You're trying to get me killed, aren't you? Who put you up to this? Caleb? Lucas?"

"Nobody put me up to anything. I don't even know Caleb or Lucas. I can walk, but I thought it would be more efficient if you flew me there. Let's go then. If Erik's not there, I'll go home."

They took the long route and stayed under the covered walkway to avoid the rain, chatting about some of Ellis's favorite chefs and cooking competition shows.

Ellis, you must've been popular when you were younger. Emmeline admired his animated way of talking and the ease and comfort he was in his skin. *I wonder what you would've chosen to do with your life if it hadn't been picked for you.*

They finally reached the base of the tower, and Emmeline looked up at the old staircase.

"How far up does this go?"

"About eight stories."

"Elevator?" Emmeline asked hopefully.

"You wish."

"Are you sure you can't fly me up?"

"Nope, but at least it'll be good exercise!"

Emmeline groaned. "I'll go up myself. I'll message you when I'm done. And before you insist on accompanying me, I'll save you some time. I think it'll be safer if I go by myself."

"You can't be serious," Ellis sputtered.

"I'm very serious."

Ellis sighed. "I'll wait here and fly up if I hear anything."

"Oh, now, you want to fly."

"This isn't going to end well for me, is it?" Ellis closed his eyes and rubbed his temples. "Are you sure you want to do this?"

Emmeline nodded. "I'll message you."

She turned and looked up at the stairs.

The real question is, can I make it up all these stairs?

Emmeline stood at the edge of the tower and looked out over the courtyard. The rain had stopped, but a fine mist held on, filling the air with cool humidity. Thick clouds covered the moon, but the lights from the courtyard and the surrounding buildings gave off a soft reflection throughout the Sanctuary.

Emmeline looked around, but there was no sign of Erik. She walked to one of the two open doors leading to the uneven rooftops. She looked closer, and a dark figure was crouched several rooftops away. He was still, and his wings were spread out behind him.

"Erik?" Emmeline called out, but the figure didn't acknowledge her.

"Erik?" she called out louder, but still, there was no response.

She took a tentative step out onto the rooftop and held on to the doorway for support. She could feel the slippery stone beneath her flats.

"If you can hear me, please come back to the tower. I can't come to you; it's too dangerous."

Erik turned his head to her, and his irises were dull. His armor and outfit looked like it was soaked through from the rain. He turned his head back to face the city and became still again.

"Fine, I'll come to you."

Emmeline took a deep breath and let go of the doorway. The top of the roof was about a foot wide with steep drops on both sides. Cautiously, she stepped forward and looked down at the slopes, her calm immediately turning into panic. Her feet wobbled, and she let out a short yelp as her body tilted to one side.

"Erik, help!" Emmeline's hand reached out to him as she struggled to keep her balance.

Erik's head whipped around, and he leaped up, his wings lifting him into the air. He flew toward her, grabbed her hand, hoisted her up, and wrapped his other arm around her waist.

Emmeline gasped at being lifted into the air and gripped Erik's shoulder. She squeezed her eyes shut and pressed her face into his neck.

"I'm scared of heights!"

Erik quickly lowered them back to the tower and ducked inside before loosening his grip on her waist.

"Are you out of your mind? Why would you do something like that?" Erik snapped.

Emmeline slumped against the cool stone wall. "I was worried about you."

"Go home."

Erik turned back to the tower doorway, but Emmeline reached out and grabbed his hand before he could leave. He stilled and looked down at her hand.

"Come sit with me, Erik."

"You can't save me."

"I'm not trying to."

Maybe just a little bit.

Emmeline tugged at his hand. "I just don't want you to go through this alone if you don't have to."

Erik sighed, took off his helmet, unhooked his blades, and tossed everything to the side. He sat beside Emmeline and leaned his head against the stone wall.

"Did you come up here to avoid me?" Emmeline asked, but Erik didn't answer and just stared straight ahead. "Are you able to change back to human form?"

Erik shook his head. "Soon. I've been back for a while now."

"How many tonight?"

"Four."

"Where are the bodies?"

"I already brought them back. They should be in the incinerator by now."

Emmeline bit her lip and reached over to put her hand in his. Her heart skipped as his long fingers closed over hers, barely touching her skin. She could feel the warmth in his hand and found it oddly comforting.

"What are you feeling right now?"

"Dull pain in my head, and my lungs feel like they're being squeezed from the inside out. It was worse earlier, but it's starting to subside." He grimaced as his chest constricted.

"What did you feel from the raizour?"

Erik closed his eyes. "Fear and hatred. They were terrified of me, but they hated me more."

"Why?"

"Because they knew who I was and that they were going to die."

Emmeline felt her heart tighten. "Why do you act as if this were nothing?"

Erik's eyes snapped open, and he ripped his hand away. He staggered to his feet, leaving Emmeline alone on the cold floor.

"This is who I am. Are you still surprised my entire life has been dedicated to cold-blooded murder?" he sneered. "This is what I do. I take lives."

Emmeline shrank back against the wall, bringing her knees up to her chest. "That's not what I meant."

Erik knelt in front of her and brought his face inches away, his irises filled with anger and self-loathing. "Are you terrified of me? Do you hate me too? Because you should."

Emmeline turned her head away from him.

Don't let him see your fear.

Tears fell from Emmeline's eyes, and she squeezed them shut. All she could hear was the sound of blood in her ears and Erik's harsh breathing.

No wonder others are scared of you.

She felt the lightest touch against her chin, and she opened her eyes, but her vision was blurry from her tears. Erik dropped his hand and stepped back before sitting in front of her.

"That was uncalled for," Emmeline bit out.

"I'm sorry. You've been nothing but kind to me. And brave." Erik reached over and brushed the tears off her cheek. "Don't ever cry because of me."

Emmeline looked away. "All I meant was that you act like what you do doesn't impact you. Not only can I see how much it affects you, but I can also feel it." She pointed to her chest.

"You can feel it? Figuratively or literally?"

"Literally." Emmeline looked at her hands. "Last time, I could feel your pain, and I wished it would go away. I'm probably not explaining it properly, but I think that's what magic feels like to me."

"I felt it, too, but I couldn't tell if it was my imagination."

"Would you let me try again?"

Erik nodded, and Emmeline held out both her hands. She closed her eyes as he took her hands, willing the darkness into her mind. Strands of brilliant light came into her sight, and a dark, cloudy aura swirled around it. Her fingers tightened around

Erik's as she felt the excruciating pain and hatred raking through him.

Let me take some of it away.

Emmeline's hands warmed, and she watched Erik's aura smooth out to a calm wave. He squeezed her hands, and her eyes flew open. She stared at him with wide eyes, and he looked back at her in a daze.

"Erik, you're back in human form!"

"So it seems." Erik stared at Emmeline's hands in his. "How did you do that? Does Javier know you can do this?" He looked at her in shock.

Emmeline shook her head. "I wasn't even sure until now. I don't plan on telling Javier yet, so please don't say anything."

I don't want him or anyone to use this as an excuse to push you harder.

"I won't."

"I should get home. With all the late nights I've been pulling, Ms. Rose is probably worried about me."

"I'll escort you home." Erik stood up and pulled Emmeline to her feet.

"Ellis is waiting for me downstairs. Poor guy's also probably losing his mind with worry. He was adamant that I shouldn't come up here to find you, though I think he was more worried about facing Anja than anything else."

"Smart man. I wouldn't want to face my sister either." Erik cleared his throat. "I'll fly you down so you don't have to take the stairs."

"Are you saying I didn't have to walk up eight flights of stairs? Ellis refused to fly me up here. Isn't it against the rules?"

Erik rolled his eyes. "Technically, yes, but what's anyone going to do about it? Those rules are more for outside the Sanctuary. It'll be much faster if I fly you down."

He held out his palm, and his fingers unfurled gracefully, beckoning her to take his hand and follow him into the night. Emmeline's heart raced as she slipped her hand into his and let him lead her back out to the edge of the rooftop.

"Ready?" Erik asked.

"I'm ready."

Erik pulled Emmeline into his arms and she leaned into his warmth. She closed her eyes, breathing in the light scent of citrus and cedar. Before her eyes could open, they were in the air and descending to the courtyard. She felt Erik's feet touch the floor as he gently set her down.

"You can breathe now."

"Thank you, Erik. That was much faster."

Emmeline's heart pounded in her chest, and she looked at him as he stared back at her. She couldn't stop the small breath from being pulled out of her lungs as his irises darkened until they mirrored the gathering storm clouds above.

"You're welcome, Emia."

But Erik didn't move from his spot, and his arm stayed wrapped around her waist. His long fingers splayed around the edges of her rib cage, like he wanted to keep her there with him.

I like it here, in his arms.

Emmeline snapped herself out of her daze.

What am I doing?

She let go of Erik's arm. "I should go. Ms. Rose will be worried," she repeated

He blinked and pulled his arm away just as Ellis jogged over to meet them.

"Ellis, get her home safely."

"You got it. Come on, Emmeline. Let's get you home."

Emmeline walked with Ellis across the soft grass of the courtyard, only half-listening to his animated chatter. She thought she felt Erik watch her leave, but when she turned to look over her shoulder, he was already gone.

PART V:

SECONDS

CHAPTER THIRTY-EIGHT

WHEN MONSTERS FOLLOW

Ellis whistled as he got in Emmeline's car and closed the door. "Nice ride. All electric too. You and your brother don't mess around with your vehicles."

"My brother takes it to the next level. I have two vehicles—this one and a hybrid. Next time you see Mattie, ask him what he's housing," Emmeline grumbled. She started her car and drove up the steep ramp that led out of the parking garage.

"It must be nice to have money."

"We have our issues, but I'm aware of how privileged we are." Emmeline glanced at Ellis before making a left turn onto the road. "What was your childhood like?"

"Very middle class." Ellis half-smiled. "My parents were first-generation immigrants and had to work a lot, so my younger brother and I were alone most of the time. I think we turned out all right. Well, my brother did. He's my parents' dream child, and he became a pediatrician."

Emmeline laughed. "I'm sure your parents would be proud of you, too, if they knew what you did."

"I doubt *proud* is the word they'd use to describe it. Terrified, petrified, appalled. Need I go on?" Ellis snickered.

"If this life hadn't been chosen for you, what kind of career do you think you would've chosen for yourself?"

"I don't know. Maybe a chef or a linguistics teacher. Or maybe even a speech-language pathologist."

"Mattie worked with several speech-language pathologists for many years, all the way until he entered secondary school. I have a lot of respect for them." Emmeline signaled to make a right turn. "Can you tell me how one becomes a nainthe?"

"It's a terrible process. You get ill, almost die, and wait for the nainthe to find you and wake you up."

"Really?" Emmeline gripped the steering wheel, and questions raced through her head as she squinted at the slick roads. "How do you die? And what if no one comes to find you? How long can you be dead for?" The following thoughts horrified her even more. "What happens if someone tries to do an autopsy on you? Or embalms or cremates you?"

"When we first get ill, it's like our body prepares for heart failure. We feel pressure, tightness, nausea, and have trouble breathing. Then, we go into cardiac arrest, and our body sort of goes into a holding mode, where everything slows down to an undetectable level."

"But that's impossible. Unexplained deaths get autopsies, and bodies are embalmed before being buried." Emmeline could almost feel her brother losing his mind.

Ellis turned to face Emmeline. "This is why everyone's so uptight about you being here. From when a nainthe's identified to when they can be rescued is a very short period. Otherwise, they die for real."

"Do you mean all the potential nainthe over the past twenty or so years have all died?"

"Yes. There were a few we came across just by sheer luck, but the rest are dead. That's why we need you. You need to find the potentials so we can get to them. A potential can only be identified shortly before they get sick."

"Don't families look for the bodies of their loved ones?"

Ellis nodded. "It's destroyed countless families. I know my parents barely survived losing me. After being rescued, a nainthe stays in holding mode for a few months to over a year for the transformation to occur. When I woke up, I watched my parents suffer from a distance. There was nothing I could do about it without risking everything other nainthe had sacrificed their lives for. It was the hardest thing I'd ever been through, and I was only nineteen."

"I'm sorry, Ellis. No one should have to go through what you and the rest of the nainthe go through."

"Every nainthe has a unique but similar story, and we all cope differently. We all accept our fate at some point in the grieving process."

Suddenly, Ellis sat up straight and gripped the blade on his lap. His eyes darted back and forth across the windshield and then up through the moonroof.

"What's wrong?" Emmeline looked at him with alarm.

"There are raizour here. Call Erik. I need backup. There are a few raizour, but I don't know how many."

Ellis opened the moonroof, and the wind and rain rushed into the car. He hoisted himself partway through the moonroof, and his dark irises filled his eyes.

"Call Erik Loren." Emmeline voice-activated her car's calling function.

The phone rang, and he picked up immediately.

"What's wrong?"

"I'm driving home, and there are raizour close to us. Ellis needs help. Can you come or send help?" Emmeline looked out the windshield of her car.

"Coming." The line went dead.

Ellis crouched down in the car. "Keep driving but don't go home. Stay on the main roads and don't stop, no matter what. I mean it. No matter what happens, you keep driving! I'll try to keep them away from you. Lock the doors and drive fast."

Ellis changed into his nainthe form and leaped out of the moonroof with his blade brandished.

"Keep driving. Focus, focus, focus," Emmeline muttered to herself as she kept her eyes on the road.

She turned off the roads that led home and took to the main street, running several red lights as she sped through the slick lanes. She kept glancing into the rearview mirror, hoping to catch a glimpse of Ellis.

Where is he?

Without warning, a large object crashed onto Emmeline's car and shattered the moonroof, raining shards of glass over her. Her hands left the steering wheel to cover her head, and she slammed on the brakes, making her car skid and flip onto the passenger side.

Emmeline screamed and squeezed her eyes shut.

There was an explosion and a burst of force as all the airbags deployed. The car screeched as it slid against the pavement until the trunk slammed into a light post, bringing it to a sudden halt. Glass burst and hung suspended in the air before dropping.

And then everything fell silent.

Emmeline whimpered as she moved her hands from her head and opened her eyes. The ringing in her ears vibrated, and she shook her head to gather her bearings.

Am I alive?

She touched her head and arms and moved her feet. A shriek echoed from above, and she craned her head to look around.

I need to get out of here.

She unbuckled her seat belt and braced herself as her body fell to the side. She grabbed her tote bag and used it to remove the sharp edges left around the moonroof before staggering out of her car. Nausea hit her as she stumbled to the sidewalk, and she leaned against the window of a small shop to steady herself.

Where do I go?

She spotted a body behind her car. Broken wings lay on the ground, and a trail of deep blue liquid pooled beneath it.

A raizour fell on top of my car.

Emmeline stayed close to the shops lining the street and ran in the opposite direction. Another shriek pierced the air, and she looked up as she tried to locate the sound. She stopped in her tracks as a raizour landed several feet in front of her. The streetlights reflected off its translucent skin and diffused through its outstretched wings. Two other raizour dropped down behind it, both bigger in stature. They stared at her with unblinking pitch-black eyes and snapped their jaws.

"Ellis!" Emmeline screamed.

The smaller raizour clicked its teeth. *It is you—the last one. You are the one we have been looking for.*

"What do you want with me?" Emmeline backed up as the raizour advanced on her.

I cannot decide if I want you dead or alive.

Dead, another raizour growled.

A bit of a curiosity though, is it not? The first raizour cocked its head.

"Why do you want me dead? And why do you keep calling me the last one?"

Such a terrible and obvious question. It is because you help find the disgusting nainthe who hunt us.

"But why do you call me the last one?"

Emmeline felt laughter in her head, and she tried to shake it out.

You do not know, seeker? But it does not matter because I have decided I want you dead.

The first raizour was about to leap at Emmeline when Ellis slammed down in front of her. He held the body of another raizour by the neck, its throat slit open.

"Are you okay, Emmeline?" Ellis panted. He threw the raizour body at the feet of the others, and they snarled.

"I think so."

"I'm going to try to take all three. When I do, you run in the opposite direction. Got it?"

"You can't take all three. They'll kill you!"

"Better me than you. At least it'll give you a chance to get away." Ellis stopped and looked up at the sky with relief. "Erik's here."

On cue, Erik landed beside Ellis. His clothes were soaked from the rain, and he held a long blade in each hand. All three raizour howled and crouched down, ready to attack.

"Ellis, stay on guard and don't leave Emia's side," Erik commanded.

He stalked forward, and the raizour circled him and snapped their sharp teeth. The largest one leaped at Erik, its claws bared and swiping at him in quick, vicious movements. Erik ducked and ran his blade across its torso, slicing it open through its neck. Dark blue liquid ran down its body in a straight line as it gurgled and slumped over onto the pavement.

The two remaining raizour howled and attacked Erik at the same time. One of the raizour twisted its body and tried to strike him with its sharp wings, but he bent backward, barely avoiding it. He flipped over the raizour and brought his blades down in a cross against the raizour's neck, decapitating it. Its head dropped off its neck and rolled along the pavement until it hit a raised curb.

Erik's eyes blazed as he turned to the last raizour. He flipped the blade in his right hand to grip it like a spear and launched it. The blade sliced through the air and embedded itself into the raizour's chest.

Seeker, the raizour choked and clawed in Emmeline's head, *you should not exist.*

Emmeline gripped her head and fell to her knees as pain pulsated behind her eyes. Tears fell down her face and onto the pavement alongside the rain.

"Get out of my head," she screamed.

Erik's head snapped to her as she doubled over in agony. He turned back to the last raizour and sprinted forward. As he passed the raizour, he whipped out his left hand, and the raizour's throat opened up. Dark blue liquid poured out of its neck like a grim, wicked smile. Erik grabbed the blade embedded in the raizour's chest and pushed its body off with his boot.

The pain in Emmeline's head dulled to a throb, and she looked up at Ellis's concerned face.

"I think I'm going to be sick," Emmeline muttered, and she put her head between her knees.

Several sets of feet hit the pavement, and Emmeline shielded her eyes from two flashes of light as three nainthe stood in front of her. The only one she recognized was Sophia, who ran over to Ellis.

"Ellis …" Sophia touched his arm and looked at him with concern. "I should've come with you! There's no way you could've taken all five of them on your own."

"I'm okay. Erik came just in time." Ellis flushed at Sophia's concern.

Erik changed back into human form and stalked over to join the group.

"Five bodies, four here and one back over there." Erik pointed down behind Emmeline's battered car.

The three nainthe nodded, and one turned to Emmeline. Emmeline found herself looking into the bluest eyes she had ever seen. Straight chestnut-brown hair framed a delicate heart-shaped face and plush pink lips.

She's beautiful.

"You must be Emmeline," she said sweetly. "I'm Aria, and this"—she pointed beside her to a nainthe still in nainthe form—"is Olivia."

Aria, what a beautiful name.

Recognition hit Emmeline as another wave of nausea washed over her.

Oh, wait, you must be that *Aria.*

"Nice to meet you, Aria and Olivia." Emmeline tried to steady her stomach. "I'd stand up and shake your hands, except I think I might throw up."

"We'll talk later. I need to get these bodies out of here before the cavalry shows up."

Shit. The police and fire department. Cameras and witnesses.

Emmeline cringed as she started to think about damage control while sirens rang in the distance.

"Let's go. Get the bodies back to the Sanctuary. I'll fly Emia home," Erik snapped.

"No, I need to stay. I can't leave the scene of an accident. You guys go. I'll handle it from here." Emmeline looked up, and her vision swam. "Ellis, can you see if my phone's intact? It's somewhere in my car."

Erik looked at Emmeline's car, and his irises widened. "How did you walk out of that?"

"What can I say? Seat belts save lives, and don't you dare think about rolling your eyes at me."

Erik knelt beside her and checked her face and body. He cupped her chin, and she leaned into his palm. "I'm glad you had a seat belt on. How are you feeling?" he asked.

"Nauseous, but I think I'm fine, or it hasn't hit me yet." Emmeline looked at Erik. "Are you okay? You don't look like you're out of your mind."

"Maybe it's the residual effect from earlier."

"Go to my house and wait for me there. Saadah's there as well."

The sirens started to get closer.

"Erik, you need to go. Don't let anyone see you."

"Found it!" Ellis called out and ran back over, handing Emmeline her phone. "I can't believe your phone isn't broken. I can't believe *you* aren't broken."

Erik let go of Emmeline and stood up. "Ellis, go back to the Sanctuary and tell Javier what happened. I'm going to make sure Emia gets home safely."

Ellis leaped up and disappeared into the night.

"I'll be up there." Erik pointed to a tall building on the opposite side of the street before disappearing into the darkness.

Emmeline unlocked her phone and dialed the one number she always did whenever she needed help.

"Hello?" a sleepy voice answered.

"Ms. Rose? I'm sorry to wake you. I think I'm in trouble."

CHAPTER THIRTY-NINE

REALIZATIONS

Paramedics surrounded Emmeline by the time Ms. Rose and Matthew arrived. As soon as Matthew parked Ms. Rose's SUV at the side of the road, the older woman ran out of the car and rushed to Emmeline's side.

"Emia, are you okay? Are you hurt?" Ms. Rose pushed one of the paramedics to the side.

"I'm just a bit shaken up. Dave has checked me over, and all I have are some scrapes and bruises." Emmeline gestured at the poor paramedic.

"Um, I also said to look for signs of back, neck, and shoulder pain. Headaches and abdominal pain can also be delayed injuries," Dave piped up. He looked warily at Matthew, but recognition dawned on him. "Dr. Taylor-Wu, is Emmeline your sister?"

"Yes, she is. Thank you for taking care of her. How is she?"

Emmeline turned back to Ms. Rose as Matthew and Dave talked.

"I'm fine. No need to be worried."

Ms. Rose looked at Emmeline's car in horror. "Look at your car! You were in that? What the hell happened?"

"Stop talking," a deep voice commanded.

Ms. Rose spun around to face one of their family lawyers. "Oh, Peter, thank goodness you're here. Please get this all taken care of. If it's safe, I want to take Emia home."

A police officer came up to the group. "Ms. Taylor-Wu, I'd like you to take a breathalyzer test. We also have some questions for you."

"I'm Ms. Taylor-Wu's lawyer, Peter Zhao, and we decline to take the test. There's no basis for your request."

"Peter, I don't drink alcohol, and I'm not high. If it's easy to cross off the list, then let's do it." Emmeline nodded to the police officer. "Officer, please go ahead."

The officer administered the test, and the results came back as expected.

Peter frowned at the officer. "If you have any questions, direct them to my office. I will personally be taking care of this file. Can Ms. Taylor-Wu go home now? I've requested a private towing service and a specialized firm to investigate the vehicle. They should be here within minutes, and I'll stay behind to assist."

The officer looked unimpressed. "Dave, is she cleared to go home?"

Dave nodded, and the officer sighed.

"Ms. Taylor-Wu, you're free to go."

If it wasn't unethical, I'd send them a gift basket for always having to deal with people like us, Emmeline thought as she hooked her arm into Ms. Rose's for support.

She looked at her brother as they slowly walked back to Ms. Rose's car.

Shit, Mattie looks pissed.

Emmeline buckled in her seat belt and looked out the window, her eyes darting upward. She closed her eyes to focus her mind, and a familiar light and aura came into her view. It stayed with her as Matthew peeled through the slick city streets.

She looked at her brother's stoic profile. "Mattie, why are you so quiet?"

Matthew kept his eyes on the road. "What happened back there?"

Emmeline glanced at her side mirror. Ms. Rose sat quietly in the back, but Emmeline knew she was listening and waiting for an explanation.

"I think a large bird fell on top of my car, and I lost control," Emmeline said lamely.

"A bird fell on top of your car," Matthew repeated.

Don't be so dense. Emmeline gave him a look.

Ms. Rose's stern voice came from the back. "Emia, I'm thankful you're okay, and you're lucky you didn't hurt anyone else. Do you need a defensive driving refresher? Or a chauffeur? And why were you out so late again?"

"I know I'm lucky," Emmeline murmured. She shivered at the memory of the raizour stalking her with their sharp teeth and claws. "And I don't need a refresher or a chauffeur. I was helping a friend tonight."

"I'd like to know who this friend is who almost cost you your life," Ms. Rose snapped.

Emmeline turned around to face Ms. Rose. "It's not his fault, and you know it." She turned back to look out the passenger window. "Can we all just let it go? I'm fine."

Matthew gave her a firm look of disapproval.

"Sorry, Ms. Rose." Emmeline felt like a child again.

Matthew parked Ms. Rose's car in the underground garage, and they all trudged back into the house, where Mr. Jae was waiting at the top of the stairs. He didn't say anything and only gave Emmeline a gentle hug when she reached him.

"Everyone, kitchen first," Matthew ordered. He went to his office and returned with his bag. "Emia, sit at the table."

"Okay, Mr. Bossy," Emmeline grumbled.

She didn't bother fighting her brother, especially not with Ms. Rose and Mr. Jae both standing beside him with their arms crossed. She let Matthew check her all over again until he was satisfied that the paramedics hadn't missed anything.

Ms. Rose let out a breath after Matthew was done. "Everybody to bed. Emia, we'll talk about this in the morning. Go take a shower and get some rest." She turned on her heel and left the kitchen with Mr. Jae following closely behind her.

"Mattie, I think Ms. Rose is mad at me," Emmeline said.

"Can you blame her?"

"I guess not."

"What happened tonight?"

"Ellis was accompanying me home when we were attacked by several raizour. I called Erik for help because Ellis couldn't fight all of them. Erik didn't even have time to put on his armor. When Ellis killed one of the raizour, its body landed on the roof of my car, and that was how I lost control."

"What are we going to do about the potential fallout? There are cameras everywhere, and everybody has a phone."

"I don't know. The nainthe don't show up well on camera, as they are camouflaged under the moonlight. I think it has something to do with their magic. There's nothing I can do about the cameras and witnesses. All I can do is play dumb and call it a day. I guess I could always pretend to faint or something. The press would eat that up." Emmeline looked at her phone. "Erik's waiting for me on my balcony. Do you have some clothes you could lend him?"

Matthew avoided looking at Emmeline and busied himself with packing his bag. "Yes, I'll bring it to your bedroom."

"Why are you being so weird? What's going on?"

"Anja's here too." Matthew's face proceeded to turn an interesting shade of pink.

"Anja? I thought it was Saadah's night?"

"Saadah's in the guest room."

"Where's Anja staying?" Emmeline's eyes widened with realization. "Oh, Mattie." She put her face in her hands. "I'm not going to say anything to Erik because that's between you and Anja, but I can tell you, I wouldn't want to be the one to tell the unstable-yet-*extremely-proficient-with-sharp-objects* older brother that you're sleeping with his sister."

"I'll bring you some clothes," Matthew muttered and stomped out of the kitchen.

∿

Emmeline moved the heavy drapes aside and looked through her glass balcony doors. The rain had stopped, and the clouds had started to clear, revealing a smattering of stars dotting the night sky. Erik was reclined across one of the loungers, and his head rolled to one side, fast asleep.

You must be tired, Erik. Should I wake you? You'd be much more comfortable in one of the free guest rooms.

Emmeline went to her closet to find an extra blanket when she heard a knock on her bedroom door. When she opened the door, there were a pair of black fleece joggers, a T-shirt, and a new pair of socks on the floor. She looked down the hallway, but it was empty.

I thought you weren't scared of anything, Mattie.

Emmeline snickered and shook her head as she picked up the clothes. She stacked the clothes on top of the blanket and slid open the balcony door as quietly as possible. Stepping out onto the covered balcony, she watched Erik sleep, his chest slowly rising and falling with each breath. The air around him seemed to crackle with electricity, and Emmeline felt a light prickle against her skin. She set the clothes on the small table beside him and shook out the large blanket, draping it over his body. Erik's eyes snapped open, and his hand shot out to grip hers.

"Erik, it's just me, Emia," Emmeline gasped.

"Sorry."

Erik loosened his grip on her hand, but his fingers lingered against hers. Suddenly, he let go of her hand and looked away.

"I didn't want to wake you up. I figured you must be exhausted, so I decided to try and let you sleep instead. That didn't work, and I still woke you up," Emmeline said.

"I'm a light sleeper."

"I brought you some of Mattie's clothes. You're a bit taller than him, but you look about the same size. At least it'll get you through the night so you don't have to sleep in wet clothes. You don't have to stay if you don't want to. Saadah's here."

"I'd feel better if I stayed. Tonight was unexpected, and I should've sensed that raizour were nearby. The raizour were waiting for you, though I don't think they counted on Ellis or me being there."

Emmeline stared at Erik in shock.

"Do you want to sit?" Erik shifted to one side of the lounger and held out his hand.

Emmeline gripped Erik's hand and perched on the side of the lounger as wild thoughts raced through her head.

"This whole situation is ludicrous. How did I even get mixed up with the nainthe and raizour?" Emmeline asked.

"I don't know how any of us were chosen for this life."

"What have I gotten myself into? I'm going to die, aren't I?"

"You're not going to die. I promise I'll protect you with my life."

"I don't want anyone protecting me with their life. I don't want anyone to die because of me," Emmeline insisted.

"I know."

Erik looked down at her hand and ran his thumb across the top. Emmeline shivered, aware of their closeness and the feel of his fingers against her sensitive skin.

Erik blinked, and his eyes were clear again. He stood up and let go of her hand.

"It's late. You should get some rest."

"Do you want a guest room?"

"I can share with Saadah." He picked up the dry clothes and his blades. "Just the next balcony?"

Emmeline nodded.

"Good night, Emia."

"Good night, Erik."

Her heart skipped, and she clutched her hands to her chest as Erik jumped over the railing and landed on the next balcony. He looked over his shoulder, and his eyes burned bright against the moonlight before he turned and melted into the shadows.

CHAPTER FORTY

LINES CROSSED

Emmeline was startled awake by her phone buzzing in her ear.

Why am I constantly being woken up by my phone? I need to start putting this thing on silent, she grumbled.

Ms. Rose: Emia, darling, how many people stayed over last night? I thought you had one friend staying over. There are a bunch of people in the garden right now. I should order some food.

Emia: Good morning, Ms. Rose. How many people?

Ms. Rose: There are six, including Mattie.

Why are there six? I'd better get downstairs.

Emia: On my way. Sorry about that. It must've slipped my mind. Yes, please order some pastries. Can you bring out coffee, tea, and water?

Emmeline threw herself out of bed and flew through her morning routine. She grabbed her phone and tablet and hurried downstairs to the kitchen, where Ms. Rose was preparing a cart of beverages. Emmeline walked up to her and kissed her on the cheek.

"Are you still upset with me, Ms. Rose?"

Ms. Rose gave her a stern look before she stopped what she was doing. "Upset? No. Concerned? Yes." She sighed. "I promised your parents that I would watch over you and Mattie and keep you both safe for as long as possible. Last night, it crossed my mind that I was very close to breaking that promise."

"It wasn't your fault. How would you have stopped a bird or whatever it was from landing on top of my car? You can't protect us forever, but I'm grateful for you." Emmeline gave her a big hug.

Ms. Rose sighed again and patted Emmeline on the back. "Your friends are outside, waiting for you."

Emmeline looked out the patio window, and her eyes widened in surprise.

"I don't recognize anyone, except Saadah and the strange man who was in our kitchen last time. Who are the others?" Ms. Rose asked.

"You know Saadah?"

"Yes, sometimes, he stays in the guest room." Ms. Rose raised an eyebrow at Emmeline. "Why are you surprised? Did you think I'd wait for you to do introductions?"

Emmeline stared at Ms. Rose before shaking her head. "I'll introduce you to the others when we get outside."

Emmeline's phone vibrated against the kitchen counter.

Gus: Eva and I are almost at your house. Can you open the gate and garage for us?

Emia: What do you mean? Why are you coming over?

Gus: I'll explain when we get inside. It's important.

Emmeline groaned. There was no stopping them. *What am I going to do?*

Emia: It's open. I have friends over right now. Just go straight to the garden.

"Ms. Rose, better change that breakfast order to account for nine. Eleven, including you and Mr. Jae."

~

Emmeline walked onto the patio, and Ms. Rose followed with the beverage cart. Emmeline made eye contact with Matthew, and his face was blank, but his eyes screamed for help. Emmeline would laugh if she didn't feel so bad for him.

To Matthew's left was Anja, in front of him were Erik and Javier, and at the end of the table were Ellis and Saadah. Emmeline looked amusedly at Ellis, who appeared oblivious to the awkwardness at the table.

"Good morning, everyone," Emmeline said before gesturing to Ms. Rose. "I'd like to introduce you to Ms. Rose. She's our governess."

"Don't mind my dear Emia. I was their governess up until they were in their teenage years. Now, I'm their glorified housekeeper, picking up after their messes."

"Ms. Rose, you know Saadah, and you remember Erik?"

Erik stood up to his full height and shook her outstretched hand. He glanced at Emmeline before turning back to Ms. Rose. "I'm sorry for intruding so early. Please don't bother yourself with us. We'll be on our way soon."

"Nonsense. I've already ordered catering, and it'll be delivered in the next fifteen minutes."

"Ms. Rose, this is Javier, Ellis, and Anja," Emmeline said.

Everyone took turns, shaking Ms. Rose's hand.

"We've been working on a new charity project together, but it's still in its infancy stage." Emmeline cringed as she lied.

There was a light cough or perhaps a choke around the table, but she didn't dare look to see who it had come from. Ms. Rose raised an eyebrow at Emmeline.

She knows I'm lying. How does she always know?

"Beverages are on the cart. I'll bring out the pastries once they arrive." With that, Ms. Rose swept back inside the house.

As soon as Ms. Rose disappeared through the doors, Anja jumped up and ran over to the cart to pour herself a large cup of coffee.

Emmeline took a seat beside Matthew. "Javier, what brings you to my home?"

"I'm concerned for your safety. Last night was unheard of. In all my years, I've never seen such a brazen attack on an elystier. I want you to reconsider moving to the Sanctuary."

"I'm sorry, but I can't. I'm not leaving my home or my family."

"Do you understand how close you and Ellis came to dying last night if Erik hadn't made it there in time?" Javier asked.

Ellis spoke up. "I know it's not for me to say, but I also think you should move to the Sanctuary. If last night was a sign of what's to come, we will need a team following you to keep you safe. I don't think I could've protected you on my own."

Emmeline looked at her hands. "I'll think about it, but no promises."

The patio doors slid open, and August and Eva stepped into the garden. They stopped at the sight of all the people around the table and looked at Emmeline with wide eyes.

"Eva, Gus, don't be shy. Pull up a chair," Emmeline said.

Every person, including Matthew, turned to look at Emmeline, but she only shrugged.

"This was bound to happen sooner or later. Might as well get it over with."

"Get what over with?" August asked as she and Eva sat down.

Javier stiffened. "Emmeline," he warned.

Eva leaned forward and narrowed her eyes at Javier. "I don't like the tone of your voice. Don't talk to Emia like that."

Emmeline lay a hand on Eva's arm, and Eva leaned back in her chair, her sharp eyes never leaving Javier's face.

"Javier, for future reference, you should know that no one in my life takes even the slightest hint of a threat well," Emmeline said.

"It wasn't a threat. It was a precaution."

Emmeline turned to Eva. "Javier and I are still learning how to communicate effectively with each other. It's a work in progress."

"Why do you need to learn how to communicate with him at all?" August asked as she eyed Javier down.

"Let me do a round of introductions first, and then I'll explain." Emmeline introduced each person around the table and let everyone settle down with a drink.

She took a deep breath and exhaled.

This is going to be fun.

"Javier, August and Eva are my two closest friends, and I consider them my family. Gus is the director of my family foundation and oversees all financial aspects, including audits. Eva runs her own private technology firm and handles all non-physical security-related dealings for my family and our businesses. Eva's been investigating the small matter of me being followed."

Eva tapped the table. "Actually, it's not a small matter."

August shook her head. "No small matter."

Emmeline glanced at Eva and August. "Let me tell you more about the people around the table, and then you can fill us all in." She gestured to Javier. "This is Javier and his team of private security experts. I didn't tell you guys earlier because I didn't want to worry you, but there's another separate threat against me."

"What?" Eva glared at Emmeline.

August gasped. "What do you mean?"

"Ms. Rose and Mr. Jae don't know yet, and I'd like to keep it that way. Obviously, Mattie knows."

"Oh great, Mattie knows. That's fabulous. What's he going to do about it? Protect you with his stethoscope?" Eva asked sarcastically.

"I like her," Anja snickered.

Matthew rolled his eyes. "Did you pick a stethoscope because that's the only piece of medical equipment you know?"

"I'm trying to make a point," Eva snapped at Matthew, but her glare remained on Emmeline. "What's this other threat?"

The patio doors slid open again, and Ms. Rose came out, carrying an enormous tray of pastries. Eva clammed up, and both she and August pasted smiles on their faces. Erik stood up and took the tray from Ms. Rose and set it in the center of the patio table.

"Thank you, Erik." Ms. Rose turned to Emmeline. "I ordered a new car for you. It'll be delivered here within the next two hours."

Ellis sat up. "A new car? What did you get?"

Javier gave him a withering glare, and Ellis sank back into his seat.

"Sorry, not the right time," Ellis mumbled.

He's going to be disappointed when he finds out I ordered the same car.

Eva's smile faltered, and she looked at Emmeline. "Why did you get a new car?"

Emmeline froze, and her eyes darted around the table. Everyone seemed to be looking somewhere else, except at her or Eva.

Ms. Rose pulled out her phone and tapped into her photo album. "Oh, Emia didn't tell you yet, Eva? She was in a car accident last night. Apparently, a *bird* fell on top of her car. A big one. Let me show you what happened to her car."

Ms. Rose handed her phone to Eva, and August leaned over to see. August's hand immediately went to cover her mouth.

"What the actual fuck, Emia?" Eva snapped.

Eva handed the phone back to Ms. Rose, and Emmeline could tell she was getting angrier by the second.

"Thanks a lot, Ms. Rose." Emmeline rubbed her temples.

"Always a pleasure, Emia, darling." Ms. Rose turned on her heel and walked gracefully back into the house.

Eva crossed her arms and waited for Emmeline to talk.

"Last night, I was run off the road. I had hired Javier and his team a few weeks ago for extra protection. Completely off the books. It was a good thing Erik and Ellis were following me. They took care of the threat, though my car didn't survive the attack."

"Who ran you off the road?"

"I don't know. Javier and his team are working on it."

Eva looked at Javier and didn't flinch when Javier challenged her with his own glare.

"What's the name of your company?" Eva asked.

"We don't have a name," Javier replied.

Emmeline reached over and took Eva's hand. "This is part of the reason why I didn't tell you. This needs to stay off the record, and you'll have to trust me on this. It's also for your safety. If something happens, you truthfully won't know anything. Do you understand?"

Eva stared at Emmeline for a long time before nodding.

"Eva, promise me. No more questions. I need to hear you say it," Emmeline pleaded.

"I promise," Eva said through clenched teeth.

"This is also why I've been absent in so many things lately, and it'll continue for the next while." Emmeline turned to August. "Gus, I need you to take a bigger role in the family foundation. I'll still do some face time for our title sponsorships, but otherwise, I will take a step back. You can hire any resources you need to help you with the workload."

August nodded and pressed her lips together.

"Eva, can you monitor our networks and ensure that our security is constantly updated? Not just for my protection, but also for Mattie, Ms. Rose, Mr. Jae, and Gus."

"I already do that," Eva said.

Emmeline smiled at her best friend. *That's my girl.*

"Now that we've gotten that out of the way, do you want to talk about my other problem?" Emmeline asked.

August frowned. "With everybody here?"

Emmeline nodded.

Eva clicked on her tablet. "I was able to figure out who had ordered you to be followed."

"Is it who I thought it was?" Emmeline asked.

"Yes, it was Philip."

Emmeline pushed her chair back and stood up. She strode out to the garden and crossed her arms against her chest.

Why would Philip do this to me? she thought, angry tears prickling her eyes. *Emmeline, you're so stupid sometimes. You should've trusted your gut. Mom always told you to trust your gut.*

She felt Erik's presence beside her, and she wiped her eyes with the back of her hand.

"I can take care of him for you."

Emmeline didn't look at him. "You're kind, Erik. At least in your threatening and frightening way. Anja already offered to do the same last night. She didn't even wait for confirmation."

"Her intuition's usually good." Erik waited beside her while she composed herself.

"I'm ready to go back."

Erik stepped out of her way and followed her back to the patio.

Emmeline sat back down. "My apologies. Eva, please continue."

"Philip's had you followed for some time now. Since before the Royal Children's Rehabilitation Hospital gala," Eva said.

Matthew cleared his throat. "This asset management firm, how serious are they?"

"Their investigators are all on payroll, and I did a background check on most of them. Some are legitimate private investigators, and some are ex-military. I only found instructions to follow Emia and report on all her activities. I also didn't find any official priors on the mayor, but there are rumors that he has a temper. It's one of the unofficial reasons for his separation from his ex-wife."

"Did he hurt her?"

"No official charges, so I can't say. But you know what they say about smoke and fire."

"Do you know why he's having me followed?"

Eva shook her head. "Nothing concrete, but I think Gus might have some theories."

"I did some checking on the foundations he supports." August looked at Eva, who nodded encouragingly. "Eva might or might not have gotten access to the financial records of said foundations. He's funneled some of the money from the foundations to his accounts. This guy has a shitload of debt and uses this scheme to keep creditors at bay. I think he has his eye on you because of who you are and your wealth."

He thought I was the dumb heiress who would maintain his extravagant lifestyle. But why me? There are many wealthy women out there. Emmeline answered her own question, *Because he thought you, Emmeline Taylor-Wu, the reclusive heiress, would be desperate enough not to see through his lies.*

"Emia, are you okay?" August asked.

Emmeline blinked. "Yes."

"What would you like me to do?"

"Can you send me proof of him embezzling funds?"

"I can, but you can't use that information. Not legally anyway."

"You let me and my lawyer worry about that," Emmeline bit out. She struggled to quash the fury threatening to erupt at any moment. "Eva, Gus, thank you for your help, but I don't want you looking into this any further. I know I asked you to cross a line, which wasn't right of me."

"No," Eva snapped.

"I'll do this through different channels, and don't worry; I'll get even."

"No," Eva repeated herself.

"Think about Sally and Gus and all the people our family foundation helps. I don't want to jeopardize any of that, so no more. I want you to promise me."

Emmeline knew she'd hit the mark when Eva's face fell. The foundation and her loved ones were always her weak spot.

"I promise," Eva said grudgingly.

Emmeline looked expectantly at August.

"I promise," August mumbled.

"Good."

"Eva and I should get going. With all that's going on, are you still going to attend the Million Lanterns fundraiser?" August asked.

"I already promised the hospital administration that I would. Philip asked me to accompany him, but that will no longer happen."

"Do you want me to come with you?"

"No, I'll be fine. I've been doing this alone for a long time, and nothing has changed. I won't let some wannabe stalker ruin what our foundation has worked so hard for."

Javier regarded Emmeline before speaking. "Anja, I'd like you to attend the fundraiser with Lesedi, under your existing cover. Erik, you're on perimeter guard and watching for two threats.

Emmeline, Saadah will be your official bodyguard at the event. I wouldn't mind giving your other problem a good scare."

Ellis perked up. "Instead of Saadah, I could go with Sophia, and we could be Emmeline's bodyguards. It'd give me a chance to take Sophia somewhere fancy even though we'd technically be working."

Javier narrowed his eyes at Ellis.

"Never mind," Ellis muttered.

"Ellis, you're to patrol Emmeline's residence. If Sophia wishes, she can do patrols with you."

Eva looked happy with the arrangement, which made Emmeline feel better. Eva and August packed their bags and stood up, each giving Emmeline a quick hug.

"Be safe, Emia," August whispered in her ear.

Emmeline felt her heart tug as her two best friends vanished back into her house.

Abruptly, Matthew pushed back his chair and stood up.

"I need to get to the hospital. I'm already late." He stalked back into the house.

"Is Matthew upset?" Ellis asked.

Emmeline tried to downplay her brother's rudeness. "He doesn't like to be late for anything."

I think my brother is jealous of Anja attending the fundraiser with Lesedi.

Emmeline watched as fleeting emotions ran across Anja's face before she pressed her lips into a frown.

Ellis changed the topic. "Does anyone else find it odd that both these issues are happening at the same time?"

"Probably just my bad luck," Emmeline muttered. She unlocked her phone, and her finger hovered over her messaging app.

Emia: Philip, we shouldn't see each other anymore. It was fun while it lasted, but it's not going to work out.

Philip: What brought this on? Let's talk about this like adults. I can't call you right now, but I'll come over after I'm done with my meetings. Don't make any rash decisions.

Emia: I've made up my mind. Don't come over. My security team will stop you from entering the premises.

Philip: You're making a big mistake.

Emia: You made the first mistake when you hired private investigators to follow me. Don't forget to find someone else to accompany you to the Million Lanterns fundraiser.

Philip: You're going to embarrass me at one of the year's most important events. Who do you think you are?

Emmeline blocked Philip's number and slammed her phone on the patio table. She heard a crack and flipped her phone over, groaning at the shattered screen.

This will be my third phone in a few weeks.

"Well, the smaller of my problems should no longer be a problem. Javier, are we done here?" Emmeline could feel her anger swirling inside her, threatening to burst at any moment.

"We can be. I hope you'll come by the Sanctuary tonight. Also, don't assume that the mayor will give up so easily. You should plan that he still has people following you," Javier replied.

Emmeline stood up and clenched her jaw. She couldn't bring herself to say anything more.

Don't let them see you cry. Wait until you get to your room.

She composed her features and turned away. She felt Erik watching her as she walked back into her family home.

⁓

Emmeline heard a knock on her bedroom door and debated on ignoring it. Her eyes were puffy and red from crying, and she was in an extremely foul mood.

I'd better get the door before Ms. Rose gets Mr. Jae to take it apart.

She opened the door, and Ms. Rose looked at her with alarm.

"Emia, darling, what's wrong? What happened?"

"Don't worry; I'm not going to cry anymore. I don't have any tears left. I'm just dehydrated now."

"That doesn't answer my question about what happened." Ms. Rose took out her phone and dialed a number. "Mr. Jae, can you bring some warm water to Emia's room?"

"I can walk to the kitchen. You didn't have to send for Mr. Jae."

"Knowing you, you'd rather die of dehydration than leave your room. Before I forget, here's your third new phone. Everything's set up already." Ms. Rose held out a new device, and Emmeline mumbled her thanks with embarrassment.

"Now, sweetheart, tell me what happened."

Emmeline proceeded to tell Ms. Rose everything about the mayor.

"I'm so angry with myself. Why am I so stupid?"

Ms. Rose pulled Emmeline into a hug. "Oh, darling, love is hard to find. Your heart is so kind, and your parents did a wonderful job raising you and Mattie. Many people out there can't see beyond all this other stuff that surrounds you."

"I didn't even like Philip that much!"

"I know, sweetheart." Ms. Rose ruffled Emmeline's hair.

"It was nowhere close to how I felt about Sam all those years ago. Did you know Sam's married now? He has two beautiful kids, and his wife is lovely. I met her at one of the charity galas." Emmeline wiped her eyes.

"Emia, you are extraordinary. You and Mattie both. Don't forget that, because when you find that special someone, you'll know. And you'll know because he'll see that beautiful light inside you, and you, in turn, will see his. He'll share the same values, and he'll be your equal in all aspects. Don't settle for anything less." Ms. Rose rested her cheek on Emmeline's hair. "Can you trust me on that?"

Emmeline nodded and let out a breath.

"I'll order something you love for dinner tonight. Do you know if Mattie will be joining us?"

"I doubt it. He was upset when he left for work this morning and will probably drown himself in paperwork until midnight."

"I worry very much for Mattie." Ms. Rose sighed and stood up to leave Emmeline's room. "I'll see you for dinner."

"Ms. Rose?"

"Yes, Emia?"

"I love you."

Ms. Rose smiled. "I love you too, sweetheart."

CHAPTER FORTY-ONE

RIGHT BESIDE YOU

Erik: Emia, I can pick you up if you're coming to the Sanctuary tonight.

Emia: I'm having dinner at home, and I need to take care of some things afterward. Can you pick me up at ten?

Erik: Yes. I'm going to take a motorcycle, so dress appropriately.

Emia: I don't have a helmet.

Erik: I'll bring you one. Don't worry; it'll be new.

How does one dress appropriately for riding a motorcycle?
Emmeline flopped back down on her bed and rubbed her eyes.

It's almost dinnertime. I'd better get ready. I will let security know Erik's coming.

Emmeline hopped in the shower and soaked under the scalding hot water, letting her anger drain away from her earlier interaction with Philip. After a quick web search on motorcycle outfits, she picked out a pair of black jean leggings, a fitted cross-back tank, and a cropped leather jacket. She went back to the bathroom and looked at her face in the mirror. Her eyes were still puffy and red, so she tried to dab on a bit of concealer to hide the mess, but it was futile.

I give up.

She sighed and went downstairs for dinner.

~

Emmeline heard the rumble of a motorcycle outside her home and grabbed her backpack and leather jacket.

"That sounds like a motorcycle outside. Let me guess. Erik's here to pick you up?" Ms. Rose said as she put the dishes away into the cupboards.

"How did you know?"

"It's not rocket science." Ms. Rose stopped what she was doing. "He seems very serious. Is he a good person?"

"I don't think I'm in any position to judge whether someone's a good person or not. I haven't been doing a good job of that lately," Emmeline muttered.

"It was one person. Don't let one person overshadow everyone and everything else, especially your trust in your own judgment."

"I think he's a good person. He's been a good friend to me."

Ms. Rose peered over her glasses. "Emia, that man wants you as more than a friend."

Emmeline turned pink, and she looked away. "No, he doesn't."

"I see it in the way he looks at you." Ms. Rose raised an eyebrow. "I've only met him twice. The first time was just"—she paused—"odd. But this morning, I could see it in his eyes. I'm just not sure how I feel about him."

"I don't think I'm his type, and he's not really my type."

"You gave the mayor a chance, and he wasn't your type."

"And look how great that turned out," Emmeline replied sarcastically, earning a stern look from Ms. Rose. "Sorry," she mumbled.

"I don't get the sense Erik's anything like Philip. They're probably as far opposite as opposites could get. I'm not trying to convince you that you should date him. I just want you to be aware that he doesn't want you as just a friend."

Emmeline shifted uncomfortably, and she stared at her hands.

"Do you like him?" Ms. Rose asked gently.

Emmeline opened her mouth and then closed it, her cheeks flushing deeper.

Ms. Rose smiled and patted Emmeline's hand. "I assume Erik's bringing you a helmet. You know how I feel about motorcycles."

Emmeline nodded and kissed Ms. Rose on the cheek. "I'll be home late, but he'll make sure I get home in one piece."

"I'm sure he will. Be safe, sweetheart."

"I'll try, Ms. Rose." She grinned and earned herself another stern glare from her forever governess.

Emmeline locked the front door and nodded at Tom, the security supervisor she had hired.

"Tom, it's warm outside. Make sure you and Hannah have enough water and take your breaks."

"Mr. Jae always takes care of us. Have a good night, Ms. Taylor-Wu," Tom replied.

Emmeline turned to look for Erik. He had his full face helmet on and was sitting on his sport bike, waiting patiently for her. She found it disconcerting not to be able to see his gray eyes through the darkly tinted visor.

Erik. Emmeline smiled shyly at him.

He got off his motorcycle and removed his helmet, his icy eyes warming as they found hers. The air crackled between them, and Emmeline tucked her hair behind her ears as she walked down the steps to meet him. Erik unhooked a second helmet from the lock underneath the backseat and took several long strides to meet her.

"Why have you been crying?" Erik asked, his eyes lingering on her face.

"I don't want to talk about it."

"Was it because of what happened this morning? Because you ended your relationship with the mayor?"

Emmeline gave him a withering look. "Yes."

"It seems that you're crying every time I see you."

"Well, that's because you cause the majority of it," Emmeline retorted.

Hurt flashed across Erik's eyes, and he stepped back, but the look disappeared as quickly as it had appeared.

Emmeline instantly regretted her harsh words. "I'm sorry, Erik. I'm in a terrible mood, and I just took it out on you. Really, I'm sorry."

"Don't ever apologize for speaking the truth," Erik replied and looked down the driveway. "Someone in a white car is watching your house from down the street. Would you like me to take care of them?"

"No, it's time for this nonsense to end." Emmeline turned back to Tom. "My friend says someone's staked outside the property."

"We're aware, Ms. Taylor-Wu. Our head office is on it, and the police will be here in three minutes."

Emmeline pulled out her phone from her backpack and dialed her lawyer. "Peter, I'd like you to have an off-record conversation with the private asset management firm the mayor is with. Let them know I'm aware of their arrangement and I expect them to cease all surveillance of my family and me. If not, several of their prominent clients will be publicly liquidating their assets from their portfolio."

"I will make an in-person visit. How long do they have to execute this?" Peter asked.

"Confirmation within forty-eight hours. The clock starts after your visit."

"Very well. Anything else?"

"That's it."

"Consider it done."

Emmeline clicked off her phone and looked up at Erik. "Let's hope this works. I'm out of tricks if it doesn't."

Erik eyed her. "Remind me not to get on your bad side."

"Funny, that's how I feel about your sister."

Erik's eyes crinkled, and he laughed. Emmeline's heart warmed, and her mouth tugged at his musical tenor.

I like hearing him laugh.

"We should get going. I don't want you to be late for training."

Erik snapped on his helmet and got back on the motorcycle. Emmeline followed suit and climbed onto the backseat.

"Hold on tight." Erik started the engine and the motorcycle growled to life.

Emmeline wrapped her arms around Erik's waist as he knocked back the kickstand. Revving the engine, he took off down the steep driveway.

~

The motorcycle roared through the underground parking garage and stopped beside several other motorcycles. Emmeline let go of Erik and hopped off the backseat. She pulled off her helmet and shook out her long hair.

"That was fun!" Emmeline felt exhilarated and refreshed.

Seeing the city from the back of a motorcycle was amazing. I needed that.

Erik shrugged off his leather jacket and removed his helmet, tucking both under his arm. "I'm glad you enjoyed it. I'll probably use the motorcycle more often since it's more maneuverable than a car." He held out his hand to Emmeline. "I can carry your helmet, if you'd like."

Emmeline handed Erik her helmet and shrugged off her own leather jacket. She stole a glance at Erik's serious profile as they walked in silence through the courtyard. He moved slower than usual, staying close beside her and matching her steps as they made their way to Ember's studio.

"How long will you be staying tonight?" Erik asked.

"I only have training. There are a few things I want to test with Ember. I noticed you have a distinct aura, and I want to see if I can tell the difference with others." Emmeline paused. "Are you going on a hunt tonight?"

Erik nodded, and Emmeline furrowed her brow.

"What's wrong?" Erik asked.

Emmeline hesitated. "Don't get upset. I might have mentioned to Javier that the rest of the nainthe need to pull their weight around here and take on more of the nightly hunts."

She braced herself for Erik's indignation and anger, but nothing came. She peeked up at him, but he just stared straight ahead.

Silence is usually worse.

"Are you mad?"

Erik shook his head. "Anja already told me. Javier did speak to me about it, and so did Maira."

Emmeline breathed a sigh of relief, but annoyance quickly followed. "So, why hasn't Javier done anything about it?"

"Because I told him not to. I don't want anyone to die because I need a vacation. Nobody's forcing me to do this, and it's my choice. Can you respect my choice?"

Emmeline's heart fell, but she nodded. They stopped in front of Ember's studio, and Emmeline held out her hand to take back her helmet. Erik handed it to her and stood there awkwardly.

"Emia, would you be able to stay until I come back from my hunt?"

"Of course I can. You don't even need to ask."

"You can't be as careless as you were the last few times. If I don't recognize you, you must get away as fast as possible. I will ask Anja to accompany you, just in case."

"That's a good idea. Anja usually comes with me to meet with

Ember if she's not scheduled for a hunt, so I'll stay with her until you get back." Emmeline looked up at Erik, and his icy-gray eyes deepened as they met hers. Her heart raced, and she tried to look away but couldn't.

He's standing so close to me.

"Emia, after I come back and if I'm okay, would you like to grab something to eat together?" Erik asked. "But only if it's not too late for you," he added hastily.

Is this his version of asking me on a date? Emmeline blushed and mentally shook herself. *Don't be silly. It's just food.*

"I'd like that, Erik."

"What are you guys talking about?" A voice came from behind Emmeline's ear, and she shrieked.

"Anja, don't do that! I hate it when you do that." Emmeline clutched her chest.

Erik rubbed his ear and glared at his sister. "Was that necessary?"

"Sorry. It's hard to resist sometimes. You need to work on your jumpiness, Emmeline."

"I don't know how you expect me to work on my jumpiness," Emmeline snapped.

Anja glanced at the helmet in Emmeline's hand and then at Erik. "Good. You got her on a motorcycle. So, what were you guys talking about?"

Emmeline scanned the courtyard to make sure nobody was in the vicinity. "I'm going to stay after my session with Ember and wait for Erik to return from his hunt. I'm not completely sure yet, but I think I can remove the pain Erik feels after a hunt."

"What do you mean?" Anja looked at her and Erik in confusion.

"The first time I did it, it was an accident. It was the second time I went to find Erik, after he lost his mind, that I noticed it."

"I'm standing right beside you," Erik said dryly.

Emmeline ignored him and continued, "I didn't think much of it, but the third time I went to find Erik, it worked again! I was able to help him change back to human form."

Anja's mouth fell open, and she looked at her brother with hope in her eyes. "Really? That's amazing! But how?"

"I don't understand how it works, so I want to test it on him a few more times."

"Why don't you want to tell anyone?"

"I want to be sure first. I haven't even told Mattie yet. Though he's been a bit preoccupied lately." Emmeline raised an eyebrow at Anja, who flushed and turned away.

"Anja, I want you to wait with Emia. If I don't recognize her, you need to get her out. Fly her out if you must, but don't let her stay. She's incredibly stubborn." A small smile pulled at Erik's mouth.

"I'm standing right beside you, Erik," Emmeline mimicked him and made a face.

Erik gave her a stern look, but his eyes lit up brilliantly against the darkening sky. Emmeline's heart quickened as she looked up at him again.

"Emia, you're going to be late for your training session."

CHAPTER FORTY-TWO

AMBUSHED

"What do you see?" Ember asked.

Emmeline let out a breath. "I see you close to Anja and farther away from me."

"Now, picture yourself moving and the world stretching with you."

Emmeline watched as Ember's aura came into focus and Anja's aura floated closer, swirling around Ember.

"I see you near each other."

"Are you able to tell us apart?" Ember asked.

Emmeline nodded.

"How?"

"You look the same, but you feel different. I can't describe it, but I can tell you're you and Anja's Anja. It's obvious when your auras are side by side."

"Okay, stretch out your mind again. Stay focused and try to let it wander at the same time. I'm not going to ask you any more questions."

Emmeline let her body relax as she moved through the darkness. She reached out with her hand and ran her fingers through its silkiness. Suddenly, a familiar aura came into view. It contorted in the darkness, its light threads flickering viciously.

"Emmeline!" Anja shouted.

Emmeline blinked, and the chaotic aura and blazing light threads disappeared. She gripped Anja's arm for support.

"It's okay. Slow down and take a deep breath," Anja said.

Ember knelt beside them. "You were screaming. What happened?"

Emmeline struggled to get the words out.

"Erik's in trouble. I saw him, and he was burning."

"What do you mean?" Anja looked at Emmeline with alarm.

"I can recognize Erik's aura, just like I can distinguish yours and Ember's, but I think my connection to him is stronger than any other I have. You need to trust me; something's very wrong." Emmeline's voice rose.

"But he's on a hunt right now."

Anja stopped and horror crossed her face. Her irises widened, and she changed into nainthe form. Running to the exit, she bent down and swept her blade off the floor.

"Anja, you need to get your armor!" Ember cried out.

Anja ignored her and disappeared out the door and into the night.

"Shit!" Ember grabbed her phone and dialed frantically. "Erik's in trouble, and Anja went to look for him. Send the emergency teams out. I don't know which direction she went." She hung up. "Emmeline, I'm going to bring you to Javier."

"No. I'm going to the courtyard to wait." Emmeline picked up her backpack and ran to the exit.

"It's too dangerous!"

Emmeline ignored Ember and sprinted outside. She craned her neck and looked around the dark sky, hoping for a glimpse of Erik or Anja. A team of nainthe in full gear came running out into the courtyard, and with a few short commands, they flew out into the night sky in quick succession.

Please find him.

Emmeline closed her eyes and tried to concentrate, but she couldn't.

Ember picked up both her hands. "Ignore the chaos and focus on my voice. Breathe."

Emmeline slowed her breathing and let Ember come into her vision.

"Let your mind calm and stretch. You know Erik's and Anja's auras." Ember paused before gently continuing, "Now, find them."

"Incoming!" a loud voice shouted.

Emmeline jolted out of the darkness, and her eyes snapped open. Several nainthe landed on the grass and sheathed their blades. Emmeline recognized Julian from the unruly brown curls that fell out as he removed his helmet. He turned his head to the sky, and the moonlight glossed over his boyish features, highlighting his prominent nose and moss-green eyes.

"Julian! Where are Erik and Anja?" Emmeline asked.

Julian pointed to the sky. "Right behind us."

Erik slammed into the ground and was followed by Anja, who held on to his blades. Anja changed into her human form and ran to Erik's side.

Erik dropped to his knees and groaned in pain. He flung his helmet off as Anja tried to help him remove the rest of his armor. Emmeline pushed her way past several nainthe and ran to them.

"What happened?" Emmeline's eyes darted between Erik and Anja.

Within seconds, Ben appeared beside her with a large duffel bag, and Lucia followed with a stretcher underneath her arm.

"I'm sorry, Emmeline, but you need to move," Ben said breathlessly.

Emmeline staggered out of the way and watched as Anja and Ben helped Erik remove his remaining armor. It looked like it had been shredded and split apart at the seams. Erik pulled off his shirt, and there were deep cuts across his torso and arms. A thin jellylike substance covered each wound, blistering the skin around it.

Ben panicked. "Erik, you need to change back! I can't treat you in nainthe form."

"I can't." Erik gripped his chest and looked around desperately. "Emia, help me," he choked out.

Emmeline pushed past Ben and fell beside Erik. His face contorted in pain as she cupped it in her hands.

"Erik, do you recognize me?" she breathed.

He nodded and squeezed his eyes shut.

Emmeline closed her eyes and leaned into him, resting her forehead against his. She focused on him and touched his aura.

"Emia, please," Erik choked out her name again.

Her hands warmed as the sensation of magic filled her. The slow vibration of hatred and violence ebbed and flowed away from Erik, smoothing out his aura. Gasps echoed around her, and she opened her eyes to find him back in human form.

"How are you feeling?" Emmeline ran her fingers gently across his cheekbones.

"Better, but still in pain," Erik gasped.

Julian's mouth dropped open, and he looked troubled. "How did you do that? How's that possible?"

Emmeline turned to Ben, who was staring at her and Erik in shock.

"Ben, pay attention!" Anja snapped.

Ben blinked out of his daze and pulled out a syringe filled with light-blue liquid. "Sorry, Erik, this is going to hurt. A lot."

Erik squeezed his eyes shut as Ben pushed the syringe into his left side. Tiny droplets of blue dripped down Erik's side, and he took a shallow breath before collapsing to the ground.

Emmeline followed Ben and Lucia as they brought Erik's unconscious body to the infirmary.

"What happens now?" Emmeline asked Ben.

"There's nothing else we can do for him. It's up to his body to fight the raizour poison. I gave him a dose of their antibodies."

"Have you done this before?"

Ben nodded. "Our bodies can fight scratches and minor cuts from raizour wings, but deep cuts, like what you saw on Erik, require the raizour antibodies to help speed up the healing process. If we don't use the antibodies, we won't heal fast enough to counter the poison."

"Does it always work?"

"No," Ben replied.

"It will. I've seen Erik recover from worse," Anja said confidently, but her eyes were filled with worry as she stood beside Erik's bed.

Emmeline's phone vibrated.

Mattie: I'm here. Infirmary?

Emia: Yes. Anja's here too.

Mattie: I expected so.

"Anja, I asked Mattie to come. He's walking over from the parking garage," Emmeline murmured.

Anja stared at Erik's unmoving body. "He was willing to come? He didn't answer any of my messages today."

"He was probably tied up at the hospital."

"He always answers my messages."

Emmeline's heart tightened, but she couldn't tell for who. "It's harder for him than most people. He processes things differently than you and me."

"I know."

There was a sharp knock on the door, and Matthew entered the room, carrying his backpack and duffel bag.

"Ben, I'll be in the office," Lucia said and stalked past Matthew without another word.

"She doesn't like that I'm here," Matthew stated as he pushed up his glasses.

"It's okay. I don't like that she's here either," Emmeline said. *She judged you from the moment she met you and hasn't given you a chance.*

"Dr. Taylor-Wu, it's nice to see you again. I hope this isn't a waste of your time. I don't think there's much you can do for Erik," Ben said.

"What happened?" Matthew asked.

"Erik was ambushed as he left for a hunt. He was attacked multiple times by raizour wings, which are coated with poison. As I just explained to Emmeline, our bodies can usually fight off minor cuts, but if they are significant, we need help. That's where raizour antibodies come in."

"Raizour antibodies?"

"We harvest it from their bodies before we burn them."

Matthew glanced over Erik's still body. "How did you give him the antibodies?" He looked around for an IV drip. "By injection?"

Ben nodded. "Directly into his spleen."

"What?" Matthew whirled around and stared at Ben.

"We don't know why, but it's the only way the antibodies work. Injection anywhere else doesn't work."

"How did you find the spleen?"

"Nainthe fundamental—know where your spleen is. We all have our spleen location marked on our bodies." Ben lifted the back of his shirt. A small *X* was tattooed on the left mid-side of his back.

"Fascinating," Matthew muttered. He looked at Anja's back and then at Emmeline.

Emmeline returned her brother's gaze, subtly casting her eyes toward Anja. *She needs you right now, Mattie.*

Matthew walked up to Anja and stood close beside her. He glanced back at Emmeline, and she nodded encouragingly at him. He turned back to Anja and threaded his fingers with hers. Anja looked up at him, and there were tear streaks on her cheeks. He bent his head and murmured something low in her ear.

Oh, Mattie, I know how much this hurts you.

Anja leaned into Matthew's shoulder, and he brushed her hair out of her face.

You must really like her a lot.

∼

Emmeline groaned.

My back and neck.

She lifted her arm and used her hand to pull her head off the back of the chair.

I should've slept on the floor instead.

She rubbed her eyes and sat up. A thick flannel blanket fell off her chest and landed on her lap.

Where's my jacket?

Emmeline spotted it folded on top of her backpack. She glanced at the bed, where Erik had been last night, but it was empty. Matthew and Anja were on the bed next to Erik's empty one. Matthew's eyes were open, and he stared at the ceiling while Anja was tucked into the crook of his arm, fast asleep.

"Mattie, where's Erik? Did they take him somewhere?" Emmeline whispered.

Matthew glanced down at Anja before whispering back, "I don't know. I just woke up not too long ago. I don't want to wake Anja. She's very tired."

Emmeline got up and unplugged her phone from the wall charger. She flipped through her messages.

Erik: Emia, thank you for staying last night. I went back to my room. I was worried you would get cold, so I got you a blanket. I'll message you later.

Emia: How are you feeling? Are you okay? How's it possible you were able to get up and walk out of the infirmary? You were unconscious!

Emia: I didn't mean to barrage you with questions. I'm glad you're feeling better.

    Emmeline waited a little bit but didn't hear back from Erik. She went through a few other messages when another caught her eye.

Peter: It's done.

    Emmeline didn't reply; she knew Peter would not expect her to.
    Good. I never want to see Philip ever again.
    A rap on the door startled her, and she looked up to see Javier at the doorway. Matthew raised a finger to his lips and glared at Javier.
    Mattie, did you shush the leader of the nainthe?
    Javier leveled a glare back at an unblinking Matthew, and Emmeline rolled her eyes. She gestured to Javier to step out of the room and closed the door behind her.
    "Emmeline, why didn't you tell me about your special ability? Did you not think it was something important I should know about?" Javier asked angrily.
    Emmeline looked away and didn't say anything.
    I don't have a good answer for him.
    Javier raised his voice in frustration. "This is not a game you're playing. There are lives at stake. How many times do I need to tell you this? When will you start to trust us?"

"I don't know who to trust. The only person who knew about this was Erik, and it was only by accident we discovered it."

Javier glared at her for the longest time before his face fell. He walked over to a small desk and sat down, gesturing for Emmeline to join him.

"It's unfortunate you feel this way, and I don't know how to change your mind. But I'm thankful you were there to help Erik. If he hadn't changed back to his human form, the poison would've had more time to work through his system."

"Ben thinks Erik was ambushed. How could that happen? I thought he could sense raizour presence."

"I don't know. Sometimes, Erik's ability isn't completely within his control, but it's extremely rare that it isn't. He's the strongest nainthe I have ever come across, and no one comes close to his abilities," Javier replied.

"Did the nainthe catch the raizour that ambushed Erik?"

"Anja and the emergency team got a few of them, but most got away. Their priority was to get Erik back to the safety of the Sanctuary. After they did that, they went out in two teams, but couldn't locate the raizour that had escaped. They found a large tear in the barrier and closed it."

"It's like they knew to wait for Erik."

"I agree." Javier regarded Emmeline. "Have you taken care of your other problem?"

"I think so."

"I'll take my leave now. I know you are tired and would like to go home," Javier said. He looked worn down, as if he hadn't slept all night.

Just as he was about to leave, the door opened, and Anja and Matthew stepped out.

"Anja, Dr. Taylor-Wu, I was about to head back to my office." Javier turned to Emmeline. "Who would you like to escort you home? I'd suggest Anja, but I'm sure she'd like to see her brother and get some rest too."

"I don't think we need an escort to go home. It's late morning, and nothing's going to happen now. Mattie can be my escort. I've hired security at my house for my other problem."

"Very well. I'll see you later." Javier turned and left the room.

"I'm going to go check on Erik." Anja looked guardedly at Matthew. "Will you come by later if you have time?"

Matthew nodded.

"I'm going to give you a kiss, Mattie."

Matthew leaned down, and Anja kissed him on the lips. She then rounded on Emmeline and engulfed her in a hug.

"Thank you for saving Erik. If he gets to call you Emia, I will call you that as well."

"You're welcome. Tell Erik I hope he feels better soon."

Matthew picked up his bags, and for the first time, Emmeline noticed how tired he looked.

Everyone's tired. We should all take naps.

Emmeline smiled wearily at Matthew. "Shall we go home?"

CHAPTER FORTY-THREE

RECKLESS

"Do you want me to drive?" Emmeline asked Matthew.

"I'm tired, not delusional."

"Fine." Emmeline rolled her eyes and slid into the passenger side, buckling herself in.

They drove in silence for most of the ride.

Mattie's in his own world, yet he's also entirely focused on the road. I wonder how he does it.

"Mattie." Emmeline waited for him to acknowledge her. "Mattie," she repeated herself.

"Yes?" Matthew blinked and glanced at Emmeline.

"Are you okay?"

"Why wouldn't I be okay?" Matthew gripped the steering wheel tighter. "My life's a mess. I'm emotionally incapacitated. My sister is mixed up with some strange people and gets attacked by monsters from another world. I think I'm in love with someone I shouldn't be in love with, and I'm not sure I even know what love is. I don't understand anything that's happening, and nothing makes sense."

Emmeline's eyes widened. *I can't remember the last time Mattie had an outburst. I didn't think of how all this madness might impact him.* She paused. *Wait, did he say love?*

"Mattie, stop the car."

"I'm fine."

"You're not fine. I mean it. Stop the car."

Matthew signaled to the right, pulled his car to the side of the road, and turned off the ignition. He stared out the windshield, and his eyes flickered back and forth between different focal points.

"Mattie, you're not emotionally incapacitated or challenged or whatever word you want to use to describe it. Just because you feel emotions differently doesn't mean that it's bad. It's just different." Emmeline smiled at her brother. "Anja doesn't seem to mind at all. In fact, I find her quite protective of you. She was upset when you left yesterday morning and didn't talk to her all day. She didn't blame you though."

"I can't understand why."

"Maybe she sees you for you. Smart, kind, brave, and handsome. Like the way I see you."

"Why would she want someone broken, like me?"

"You're not broken. Different doesn't mean broken. Mom and Dad would be so disappointed in you if they heard you say that. I'm disappointed in you." She crossed her arms and exhaled.

Matthew sat still with his hands wrapped around the steering wheel. Emmeline could picture him filling a little box with questions and emotions before closing the lid and filing it away in his head.

"Do you love Anja?" Emmeline asked.

Matthew's jaw tensed. "I don't know. I don't even know what love is, and I know you know what I mean by that."

"I'm not sure I could tell you what love is either."

Matthew looked at Emmeline, and desperation flickered across the gold accents in his midnight irises. "Never have I ever wanted so badly to be normal. To be normal for her."

"Oh, Mattie, you're the most selfless person I know. That's what the world needs and not this perception of what normal should mean. How do you know Anja would feel the way she feels about you if you weren't you?"

They sat in silence for what seemed like an eternity.

"I'm okay now," Matthew finally said after some of the earlier tension left his shoulders. He pushed the ignition button and pulled back onto the road.

And I guess we're done with this conversation.

Emmeline sighed.

Matthew glanced up at the rearview mirror. "Someone's following us."

Emmeline turned to look out the back window and recognized the blue sports car behind them. "That's Philip." Her heart dropped, and she grabbed her phone to dial security. "Tom, the mayor is following us. We'll be home in a couple of minutes."

"Gate is open for you, Ms. Taylor-Wu. Hannah and I are at the entrance, ready and waiting."

Emmeline hung up, and the palms of her hands started to sweat.

Is Philip crazy enough to follow us home?

Suddenly, Philip's car roared past them and swerved right in front of Matthew's car. Matthew slammed on the brakes, and the car screeched to a halt, narrowly missing Philip's car. Philip leaped out of his car and ran to Emmeline's passenger door, his features ugly and laced with fury.

"Who do you think you are?" Philip smacked his hand against Emmeline's window. "I'm the mayor of this fucking city! My investment firm just dropped me as a client. Who the fuck do you think you are?" He took his fist and slammed it again against the window. Screaming in frustration, Philip kicked the door with his heel.

"He'll break his hand before he breaks the window," Matthew said. He undid his seat belt and opened the driver's door.

"Mattie, are you insane? Get back in the car!"

Emmeline reached over and tried to grab Matthew's arm and pull him back inside, but he was too fast for her. Emmeline scrambled over the center console and out the driver's side after him. She looked up the road, and Tom and Hannah were sprinting down the hill.

"Emia, get back in the car and lock the door."

"You get back in the car!"

Philip stalked around the car, and Emmeline slipped behind her brother. Philip tried to reach around Matthew and grab Emmeline, but Matthew deflected his hand. He twisted Philip's arm behind his back and slammed his body onto the hood of the car.

"Let go of me, you freak!" Philip spat as he struggled against Matthew's grip.

Footsteps pounded against the asphalt, and Emmeline breathed a sigh of relief as Tom and Hannah came to a stop.

"Dr. Taylor-Wu, we've got it," Tom growled.

Matthew let go of Philip and moved back, allowing Tom and Hannah to step in between him and Philip. Tom was built like a linebacker, and Hannah had an ex-military background. They both stood intimidatingly in front of Philip, blocking him from Matthew and Emmeline.

"Ms. Taylor-Wu, would you like us to notify the police?" Hannah asked, her eyes never leaving Philip.

Emmeline grabbed her phone and took a few pictures of the scene. "What do you think, Philip? Should I call the police and have some charges filed? The press would have a field day with this."

"Who were you with this morning? I saw the pictures of you getting onto the back of a motorcycle. Who was he? You can't do better than me at your age."

Emmeline's blood turned to ice. "He's none of your business. Instead of stalking me, maybe you should focus on finding a new asset management firm."

"You think your family money makes you invincible? You're just a rich little princess. Believe me, there are way more powerful people than me who'll eat you alive," Philip sneered.

"They can talk to me when they're ready. I don't need to waste my time with you," Emmeline snapped back.

Philip's face turned red, and he tried to lunge at Emmeline, but Tom shoved him in the chest, knocking him to the pavement.

Emmeline stood as straight as she could. "This is my absolute last warning, Mayor Vil. If you ever threaten me again, I'll personally see that your political career is ruined." She walked around the car and stood by the passenger door. "Oh, and, Philip? I know you've been embezzling money from two charities, and I suspect there are more that I don't know about yet. I'm sure I'll find more if I want to. Return all the money you've stolen, or I'll leak everything to the press. You have three months."

"You wouldn't dare. You're not the only one with friends in the media business."

"Then, don't return the money and see what happens."

"I don't have enough liquidity to do it so quickly. I need more time," Philip growled.

"Fine, you have six months. I also suggest you use some of that time to take an anger management course or two." Emmeline threw him a sweet smile and opened the car door. "From now on, any contact required to close this agreement will come from my lawyers. I recommend you be prompt in responding to their requests. The evidence is already in their hands."

Emmeline got back into the car and slammed the door. Matthew got in after her and started the engine. He backed up and drove around the mayor.

"Your tongue has gotten much sharper than I remember," Matthew commented.

"I won't be a doormat."

"I never said you were one." Matthew turned into their driveway and waited for the garage door to open. "But six months?"

"I want him to pay the money back to the charities, and he'll need time to come up with the funds." Emmeline glanced at Matthew. "Sorry about your car door."

"That's an easy fix. Problems that can be solved with money are not problems—at least, not for us."

"You shouldn't have gotten out of the car. What if he'd had a knife or a gun? Why did you get out of the car? That was reckless."

"I didn't like what he was saying," Matthew replied.

CHAPTER FORTY-FOUR

UNFINISHED BUSINESS

After a hot shower, Emmeline wrapped herself in a long robe and walked to the room opposite her bedroom.

What should I wear tonight to the Million Lanterns fundraiser?

Several years ago, she had turned one of the spare bedrooms into another closet to house some of her formal and couture wear. One of the walls was dedicated to displaying her shoes and handbags.

I barely use most of these items. I should auction some of it off, though Gus and Eva might get upset since they love to borrow from this room.

Emmeline flipped through a rack of dresses, but nothing caught her eye. She messaged August.

Emia: Hey, sweetie. What should I wear tonight to the Million Lanterns fundraiser?

Gus: What vibe do you want to give off?

Emia: Confidence.

Gus: Got it. Give me a minute.

Emmeline grinned.

She's probably going through several pictures of my closet and putting together outfits.

Gus: On the rack just to the right of the gigantic mirror, there's a high-neck halter gown, embroidered with gold, copper, and navy. It's backless with a side slit that's barely decent. That's the one.

Emmeline plucked out the dress and examined it. The elaborate embroidery had a subtle Chinese influence and shimmered under the lights.

This is perfect since the fundraiser celebrates the mid-autumn festival. I don't think I've worn this dress before. I hope it fits.

Gus: On your shoe rack, third row from the bottom, there's a pair of pale matte-gold slingbacks. You can also use that gorgeous dark cream cashmere shawl that ties perfectly into a bow off your shoulders. Don't wear it unless you're about to freeze to death and you have frostbite to prove it. In the display cabinet, there's a navy leather envelope clutch just big enough for your phone, ID, and lipstick. Everything else, have your security carry it.

Emmeline gathered each item and arranged it on the area rug. She took a picture and sent it to August.

Emia: Like this?

Gus: Perfect. You'll knock everyone dead on their feet.

Emia: Hair, makeup, and jewelry?

Gus: Do the classic low bun you love; it always looks fabulous on you. Minimal makeup, but do your famous smoky eyes. Gold waterfall earrings and your mom's gold bangles. Don't forget your mom's massive crystal-clear emerald-cut diamond ring.

Emia: You're amazing.

Gus: That I am. Remember, you don't take shit from anybody.

Emmeline laughed.
I love you, Gus.

~

Emmeline inspected her reflection in the floor-length mirror.
Gus really knows how to pull together an outfit.
The dress had a structured bodice and flowed from the waist, spectacularly showing off her lithe figure. The high side slit made her legs look miles long and toed the line on decency. She slipped on a pair of flats and carried her heels downstairs.
"Emia, darling, you look beautiful!" Ms. Rose gasped as Emmeline walked into the kitchen.

Emmeline grinned and gave a small twirl that ended in a dramatic curtsy.

"Mattie, doesn't your sister look fabulous?"

"She looks great." Matthew didn't look up from his tablet as he swiped through several screens before jotting down some notes on a notepad.

"Mattie, are you sure you don't want to come?" Emmeline asked.

"I'm positive I don't want to be there." Matthew glanced up. "Unless you want me there. Will Philip be in attendance?"

Emmeline nodded. "It's one of the biggest events this year. I know you don't want to go, so don't worry about it. Saadah's going to be my security detail."

Ms. Rose clapped her hands with delight. "Oh good. I like Saadah very much. He's polite but looks scary. He's perfect for tonight."

"You like him?" Emmeline asked.

"Yes, sometimes, we have coffee together in the morning before he leaves. He's a nice young man."

Ms. Rose, if you only knew what Saadah is and how old he is. Emmeline smirked.

Ms. Rose handed Matthew a packed meal. "How come you don't want to go to the fundraiser? I know you don't like going to these things, but you seem extra against going this time. You could go with that nice girl who comes over at night."

Emmeline's grin widened. *Very subtle, Ms. Rose.*

Matthew refused to look up. "That nice girl is going to said fundraiser with someone else."

"Someone else?" Ms. Rose raised an eyebrow.

Emmeline piped in, "It wasn't Anja's decision. She's representing her company, and her boss requested her to do so. It just so happens that the other representative is her ex-lover."

"Doesn't mean I want to see them together even if they aren't together." Matthew continued to write notes as he studied his tablet.

It's not fair that he can multitask like that.

Ms. Rose looked thoughtful. "Mattie, what you're feeling is jealousy, and it's completely normal. I want to meet Anja properly. Can you bring her home for dinner one day?"

Matthew stared at his tablet. "Maybe one day."

Emmeline eyed the meal Ms. Rose had packed for Matthew. "Are you going to the hospital now? It's almost dinnertime."

"Just for a bit."

"Make sure you come home at a decent time. We still haven't had a conversation about work-life balance. If you promise to come home at a proper time, I'll spare you the conversation for another short while," Emmeline said.

"Yes, I'll come home at a decent time."

"Good. Now, where's Saadah? We're going to be late."

～

Saadah strode into the kitchen, handsomely dressed in a slim, navy suit.

"Saadah, you clean up well. You're going to drive all the aunties wild. They'll be all over you to line dance with them," Emmeline said.

"What's line dancing?" Saadah asked.

"Trust me, you don't want to do it," Matthew muttered, shaking his head.

"Mattie has lots of experience doing it and evading it. He's been practicing both since he was an awkward teenager," Emmeline giggled, and Ms. Rose snorted.

Saadah looked like a deer in headlights, and Emmeline patted his hand.

"Don't worry; I'll protect you from the aunties."

"She's lying to you. No one can protect you from them," Matthew grumbled.

"Mattie, can I take your car tonight?" Emmeline asked.

"No."

Ms. Rose winked at Emmeline. "Now, Mattie, all you're doing is going to the hospital to work, so you can take Emia's car or one of your other cars. Emia's going to a fundraiser, and your car would complement her fabulous outfit perfectly."

"Fine, but I just got the door fixed. Any damages, and you're paying for it. You know where the keys are. I'm surprised you asked me first this time." Matthew closed his tablet and packed up his backpack.

"Thank you, Mattie."

Matthew muttered something unintelligible and left the kitchen. Emmeline could hear his footsteps heading down to the underground garage.

Ms. Rose turned somber. "Emia, darling, I want you to be careful tonight. After what happened with the mayor a few weeks ago, I don't like the idea of him being anywhere close to you."

"Don't worry, Ms. Rose; I'll look after Emmeline," Saadah said. "I need to get my dress shoes. Emmeline, I'll meet you downstairs?"

"Yes, I'll be down in two minutes."

After Saadah left, Ms. Rose took Emmeline's hands.

"Emia, I'm so proud of you, and I know your parents would be too. You have a strength I don't think you realize you have." Ms. Rose brushed a few strands of hair away from Emmeline's face. "You outgrew your governess so many years ago."

"Never. You're my forever governess." Emmeline hugged Ms. Rose.

"I'd normally tell you to have fun, but I know you're not going to tonight. So, instead, I want you to show everyone what a Taylor-Wu is really made of."

"Nice pep talk, Ms. Rose." Emmeline couldn't stop the grin on her face.

"I try."

∽

"Do you want to drive, Saadah?"

"Nope. I couldn't afford to repair a broken side mirror on this car." Saadah walked over to the passenger side. "And I can't drive manual."

"I thought you would've jumped at the opportunity to give poor Ellis a heart attack."

Saadah rolled his eyes. "I'd never hear the end of it."

Emmeline hiked up her dress and slid into the luxury sports car. As the palms of her hands glided over the leather-covered steering wheel, she couldn't help but smile. She pushed the ignition button and reveled in the deep growl as the engine came to life.

I know why I like this car so much. It makes me feel powerful.

She drove out of the underground garage, purposely leaving the driver's window open so she could hear the engine as she moved between the gears. The air around her pulsated with the engine's rhythm, humming against her bare skin.

"Saadah, are you armed?"

"I have a short blade with me. My jacket has a long pocket on the inside, and the short blade fits in it perfectly. It's effective on both raizour and humans, if that's what you're worried about."

"You're carrying a concealed weapon? Are bodyguards allowed to do that?"

"Don't worry; I've got it covered. Erik said you were a worrier," Saadah replied.

"I'm not a worrier, and how would he know?"

"I can see how he came to that conclusion." Saadah shrugged and earned himself a glare.

Emmeline turned into the Grand Metropolis Hotel entrance and stopped at the front. She changed into her heels and grabbed her clutch before pushing the door latch and letting it slide toward the clear night sky. Stepping out of the car, she was aware of the heads turning in her direction and the curious whispers that followed. She handed her key fob to the valet and walked around the car with Saadah following close behind her. The warm air continued to hum and wrap itself around her bare shoulders and legs, and she shivered.

"Saadah, something feels unsettled," Emmeline murmured.

"It's probably nerves. Don't worry; we've got you. Anja and Lesedi are already inside and making their rounds. Erik's on the roof, probably dying of boredom and half-asleep."

"You're right. I'm sure everything will be fine."

Emmeline pasted a smile on her face and pulled her shoulders back.

Let's get this over with.

∽

Emmeline gasped as soon as she walked into the magnificent foyer. The foyer had been transformed into a traditional Chinese village, and red paper lanterns hung in waves from the ceiling.

The organizers outdid themselves this year, and from what I heard, they stayed under budget. Good job.

Emmeline caught sight of Philip a few steps away, and he had his arm around the waist of a stunning blonde. Panicked, she hurried away in the opposite direction.

"Are you okay?" Saadah kept his voice low so that others could not hear him.

"As long as Philip doesn't come near me, I'll be fine. I don't want to be on the receiving end of his temper again."

Emmeline walked up to the concierge, and a fundraiser attendant recognized her immediately.

"Ms. Taylor-Wu, we're honored you're joining us tonight. Let me show you to your table. I'll let Mr. Huang know you're here."

The attendant escorted Emmeline up the elevator to the top floor, where the fundraiser was being held. After showing Emmeline to her seat, the attendant looked at her tablet with embarrassment. "I don't have a spot for your friend."

"He's my security detail."

"I'm sorry, but I cannot shift the seats. Let me see if I can find something nearby."

Saadah spoke up. "No need. I'll stay by the window where I'll have a direct line of sight to Ms. Taylor-Wu."

"Very well." The attendant tapped her tablet. "Mr. Huang has been notified that you've arrived and will be here in a few minutes."

"Thank you." Emmeline turned to Saadah after the attendant left. "You don't need to stand by the wall. You're not actually working right now. You're just *pretend* working."

"I'm fine with standing."

"It's going to be a long night. Are you sure?"

Saadah nodded and glanced up. "I'm guessing that's Mr. Huang walking over." He moved away and took his position by the wall.

Emmeline turned and beamed at the short, bald man with thick-rimmed glasses. Mr. Huang was one of her father's oldest friends.

"Uncle Jack!"

"Emmeline! Look at you." Uncle Jack grasped her shoulders and kissed her on both cheeks. "I can't believe how much you look like your mother. How are you doing? How's Matthew?"

"We're doing well. You know Mattie, always a workaholic. Then again, you're a workaholic too, so you can't go around judging anybody else," Emmeline teased.

Uncle Jack snorted before turning serious. "Auntie Peggy and I will be at your table tonight. Ms. Rose told me to make some arrangements in the seating so that you're not at the same table as a certain someone else."

"Ms. Rose told you? How much did she tell you?" Emmeline flushed with embarrassment.

"Enough to know I should keep an eye out for you. You're my late friend's daughter, and it's my duty." Uncle Jack nodded to Saadah. "Who's that man you came with?"

"He's my security detail."

"Smart. I feel more at ease, knowing that." Uncle Jack looked hard at Emmeline. "People talk, and Philip Vil doesn't have a good reputation. Next time, you should talk to the aunties first. They know everything about everyone."

"They're the last people I would talk to about my love life. The first thing they'd point out is how it's nonexistent."

"No, the first thing they'd do is call up all their friends who are eligible lawyers, doctors, engineers, and accountants and set you up on blind dates," Uncle Jack cackled.

Emmeline laughed. "Maybe, one day, I might take them up on their offer."

They chatted for a bit longer before Uncle Jack had to make a few rounds. Another couple sat down at the table, and Emmeline recognized them as a wealthy pair who had newly immigrated to Canada. They made some small talk, but Emmeline had trouble keeping up with their rapid, fluent Mandarin.

Sorry, Mom, I think I've embarrassed you again.

She was about to take her phone out of her clutch when the air around her cooled. Emmeline stiffened and looked up. Philip stood in front of her, and his fingers gripped the banquet hall chair beside her.

"I see you've come alone tonight," Philip sneered.

"I've been doing this for a long time, and I always attend these functions alone. This one's no different. My life didn't change because of you," Emmeline said as calmly as she could.

Don't let him see that you're afraid of him.

She put her clutch down and stood up, holding her head high.

Saadah, where are you?

Philip leaned toward her, and she stepped back.

"You blew it, Emmeline. I would've given you everything you ever wanted: status, influence, privilege, family, and children. But now, the reclusive heiress will never have that, will she?"

Philip cocked his head at her, and she saw his fingers twitch.

"The first three, I already have and are things I'd have given you, not the other way around. Isn't that why you wanted me? To get all the things you don't have?" Emmeline tried to keep her voice from shaking. "The last two, no matter how badly I want them, I wouldn't want them with someone who's a fraud. Someone like you."

"You bitch," Philip spat.

"I warned you about coming near me. You'll be hearing from my lawyer," Emmeline retorted.

A hand appeared, and Saadah stepped in between them. "Move away from Ms. Taylor-Wu," he commanded.

"A security detail? You're pathetic," Philip mocked.

Saadah pushed Philip back. "I only need one move to incapacitate you. Would you like me to demonstrate? Then, we'll see who's the pathetic one."

Philip stepped back and turned to walk away. He looked over his shoulder, and his eyes were filled with loathing. "You'll regret the day you made an enemy out of me."

CHAPTER FORTY-FIVE

THE CONNECTION

Emmeline let out a sigh.

The tension from her earlier interaction with Philip made it difficult for her to concentrate on mingling with other donors. They were now on a programming break, giving everybody a chance to get up and socialize. The house band played light jazz in the background, and the lanterns draped across the ceiling made the room glow. A few couples made their way to the dance floor, showcasing their skills and working off calories from the first two courses.

Auntie Peggy nudged Emmeline. "Do you want to accompany me and the aunties on some table rounds? The gossip will do wonders for your mood. Even Uncle Jack is joining me."

Emmeline leaned in beside Auntie Peggy's ear and whispered back in a grave voice despite the wide smile on her face, "Auntie Peggy, I'd rather eat a rusty nail."

Auntie Peggy threw her head back and laughed. "Can't say I didn't try! Will you be okay here by yourself?"

"I'll make some rounds later. Don't worry about me." Emmeline gestured in Saadah's direction. "My security is keeping watch and will accompany me anywhere I go."

"At least you picked a good-looking security detail. So very handsome." Auntie Peggy eyed Saadah and fanned herself.

"Yes, that's what the criteria was." Emmeline nodded solemnly.

"I have a wonderful corporate lawyer I'd like to introduce to you. Will you let me? He's ambitious and handsome, and he works a lot, so he won't bother you much. He's perfect!"

"Go find the other aunties! I think they're all waiting for you. They can't start unless Auntie Peggy is there." Emmeline nudged her, teasing.

"One day, Emmeline, I'll succeed." Auntie Peggy stood up and waved to someone in the distance. "I'll be back soon!"

Emmeline scanned the hall and relaxed.

Good, Philip isn't around.

Emmeline closed her eyes and focused on finding all the nain-the in the room. In the darkness, she found Anja's aura. Close to Anja, she felt another gentle and steady aura.

That must be Lesedi. I've never seen her aura before.

Emmeline turned her attention to Saadah.

This is getting much easier to do. Let me find Erik.

Emmeline reached out and searched for Erik. Almost immediately, she found him and the bright threads of magic that were uniquely his. She smiled to herself.

I wonder if he can feel me if I'm not physically touching him.

Emmeline reached out to him again.

Erik?

She felt his warmth pulse against her, and her eyes flew open with excitement. Her phone buzzed with a message.

Erik: I think I just felt you try to reach me. Did you?

Emmeline fumbled for her wireless earbuds and popped them into her ears. She dialed Erik and started talking as soon as he picked up.

"I tried to reach you, and you felt it. I felt you too. This is amazing! What did it feel like?" Emmeline asked.

"Hard to describe. It just felt like you."

"Well, I hope it felt good." Emmeline reddened as soon as the words left her mouth. "That didn't come out the way I'd intended, but you know what I mean."

Erik didn't say anything, but Emmeline could feel him smiling.

"Go on, Erik. You can laugh at me. I can handle it."

"I wouldn't dare. How are you doing down there? Saadah told us what happened with the mayor."

"He told all of you? When did he have time to do that? He's on the clock right now."

"We have a group chat," Erik said.

"Really? You don't strike me as a *group chat* type of person. Can I be a part of it? Oh, and Mattie too."

"I'm sure Matthew has no interest in talking to any of us—with the exception of one."

"You're right. Just add me then."

Erik changed the subject. "If the mayor tries to lay a hand on you, I'll take it—and more—from him."

"I believe you." Emmeline blushed. "How's everything outside?"

"It's quiet up here, though I can hear everything happening at the party. It sounds boring, but at least the band is good."

"Welcome to my world. Usually, the band's the best part." Emmeline peeked around the room. "I should go and mingle a bit. I wouldn't want to give people more ammunition to call me reclusive. I'll bring you some food after the main course is served."

"Thank you."

Emmeline smiled, and her eyes brightened.

I can't wait to see him.

"Anja, I can feel you beside me," Emmeline said.

Anja pouted and sat down in Auntie Peggy's empty chair.

"You both look beautiful and stunning, as always," Emmeline said as she assessed Anja's and Lesedi's outfits.

Lesedi was in a black sequined tuxedo, and Anja was in a long, strapless deep-red dress.

I think Mattie would just about die if he saw Anja right now.

"Lesedi, can you take a picture of Anja and me?"

Emmeline handed her phone to Lesedi and pulled Anja beside her. After Lesedi handed back her phone, she forwarded the photo to Matthew and saw the Read receipt pop up beside the picture, but he didn't respond to her.

Interesting.

Anja's phone lit up with a message, and she smiled as she read it.

"I'm going to get a drink. I'll bring you both back something," Anja announced without looking up from her phone. She walked away before either Lesedi or Emmeline could respond.

I'm willing to bet I'll see Anja after this party, Emmeline thought smugly. *You're welcome, Mattie.*

Emmeline and Lesedi sat in uncomfortable silence as they waited for Anja to return.

I should say something.

"Lesedi, I know it's a little awkward, but we might as well get it out of the way," Emmeline said. "I'm sorry things didn't work out between you and Anja."

"I haven't had a chance to talk to you since the Inspire Gala. It's been hard to see Anja move on," Lesedi admitted.

With your brother.

The words hung unspoken in the air between them.

"I understand. Please don't hate Mattie."

"I've been around a long time, and hate hasn't solved a single problem in this world. I don't hate Matthew—far from it. If it wasn't for Matthew, I probably wouldn't be sitting here beside you. He came to my aid even though we weren't kind to him." Lesedi sighed. "If Anja's happy, that's all that matters. Matthew's heart is good and strong, and he might not understand it, but I can see it. He's completely devoted to her."

Emmeline felt a burst of pride for her brother.

Mattie, people do see you. I wish I could show you so you could see it too.

"I was the one who wanted an open relationship with Anja, but there has never been another, except her. The thought has crossed my mind that it might have impacted how our relationship deteriorated over time," Lesedi murmured.

Emmeline couldn't help herself, and she reached around Lesedi to give her a hug.

"Anja warned me that you're a hugger." Lesedi hugged her back.

"If that's my reputation, I'm fine with it."

"One day, the good doctor and I might end up as friends, but right now, it's just too hard."

They both looked up just as Anja walked back with two glasses of wine and a bottle of sparkling water. She placed the drinks on the table.

"I saw the mayor and that ridiculously hot blonde at their table. Shall I walk by and spill a drink or two in his lap?"

Lesedi sighed. "You're so immature sometimes. Just trip him when he gets up and be done with it."

Anja snickered, and Emmeline covered her mouth and laughed.

Maybe this night isn't going to be so bad after all.

~

"Excuse me." Emmeline raised her hand as an attendant passed by.

"How can I assist you, Ms. Taylor-Wu?" The attendant bent down beside her.

"Could I get two boxed meals with some cutlery? One vegetarian and one chicken. No need for bags, and you can send me the bill."

"Absolutely. I'll be back shortly with your items."

The attendant headed for the kitchen, and Emmeline leaned back in her chair and watched the dance floor.

One more course, and then the draw for the grand prize. Then, I get to go home. Poor Saadah. I bet he didn't sign up for this. Emmeline almost laughed at the glazed look on Saadah's face.

The band started a new set of popular songs, and Emmeline watched with amusement as Uncle Jack and Auntie Peggy ran to the dance floor with their friends.

They're having so much fun. Maybe I'll join them later.

Emmeline searched the room and found Philip and his date, but she quickly looked away before he could catch her watching.

"Ms. Taylor-Wu, here are the items you requested. Let me know if there's anything else I can help you with." The attendant placed two cardboard takeout boxes on the table.

"Thank you very much."

Emmeline stood and balanced the containers and cutlery with one hand and held on to her clutch with the other. She walked over to Saadah, and he looked at her in surprise.

"You must be hungry and bored." Emmeline used her chin and motioned to the boxes in her hand. "Take the top box. It's a vegetarian pasta and a side of arugula salad."

Saadah eyed the box. "I'm technically working, so I shouldn't eat. I can eat when we get back to your home."

"You and I both need a break. I'm going to bring the other box upstairs to Erik. You can eat and make sure no one sees me go to the roof. If you don't eat, you won't have the energy to be my knight in shining armor," Emmeline urged.

Saadah happily took the boxes and cutlery from Emmeline's hands, and they walked out into the hallway. Emmeline picked up one of the red paper lanterns and switched off the LED bulb. Saadah looked around and nodded to Emmeline before she pushed through the emergency stairwell door. Her heart fluttered in anticipation as they made their way up the two flights of stairs leading to the roof.

"I'll wait for you in the stairwell and warn you if anyone's coming up."

"Do you promise me you'll eat?"

"Yes, boss." Saadah mockingly saluted her.

"Very funny. Oh, and to warn you, the food probably doesn't taste amazing, but it'll get the job done."

"It's fine. I'm not picky."

Saadah handed the bottom box back to Emmeline, and she tucked it under her arm. Saadah pushed open the rooftop door for her, and she stepped out into the night.

CHAPTER FORTY-SIX

BENEATH THE MID-AUTUMN MOON

High up above the city skyline, the roof of the Grand Metropolis Hotel offered a spectacular view of the beautiful city Emmeline called home. As far as her eyes could see, millions of lights glimmered and illuminated the night sky. There wasn't a single cloud in sight, and the air had cooled from the earlier warmth. Emmeline closed her eyes to search for Erik and jumped when she felt him right behind her.

"Erik, don't do that!"

Emmeline's heart skipped as Erik leaned over her shoulder, his cheek almost touching hers.

"Anja's right; it's fun, watching you jump."

Someone's in a good mood today.

"I almost dropped your food."

"Thank you for bringing me dinner," Erik murmured beside her ear.

He reluctantly pulled away from her and reached over to take the cardboard box and paper lantern. He was in his usual black ensemble and had his armor and blades on, but his helmet was absent.

"I hope you have low expectations. It's just chicken and salad. Dessert hasn't been served yet."

Erik looked at the box and shrugged. "I've had worse." He inspected the paper lantern. "What's this for?"

Emmeline reached inside the lantern and turned on the LED bulb. "It's the mid-autumn festival, and paper lanterns are used as part of the celebration."

"What's the mid-autumn festival?"

Emmeline pointed to the full moon that looked close enough for them to touch. "The festival celebrates the end of the autumn harvest, and the moon is especially round during this time." She turned to Erik and smiled. "I thought the lantern was pretty and figured you could use some mood lighting for your meal."

"Do you need to go back downstairs?"

"Not yet, but I need to be back for the grand prize draw. Our foundation donated it, so I should be there to congratulate the winner."

"Will you sit with me for a while?" Erik asked.

Emmeline nodded, and Erik held out his hand to her. She slipped her hand into his and flushed as he wrapped his long fingers around her hand. He led her to a small area with a smooth, raised concrete ledge and set down the lantern. The bulb flickered through the translucent red paper, matching the night air that seemed livelier on the rooftop as music and laughter wafted through the vents. Erik sat down on the ledge, and Emmeline lifted her dress to sit beside him. He opened his box and started to eat from it.

"It's not too bad." He chewed thoughtfully, making a slight face as he swallowed.

"Just eat. You need your energy," Emmeline chided him. "After the party, come back to my house, and I'll ask Ms. Rose to fry up some of her homemade dumplings. I promise it'll make up for this meal."

"Deal."

"Do you feel anything?"

"What do you mean?"

Emmeline felt flustered. "I mean, do you feel any raizour?"

Erik shook his head. "It's been quiet, but it's still early."

"There hasn't been much activity over the past few weeks. Is that normal?"

"No, it's not. I don't know what's going on." Erik looked up at the sky.

"Is this what's been impacting your mood? You've come back from a few hunts empty-handed, and I haven't had to help you as much. The past few times I've seen you, you've been …" Emmeline paused to search for the right word. "You've been less intense. Lighter."

Erik put down his box and wiped his mouth with a napkin. "I think each time you help me, the effect lasts a little longer than the last time. I feel less pain and don't get headaches anymore."

"I'm glad I'm able to help you. At least I'm not completely useless to the nainthe. Though I still think you should take more breaks." Emmeline followed his sight line and looked at the iconic tower in the distance. "What if, one day, I'm not around to help you? What will happen?"

"Then, I'll go back to what I've been doing for the past fifty-odd years. You don't ever need to worry about me. I've survived so long, living like this. What's another few years or decades?"

Emmeline's emotions swirled inside her, and she changed the subject, flashing him an easy smile. "How come your clothes and armor don't get affected by your wings when you change between human and nainthe forms? Are your wings magic?"

Erik nodded. "They're magic but also as solid and sharp as they come." He turned his body so that Emmeline could see his back. "There are slits in our armor and most of our clothes. If we didn't do that, our clothes would be torn to shreds each time. It would just be awkward for everybody."

Emmeline laughed and touched his armor, lightly tracing her finger over the almost-invisible opening. The band finished their current set and shifted to classical Chinese music, and comfort settled over her at the familiar tunes.

"Why are you smiling to yourself?" Erik nudged her.

"This music reminds me of my childhood. My mom used to listen to many of these songs, and I often heard them when we went to galas and fundraisers."

They sat in silence as they listened to the music together. There was a pause and some light clapping. Emmeline's heart lifted as the pure vibration of an exotic string instrument drifted upward.

"The erhu." Erik tilted his head toward the vents.

"You know the erhu?"

"I've never played it, but I know the sound."

"Are you musically inclined? I'm not, and neither is Mattie, and we both endured fifteen years of weekly piano lessons. We're a great disappointment on the musical front."

Erik laughed. "I guess you could say I'm musically inclined." He sobered. "I used to play the violin, but I don't anymore. I haven't for a very long time."

"Reminds you too much of your past?" Emmeline asked.

"Too much of my family and my home."

Emmeline reached over and covered the top of his hand. Erik turned his hand around and closed his fingers over hers.

"Where was home for you, Erik?"

"I grew up on the East Coast, in a small town in Nova Scotia." Erik looked at her hand in his. "Both my parents passed away many years ago. I have a younger sister, whom you know. I also have a younger brother, Arthur, who still lives out east with a family of his own. I have two nieces, who will be going to university soon." He gave Emmeline a wry smile. "Arthur's quite a bit younger than Anja and me, and he had two kids late in his life. We used to poke fun at him and call him 'the mistake,' but he wasn't. He looked after our parents when Anja and I couldn't be there."

"Do you see your brother?"

"Anja and I go back home maybe once or twice a year. We watch from afar." Erik paused. "I don't think Arthur's doing too well. The last time I saw him, he made a few trips to the hospital. I've been meaning to go visit again."

"I hope Arthur's all right," Emmeline murmured and squeezed his hand.

They settled into silence, listening to the soloist pull their bow over the dual strings. The song ended, and enthusiastic claps echoed through the vents. Calls for an encore followed and then quieted down in anticipation. Emmeline sighed with happiness when the soloist pulled the first few bars of a haunting melody.

"I take it, you like this song?" Erik asked.

"I adore this song. It was one of Mom's favorites."

A clear, silky soprano joined the call of the erhu, and Emmeline closed her eyes, letting the music bring back some of her happiest memories of her parents. She felt a gentle tug on her hand and opened her eyes to see Erik standing in front of her, holding out his hand. He seemed unsure of himself, as if he was just as surprised at his request.

"Emia, would you dance with me?"

I would follow you anywhere.

Emmeline's heart pounded in her chest, and she flushed as she took his hand. She stood and shook out her dress, making it glimmer under the bright moonlight. Erik placed his hand on her back, and her arm rested on his. She shivered from the warmth of his fingers as they skimmed over the bare skin of her back.

"Are you cold?"

Emmeline shook her head and looked up at Erik, her breath catching in her throat as her eyes roamed over his strong cheekbones and how his black hair offset his pale Scandinavian skin.

He's quite handsome, isn't he? Tall and strong. Funny and kind. She mentally shook herself and flushed even deeper. *He's also terrifying and called Executioner for a reason.*

Erik pulled her a little closer to him. "What's this song about?"

"It's the perfect song for the mid-autumn festival." Emmeline looked wistfully at the moon. "The heroine laments to her lover that her love for him is deep and true. She tells him to look toward the moon as a symbol of her devotion, even when she's not there. Her heart is like the moon, bright and full, belonging to only him." Her cheeks flushed again. "At least, that's what my interpretation is. My Mandarin's a little spotty."

"A little?"

"Okay, a lot."

Emmeline tapped Erik playfully on the arm, and she gave him her most devastating smile. His stormy eyes deepened against her bright midnight ones, and the air around them crackled with electricity. Emmeline's heart pounded in her ears as Erik's fingers moved lightly across her bare skin, sending sparks up her spine.

"You look beautiful tonight."

Emmeline smiled shyly. "Just tonight?" she teased.

Erik's mouth twitched, and he quickly corrected himself. "Always. You look beautiful always."

Emmeline blushed and looked away. Erik let go of her hand and tilted her chin to look at him, his thumb running lightly against her cheek. His eyes darkened, and Emmeline's heart stopped in her chest.

"Emia, may I kiss you?"

Emmeline nodded mutely, and her voice died beside her heart.

Erik bent his head and pressed a light kiss against her lips. She gasped as his mouth burned against hers, and a spark jolted through her heart. Erik sighed, and his breath was sweet and intoxicating as the soloist played the last chord of the haunting love song, drawing it out and letting the dreamy yearning for love remain in the air.

There was silence, and then thunderous applause erupted from partygoers. Erik stepped away from Emmeline and kissed the top of her hand, his mouth lingering against her skin before letting go.

"Thank you for the dance."

Emmeline reddened and looked at her hand as she twisted her mother's ring on her finger.

"I should get back. They'll be doing the grand prize draw soon." Emmeline picked up her clutch and made her way to the door with Erik following closely behind her.

"I'll see you later." Erik pulled the heavy metal door open for her.

Emmeline only nodded and stepped over the threshold, leaving her chaotic feelings amid the magical city lights on the rooftop of the Grand Metropolis Hotel.

Saadah sat several steps down, his eyes glassy as he scrolled through his phone. Emmeline held her long dress in her hands and walked down the stairs.

"I'm sorry, Saadah. I completely lost track of time."

"No worries. Sitting here was better than standing in the hall. Everything okay with Erik?" Saadah asked.

"Yes, we just got caught up in conversation. Let's get back downstairs. It'd be embarrassing if I missed the grand prize draw."

They made their way downstairs as quickly as Emmeline's heels would allow, and she paused at the entrance to the banquet hall to take a deep breath and calm her nerves. She schooled her face into friendly indifference and held her head up with practiced confidence. Saadah took his place by the wall, and Emmeline rejoined Uncle Jack and Auntie Peggy at their table.

CHAPTER FORTY-SEVEN

COLLATERAL

After Emmeline congratulated the winner of the grand prize of two first-class round-trip tickets to Shanghai, she made a beeline for Saadah.

"We're free!"

"Thank goodness. Let's get out of here," Saadah muttered.

"Let me say good-bye to a few people. Come with me?"

Saadah nodded, and Emmeline led the way. She bid her tablemates a good night and gave Uncle Jack and Auntie Peggy a hug.

"Take care of yourself and Matthew." Auntie Peggy kissed Emmeline on the cheek. "I've started a list of eligible bachelors. You let me know when you're ready."

Emmeline laughed and gave Auntie Peggy an exasperated sigh. She glanced over to Philip's table, but he was nowhere to be seen despite his date sitting at the table with an idle drink in her hand. Emmeline felt a tinge of pity for her.

She has no idea what she's signing up for.

"Auntie Peggy, could you do me a favor?"

"Anything you need, dear."

"Can you have one of the other aunties float a rumor into the ear of the mayor's date? I want her to know what she's dealing with. I don't want her to find out about his ugly side the way I did. Or worse, when no one's around."

Auntie Peggy looked thoughtful, and then a calculated gleam waltzed into her eyes. "I have an idea."

Emmeline held up her hands. "I don't want to know about it. I trust you to work your magic."

She kissed Auntie Peggy again, and she and Saadah made their way to the lobby of the hotel.

"Ms. Taylor-Wu, your car is waiting for you." The valet walked Emmeline outside and pressed the key fob to open both car doors.

Emmeline climbed into the driver's seat, and the car door glided down, securing itself into place. She slipped on her ballet flats and then took out her phone to send a few messages.

Emia: Ms. Rose, Saadah and I are on our way home. I might have a few friends joining us. Can you pan-fry a bunch of your famous dumplings for us?

Emia: Mattie, are you home yet? We're on our way back from the fundraiser. See you soon.

Emia: Anja, are you coming by my house? I asked Ms. Rose to make her famous dumplings, and I'm sure you could use a coffee.

Anja: Yes, please. We will leave the party soon, and I'll drop Lessie home first.

Emmeline hesitated for a moment as her fingers hovered over her phone.

Emia: Saadah and I are leaving now. Will you come by after?

Erik: Yes, I'll see you soon.

She put her phone on the center console and lowered her window before starting the engine. Her entire body relaxed at the rumble of the car engine.

I wonder what Erik's thinking right now. Do I feel this way because of our connection? I don't even know what I'm feeling.

Emmeline touched her lips.

Liar, you know exactly what you're feeling.

"You look like you have a lot on your mind," Saadah commented as Emmeline drove through the city streets.

"Just a few things." Emmeline glanced at Saadah. "Thank you for staying with me the whole night. The life of a reclusive philanthropist is very exciting."

Saadah snorted. "I can't understand how you do this all the time. I almost fell asleep, standing up."

"It's necessary if I want to continue my parents' work. It's not all bad. I've met some nice people who work tirelessly to raise funds for worthy causes, and the music's usually pretty good."

Emmeline turned into her driveway and opened the gate when Saadah stiffened.

"What?" Emmeline looked at Saadah with alarm.

"I'm not sure."

Emmeline drove up the driveway and slammed on the brakes when Ellis and Sophia landed in front of her car. They were both armed, and Ellis held a set of armor in one hand and a single long blade in the other. He tossed everything to Saadah as soon as he exited the car.

"Do you feel it too?" Saadah asked Ellis as he shed his blazer and strapped on his armor over his dress shirt. He slid his long blade into the harness along his back.

"I do, but I don't know what it is." Ellis looked up at the sky. "We just came back from another perimeter check, but we didn't want to stray too far from the residence."

"Let's go do another round."

Ellis nodded. "Emmeline, get inside the house. We won't be too far away."

Something's wrong. I can feel it too.

After parking Matthew's car back in his favorite spot, she hurried up the stairs and kicked off her flats before dropping her clutch onto the hallway console table.

Why is the house so quiet?

"Ms. Rose? Mr. Jae?" Emmeline called out. "Mattie?"

Where is everybody?

Her phone vibrated in her hand.

Erik:	I'm going to do a patrol first. I feel something in the air. I'll message you soon.
Emia:	Saadah, Sophia, and Ellis are doing a perimeter check. They said they felt something as well, but they're not sure what it is. Be safe out there.
Erik:	I will.

Emmeline walked by Matthew's office, but it was empty. His backpack was on his desk, and his blazer was draped over his chair.

Maybe he went to take a shower.

"Ms. Rose?" Emmeline called out again, but all she got was silence.

She walked over to the kitchen and poked her head in, but it was also empty. A large pan, filled with uncooked dumplings, sat on the stove, and mixing sauces and utensils were laid out on the kitchen island. She was about to check the great room when she noticed the patio doors were ajar.

She slowly approached the patio doors.

"Mr. Jae?"

Where are the security guards?

Emmeline pushed open a door and stepped out, barefoot, into the garden.

"Hello, Emmeline."

She froze.

Philip.

Emmeline whirled around and found Philip grinning at her. He was still in his tuxedo from the party, and his features were cold and twisted.

"Emia, get out of here!" Mattie's frantic voice came from behind Philip.

Philip moved out of the shadows, and behind him were Matthew and Ms. Rose, tied up on the floor with their hands and feet bound.

"No!" Emmeline ran toward her family.

Philip clicked his tongue, and Emmeline stopped in her tracks as she heard the distinct cocking of a gun. He smiled and pointed his gun at her chest.

"Philip, are you crazy? What are you doing?" Emmeline cried.

"Am I crazy? AM I CRAZY?" Philip shouted at her before forcing himself to calm back down. "No, I'm not crazy. I just want to get what I want, and I always do."

Emmeline looked desperately at Matthew, who had a gash on his forehead. A large bruise was starting to form around the wound, and a thin streak of blood dripped down the side of his cheek.

What do I do, Mattie?

Too late to run. Try to de-escalate. Matthew seemed to nod to her.

Emmeline watched her brother's face change from panic to calm to mirror what he wanted her to feel.

"What do you want, Philip?" Emmeline asked. "I'll give you anything that's in my power to give. Is it money? Business connections? All you have to do is ask."

Philip waved his gun at her. "Too late for that. I might have wanted that from you before, but there are other ways to get those things. You really fucked things up for yourself, and now, your family's collateral damage."

Emmeline's heart stopped, and her eyes flickered fearfully to Matthew.

Stay calm. Try again, Matthew said silently.

"How are you going to get what you want?" Emmeline asked.

Philip grinned. "Others told me about you and how you'd make an excellent wife. Rich, isolated, and with no family. Well, I guess there's the exception of your freak brother, but that would've been easy to remedy. No in-laws to deal with and no parents holding control of the family money. What an incredible opportunity."

Emmeline was about to retort when she caught Matthew's eye.

Hold your tongue. They're just words. Matthew blinked deliberately.

Philip stalked up to Emmeline and lifted a finger to stroke her cheek. "I decided to learn more about you, but it wasn't easy. I knew you'd be at the gala, and when I met you, you were more beautiful than any picture I had seen. That sealed the deal for me."

Don't let him see your fear.

Philip continued, "Things lined up quite nicely. Imagine me, coming home after work to a beautiful, obedient, and loving wife. My children running into my arms. Me making love to my dutiful wife every night."

Emmeline softened her voice. "Is that something you still want?"

"Oh, Emmeline, you really hurt my feelings. After that little stunt you pulled earlier, do you think I'd be that stupid? Do you have any idea how much money I lost because of what you did?"

"Money can be replaced."

Philip tapped her nose playfully, as a friend would. "But no matter because, shortly after I met you, someone else decided they were also interested in you, and that's how I found myself a nice little benefactor. All I had to do was keep you close and report on your movements. How perfectly did that work out for me? I was already having you followed, and now, I would be paid for it."

"Who's your benefactor? Whatever they offered you, I'll double it."

"Too late. Your offer's tempting, but my benefactor isn't the forgiving type, and he's not someone I would double-cross. I'm to deliver you to him tonight."

Matthew looked at Emmeline and then pointed his chin at the patio door. *Wait for the moment he's distracted and get out of here.*

"Philip, this is a crime you're committing. Is it worth it? Tell us who your benefactor is, and we'll take care of it," Matthew said. "My sister has offered you double what your benefactor has promised you without even knowing what you've been promised. That means, you can essentially name your price. It's completely logical to take her offer."

Philip turned to Matthew. "You people! You think money can solve all your problems, don't you? Just throw money at us peasants, and we'll do anything you ask," he sneered.

Don't antagonize him, Mattie. Don't do it! They're just words, remember? Emmeline screamed silently.

Matthew ignored Emmeline's stare and tilted his head to the side, arrogance taking over his features. "Don't be a hypocrite. Isn't that what this has all been about? Money? You want to be one of us and reap all the privileges that come with it. There's no need to pretend that you can't be bought. Everyone can be bought."

Philip took three long strides forward, pulled his hand back, and struck Matthew across the temple with the grip of the gun. Emmeline and Ms. Rose both screamed as Matthew fell to the floor.

"The great Dr. Taylor-Wu. I wonder how many of your patients would still want you as their doctor if they knew about your condition. They'd all leave you," Philip spat.

Matthew looked wildly at Emmeline as he lay on the floor. *Go! Run!*

Philip lifted his leg and kicked Matthew's abdomen, making him gasp in pain.

"Stop it!" Emmeline cried out.

She ran at Philip and threw her entire body at him, knocking him to the ground. The gun fell out of his hand and skidded across the patio floor. Philip cursed and grabbed Emmeline's leg, pulling her back to him.

Emmeline looked frantically for the gun and spotted it close to the patio doors. Glancing back at Philip, she raised her foot and kicked him in the face as hard as she could. Emmeline felt a crack, and Philip howled in agony.

"You broke my nose!" Philip shrieked.

Emmeline fumbled to get up, but her foot slipped on the hem of her dress. She scrambled toward the gun again, but Philip was on her within seconds. He grabbed her shoulders and flipped her onto her back, straddling her as she struggled to escape from under him.

"Leave her alone!" Ms. Rose cried out, tears streaming down her face. "Please leave her alone. I'm begging you, please."

Philip ignored Ms. Rose's cries and grabbed both of Emmeline's hands as she tried to claw at him. He held both her wrists in one hand and raised his other hand high up, bringing it down hard against her cheek. The sound echoed like a whip across the garden, and the force of the impact stunned Emmeline.

"You bitch!" Philip seethed. His chest heaved as blood dripped down his nose and onto her dress. "Not so powerful now, are you? Where's your security? Your bodyguards? Not even your brother can protect you."

He grabbed her chin with his hand and forced her to look him in the eyes. A salty, metallic taste filled Emmeline's mouth.

"You're a monster. I wish I'd never met you."

Philip let go of her chin and slapped her with the back of his hand. Tears stung Emmeline's eyes, and her ears rang. She made eye contact with Matthew as her cheek came to rest against the patio floor. Blood was streaked across his forehead, and his eyes were hard, but there was a trail of wetness along his cheek.

Focus on surviving. Nothing else, Matthew urged her.

"Isn't it funny how I feel the exact opposite? Meeting you has changed my life." Philip smiled wickedly and leaned in close to her ear. He ran his hand up her bare leg, pushing her dress up to her hips. "If my benefactor didn't want you delivered tonight, I would take you home first. Think about how much fun I would have, pretending you were my obedient wife for a night. Maybe I should still consider it. I have time."

Emmeline turned her head and bit down hard on Philip's ear and ripped it from his head. He let out a bloodcurdling howl and let go of her hands. He clutched at the side of his head, as blood poured out between his fingers. She spat his ear out onto the floor.

Emmeline balled up her fist and punched Philip in the chin. She twisted her body to try to unbalance him and push him off her, but he was too heavy.

"Get off me!" Emmeline tried to punch him again.

"You fucking bitch!"

Philip used his free hand and grabbed her chin again. He lifted her head off the ground and slammed it against the wooden patio floor. Emmeline cried out in pain, and her vision swam.

"Stop it! You're going to kill her! You need her alive, don't you?" Ms. Rose begged Philip.

Philip picked up Emmeline's head and hit it against the ground again. He cursed in pain as he got off her. Emmeline choked, and her vision darkened and closed in.

Erik, help! Please help me.

"Emia, don't close your eyes. Stay awake," Matthew begged.

Emmeline heard her brother call out to her, but she couldn't focus on where he was. Her head rolled to the side, and her arms lay limp against the patio floor. Her fingers unfurled, as if reaching for something in the distance, and she stared out into her beautiful garden as time slowed to a standstill.

Out of the darkness, the air split, and strands of light flashed around Emmeline. She watched as the air tore at itself, like a seam ripping open on a dress. A sharp claw appeared, followed by a translucent body and wide black eyes.

Emmeline wanted to scream, but she couldn't.

No.

CHAPTER FORTY-EIGHT

TWO OF TWO

Blood pooled at the back of Emmeline's throat, and she spat it on the floor. She propped herself up on her elbows, and her head swam as she tried to focus. A raizour landed in the garden and trained its deadly eyes on Emmeline, but it didn't move from its spot.

"What the hell is that thing?" Philip stared at the raizour.

"Emia, look at me!" Matthew shouted.

Emmeline slowly turned to Matthew's voice.

"Get inside to the safe room. Go!" Matthew pleaded. "Emia, you have to get up." He looked around. "Philip, get her inside. That thing will kill us all. You won't be able to deliver Emia to your benefactor if she's dead!"

Philip didn't acknowledge Matthew and stared open-mouthed at the creature before him. Emmeline tried to push herself toward the patio doors, but her head felt like it was about to split open.

Do not move, seeker. If you do, I will kill the others. You might live, but they will not, the raizour growled.

Emmeline froze in her spot. "What do you want?" she choked out but was met with silence.

"Don't listen to it, Emia. Get inside now!" Matthew begged, and Ms. Rose whimpered behind him.

Emmeline kept her eyes trained on the raizour. "I can't. It threatened to kill you and Ms. Rose if I try to leave."

More raizour filed out behind the first one, and they stood in perfect rows. None of the raizour moved, and they all trained their unblinking eyes on Emmeline. Finally, no more raizour came through, and all went silent.

What are they doing? Why are they just standing there?

Emmeline felt the air grow electric and heavy, and the center line of raizour moved aside for something else that entered the atmosphere. A raizour, bigger and more menacing than the others, stalked to the front, and another figure behind the large raizour glided into the light. The figure studied her as he sauntered over, and she recognized his magic like she would a loved one.

The second seeker.

He was tall and lanky, and he looked to be around Emmeline's age. The moonlight bounced off his sallow skin, and his straight dirty-blond hair was slicked back, framing his narrow face. Dark green eyes glinted against the night as he assessed his surroundings. He was dressed in black, and it stood out against the slippery, translucent skin of the raizour that surrounded him.

The seeker leaned over and spoke to the large raizour in a voice too low for Emmeline to hear. The large raizour trained its eyes back on her and lifted a sharp claw to motion to a second raizour. The second raizour stalked through the garden and made its way up the patio steps.

Emmeline whimpered and turned her head to the side as it came up and snapped its sharp teeth at her. It bent beside her and wrapped its claws around her neck, the tips of its claws pricking her skin. It lifted her up by her neck until her toes barely grazed the floor.

"Let me down!" Emmeline bit out as her feet struggled to reach the floor.

Be quiet, it commanded.

The seeker sauntered up to Emmeline, and his green eyes roamed over her face. "So, you're the last one. You're the one that shouldn't exist," he said. His sunken eyes raked over Emmeline. "Your ability's weak. I can barely feel it."

"Who are you?" Emmeline gasped.

He tilted his head arrogantly. "You know who I am, but you can call me Rowen if you need a name."

"Why are you with the raizour? You're supposed to help the nainthe. They've been looking for you for decades!"

"Helping them holds no benefit for me, though you might be of some use."

We should kill her, the large raizour growled.

"No, Daimai. We might have more use for her alive than dead. If she proves useless, you can kill her," Rowen replied.

She should not exist, Daimai countered.

"Perhaps, but that doesn't mean she won't be useful." Rowen paused as he eyed Emmeline's bruised face, and his eyes flickered over to Philip, coolly looking him up and down before returning to Emmeline. "Bring her home." He turned and walked off the patio.

Emmeline wrapped her hands around the raizour's claws and tried to pry them off her neck. She kicked back but couldn't get enough leverage to make any impact. The raizour tightened its grip around her neck, and she gasped for air as she clawed against its grip.

Suddenly, a pair of boots crashed to the patio floor, and in a flash, a short black blade sliced open Emmeline's captor's throat, decapitating it. The raizour's claws loosened around her neck and its body collapsed. Strong arms caught Emmeline, and her eyes closed with relief.

Multiple boots slammed to the ground, and Emmeline looked up to see Ellis, Sophia, Saadah, Anja, and Lesedi, all in their nainthe form, armed and ready.

Erik changed into his human form and cradled Emmeline's head in his hands. "I came as soon as I felt you reach out to me." He tried to wipe some of the blood off her face with his fingers.

Emmeline looked around at the scene in front of her. "There are only six of you. There's no way you can fight your way through all those raizour!"

"Lesedi's notified the Sanctuary, and help is on the way."

"Erik, you need to move Emia now!" Anja hissed, her cold eyes trained on the raizour in front of her.

Erik gathered Emmeline in his arms and moved her to the far end of the patio. He flipped his short blade and pressed the handle into her hand before covering it with her dress.

"No hesitation, Emia. Hesitation will cost you your life. Use the element of surprise."

Emmeline nodded shakily, and her hand closed around the grip of the blade.

Sophia ran over to Erik. "I'll guard Emmeline and her family. I'm the least experienced in battle and the weakest here." She looked worriedly at the wall of raizour. "Erik, go!"

Emmeline grasped Erik's hand as he turned to leave. "The second seeker's here. He's with the raizour."

Surprise flashed across Erik's eyes but disappeared quickly. Pulling out his two long blades, he changed into nainthe form and dragged the tips of the blades on the patio floor as he stalked toward the raizour. His dark, leathery wings unfolded around him, and the others followed suit, their sharp blades ready at their sides. For the first time, Emmeline realized the breadth of power and horror in front of her.

I've never seen them in battle. They're terrifying.

Emmeline looked at Matthew, who watched the scene with fascination. Her eyes darted to Philip, and he was still frozen. His ear had stopped bleeding and was now a sticky red mess.

Just wait until we're done here, Philip. That ear's going to be the least of your problems.

"It's nice to finally meet you, Executioner," Rowen drawled and stepped back into the light.

Daimai stood taut and snarled at Erik, its claws flexing at its sides. Erik's icy irises assessed Daimai, but his features stayed blank.

Lesedi moved beside Erik and addressed Rowen. "I know you are a seeker. Why are you with the raizour? Are you with them by choice or against your will?"

"Do I look like I'm being held against my will?" Rowen raised an eyebrow.

"Then, my first question still stands. Why are you with them?"

Rowen just grinned and stepped back again with Daimai. He tipped his head, and the rest of the raizour crouched and leaped up, raining down on the nainthe.

Emmeline watched as the nainthe fought against the onslaught of claws, teeth, and wings. Saadah and Ellis worked as a team, guarding each other's back and working in synchronization as they dispatched one raizour after another. Anja and Lesedi made sure they covered each other from all angles. They gave Erik a wide berth to work with, drawing raizour away from him but leaving him the bulk of the fight.

Emmeline held her breath as Erik slaughtered raizour after raizour, his movements precise and unforgiving. For every one the others took out, Erik went through three.

I see why he works alone. They wouldn't be able to keep up with him.

Emmeline's eyes snapped to the side as a dark outline slunk across the patio. A raizour came out of the shadows, its black eyes never leaving Emmeline's face. Sophia shifted her body and stood in front of Emmeline, holding her blade at her side. Philip picked up his gun and rushed toward Emmeline.

Philip pointed his gun at the raizour. "I still need to get you to my benefactor."

"The gun won't work on them!" Emmeline cried.

Philip ignored her and pulled the trigger. He fired two shots at the raizour, but the bullets ricocheted off its slick skin.

"What the hell?" Philip looked at his gun and fired continually until he emptied his clip, but it didn't hurt the raizour.

Move, human, the raizour clicked and snapped its jaw at Philip.

Sophia growled and stomped over to Philip as he fumbled to reload his gun. She grabbed Philip by his collar and threw him through the glass patio doors. Emmeline screamed as Philip crashed to the floor and glass shattered around him.

Sophia turned to the raizour. "Hurry up," she hissed and moved out of its way.

She can speak the raizour language.

Emmeline's eyes widened in horror, and she looked back and forth between the raizour and Sophia.

They know each other.

"Sophia! How could you betray the nainthe like this? How could you do this to Ellis?"

"Things need to change, and you're in the way. Unlike the rest of the nainthe, I won't spend my life hiding away like a coward," Sophia replied coldly.

The raizour materialized in front of Emmeline, its sharp teeth gleaming under the moonlight. She steadied herself and gripped Erik's blade, hidden in the folds of her dress. Before she could scream, the raizour grabbed her throat and lifted her into the air.

No hesitation!

Emmeline thrust the blade deep into the raizour's abdomen. It slid through the raizour's outer skin and embedded itself into a mixture of muscle and organs. She pulled the blade upward with both her hands until she hit something hard. She tore the blade out of the raizour's body, and its wicked grin faltered into shock. It looked down at the dark blue liquid seeping out of its abdomen.

You piece of shit.

Emmeline fell to her knees and gulped down air as the raizour slumped over in front of her. Before she could catch her breath, sharp fingernails laced through her hair and pulled her head back. She whimpered as the coolness of a blade touched her bare throat.

"Don't resist me, seeker," Sophia hissed. "Do anything, and they'll kill your brother." She dragged Emmeline to her feet and pushed her toward Rowen and Daimai. "Walk."

Erik! Help!

Erik whirled around and jumped into the air, his icy irises sparking wildly as he crashed in front of Sophia. The raizour stopped their assault, and Rowen put his hands in his pockets.

"Isn't this interesting?" Rowen laughed. "Bring her to me."

"Sophia, what are you doing?" Ellis ran up beside Erik. He tried to step forward, but Erik blocked his path with his blade.

"Let her go, Sophia," Erik growled.

"Either I take her alive to Rowen or you can watch me kill her right here," Sophia sneered.

"Then, I'll kill you either way. You won't leave this place alive," Erik replied.

"I'm not afraid of dying, and I'm done hiding. Anything is better than this so-called nonexistence." Sophia tightened her grip on Emmeline's hair.

Suddenly, there was a thunderous echo of wings from above. Emmeline squeezed her eyes shut as flashes of light burst around her. Nainthe dropped in front of her and all over the garden, ready with their blades poised.

You are taking too long, nainthe, Daimai growled.

Sophia pushed Emmeline forward. "Move!"

Emmeline looked desperately at Erik. *Wait for it! I hope this works.*

Erik flexed his fingers around the handles of his blades, and his eyes sharpened.

Emmeline let her long dress tangle with her feet and cried out as she pretended to stumble. Her knees buckled, and her body fell hard to the side, away from the blade. The force of her fall surprised Sophia, and she released Emmeline for barely a second before catching her.

But a second was all Erik needed. He lashed out, his blade whipping through the air and slicing through Sophia's neck. Sophia went still, and a look of silent shock flickered across her face before her body and head fell to the patio floor, separating as they collided against the ground.

"It's time to go," Rowen announced, and the tear in the sky reopened up.

Erik unhooked something small from his armor and launched it at Rowen. It cut through Rowen's shirt, drawing blood from his arm.

Rowen hissed, and his eyes turned hard. "For an executioner, you aren't very good at your job. Don't worry; your time is coming soon."

Daimai picked up Rowen, and they disappeared through the tear. The remaining raizour raced to follow them, screeching into the night as they vanished.

PART VI:

THE CATASTROPHE OF OATHS

CHAPTER FORTY-NINE

THE BEGINNING OF THE END

Emmeline stood in shock on the patio and slowly sank to her knees. Her stomach turned as she stared at Sophia's body.

Lesedi changed into her human form. "Get the bodies back to the Sanctuary," she commanded.

The rest of the nainthe obeyed, each picking up two bodies before leaping into the night. Another nainthe, smaller in stature, sheathed her blade and pulled off her helmet.

Maira.

Maira walked up to Lesedi. "Sophia was working with them. And what was that large raizour? I've never seen one like that before."

"This wasn't an attack against the nainthe. They were here for Emmeline." Lesedi furrowed her brow. "The second seeker has been with them all this time. Willingly."

"I don't understand how that's possible. How did the raizour find the seeker? Or did the seeker find them? And why would he be helping them?" Maira looked troubled. "I have too many questions and need to get back to the Sanctuary to speak to Javier. Will you be coming back or staying here? It would be good for you to come with me. We could use your help."

Lesedi glanced over at Anja, who was helping stack raizour bodies for returning nainthe to bring back to the Sanctuary.

"I'll come back home. Anja and Erik will stay back and help look after Emmeline and Matthew," Lesedi confirmed. "We need to be cautious. There might be more like Sophia among us."

Maira's eyes hardened. "We will find them. I'll see you in Javier's office."

Maira picked up Sophia's body and head before changing back into nainthe form. Her wings expanded behind her, and she flew into the air, disappearing into the night.

Erik sheathed his blades and knelt beside Emmeline. "Are you okay?"

Emmeline let a breath out. "I think so."

"Can you do your thing for me?"

Emmeline shifted closer to Erik and took his face into her hands. She closed her eyes and felt fury and violence seep into her skin. For the first time, she felt the threads of his magic move against her aura.

I can feel Erik's magic.

Emmeline opened her eyes, and he was back in human form. She ran her thumb over his cheek.

"How do you feel?" Emmeline asked.

"As long as you're here, I'm fine." Erik exhaled. "I'm sorry I took so long to come."

Erik wrapped his arm around Emmeline's waist and pulled her close to him, resting his forehead against hers. After a moment, he pulled away and studied her face. His warm fingers lifted her chin, and he traced the bruising on her cheek and mouth.

"Did the seeker do this to you?" Erik's irises swelled with fury.

Emmeline shook her head. "It was Philip. He was here at the house. He was waiting for me when I got home and tried to kidnap me. He said someone paid him to keep tabs on me, and he was supposed to deliver me to him tonight." She touched the back of her head and studied the viscous liquid that coated her fingertips. "I think I might be at risk of a concussion. You should be very proud of me; I broke his nose and ripped his ear off."

"Where is he?" Erik stood up, and his irises expanded to cover his eyes. He reached down and pulled a short blade from his boot.

"Sophia threw him through the patio doors, so he's either injured on the kitchen floor or long gone." Emmeline gripped Erik's hand. "She threatened Mattie's life and said if I didn't cooperate, another would kill him. She didn't say if it was another nainthe or raizour."

Anja sprinted over, fear lining her features. "Emia, you need to come over. Mattie needs you."

Emmeline stood up and they ran over to Matthew and Ms. Rose. Matthew's binds were undone, and he knelt on the patio with his back to them. There was a tear in his white dress shirt, and his blood had soaked through it.

"Mattie?" Emmeline called out.

As she got closer, she saw Matthew hunched over a body. Its arms were limp, and long, manicured fingers lay open and lifeless on the floor. Vacant eyes stared at the quiet sky, and a large pool of blood trickled across the patio floor.

When Matthew spoke, his voice was dull. "She's gone."

Emmeline fell to her knees beside Matthew.

"No, no, no!" She wrapped her hands around Ms. Rose's face. "Ms. Rose, please come back. I can't live without you. Please, Ms. Rose, please," Emmeline begged. Hot tears fell from her eyes and dripped onto Ms. Rose's cheeks. She looked over her shoulder, but couldn't see through her tears. "Someone, call an ambulance!"

Matthew stared at Ms. Rose's face. "It's no use. She's gone."

Emmeline whirled around to face her brother. "Did you try to save her? Did you?" she screamed. "How could you be so heartless and cold? This isn't one of your damn patients. It's Ms. Rose!"

Emmeline screamed again and shoved Matthew as hard as she could. Matthew fell backward, and his eyes never left Ms. Rose's face. Emmeline looked down at Matthew's hands, and her anger turned into panic. His hands were covered with blood, and his fingernails dug into the palms of his hands, cutting into his skin.

Emmeline turned and stared at Ms. Rose's body. Bloody handprints covered the middle of her shirt, and blurred thumbprints were smeared across her jawline and around the wound on her neck. Emmeline looked up at Matthew, but he was motionless.

"Mattie, I'm sorry," Emmeline wept. "I know you tried; I know! I didn't mean what I said. Please, Mattie, don't disappear on me again. Don't shut me out. Don't leave me here by myself." She pulled Matthew into her arms and pressed his head into her shoulder.

I'm sorry, Mattie. Please come back.

Anja knelt beside Matthew, and she wrapped her arms around both Emmeline and Matthew.

"Mattie, we're both here. We need you. Please come back to us," Emmeline whispered.

Matthew lifted his head, and Emmeline's heart squeezed hopefully. She took his face in her hands and searched his eyes. Then, he blinked, and recognition flickered across his irises. She let out a sigh of relief and hugged him again.

"I'll take care of everything. Let's get you off the floor," Emmeline said.

Matthew nodded slowly, and Emmeline and Anja helped him move away from Ms. Rose's body.

How am I going to face Ms. Rose alone?

Emmeline pushed a stray hair off Ms. Rose's face.

I'm sorry you got caught up in this mess. I was the one who was supposed to die. Not you.

Emmeline tried to wipe the tears off her face, but the tears kept coming.

How am I going to live without you, my forever governess?

Erik crouched down beside Emmeline. "I'm sorry, Emia."

"Ms. Rose became my mother when Mom passed away. She cared for Mattie and me, even when we were at our worst. She made sure we ate, that we were safe, and she always made sure we knew we were loved." Emmeline leaned on Erik's shoulder, her tears falling lightly onto his armor. "She loved my parents too. Having her almost made it feel like Mom and Dad were still here sometimes."

Erik touched her face and gently wiped the tear streaks off. He surveyed the grounds, and his eyes were sharp when he looked back at her.

"What happened to your security team?"

Emmeline's eyes widened. "Mr. Jae! Where is he? And Tom and Hannah!"

"I'll go look for them. You stay here." Erik called out over his shoulder. "Lessie, can you stay close? I need to search the grounds for Mr. Jae and the two security guards."

Lesedi nodded, and Erik sprinted off.

"What are you going to do now, Emmeline? How can I help?" Lesedi asked kindly.

Emmeline closed her eyes and took a deep breath.

Time to take care of business. You can cry later.

"Can you ask someone to go into my house and get my shoes and phone? I left both by the console table at the top of the stairs that go to the basement. I'd get them myself, but I have no shoes, and there's glass all over the floor. All the raizour bodies and nainthe need to be cleared out in the next few minutes so I can call the police and emergency services," Emmeline said.

Lesedi relayed the message to the remaining nainthe on-site.

"I can stay with you while the police are here," Lesedi offered.

Emmeline shook her head and took Ms. Rose's cold hand in hers. "That'll raise more questions. You must go back to the Sanctuary and figure out what the hell happened tonight. I want to know who Rowen is and what he wants with me."

Saadah came by with Emmeline's items and handed them to her. "I'm sorry for your loss. Ms. Rose was kind to me, and I will miss her very much," he said in a low voice and pressed his hand to his heart.

"Thank you, Saadah," Emmeline murmured.

"We're done here. You can call the police." Saadah gave her shoulder a squeeze. "Take care of yourself."

Emmeline watched as, one by one, the nainthe disappeared into the night sky. Erik came running back just as the last nainthe left.

"I found Mr. Jae and the two security guards. They were tied up in the garden shed. I freed them, and they're resting on the lawn," Erik said.

Emmeline let out a sigh of relief. "I need to call the police." She looked up at Erik. "Will you stay?"

"Anja and I will watch from the roof. I looked for Philip, but couldn't find him. There's blood on the glass from the patio doors, but no trail."

Emmeline felt a sharp stab of fury. "I'll worry about him later." She dialed emergency services.

"Nine-one-one. What's your emergency?" the operator asked.

Emmeline closed her eyes.

"I'd like to report a murder."

∽

Emmeline hung up with emergency services and dialed another number.

"Peter, you'd better come to my house." She tried to tell him what had happened, but it came out as a disjointed series of sentences.

In the distance, she could hear the sirens getting closer.

"Erik, you and Anja need to hide. The police will be here in less than a few minutes, and this place will be swarming with the press. You need to stay hidden," Emmeline said. Even to herself, her voice sounded far away.

Erik knelt beside her and gently turned Emmeline's face to him. "Emia?" His eyes searched her face.

Emmeline struggled to speak. "I need to be strong enough for me and Mattie." She looked to the entrance of the garden. "They're here. You need to go."

"I'll be close by." Erik motioned to Anja, who reluctantly left Matthew's side.

Erik ran out into the garden and bent down to pick up something sharp off the grass. Holding up a small diamond-shaped black object against the moonlight, he inspected it before walking back to Anja's side. They both changed into nainthe form and disappeared over the roof of the house.

"Ms. Taylor-Wu, we're posting several officers around your home, and an APB has been put out for the mayor. We found his car down the road, so he couldn't have gotten very far. He's highly recognizable, and we'll find him," the detective said. "We're going to see if there's any video footage we can use to identify the individuals who helped him get inside your residence. My officers did a walk-through of your house, and it's safe to go back in." He nodded at Peter in acknowledgment. "I'll be in touch with Mr. Zhao tomorrow on the next steps. I hope you're able to get some rest tonight."

"Thank you, Detective Caron."

"Are you sure you don't want to go to the hospital?"

Emmeline shook her head and stood up, signaling the end of the discussion. She waited for the detective to leave before speaking to her lawyer.

"Peter, you have your work cut out for you. I'd like you to hire private investigators to help augment the search for Philip and his benefactor. Follow the money. Eva will assist you."

"I'll have someone on my team take care of all the required paperwork. Do try to get some rest tonight."

"Good night, Peter."

Emmeline didn't wait for a reply and walked back into the house.

CHAPTER FIFTY

DENMARK

Emia: Anja, has Mattie gone to bed yet?

Anja: Yes, he's sleeping now. Do you want me to wake him up?

Emia: No, let him rest. Thank you for staying with him. I'm going to bed.

Emia: Erik, where are you?

Erik: I'm on the roof, keeping a lookout.

Emia: I've unlocked my balcony door. You don't need to keep a lookout. There are officers on the ground.

    Emmeline heard the balcony door handle click and the heavy door slide open. Erik stepped into her room and unhooked his blades, placing them against the wall.
    "You're covered with raizour blood." Emmeline grimaced at the sticky liquid that coated his armor and clothes. "Please take off your shoes and do not touch or sit on anything."

Erik looked down at himself. "Now, you know why I sometimes wear a face mask. It gets everywhere and tastes bad."

Emmeline covered her mouth and smiled. Guilt hit her like a wave, and she looked away.

"It's okay to smile and grieve at the same time, Emia."

Emmeline wiped under her eyes and blinked hard. She went into her closet and came back out with a pile of clothes.

"These are from the last time you were here. Why don't you get cleaned up in the guest room? It has a large en suite, and there's a bathtub you can use to wash your armor and blades." She looked down at her bloodstained dress. "I'm going to take a shower."

"Do you want me to come back after? If not, I'll stay in the guest room."

Emmeline stared at her bloodied hands and twisted her mother's ring around her finger.

Erik answered for her and motioned to the built-in daybed Emmeline used for reading. "I'll come back and sleep here."

"Thank you," Emmeline murmured.

Erik nodded and took the clothes from her hands. He picked up his blades and pulled open the balcony doors.

"Erik, what are you doing?"

"I'm going to the guest room."

"From the balcony?"

"That's what I did last time."

"This is a house. You can get to the guest room from the hallway." Emmeline walked over to her bedroom door and opened it.

Holding his head high, Erik walked past Emmeline and left her bedroom.

~

Emmeline looked at herself in her full-length mirror. Her hair was undone and matted with blood, her face was bruised, her neck scabbed where the raizour's claws had been, and blood covered most of her dress.

Maybe I shouldn't have judged Erik.

She turned on the hot water and let it steam up the bathroom. She pulled out the pins still stuck in her hair and stripped off her dress and undergarments, leaving them in a pile on the floor. The hot water burned as it ran through her hair and down her skin, taking with it streaks of bright red against the white-marbled floor. Emmeline watched the blood swirl around the drain.

I don't even know how much of that blood is mine or Ms. Rose's. Some of it probably belongs to Philip.

Emmeline placed her hands over her eyes, and the hot water burned her fingers. She started to heave, and soon, her entire body was racked with sobs.

I'm sorry, Ms. Rose. Will you forgive me?

She covered her mouth to muffle the sounds of her crying and squeezed her eyes shut.

If you were here, I know you'd tell me you love me and there's nothing to forgive. You'd call me darling or sweetheart and give me a hug. Who's going to hug me now? What am I going to do without you? What's Mattie going to do without you? You didn't deserve this.

She rubbed the water out of her eyes and took a few shaky breaths.

Be strong, Emmeline. Be strong for Mattie. Be strong for Ms. Rose.

Emmeline stepped out of the shower and towel-dried her hair. She looked at herself in the mirror and flinched at her reflection. The bruises on her lower cheek and mouth had darkened into a deep red.

It looks worse now than before I showered.

She opened her medicine cabinet, and her hand hesitated before picking up a bottle of pills. Turning it around, she found the expiration date and sighed. She threw the bottle into the garbage can.

I'll order some tomorrow.

⁓

Emmeline wrapped her robe around her body and tied it with the wide sash. She left her bathroom and found Erik standing by her bookshelf, perusing her collection. His hair was still damp, and he had it slicked back. She could see the slight waves in his hair starting to form as it dried.

He looks much less intimidating when he's not dressed like Batman.

Emmeline noted the softcover book in his hand. "The library downstairs has a much more extensive collection if you're looking for something to read. There's even a wide collection of medical textbooks, if that's what floats your boat."

"I see you love your murder mysteries." Erik put the book back on the shelf. He turned to her, and his eyes darkened at the wounds on her cheek. "Does it hurt a lot?"

Emmeline nodded. "It'll be better in a few days."

"How's the back of your head? Do you mind if I take a look?"

"Sure, though the paramedic said I'll be fine."

Erik walked over to her and gently moved her hair away from her scalp. "There's a split in your scalp, but it's already scabbing over. You're lucky."

"Maybe I was too lucky."

"It seems our lives are ruled by some combination of coincidence and choice, though I haven't quite figured out which one has the upper hand," Erik murmured.

"You don't believe in luck?"

"Not usually." Erik glanced at the clock on her nightstand. "You should try to sleep."

"Let me change and get you a blanket and pillow."

Emmeline went into her closet and switched her robe for a light tank dress. She handed Erik a pillow and blanket and crawled into her bed, wrapping the comforter tightly around her.

"Thank you for staying, Erik. Good night."

"Good night, Emia."

∼

Emmeline stared at the ceiling.

I don't mind the darkness. At least I don't need to be careful with my facial expressions or be watchful of my body language. I don't need to pretend and make sure everyone else is fine.

A few tears rolled down her temples. She willed herself to even out her breathing and wiped her cheeks with her fingers.

I don't want to wake Erik up. He needs his rest too.

She turned to face the wall.

Ms. Rose has some distant family in Europe. I need to find a way to notify them, and I also need to find a burial spot for her. I'll see if Mattie's okay with giving her a place in the family mausoleum.

Warm tears dripped off the bridge of her nose and onto the pillow.

Eventually, everyone leaves me—Mom, Dad, Ms. Rose. Mr. Jae will return to South Korea to be with his family. I don't blame him. There's nothing left for him here.

Emmeline hiccupped into her pillow.

Ms. Rose, I wish you were here to tell me what to do. I'm so lost without you.

She struggled to swallow the air caught in her throat. She heard the daybed creak as Erik got up. She squeezed her eyes shut and held her breath as more tears fell, her lungs forcing her to take short gasps of air. Erik knelt beside her bed, but she didn't turn around.

"Emia," Erik called to her softly. "You're doing a terrible job of hiding your crying."

Emmeline wiped her face. "I know. I'm sorry for waking you."

She heard Erik walk away and the rustle of him removing cushions from the daybed. He was back within a few seconds, propping pillows against her nightstand. He sat on the floor beside her bed, and they stayed quietly together as the minutes ticked by. Eventually, Emmeline calmed while listening to Erik's steady breathing. She shifted to lie on her stomach and turned her head to Erik, watching his profile in the dark.

"Erik?"

"Yes, Emia?"

"Have you ever been to Denmark?"

Erik rested his head on the edge of her mattress. "Once, a long time ago. My parents talked about their home a lot, but I never got to go with them. Aria convinced me to go and see the birthplace of my parents before the chance was taken away from me. Why do you ask?"

Emmeline felt a slight pang of jealousy at the mention of Aria.

"I've never been there."

He smiled at her, making her heart skip a beat. "The great Ms. Taylor-Wu has never been to Denmark? I would've thought you'd been to every country by now."

"We did some traveling, but not as much as people would think we did. We spent lots of time in Asia and Australia, but between school, extracurriculars, and my parents' jobs, it didn't leave much time for other places."

"One day, we can go together. It would be nice to go back. It's a beautiful country." Erik looked away, and they lapsed back into silence.

"I would love to see Denmark with you," Emmeline said.

Erik tilted his head. "Maybe you can take me to Asia. I haven't been to that continent yet."

"Have you been to Australia?"

Erik nodded. "I needed to get away and picked a faraway country where I wouldn't stick out like a sore thumb."

"Anja told me you left the nainthe once. Was it during that time that you went to Australia?"

Erik nodded again, and his eyes dimmed. "Did my sister tell you why I left?"

"Just a little bit. When you're ready to, you can tell me about it."

"Maybe one day," Erik murmured.

"Erik?"

"Yes, Emia?"

"A while ago, you promised to share something about yourself with me. Can I call on that now? I'd love to hear something about you, if you don't mind."

"You know a lot about me already. More than most ever will."

"I know some things about you as a nainthe and your life now, but I don't know anything about you before that. I want to know something about you."

Erik stared ahead. "Before becoming a nainthe? It was so long ago; sometimes, I can't remember." He paused and searched his memory until his eyes brightened in the dark room. "When you were a child, everyone called you Emia. When I was a child, my nickname was Slice."

"Why Slice?"

"I'm a Canadian, born to Scandinavian parents, out in rural Nova Scotia. I was in skates before I could walk," Erik snorted. "I played amateur hockey and practically lived on the ice for as long as the season would allow. At that time and where we lived, we only had outdoor rinks. We were in a remote area, so my father and a few neighbors would get together every year and put up a huge rink for the kids to mess around in."

Emmeline tried to imagine a young Erik stick-handling a hockey puck and sliding to a stop to quickly change directions. "Did they call you Slice because you were great at hockey stops?"

"No, though I was good at that. They called me Slice because I had the best wrist shot in the province."

"The best in the province?" Emmeline raised an eyebrow.

Erik let out a short laugh. "That's what my father told me every morning before I went out for practice."

Emmeline smiled against her pillow, and her heart warmed. "Thank you for sharing that with me, Slice. We can get out on a rink when it's colder, and you can show me the best wrist shot born out of the East Coast."

"Anytime your busy schedule allows for it, Ms. Taylor-Wu."

They both fell back into silence, and Emmeline's eyes began to droop.

"Erik?"

"Yes, Emia?"

"Can I sit with you?"

"Always."

Erik shifted over and held out his hand to Emmeline. She took his hand and slipped out from under her covers and sat beside him. Erik wrapped his arm around her waist, and she molded herself against his warmth, resting her head on his shoulder.

Erik tucked Emmeline's hair behind her ear. "Ms. Rose knew you loved her, just like your parents knew you loved them. Remember that when the pain becomes too much to bear. You and Matthew were lucky to have Ms. Rose, and she was lucky to have you both."

Fresh tears fell down Emmeline's cheeks. "I thought you didn't believe in luck?"

"I do when it suits my purpose." Erik wiped Emmeline's cheek with his fingers. "I didn't mean to make you cry again."

"It's okay. I'm pretty much out of tears anyway." Emmeline closed her tired eyes.

Erik started to hum a soft tune, and Emmeline recognized it as the haunting lullaby she had once heard Anja sing to Matthew when they first came to the Sanctuary. She let the melody wash over her and calm her broken heart. Her body began to relax, and sleep weaved through her exhausted mind.

"You're very much musically inclined," Emmeline mumbled.

As sleep overtook her, Erik reached over and pulled the duvet off her bed to drape it over them. Her mind slowly turned dark, and she drifted into a deep, dreamless sleep.

CHAPTER FIFTY-ONE

CRACKED GLASS

Emmeline's sleepy mind started to wake, and she felt a hand resting on the dip of her waist. A faint, familiar scent made her heart skip, and she forced her eyes to open despite the feeble protest from her mind.

"You're up," Erik stated.

Emmeline blushed and reluctantly pushed herself up.

"I think I'm still asleep," she mumbled. She rubbed her eyes and tried to smooth her long hair with her fingers. "I should get up. I have so much to do."

"How did you sleep?"

"Like a rock."

"Good." Erik grimaced as he shifted his arm out from under her. "Because I think I've lost all feeling on the entire left side of my body."

"I'm sorry. If it's any consolation, it was comfortable for me." Emmeline shrugged helplessly.

Erik laughed, and his musical tenor filled her bedroom. Emmeline's heart lifted a little, and she couldn't help but smile.

Erik sobered. "Javier asked that we all return to the Sanctuary today. He wants to speak to you as soon as you're available. The news of the attack and the second seeker is concerning."

"I'll get ready, and we can go. Can you let Anja know? Mattie doesn't need to come unless he wants to. I want him to get his rest."

Erik nodded and picked up his phone.

Emmeline shrugged off the comforter and turned to him. "Thank you for staying. I don't know how I would've gotten through last night if you hadn't been here."

"I wanted to be here." Erik's eyes clouded over. "Go get ready. Anja says Matthew will join us. They'll meet us in the garage in an hour."

Emmeline stood up, and the hem of her sleep dress grazed the top of her thighs.

Maybe I should have worn something a little more conservative.

She blushed again and could feel Erik's darkening gaze on her.

"I'll be right back," she murmured.

She grabbed her robe from the closet and went to the bathroom. She closed the door behind her and leaned against it, letting out a breath.

What a mess everything is.

˜

Emmeline looked at her watch. "It's not time to meet Mattie and Anja yet. I'll make us coffee."

As they made their way downstairs, they passed the great room, and a lone figure sitting on the sofa caught Emmeline's eye.

Mattie.

"Erik, can you wait for me in the kitchen?"

Erik's eyes went over to Matthew, and he nodded. Emmeline slid open the doors to the great room and walked in, making sure

Matthew heard her. He didn't look at her when she took a seat beside him.

"I'm sorry you had to do everything on your own yesterday. I'm sorry I wasn't there for you when you needed me," Matthew said. He stared at the blank television screen on the wall.

"I'm sorry about what I said. I didn't mean it."

"I know you didn't."

"It's just you and me now."

"Yes, it is."

"Mattie, I don't want you involved in this nainthe-raizour business. I don't want you to come to the Sanctuary anymore. I want you to move back to your condominium, be a doctor, and save lives. That's your calling." Emmeline looked at Mattie's side, and she could see the outline of a bandage. "Last night, I came close to losing you, too, and I won't take that risk. I won't let you leave me all alone in this world."

Matthew turned to look at her, and his eyes flashed. "Now you know how I felt last night. Do you think I would leave you to fend for yourself? Have you ever thought about what would happen to me if something happened to you? Do you know how I felt as I watched Philip slam your head into the ground? Do you know how Ms. Rose felt as she watched him hit you? That was the last thing she saw before she died."

Matthew stopped talking and abruptly stood up. Emmeline started to cry as he paced the room.

"I thought Philip was going to kill you, and then the raizour came. And what the hell happened with Sophia? I thought you were going to die, and there was nothing I could do about it."

Matthew picked up the glass of water beside him and hurled it against the wall.

"But I didn't die, and I'm right here. I know you tried to protect me as best you could," Emmeline said.

Matthew sat back down and put his head in his hands.

"Mattie, I'm going to hug you."

Matthew nodded without looking up, and Emmeline wrapped her arms around his shoulders, giving him time to collect his thoughts.

"I haven't seen you like this since Mom died. Should we give your therapist a call?" Emmeline asked as the tension slowly left from Matthew's shoulders.

"Dr. Pella? What could I possibly tell her?"

"Fair," Emmeline murmured. "Do you feel a little better?"

Matthew gave her a disapproving look and didn't bother answering her.

"I guess you're coming to the Sanctuary with us, and I'm making four coffees to go." Emmeline looked at the water stain on the wall and the shattered glass on the floor. She sighed. "You'd better clean that up."

Matthew took off his glasses and rubbed his eyes. "I will."

CHAPTER FIFTY-TWO

POWERLESS

Emmeline parked her car in the Sanctuary garage, her white car standing out in the sea of black vehicles and motorcycles. They made their way through the courtyard and headed to Javier's office. The sky was cloudy and marbled, and the still air held its breath, as if it were waiting for permission to breathe.

Emmeline fell back and let Matthew and Anja walk ahead of her. Erik fell in step with her, and they both slowed their pace, widening their distance from Matthew and Anja. Emmeline watched her brother reach for Anja and wrap his hand around hers. They didn't speak but seemed perfectly comfortable in each other's company.

"Your brother cares a lot for my sister," Erik said.

"He does. I think he loves her."

Emmeline looked up at Erik as they continued their slow walk across the grassy lawn.

His eyes look warm under the gray sky.

"How do you know?" Erik asked.

"Mattie doesn't like to be touched and avoids it as much as possible. He tolerates it from Ms. Rose and me." Emmeline stopped talking and swallowed hard before she corrected herself. "Tolerated it from Ms. Rose. And even then, he only barely tolerated it."

She pointed to Matthew holding Anja's hand. "Mattie initiated it, and he doesn't do anything he doesn't want to do unless he's rationalized it in his mind, like working with patients. Anja has been good for Mattie. She gives him space to just be himself and hasn't tried to fix him."

"Because there's nothing to be fixed," Erik replied.

"You'd be surprised how many people want to fix him so he fits in with everyone else."

Erik opened his mouth to respond when a voice broke through their quiet conversation.

"Erik!" a sweet voice called out.

Emmeline looked up to see Aria jogging over, her bright blue eyes standing out against her silky brown hair. Emmeline straightened up and composed her features.

"I heard about last night from Maira." Aria was almost breathless when she reached them. She stood on her toes and gave Erik a quick kiss on the cheek.

Emmeline stiffened at Aria's display of affection, and she looked away.

You have no right to be jealous. Pull yourself together.

She forced herself to relax and turned back to face Erik and Aria.

"Emmeline, it's nice to see you again. I'm glad you're okay. It must've been a terrifying experience," Aria said kindly.

"Thank you, Aria. It's nice to see you too."

Aria's eyes fell on Emmeline's bruised cheek, and she reached out to touch it. Emmeline flinched and stepped backward.

"Sorry, I didn't mean to startle you." Aria glanced at Erik. "It looks very painful. Did the other seeker do this to you?"

"No, it wasn't him." Emmeline felt her insides twist.

I don't even want to say it was Philip. It's so embarrassing. She'll think I'm pathetic.

"I don't want to talk about it," Emmeline stammered, her composed features faltering.

I need to get out of here.

"I'm sure you and Erik have lots to catch up on. I'll see you both later."

Emmeline didn't wait for an answer and turned in the direction of Javier's office. Matthew and Anja waited for her to catch up to them.

Anja looked behind Emmeline. "Where's my brother?"

"He's with Aria. We should get started. I'm sure Erik will come as soon as he can."

Emmeline walked past them and knocked on the door to Javier's office. The door slid open and Javier stood up as soon as Emmeline stepped inside. He picked up his phone and sent a couple of messages before motioning for them to sit at the conference table.

"Emmeline, Dr. Taylor-Wu, I heard about Ms. Rose from Maira and Lesedi. Please accept my condolences for your loss. I know she was family to you." Javier pressed his hand to his heart.

The door to Javier's office slid open, and Maira and Michael appeared. They sat down at the table with grim faces. They each offered condolences to her and Matthew and waited for Javier to start.

Emmeline heard the door slide open again, and she knew Erik had stepped into the room. She felt his eyes on her, but she kept her eyes forward and didn't look at him when he sat down.

"Emmeline, can you tell me what happened last night? From when you got home. I know some of it is related to the other issue you were having, but I want to hear it all," Javier said.

The color drained from Emmeline's face, and she opened her mouth and closed it.

Matthew pulled out the empty seat beside her and sat down. "I'll try to fill in the details where you can't."

Emmeline nodded and cleared her throat. "When I came home from the fundraiser, Ellis, Sophia, and Saadah left to do a check around the house. They said they felt something was wrong. I didn't notice at the time, but my security guards were missing. When I got inside the house, I couldn't find anyone. I went outside to the backyard, and Philip was there, holding a gun, and Mattie and Ms. Rose were tied up behind him."

Javier turned to Matthew. "How did Philip get in the house? I thought you had security."

"When I looked back at the security footage, Philip had help from three people. They took out the security team and Mr. Jae; only Philip came inside the house. I never saw the others. Philip had a gun and made me disable all the security cameras. Afterward, he tied Ms. Rose and me up and made us go to the garden."

"Emmeline, what happened after you got to the garden?" Javier asked.

"We fought."

"Is that how you sustained your injuries?"

"Philip hit me twice in the face. The first time he hit me was because I'd broken his nose. The second time was because I had called him a monster and wasn't as obedient as he'd expected me to be." Emmeline swallowed, and her vision clouded over. She touched the back of her head. "He threatened to rape me before delivering me to whoever had hired him, so I ripped his ear off with my teeth. He didn't like that, so he slammed my head into the floor twice."

Emmeline stared at the wall behind Javier. She didn't trust herself to look at anyone and didn't want to see the pity on their faces. She heard Erik push his chair back and leave the room, but she couldn't turn around. Anja ran outside after Erik.

"It sounds like you put up quite the fight. You should be proud," Maira finally said.

"I didn't win."

"That's because it wasn't a fair fight to begin with."

Emmeline looked at her hands, and tears rolled down her cheeks.

Why can't I stop crying?

"Do you want me to take over?" Matthew asked.

Emmeline shook her head and wiped her face. "It was a good thing the raizour came when they did. If they hadn't shown up, maybe something worse would've happened to me. One raizour spoke to me and said that they would kill everyone else who was present if I tried to escape. So, I stayed."

The office door slid open, and Anja and Erik entered the room again. They didn't approach the table; instead, they stood by the door. Emmeline could feel the heat and tension radiating off them both.

"The other seeker was commanding the raizour, and they obeyed him. When he came up to me, he knew I was a seeker, just like I knew he was one without him having to tell me. He also knew he was stronger than I was. I think I was a curiosity to him," Emmeline added.

"Did he say why he was with the raizour and what he wanted with you?" Javier asked.

"He said there was no reason for him to help the nainthe, but I could help him. The larger raizour wanted to kill me on the spot and said I shouldn't exist, but the seeker refused. He wanted to see if I was useful, though I don't know what he meant by that. After that, Erik and everyone else showed up. If they had shown up any later, I would've already been gone." Emmeline twisted her mother's ring. "And you know the rest."

"It's obvious we were drawn away on purpose. After Emia left the fundraiser, we could feel raizour presence around her home and went to investigate. They did this to give the seeker a chance to take Emia," Erik growled.

Javier stood up. "Except for Emmeline, I'd like everyone to leave this room. I want to speak to her alone."

Maira and Michael stood and left the room, but nobody else made any effort to go.

"I'm not leaving my sister," Matthew snapped.

"Javier"—Anja's voice came from behind—"may I remind you that you're not a woman?"

"I'm aware of that. Make your point."

"She just went through multiple traumas," Anja replied.

Emmeline turned red.

Victim. Philip didn't break me. I won't let him.

Javier's face softened, and a touch of sadness fleeted across his eyes. "Yes, of course."

Anja knelt beside Emmeline. "Would you like me to stay with you?"

"Yes." Emmeline's throat closed.

Anja nodded to Matthew and Erik, and they both reluctantly left the room. She sat in the chair beside Emmeline and pulled her into a hug.

"You did good, Emia," Anja whispered. "You were braver than anyone I've ever met. Ms. Rose was so proud of you, Mattie's so proud of you, and I'm so proud of you."

"Then, why do I feel like this?"

"Because an asshole tried to make you feel powerless," Anja said, her ash eyes glittering like ice. "But you showed him that you're not. When I find him, I'll show him the true meaning of being powerless."

"Erik said he would find him."

"Philip had better hope I find him first. My brother will be much less forgiving than I am."

Javier paced the room slowly. "There are a few things that don't make sense. The other night, Erik was ambushed. How did the raizour know where he would be, and how did they escape detection? And why Erik?"

"You know why," Anja said. "Obviously, they're going to go after your strongest first. Think about how many raizour Erik has killed over his lifetime of service here. You don't think they've realized that?"

"They know who he is. Every time a raizour refers to him, it refers to him as the Executioner. The seeker knew exactly who Erik was, and it was his first time meeting him," Emmeline added.

Javier continued to pace. "And Erik's right. On the day of the fundraiser, the team was purposely lured away from your residence. How did the raizour know your schedule? Same with that night that you were in the car accident. I suspect you were purposely followed."

"Sophia knew my schedule."

Anja looked at Emmeline with horror. "Ellis. She must have targeted him because of your friendship with him."

"At first, I thought that maybe Ellis was involved, but I saw the look on his face when Sophia was holding me hostage. He'd had no idea," Emmeline said.

"Emia, do you remember what you said to me the first time you came to the Sanctuary? Right before you left?" Anja asked.

Javier crossed his arms. "What are you talking about?"

"When the raizour was talking to me, it told me that the nainthe's house was crumbling from the inside," Emmeline replied.

"Anja, did you not even think to tell me these things?" Javier glared at her. "I've given you lots of leeway, and you've gotten away with things that others have not, partially because I find your rebelliousness refreshing, but this is beyond serious. Quinn and Mihal are dead. Whoever the traitors are, they've tried to kill your brother, and they've made several attempts on Emmeline's life."

Emmeline stared at Javier. "How do I know you aren't the traitor? How do I know you aren't the one trying to kill me?"

Javier sighed and put his head in his hands. "You don't."

"It's not him," Anja said.

"How do you know that?" Emmeline asked.

"My intuition."

Right.

Javier glared at Anja. "Then, why didn't you say something?"

"My intuition didn't kick in until now," Anja replied.

Emmeline's eyes widened. "Javier, Sophia could speak the raizour language. I heard them talking to each other. This means Sophia must have been working with them for some time now.

Javier cursed and ran his hand through his hair. "I need to find out who the traitors are. Emmeline, can you make a list of every nainthe you've had contact with?"

"That's easy enough to do."

"Anja, I want you to take Emmeline's list and tell me who all the surrounding nainthe are."

"Sure, though you know I'm going to tell my brother about all of this," Anja said matter-of-factly.

Javier rolled his eyes and didn't bother responding to her. He looked thoughtfully at Emmeline. "We did learn two interesting things overnight. One, there has been a first seeker all along, and two, humans can survive in the raizour world."

"The seeker's name is Rowen, and he called the larger raizour Daimai," Emmeline said.

"I know you aren't going to like what I'm about to say, but I want you to move to the Sanctuary, even if only temporarily. At least until we have this traitor business sorted out."

"Is that smart? If the traitors are here, I would feel less safe."

"I could protect you much better at the Sanctuary. The traitors might be here, but the raizour can't get in. It's more difficult to protect you at your residence."

I don't want to be at home right now anyway.

"If I move here, you need to accept Mattie too, if he chooses to come."

Javier eyed Anja. "Dr. Taylor-Wu is as welcome here as you are, and given the opportunity, I'm sure he would come."

Anja looked away and blushed.

"You're probably right," Emmeline replied.

"Do you want me to drive? You can get some rest on the way home," Matthew asked Emmeline.

"Sure."

Emmeline handed Matthew her key fob.

"Javier asked me to move to the Sanctuary temporarily. For safety reasons and not because of training. He said you're welcome to stay at the Sanctuary too. Would you consider it?"

"Do you want me to?"

Emmeline nodded. "I know you still have to go to work, so I understand if you don't want to. Maybe you can come to stay on your days off."

"I've been thinking of taking a short sabbatical from the hospital."

"Is that what you want to do?"

"I don't want to leave my patients, but I think this is something I might need to do. I don't want to jeopardize my patients' health, and I want to spend more time with you."

"You don't have to worry about me. I have two of the world's most terrifying bodyguards looking after me." Emmeline motioned behind herself at Erik and Anja. "Though I do think taking a sabbatical, even a short one, would be good. I'd love to spend more time with you."

"Then, it's settled. I'll temporarily move to the Sanctuary with you. I'll let the hospital and my patients know."

CHAPTER FIFTY-THREE

BURDEN OF RESPONSIBILITY

Everyone sat in silence for the entire trip back to Emmeline's home, each lost in their own thoughts. Emmeline stared out the passenger window until they were back in the underground garage and Mattie parked her car beside his.

"Emia." Matthew repeated her name a couple of times.

"Sorry, I zoned out." Emmeline got out of the car and walked to the back to plug it in. "Anja, does the Sanctuary have a charging station in the parking garage?"

"No, but I'll ask to have one installed for you," Anja replied.

"I'll pay for any expenses related to our stay at the Sanctuary. Just let me know how much everything is," Emmeline said absently as she looked around the garage. "I guess we should bring two cars. What do you think, Mattie?"

"Obviously, we're bringing two cars. I'm not leaving my new car unattended."

Emmeline rolled her eyes, and she heard Anja snicker behind her.

"Mattie, I can always teach you how to ride a motorcycle," Anja drawled. "I guarantee you, it's much faster and way more fun."

"Did you forget I work in a hospital? I stay away from motorcycles and trampolines for a reason."

Trampolines? I must ask him about that later.

"Mattie, can you call Peter and let him know we're going to stay at another residence for a short while? He knows how to reach us, and we'll be available for anything he needs. Also, can you talk to the police officers outside and let them know I'd like them to leave?"

"I'll do that."

"Anja, can you help me check on the kitchen? Contractors were supposed to fix the patio doors. It's almost dinnertime, so order food if you guys are hungry."

"I'll get us some wraps and salads," Anja replied.

Emmeline steeled herself to look at Erik for the first time since their encounter with Aria. "Erik, can you help me with some suitcases?"

I don't know why Erik and Aria's relationship bothers me so much. Aria has been perfectly nice to me. Emmeline answered her own question, *It bothers you because she used to be his lover, and now, they're good friends, and you're jealous—that's why. Stop trying to pretend you aren't jealous.*

Erik followed Emmeline into the basement storage room. She pulled out two expandable suitcases for herself and two for Matthew. She stacked the smaller ones inside its matching larger one and rolled them over to Erik.

"This one's for Mattie, and the other one's mine. Can you help me bring them up to our rooms? We can use the elevator if it's easier," Emmeline said.

"Stairs are fine."

Erik took both suitcases and walked behind Emmeline as they made their way up the stairs.

"Emia?"

"Yes, Erik?"

"Are you upset with me?"

Emmeline stopped climbing the stairs and turned around. "Why in the world would you think I'm upset with you?"

"You've been avoiding me since this morning."

"You haven't done anything wrong." Emmeline turned back and continued to climb the stairs.

She stopped at the top of the stairs and pointed to the opposite direction of her room. "Mattie's room is at the end of the hallway, to the right. You can just leave his luggage in front of his door. I'll bring mine over to my room." She took her suitcase from his hand.

"I know I should've gotten to you sooner," Erik said quietly.

Emmeline looked down at her hands. "Don't blame yourself for what happened. If you hadn't come when you did, it would've been worse."

"I didn't know what Philip had done and what he'd tried to do. I should've killed him when I had the chance." Erik reached for Emmeline's cheek, and his fingers traced the large bruise.

"You can't just go around, killing humans. The police will find Philip, and it'll be over for him. He's too well known to hide for long."

Emmeline wanted to close her eyes and lean into Erik's touch. She wanted him to take her into his arms and tell her everything would be fine and that the hate, pain, and guilt she felt would disappear one day.

"Erik, you're not responsible for me. I know you think you are, but you're not. I'm responsible for me, so don't ever put that duty on yourself. It's not worth it."

Erik's hand dropped away, and Emmeline felt cold again.

"I'll wait for you downstairs. Call me when you are done, and I'll come up and help you bring your suitcases down," Erik said.

Emmeline nodded and turned around to go to her room.

Why is everything always so complicated?

CHAPTER FIFTY-FOUR

LOOK AT ME

Emmeline rolled her suitcases into her room and left them open on the floor. She methodically went through her list of technology items and packed everything into her backpack. She went through her bathroom vanity and organized her skin care and makeup into separate travel pouches.

Clothes. I guess I don't need any of my suits or evening wear for the next while. I'll pack some leggings, jeans, sweaters, and T-shirts. And underwear. Don't forget underwear.

Emmeline pulled one of her suitcases into her walk-in closet and worked until she was satisfied that she had everything she needed. She closed the top of her suitcase and pushed herself off the floor.

I need to call a service to mothball the house since I don't know how long Mattie and I'll be gone. If Mattie leaves the Sanctuary, he'll probably go back to his condominium.

Emmeline scrolled through her list of contacts to look for the company she used for more complex cleaning jobs. Her bedroom door opened, and her head snapped up.

That must be Erik. He must've gotten impatient, waiting for me.

"Erik?" she called out and walked out of her closet.

She screamed as a large hand shot out from the side and clamped down over her mouth and nose. Another arm pressed down hard on her torso and pinned her arms to her body, sending her phone crashing to the floor. Suddenly, her assailant flung her to the ground. She cried out as her hands hit the ground to break her fall.

Philip!

Emmeline looked up into his crazed eyes and bloodied face. He was still in his tuxedo from the fundraiser, and his white shirt was stained a deep red. Where his ear once had been was a mess of sticky, dried blood.

Philip pointed his gun at her, and his eyes darted back and forth between Emmeline and the bedroom door.

"Philip, what are you doing? The police are looking for you. Put the gun away! Haven't you caused enough trouble?"

"What the fuck happened last night? What were those things?"

Emmeline closed her eyes and tried to focus on reaching Erik, but she couldn't concentrate.

"What things?"

"Don't fuck around with me, Emmeline! You know what I'm talking about."

Emmeline scrambled to her feet and backed up while Philip paced around her room.

"I don't know what you're talking about," Emmeline stammered.

"Those things that came from the sky with the giant wings and big black eyes. Those things were not human. And what about the other things? I saw one of them, and he was human, and then he became a monster. He *helped* you." Philip glared at her before he went back to pacing.

"Do you know you killed Ms. Rose last night? One of your stray bullets went through her neck. You murdered her!" Emmeline shouted.

Philip ignored her and ran his hand through his hair. He started mumbling to himself before he turned back to her. He took a couple of long strides over to Emmeline and grabbed her wrist. "And you—I didn't deliver you to my benefactor. He's going to kill me. I need to take you to him."

"You killed her, Philip! I'll never see her again! You took her away from Mattie and me. Do you hear me? Do you even care?" Emmeline screamed.

Adrenaline took over, and Emmeline used her weight to twist her wrist out of his grasp. She lifted her heel and brought it down on Philip's knee. Philip hissed in pain and lashed out, striking her across the cheek with the barrel of his gun. The wound on Emmeline's mouth opened back up, and she could taste the bitter, metallic liquid, even before her body hit the floor.

"If you had just followed my plan, I could've saved you from all of this. I would've kept you safe." Philip picked her up by the arms, and his eyes were fully dilated and mad as he stared at the blood dripping down her chin.

He's going to kill me.

Philip lifted Emmeline into the air and hurled her body away from him. She screamed as she landed on top of her glass desk. It shattered beneath her, sending her crashing to the floor. Emmeline cried out as shards of glass cut through her clothes and skin.

"If I can't deliver you to my benefactor, then I'll just kill you. My life's over anyway." For the first time, Philip looked at her with clear eyes, his fingers twitching around the handle of the gun in his hand.

There was a tremor of footsteps pounding down the hall, and Erik was the first one through her bedroom door, with Anja and Matthew at his heels. Erik grabbed Philip and flung him across the room, sending him into the wall. Philip fell to the floor, and the gun tumbled out of his hand, skidding across the ground.

Panicked, Erik spun around to look for Emmeline, but Matthew stopped him.

"I'll look after my sister. You take care of Philip and keep him away from her!"

"Emia, don't move yet." Matthew rushed to Emmeline's side. "Can you feel everything?"

"Yes. The glass though," Emmeline bit out and winced in pain.

Erik stalked over to Philip and grabbed his face. Wrapping his long fingers across Philip's jaw, Erik changed into nainthe form and bared his sharp teeth. Philip stared at Erik in horror and tried to scream and get away, but Erik pinned him to the floor.

"Who sent you?" Erik hissed.

"I don't know!"

"Try harder."

"I've never met the person and only received messages on what to do."

Erik squeezed his fingers against Philip's face and pushed his head back, straining his neck. "How were you paid?"

"Cash was dropped at my office!" Philip struggled against Erik's grip. "Let me go! You're going to break my neck!"

"Where were you going to deliver Emia?"

"I was supposed to leave her in a duffel bag in the parking garage at my office!" Philip panted. "Please let me go!"

"You were going to leave her in a duffel bag?" Erik snarled. His sharp wings snapped out behind him, and he leaned down until he was an inch away from Philip's terrified face. "You're a monster and an utterly useless piece of shit, Mr. Mayor. I don't want to hear another fucking word come out of your mouth."

With a sharp jerk, Erik twisted Philip's jaw to the side and shattered it. Philip screamed in pain, and his head fell back. Erik reached behind and pulled a short blade from underneath his shirt, his pupils contracting into thin slits as he leaned into Philip's face again.

"Emia told me what you tried to do to her. Did you really think you would get away with it? With even threatening her?" Erik sneered and looked down at Philip's right hand. "Is that the hand you used to hold the gun? The same hand you assaulted her with?"

Erik reached over and turned Philip's hand palm down on the floor. Philip struggled against Erik's grip and screamed as he tried to free himself, his legs kicking at the floor. Erik flipped his short blade around and slammed it over Philip's knuckles, breaking each one on contact.

"You have no idea who the fuck I am, *Mr. Mayor*, but you will by the time I'm done with you. I'm going to fucking castrate you so you'll never be able to do this to anyone else." Erik stood and changed back into human form, fury licking beneath his icy irises.

Anja walked up to Philip and knelt beside him on the floor. She cocked her head and smiled sweetly before placing one of her legs over his body and straddling his torso. "You must like this, don't you? Does it turn you on?" She placed her forearms on his chest and leaned down to stare at him, her sweet smile remaining plastered on her cold features. "Right, you can't talk. I almost forgot your jaw's broken into many pieces. If it had been up to me, I would've just taken your tongue instead. It's a little messier, but at least it would've been permanent."

Pressing her palms on Philip's chest, Anja grinned like a cat and pushed herself upright. She grabbed the side of his head with both her hands, and he screamed in pain.

"Do you like picking on women, Philip? Do you enjoy it when you know you can win an unfair fight? If you're up for it, I can give you an unfair fight." Anja smiled wickedly and picked up Philip's head off the floor. "Do you remember how many times you hit Emia? Because I do."

A crack echoed through Emmeline's bedroom as Anja slammed Philip's head against the floor twice. Philip howled, and his voice gurgled deep in his throat.

"It would be so easy for me to kill you right now. I wouldn't even regret it." Anja dropped Philip's head and stood up.

Matthew put his arms under Emmeline and lifted her off the broken glass. He helped her sit on the edge of her bed. "There's glass embedded deep in your skin. I need to get you to a hospital."

Emmeline barely heard Matthew as she stared at Philip.

You've tried to kill me twice now, Philip. You were going to kidnap me and trade me. And for what? Money.

She watched as Philip struggled to stand up and lean against the wall. Blood dripped from his nose, and his jaw hung to the side.

"Mattie, can you get my phone?" Emmeline hardly recognized her own voice. "It's over there on the floor." She pointed to the entrance of her closet.

I already lost both my parents, and you took Ms. Rose from me. You almost killed Mattie, the last of my family.

Emmeline stood up, and she didn't feel pain anymore. She walked over to where Philip's gun lay and picked it up. She felt its heavy weight in her hand, and it comforted her.

It felt good.

It felt solid.

It's a good thing Dad taught us how to handle guns.

She lifted the gun and pointed it at Philip's head.

"Emia, what are you doing?" Erik looked at her in alarm.

"I'm going to kill him."

"Put the gun down."

"No. And don't even think about trying to take it from me. I know how to use it, and I'm a good shot." Emmeline's eyes didn't stray from Philip's face, and she stepped back from Erik and Anja.

"Once you kill someone, you can't take it back. I'll take care of Philip. Please put the gun down." Erik glanced at Matthew in panic.

"How are you going to take care of him, Erik? I know you won't kill him. You can't," Emmeline said. "No, Philip needs to die. He almost took everything from me. Ms. Rose, Mr. Jae, Mattie. Nobody has ever laid a hand on me, and he took that away from me too. I don't feel safe in my own home anymore." She cocked the gun. "He doesn't get to do that and get away with it. And I won't take the risk that he'll get to do something like this to me again."

"You'll go to jail. This is murder," Erik said desperately.

Tears slid down Emmeline's cheeks. "Do you see me, Erik? Do you see what he's done to me?"

"I do. Believe me, I do." Erik pleaded with her, "Please look at me. Look at what this life has done to me. It'll destroy you. Don't become me."

Emmeline ignored Erik, and her breathing became hard. Her vision went cloudy again, and her hand started to tremble. She saw the terror in both Erik's and Anja's faces as they looked at each other. Matthew came up beside her, but he didn't try to take the gun from her hand.

"Emia, give me the gun. This isn't who you are." Matthew held out his hand.

Emmeline's face crumpled, and she sank to her knees.

I'm not even strong enough to pull the trigger. I'm sorry, Ms. Rose.

Emmeline's hand loosened around the gun, and Matthew lifted it off her palm. She looked up at him, and her heart stopped as he measured the weight of the gun in his hand, considering it as he flipped it over.

No, Mattie.

Just as she had, he lifted the gun and pointed it at Philip.

But unlike her, he didn't hesitate.

He didn't even blink.

Unlike her, he just pulled the trigger.

Erik was instantly in nainthe form, and the bullet hit his shoulder as he shielded Philip with his body. He hissed as his body absorbed the impact of the bullet.

"Erik!" Emmeline screamed.

"Erik, you need to move. It doesn't work if you're standing in the way," Matthew said.

"Mattie, what are you doing? Don't do this," Anja choked out.

If I'd pulled the trigger, Mattie wouldn't be doing this.

"Mattie, I can't lose you too," Emmeline pleaded and shook his arm. "If I lose you too, I'll die. Do you hear me?"

Matthew didn't look at her, but she saw his mouth move before his words registered in her head.

"I'm sorry, Emia."

Matthew took her arm and pushed her toward Erik. Emmeline stumbled and fell forward, and Erik caught her. They both looked up as Matthew steadied his hand and aimed at Philip again.

Erik let go of Emmeline and pulled Philip out of Matthew's line of sight just as he pulled the trigger. Erik flicked his wrist, and a streak of black sliced through the air. Droplets of blood splattered in a line across the pristine white wall, leaving a perfectly straight trail.

He had slit Philip's throat.

CHAPTER FIFTY-FIVE

A THOUSAND LIFETIMES

Philip's throat split open, and blood poured out like a grim smile. He looked at Emmeline in shock and slowly fell to his knees before slumping face-first onto the floor.

"Erik, what have you done?" Anja dropped beside Philip's body and looked at her brother in a mixture of horror and disbelief.

Philip's blood seeped into the hardwood floor, staining it red as it followed the lines and grooves of the wide planks.

"Erik," Emmeline whispered and covered her mouth with her hand.

"His life wasn't yours to take," Matthew said.

"It wasn't yours either," Erik retorted. He walked into Emmeline's bathroom and turned on the faucet to wash his blade. When he came back out, he looked directly at Matthew. "You've saved many lives over your career. Have you ever taken one?"

"No, but I would've taken this one."

Erik sheathed his blade back into its harness, and it lay invisible underneath his clothing. "I have taken more lives than you'll save in a thousand of your lifetimes, and I wouldn't wish one death on your conscience."

"Erik, you need to leave immediately. You need to go!" Anja cried hysterically.

Erik knelt beside his sister. "I'm not going anywhere, and I'm not running. You know I can't run from this."

"Why did you do it?" Tears fell from Anja's eyes.

"You know why. It had to be done."

Anja wrapped her arms around her brother and hugged him tightly.

Emmeline stared at Philip's body. His eyes were hollow and focused on nothing.

Oh, Mattie, what have we done? You forced Erik's hand, like I'd forced yours.

Matthew surveyed the room, his eyes blinking rapidly as his mind worked in overdrive.

"Emia, you need to get to a hospital. My emergency bag is at the Sanctuary, and I don't have the right equipment here to remove the glass from your back. I can't tell how deep the glass is embedded in your skin."

"I can't go to a hospital like this. Too many questions."

Matthew fell silent, and Emmeline watched his eyes flicker back and forth.

"Erik, you take Emia back to the Sanctuary. I'll give Ben and Lucia an update on what needs to be done. Anja, I'll wrap up Philip's body, and you drive it back to the Sanctuary. Nobody can find the body, so it needs to be burned in the incinerator, where the nainthe cremate the raizour bodies. Have it burned with the raizour, not after. The gun, all our clothes, and anything that touched Philip go in the incinerator as well. If a body doesn't show up, the police will assume Philip's on the run."

Matthew went into Emmeline's closet, pulled out a blanket, and shook it out on the floor. He ran down to the kitchen and came back with plastic wrap, rolls of paper towels, and a large bottle of hydrogen peroxide. He wrapped several paper towels around Philip's throat and then covered his head and neck in multiple layers of plastic. He worked quickly and systematically as they watched him in silence.

My brother, if nothing else, is efficient.

Emmeline couldn't even move from her spot on the floor.

Matthew took off the lid to the bottle of bleach and held out his hand. "Erik, your blade, please."

Erik handed Matthew his blade, and Matthew inserted it into the bottle, letting it sit as he watched the time. He removed the blade and wiped it clean with a paper towel before handing it back to Erik.

"Anja, you take Emia's car. Erik, Emia won't be able to sit in a car properly. It would be best if you flew her back to the Sanctuary," Matthew said.

Matthew and Erik each picked up one end of Philip's body and laid him on top of the blanket before rolling it up.

"Erik, when you get questioned, don't mention the gun. Give as little detail as possible."

He's erasing all our involvement.

"Emia, Peter will have a contact I can use for a cleanup. I believe now would be a great time to do a home renovation, starting with the third floor. This will help explain why we're not living at this residence. I'll take care of it."

Emmeline only nodded.

Matthew glanced at his watch. "You guys should go now."

"What are you going to do?" Emmeline asked.

Matthew looked at the blood splatter on the wall and the pool of blood on the floor. "I'm going to do a preliminary cleanup. I know enough about blood to make it not look like a crime scene—at least, not on the surface. I'll come back to the Sanctuary as soon as possible. I trust Ben to take care of you."

Matthew looked at Anja and then to Emmeline. "This last part is important. Emia, you were unconscious after Philip threw you on your desk. Anja, you were in the garage, prepping the cars, and you didn't see what happened. All either of you saw was Philip dead on the floor. If they ask you if Erik was holding his blade, just say that it was in his harness. Neither of you saw it happen, and you only know what Erik and I told you. This way, they can't question you on how it happened. Do you understand?"

Emmeline nodded slowly, but Anja didn't acknowledge Matthew.

"Anja, do you understand?" Matthew asked sharply.

"Don't talk to me like that. You don't get to talk to me like that. Ever," Anja bit back.

She blames Mattie.

Emmeline looked up at Matthew, but there wasn't any emotion on his face.

"It's important that you understand this and do as I've said," Matthew replied.

Anja didn't respond to him and just stared at Philip's wrapped body.

Matthew straightened. "Time to get moving."

CHAPTER FIFTY-SIX

ANGEL OF DEATH

Erik landed on the grassy lawn of the Sanctuary courtyard and let go of Emmeline, being sure to avoid the wounds on her back. Ben and Lucia were both waiting for them and rushed over as soon as they landed.

"Dr. Taylor-Wu gave us a heads-up on what needs to be done. We have everything set up. Emmeline, why don't you come with us?" Ben looked at Emmeline's bloody shirt with concern and took her backpack from Erik's hand.

"I'll be there in a minute. I need to talk to Erik privately," Emmeline said.

"Yes, but not too long. I want to examine your back as soon as possible," Ben replied.

Emmeline pulled Erik away from Ben and Lucia.

"Erik, why did you do it?" Emmeline tried to search his eyes, but he wouldn't look at her.

"This is what I do. I take lives."

"That's not true. You've saved me many times now. Why do you keep saying that?" Emmeline gripped his arm. "Erik, please look at me."

"I can't talk about this right now. I'm going to wait for Anja in the garage. I need to spend some time with her."

Emmeline's heart fell.

He blames me too.

"Will you come to the infirmary after?" Emmeline asked.

"I don't know if I'll have time, but I'll try." There was an edge to Erik's voice, something simmering beneath the surface. He called Ben and Lucia over. "Please take care of Emia."

"We will. Come, Emmeline. Let's get that glass out," Ben said.

Emmeline watched Erik turn and walk away, his graceful, long strides purposeful and heavy. She noticed for the first time that he was dressed more casually than usual, his dark hoodie and slim joggers highlighting his tall and foreboding presence. She could barely make out the short blade hidden underneath his clothes—the blade that had taken a human life just moments earlier.

Erik stopped in the middle of the courtyard and tilted his head to the midnight sky, pausing to stare at the bright full moon. It seemed to her that he almost wanted to reach for it, for it was so close. The silvery moonlight reflected off his pale, angular features, making him look both ethereal and terrifying.

Like the angel of death.

Ben sat back and exhaled. "Emmeline, I'm done stitching up your skin. I'm sorry, but there'll be some scarring." He switched off the light on the magnifying lamp and pushed it to the side. "You take pain like a champ."

"Thanks, Ben." Emmeline let out a breath.

"Are your vaccinations up to date?" Lucia asked as she cleaned the wounds on her back.

Emmeline nodded.

Ben handed her a clean T-shirt. "I can take out the stitches in a week or two. We'll keep an eye out for infection."

There was a knock on the door as Emmeline carefully pulled the shirt over her head. The door creaked open, and Erik walked in. The harsh light in the infirmary accentuated the shadows under his eyes and the sharp lines against his set jaw.

"Emia, how's your back?" Erik asked.

He sounds exhausted.

"Just some minor stitches. Nothing to worry about," Emmeline replied.

"May I?" Erik gestured to her back.

Emmeline nodded, and Erik moved to the other side of the examination table. He lifted the back of her shirt to look and then let it back down.

"Ben, Lucia, can I have a moment with Emia?"

"We'll be in the office. Let us know if you need anything," Ben replied.

He and Lucia left the room and closed the door behind them.

Erik walked back from behind the examination table and pulled out a chair to sit in front of Emmeline. He sighed and put his head in his hands.

"Erik, what's wrong?" Emmeline shifted her body to get off the examination table.

"Please, just stay sitting." Erik leaned back in his chair and crossed his arms. "You asked me why I keep saying that killing is my job. I say it because it's what I've been doing for decades. I've done it for so long that, some days, I don't remember what came before it. I don't regret taking Philip's life. If I were truthful, I would say, I don't feel anything. I've felt more from taking a raizour's life than I did Philip's or Sophia's. Does that make me the monster?" He looked at Emmeline with despair. "Do you think I'm a monster, Emia?"

"You're not a monster, Erik. I know what a monster is, and you're not it. I've never felt safer than when I'm with you."

Emmeline closed her eyes, and she heard Erik stand up. When she opened her eyes, he was so close to her that they almost touched. She reached for Erik's hand.

"I know I'm the one who made you do it. You wouldn't have done it if it hadn't been for me. It's all my fault, and I'm sorry." Emmeline looked up at him as tears fell down her cheeks. "Please don't hate me. Why does it seem like everything I touch, I ruin?"

Erik lightly traced her bruised cheek and mouth, his thumb hovering over her lips.

"I could never hate you, Emmeline Taylor-Wu. You've been a bright light in my never-ending darkness, and I'm glad to have met you even if it was only for a short while. I only wish I had more time with you." He said the last part so softly that Emmeline wasn't sure she'd heard him correctly.

"What do you mean? What did you say?" Emmeline demanded.

A knock interrupted them, and Anja walked in. Her eyes were puffy and red, as if she had been crying.

"They're almost here," Anja said dully.

"What's happening?" Emmeline's eyes snapped back to Erik, and her voice rose. "What's happening? Who's coming?" She looked back and forth at both Erik and Anja.

Erik twisted a thin iron band off his last finger and reached for Emmeline's hand. He pressed his ring into her palm and closed her fingers around it. "I can't protect you anymore. Anja will protect you from now on."

"Erik, what's happening? You're not making sense! Where are you going?" Emmeline turned to Anja, but Anja wouldn't look at her. "Anja, what's going on here? Can someone tell me what the fuck is happening?" she screamed.

"Emia, look at me. Please look at me." Erik took her face in his hands. "Promise me you won't remember me as a monster. Can you do that for me?"

"But you're not a monster." Emmeline's tears fell onto his hands.

Emmeline heard the stomping of heavy footsteps, and her heart slowed to a standstill. The door to the infirmary room swung open, and several nainthe filed into the room, all armed and dressed in full armor. Javier, Michael, and Maira followed behind and stepped into the room, their faces grim.

Sorrow lined Javier's face, and his voice was rough as he spoke. "Erik Loren, we charge you with the breaking of your oath to the nainthe order by the murder of Philip Vil. You are now to be taken into custody."

Made in United States
Troutdale, OR
02/27/2024

17997539R00311